Dedication

They may be called the Palace Guard, the City Guard, or the Patrol. Whatever the name, their purpose in any work of heroic fantasy is identical: it is, round about Chapter Three (or ten minutes into the film) to rush into the room, attack the hero one at a time, and be slaughtered. No one ever asks them if they wanted to.

This book is dedicated to those fine men.

And also to Mike Harrison, Mary Gentle, Neil Gaiman and all the others who assisted with and laughed at the idea of L-space; too bad we never used Schrödinger's Paperback . . .

GUARDS!
GUARDS!

Terry Pratchett

CORGI BOOKS

GUARDS! GUARDS!

A CORGI BOOK: 0 552 15293 5

Originally published in Great Britain by
Victor Gollancz Ltd

PRINTING HISTORY
Victor Gollancz edition published 1989
Corgi edition published 1990

19 20 18

Set in Minion by Kestrel Data, Exeter, Devon.

Corgi Books are published by Transworld Publishers,
61–63 Uxbridge Road, London W5 5SA,
a division of The Random House Group Ltd,
in Australia by Random House Australia (Pty) Ltd,
20 Alfred Street, Milsons Point, Sydney, NSW 2061, Australia,
in New Zealand by Random House New Zealand Ltd,
18 Poland Road, Glenfield, Auckland 10, New Zealand
and in South Africa by Random House (Pty) Ltd,
Endulini, 5a Jubilee Road, Parktown 2193, South Africa.

Printed and bound in Great Britain by
Cox & Wyman Ltd, Reading, Berkshire.

Papers used by Transworld Publishers are natural, recyclable
products made from wood grown in sustainable forests.
The manufacturing processes conform to the environmental
regulations of the country of origin.

GUARDS! GUARDS!

THIS IS WHERE THE DRAGONS WENT.

They lie . . .

Not dead, not asleep. Not waiting, because waiting implies expectation. Possibly the word we're looking for here is . . .

. . . dormant.

And although the space they occupy isn't like normal space, nevertheless they are packed in tightly. Not a cubic inch there but is filled by a claw, a talon, a scale, the tip of a tail, so the effect is like one of those trick drawings and your eyeballs eventually realize that the space between each dragon is, in fact, another dragon.

They could put you in mind of a can of sardines, if you thought sardines were huge and scaly and proud and arrogant.

And presumably, somewhere, there's the key.

In another space entirely, it was early morning in Ankh-Morpork, oldest and greatest and grubbiest of cities. A thin drizzle dripped from the grey sky and punctuated the river mist that coiled among the streets. Rats of various species went about their nocturnal occasions. Under night's damp cloak assassins assassinated, thieves thieved, hussies hustled. And so on.

And drunken Captain Vimes of the Night Watch staggered slowly down the street, folded gently into the gutter outside the Watch House and lay there while, above him, strange letters made of light sizzled in the damp and changed colour . . .

The city wasa, wasa, wasa wossname. Thing. *Woman*. Thass what it was. Woman. Roaring, ancient, centuries old. Strung you along, let you fall in thingy, love, with her, then kicked you inna, inna, thingy. Thingy, in your mouth. Tongue. Tonsils. *Teeth*. That's what it, she, did. She wasa . . . thing, you know, lady dog. Puppy. Hen. *Bitch*. And then you hated her and, and just when you thought you'd got her, it, out of your, your, whatever, then she opened her great booming rotten heart to you, caught you off bal, bal, bal, thing. *Ance*. Yeah. Thassit. Never knew where where you stood. Lay. Only thing you were sure of, you couldn't let her go. Because, because she was yours, all you had, even in her gutters . . .

Damp darkness shrouded the venerable buildings of Unseen University, premier college of wizardry. The only light was a faint octarine flicker from the tiny windows of the new High Energy Magic building, where keen-edged minds were probing the very fabric of the universe, whether it liked it or not.

And there was light, of course, in the Library.

The Library was the greatest assemblage of magical texts anywhere in the multiverse. Thousands of volumes of occult lore weighted its shelves.

It was said that, since vast amounts of magic can seriously distort the mundane world, the Library did not obey the normal rules of space and time. It was said that it went on *forever*. It was said that you could wander for days among the distant shelves, that there were lost tribes of research students somewhere in there, that strange things lurked in forgotten alcoves and were preyed on by other things that were even stranger.*

Wise students in search of more distant volumes took care to leave chalk marks on the shelves as they roamed deeper into the fusty darkness, and told friends to come looking for them if they weren't back by supper.

And, because magic can only loosely be bound, the Library books themselves were more than mere pulped wood and paper.

Raw magic crackled from their spines, earthing itself harmlessly in the copper rails nailed to every shelf for that very purpose. Faint traceries of blue fire crawled across the bookcases and there was a sound, a papery whispering, such as might come from a colony of roosting starlings. In the silence of the night the books talked to one another.

---

*All this was untrue. The truth is that even big collections of ordinary books distort space, as can readily be proved by anyone who has been around a really old-fashioned second-hand bookshop, one of those that look as though they were designed by M. Escher on a bad day and has more staircases than storeys and those rows of shelves which end in little doors that are surely too small for a full-sized human to enter. The relevant equation is: Knowledge = power = energy = matter = mass; a good bookshop is just a genteel Black Hole that knows how to read.

There was also the sound of someone snoring.

The light from the shelves didn't so much illuminate as highlight the darkness, but by its violet flicker a watcher might just have identified an ancient and battered desk right under the central dome.

The snoring was coming from underneath it, where a piece of tattered blanket barely covered what looked like a heap of sandbags but was in fact an adult male orangutan.

It was the Librarian.

Not many people these days remarked upon the fact that he was an ape. The change had been brought about by a magical accident, always a possibility where so many powerful books are kept together, and he was considered to have got off lightly. After all, he was still basically the same shape. And he had been allowed to keep his job, which he was rather good at, although 'allowed' is not really the right word. It was the way he could roll his upper lip back to reveal more incredibly yellow teeth than any other mouth the University Council had ever seen before that somehow made sure the matter was never really raised.

But now there was another sound, the alien sound of a door creaking open. Footsteps padded across the floor and disappeared amongst the clustering shelves. The books rustled indignantly, and some of the larger grimoires rattled their chains.

The Librarian slept on, lulled by the whispering of the rain.

In the embrace of his gutter, half a mile away,

Captain Vimes of the Night Watch opened his mouth and started to sing.

Now a black-robed figure scurried through the midnight streets, ducking from doorway to doorway, and reached a grim and forbidding portal. No mere doorway got that grim without effort, one felt. It looked as though the architect had been called in and given specific instructions. We want something eldritch in dark oak, he'd been told. So put an unpleasant gargoyle thing over the archway, give it a slam like the footfall of a giant and make it clear to everyone, in fact, that this isn't the kind of door that goes 'ding-dong' when you press the bell.

The figure rapped a complex code on the dark woodwork. A tiny barred hatch opened and one suspicious eye peered out.

' "The significant owl hoots in the night," ' said the visitor, trying to wring the rainwater out of its robe.

' "Yet many grey lords go sadly to the masterless men," ' intoned a voice on the other side of the grille.

' "Hooray, hooray for the spinster's sister's daughter," ' countered the dripping figure.

' "To the axeman, all supplicants are the same height." '

' "Yet verily, the rose is within the thorn." '

' "The good mother makes bean soup for the errant boy," ' said the voice behind the door.

There was a pause, broken only by the sound of the rain. Then the visitor said, 'What?'

' "The good mother makes bean soup for the errant boy." '

There was another, longer pause. Then the damp figure said, 'Are you sure the ill-built tower doesn't tremble mightily at a butterfly's passage?'

'Nope. Bean soup it is. I'm sorry.'

The rain hissed down relentlessly in the embarrassed silence.

'What about the cagèd whale?' said the soaking visitor, trying to squeeze into what little shelter the dread portal offered.

'What about it?'

'It should know nothing of the mighty deeps, if you must know.'

'*Oh*, the cagèd *whale*. You want the *Elucidated* Brethren of the Ebon Night. Three doors down.'

'Who're you, then?'

'We're the Illuminated and Ancient Brethren of Ee.'

'I thought you met over in Treacle Street,' said the damp man, after a while.

'Yeah, well. You know how it is. The fretwork club have the room Tuesdays. There was a bit of a mix-up.'

'Oh? Well, thanks anyway.'

'My pleasure.' The little door slammed shut.

The robed figure glared at it for a moment, and then splashed further down the street. There was indeed another portal there. The builder hadn't bothered to change the design much.

He knocked. The little barred hatch shot back.

'Yes?'

'Look, "The significant owl hoots in the night", all right?'

' "Yet many grey lords go sadly to the masterless men." '

' "Hooray, hooray for the spinster's sister's daughter", OK?'

' "To the axeman, all supplicants are the same height." '

' "Yet verily, the rose is within the thorn." It's pissing down out here. You do *know* that, don't you?'

'Yes,' said the voice, in the tones of one who indeed does know it, and is not the one standing in it.

The visitor sighed.

' "The cagèd whale knows nothing of the mighty deeps," ' he said. 'If it makes you any happier.'

' "The ill-built tower trembles mightily at a butterfly's passage." '

The supplicant grabbed the bars of the window, pulled himself up to it, and hissed: 'Now let us in, I'm soaked.'

There was another damp pause.

'These deeps . . . did you say mighty or nightly?'

'Mighty, I said. *Mighty* deeps. On account of being, you know, deep. It's me, Brother Fingers.'

'It sounded like nightly to me,' said the invisible doorkeeper cautiously.

'Look, do you want the bloody book or not? I don't have to do this. I could be at home in bed.'

'You *sure* it was mighty?'

'Listen, I know how deep the bloody deeps are all

17

right,' said Brother Fingers urgently. 'I knew how mighty they were when you were a perishing neophyte. Now will you open this door?'

'Well . . . all right.'

There was the sound of bolts sliding back. Then the voice said, 'Would you mind giving it a push? The Door of Knowledge Through Which the Untutored May Not Pass sticks something wicked in the damp.'

Brother Fingers put his shoulder to it, forced his way through, gave Brother Doorkeeper a dirty look, and hurried within.

The others were waiting for him in the Inner Sanctum, standing around with the sheepish air of people not normally accustomed to wearing sinister hooded black robes. The Supreme Grand Master nodded at him.

'Brother Fingers, isn't it?'

'Yes, Supreme Grand Master.'

'Do you have that which you were sent to get?'

Brother Fingers pulled a package from under his robe.

'Just where I said it would be,' he said. 'No problem.'

'Well done, Brother Fingers.'

'Thank you, Supreme Grand Master.'

The Supreme Grand Master rapped his gavel for attention. The room shuffled into some sort of circle.

'I call the Unique and Supreme Lodge of the Elucidated Brethren to order,' he intoned. 'Is the Door of Knowledge sealed fast against heretics and knowlessmen?'

'Stuck solid,' said Brother Doorkeeper. 'It's the damp. I'll bring my plane in next week, soon have it—'

'All right, all *right*,' said the Supreme Grand Master testily. 'Just a yes would have done. Is the triple circle well and truly traced? Art all here who Art Here? And it be well for an knowlessman that he should not be here, for he would be taken from this place and his gaskin slit, his moules shown to the four winds, his welchet torn asunder with many hooks and his figgin placed upon a spike *yes what is it?*'

'Sorry, did you say *Elucidated* Brethren?'

The Supreme Grand Master glared at the solitary figure with its hand up.

'Yea, the Elucidated Brethren, guardian of the sacred knowledge since a time no man may wot of—'

'Last February,' said Brother Doorkeeper helpfully. The Supreme Grand Master felt that Brother Doorkeeper had never really got the hang of things.

'Sorry. Sorry. Sorry,' said the worried figure. 'Wrong society, I'm afraid. Must have taken a wrong turning. I'll just be going, if you'll excuse me . . .'

'And his figgin placed upon a spike,' repeated the Supreme Grand Master pointedly, against a background of damp wooden noises as Brother Doorkeeper tried to get the dread portal open. 'Are we quite finished? Any more knowlessmen happened to drop in on their way somewhere else?' he added with bitter sarcasm. 'Right. Fine. *So* glad. I suppose it's too much to ask if the Four Watchtowers are secured? Oh, good. And the Trouser of Sanctity, has anyone bothered to shrive it? Oh, you did. Properly? I'll check, you know . . . all right. And have the windows been fastened with the Red Cords of Intellect, in accordance with ancient prescription? Good. Now perhaps we can get on with it.'

With the slightly miffed air of one who has run their finger along a daughter-in-law's top shelf and found against all expectation that it is sparkling clean, the Grand Master got on with it.

What a shower, he told himself. A bunch of incompetents no other secret society would touch with a ten-foot Sceptre of Authority. The sort to dislocate their fingers with even the simplest secret handshake.

But incompetents with possibilities, nevertheless. Let the other societies take the skilled, the hopefuls, the ambitious, the self-confident. He'd take the whining resentful ones, the ones with a bellyful of spite and bile, the ones who knew they could make it big if only they'd been given the chance. Give him the ones in which the floods of venom and vindictiveness were dammed up behind thin walls of ineptitude and lowgrade paranoia.

And stupidity, too. They've all sworn the oath, he thought, but not a man jack of 'em has even asked what a figgin is.

'Brethren,' he said. 'Tonight we have matters of profound importance to discuss. The good governance, nay, the very future of Ankh-Morpork lies in our hands.'

They leaned closer. The Supreme Grand Master

felt the beginnings of the old thrill of power. They were hanging on his words. This was a feeling worth dressing up in bloody silly robes for.

'Do we not well know that the city is in thrall to corrupt men, who wax fat on their ill-gotten gains, while better men are held back and forced into virtual servitude?'

'We certainly do!' said Brother Doorkeeper vehemently, when they'd had time to translate this mentally. 'Only last week, down at the Bakers' Guild, I tried to point out to Master Critchley that—'

It wasn't eye contact, because the Supreme Grand Master had made sure the Brethren's hoods shrouded their faces in mystic darkness, but nevertheless he managed to silence Brother Doorkeeper by dint of sheer outraged silence.

'Yet it was not always thus,' the Supreme Grand Master continued. 'There was once a golden age, when those worthy of command and respect were justly rewarded. An age when Ankh-Morpork wasn't simply a big city but a great one. An age of chivalry. An age when – yes, Brother Watchtower?'

A bulky robed figure lowered its hand. 'Are you talking about when we had kings?'

'Well done, Brother,' said the Supreme Grand Master, slightly annoyed at this unusual evidence of intelligence. 'And—'

'But that was all sorted out hundreds of years ago,' said Brother Watchtower. 'Wasn't there this great battle, or something? And since then we've just had the ruling lords, like the Patrician.'

'Yes, very good, Brother Watchtower.'

'There aren't any more kings, is the point I'm trying to make,' said Brother Watchtower helpfully.

'As Brother Watchtower says, the line of—'

'It was you talking about chivalry that give me the clue,' said Brother Watchtower.

'Quite so, and—'

'You get that with kings, chivalry,' said Brother Watchtower happily. 'And knights. And they used to have these—'

'*However*,' said the Supreme Grand Master sharply, 'it may well be that the line of the kings of Ankh is not as defunct as hitherto imagined, and that progeny of the line exist even now. Thus my researches among the ancient scrolls do indicate.'

He stood back expectantly. There didn't seem to be the effect he'd expected, however. Probably they can manage 'defunct', he thought, but I ought to have drawn the line at 'progeny'.

Brother Watchtower had his hand up again.

'Yes?'

'You saying there's some sort of heir to the throne hanging around somewhere?' said Brother Watchtower.

'This may be the case, yes.'

'Yeah. They do that, you know,' said Brother Watchtower knowledgeably. 'Happens all the time. You read about it. Skions, they're called. They go lurking around in the distant wildernesses for ages, handing down the secret sword and birthmark and so forth from generation to generation. Then just when the old kingdom needs them, they turn up and

22

turf out any usurpers that happen to be around. And then there's general rejoicing.'

The Supreme Grand Master felt his own mouth drop open. He hadn't expected it to be as easy as this.

'Yes, all right,' said a figure the Supreme Grand Master knew to be Brother Plasterer. 'But so what? Let's say a skion turns up, walks up to the Patrician, says "What ho, I'm king, here's the birthmark as per spec, now bugger off". What's he got then? Life expectancy of maybe two minutes, that's what.'

'You don't *listen*,' said Brother Watchtower. 'The thing is, the skion has to arrive when the kingdom is threatened, doesn't he? Then everyone can see, right? Then he gets carried off to the palace, cures a few people, announces a half-holiday, hands round a bit of treasure, and Bob's your uncle.'

'He has to marry a princess, too,' said Brother Doorkeeper. 'On account of him being a swine-herd.'

They looked at him.

'Who said anything about him being a swine-herd?' said Brother Watchtower. 'I never said he was a swineherd. What's this about swineherds?'

'He's got a point, though,' said Brother Plasterer. 'He's generally a swineherd or a forester or similar, your basic skion. It's to do with being in wossname. Cognito. They've got to appear to be of, you know, humble origins.'

'Nothing special about humble origins,' said a very small Brother, who seemed to consist entirely of a little perambulatory black robe with halitosis. 'I've got lots of humble origins. In my family we thought swineherding was a posh job.'

'But your family doesn't have the blood of kings, Brother Dunnykin,' said Brother Plasterer.

'We might of,' said Brother Dunnykin sulkily.

'Right, then,' said Brother Watchtower grudgingly. 'Fair enough. But at the essential moment, see, your genuine kings throw back their cloak and say "Lo!" and their essential kingnessness shines through.'

'How, exactly?' said Brother Doorkeeper.

'—*might of got the blood of kings*,' muttered Brother Dunnykin. '*Got no right saying I might not have got the blood of*—'

'Look, it just does, OK? You just know it when you see it.'

'But before that they've got to save the kingdom,' said Brother Plasterer.

'Oh, yes,' said Brother Watchtower heavily. 'That's the main thing, is that.'

'What from, then?'

'—*got as much right as anyone to might have the blood of kings*—'

'The Patrician?' said Brother Doorkeeper.

Brother Watchtower, as the sudden authority on the ways of royalty, shook his head.

'I dunno that the Patrician is a threat, exactly,' he said. 'He's not your actual tyrant, as such. Not as bad as some we've had. I mean, he doesn't actually *oppress*.'

'I get oppressed all the time,' said Brother Doorkeeper. 'Master Critchley, where I work, he oppresses me morning, noon and night, shouting at me and everything. And the woman in the vegetable shop, she oppresses me all the time.'

'That's right,' said Brother Plasterer. 'My land-lord oppresses me something wicked. Banging on the door and going on and on about all the rent I allegedly owe, which is a total lie. And the people next door oppress me all night long. I tell them, I work all day, a man's got to have some time to learn to play the tuba. That's oppression, that is. If I'm not under the heel of the oppressor, I don't know who is.'

'Put like that—' said Brother Watchtower slowly – 'I reckon my brother-in-law is oppressing me all the time with having this new horse and buggy he's been and bought. *I* haven't got one. I mean, where's the justice in that? I bet a king wouldn't let that sort of oppression go on, people's wives oppressing 'em with why haven't they got a new coach like our Rodney and that.'

The Supreme Grand Master listened to this with a slightly light-headed feeling. It was as if he'd known that there were such things as avalanches, but had never dreamed when he dropped the little snow-ball on top of the mountain that it could lead to such astonishing results. He was hardly having to egg them on at all.

'I bet a king'd have something to say about land-lords,' said Brother Plasterer.

'And he'd outlaw people with showy coaches,' said Brother Watchtower. 'Probably bought with stolen money, too, I reckon.'

'I think,' said the Supreme Grand Master, tweaking things a little, 'that a wise king would only, as it were, outlaw showy coaches for the *undeserving.*'

There was a thoughtful pause in the conversation as the assembled Brethren mentally divided the universe into the deserving and the undeserving, and put themselves on the appropriate side.

'It'd be only fair,' said Brother Watchtower slowly. 'But Brother Plasterer was right, really. I can't see a skion manifesting his destiny just because Brother Doorkeeper thinks the woman in the vegetable shop keeps giving him funny looks. No offence.'

'*And* bloody short weight,' said Brother Doorkeeper. 'And she—'

'Yes, yes, yes,' said the Supreme Grand Master. 'Truly the right-thinking folk of Ankh-Morpork are beneath the heel of the oppressors. However, a king generally reveals himself in rather more dramatic circumstances. Like a war, for example.'

Things were going well. Surely, for all their self-centred stupidity, one of them would be bright enough to make the suggestion?

'There used to be some old prophecy or something,' said Brother Plasterer. 'My grandad told me.' His eyes glazed with the effort of dramatic recall. ' "Yea, the king will come bringing Law and Justice, and know nothing but the Truth, and Protect and Serve the People with his Sword." You don't all have to look at me like that, I didn't make it up.'

'Oh, we *all* know *that* one. And a fat lot of good that'd be,' said Brother Watchtower. 'I mean, what does he do, ride in with Law and Truth and so on like the Four Horsemen of the Apocralypse? Hallo everyone,' he squeaked, 'I'm the king, and that's Truth over there, watering his horse. Not very practical, is it? Nah. You can't trust old legends.'

'Why not?' said Brother Dunnykin, in a peeved voice.

' 'Cos they're legendary. That's how you can tell,' said Brother Watchtower.

'Sleeping princesses is a good one,' said Brother Plasterer. 'Only a king can wake 'em up.'

'Don't be daft,' said Brother Watchtower severely. 'We haven't got a king, so we can't have princesses. Stands to reason.'

'Of course, in the *old* days it was easy,' said Brother Doorkeeper happily.

'Why?'

'He just had to kill a dragon.'

The Supreme Grand Master clapped his hands together and offered a silent prayer to any god who happened to be listening. He'd been right about these people. Sooner or later their rambling little minds took them where you wanted them to go.

'What an interesting idea,' he trilled.

'Wouldn't work,' said Brother Watchtower dourly. 'There ain't no big dragons now.'

'There could be.'

The Supreme Grand Master cracked his knuckles.

'Come again?' said Brother Watchtower.

'I said there could be.'

There was a nervous laugh from the depths of Brother Watchtower's cowl.

'What, the real thing? Great big scales and wings?'

'Yes.'

'Breath like a blast furnace?'

'Yes.'

'Them big claw things on its feet?'

'Talons? Oh, yes. As many as you want.'

'What do you mean, as many as I want?'

'I would hope it's self-explanatory, Brother Watchtower. If you want dragons, you can have dragons. *You* can bring a dragon here. Now. Into the city.'

'Me?'

'All of you. I mean us,' said the Supreme Grand Master.

Brother Watchtower hesitated. 'Well, I don't know if that's a very good—'

'And it would obey your every command.'

That stopped them. That pulled them up. That dropped in front of their weasely little minds like a lump of meat in a dog pound.

'Can you just repeat that?' said Brother Plasterer slowly.

'You can control it. You can make it do whatever you want.'

'What? A real dragon?'

The Supreme Grand Master's eyes rolled in the privacy of his hood.

'Yes, a real one. Not a little pet swamp dragon. The genuine article.'

'But I thought they were, you know . . . miffs.'

The Supreme Grand Master leaned forward.

'They were myths and they were real,' he said loudly. 'Both a wave and a particle.'

'You've lost me there,' said Brother Plasterer.

'I will demonstrate, then. The book please, Brother Fingers. Thank you. Brethren, I must tell you that when I was undergoing my tuition by the Secret Masters—'

'The what, Supreme Grand Master?' said Brother Plasterer.

'Why don't you listen? You never *listen*. He said the Secret Masters!' said Brother Watchtower. 'You know, the venerable sages what live on some mountain and secretly run everything and taught him all this lore and that, and can walk on fires and that. He told us last week. He's going to teach us, aren't you, Supreme Grand Master,' he finished obsequiously.

'Oh, the *Secret* Masters,' said Brother Plasterer. 'Sorry. It's these mystic hoods. Sorry. Secret. I remember.'

But when I rule the city, the Supreme Grand Master said to himself, there is going to be none of this. I shall form a new secret society of keen-minded and intelligent men, although not too intelligent of course, not *too* intelligent. And we will overthrow the cold tyrant and we will usher in a new age of enlightenment and fraternity and humanism and Ankh-Morpork will become a Utopia and people like

Brother Plasterer will be roasted over slow fires if I
have any say in the matter, which I will. *And* his
figgin.*

'When I was, as I said, undergoing my tuition by
the Secret Masters—' he continued.

'That was where they told you you had to walk on
ricepaper, wasn't it,' said Brother Watchtower conversationally. 'I always thought that was a good bit.
I've been saving it off the bottom of my macaroons
ever since. Amazing, really. I can walk on it no
trouble. Shows what being in a proper secret society
does for you, does that.'

When he is on the griddle, the Supreme Grand
Master thought, Brother Plasterer will not be lonely.

'Your footfalls on the road of enlightenment are
an example to us all, Brother Watchtower,' he said.
'If I may continue, however – among the many
secrets—'

'—from the Heart of Being—' said Brother
Watchtower approvingly.

'—from the Heart, as Brother Watchtower says, of
Being, was the current location of the noble dragons.
The belief that they died out is quite wrong. They
simply found a new evolutionary niche. And they can
be summoned from it. This book—' he flourished it
– 'gives specific instructions.'

*A figgin is defined in the *Dictionary of Eye-Watering Words* as 'a
small short-crust pasty containing raisins'. The Dictionary would
have been invaluable for the Supreme Grand Master when he
thought up the Society's oaths, since it also includes welchet ('a
type of waistcoat worn by certain clock-makers'), gaskin ('a shy,
grey-brown bird of the coot family'), and moules ('a game of skill
and dexterity, involving tortoises').

'It's just in a book?' said Brother Plasterer.

'No ordinary book. This is the only copy. It has taken me years to track it down,' said the Supreme Grand Master. 'It's in the handwriting of Tubal de Malachite, a great student of dragon lore. His actual handwriting. He summoned dragons of all sizes. And so can you.'

There was another long, awkward silence.

'Um,' said Brother Doorkeeper.

'Sounds a bit like, you know . . . *magic* to me,' said Brother Watchtower, in the nervous tone of the man who has spotted which cup the pea is hidden under but doesn't like to say. 'I mean, not wishing to question your supreme wisdomship and that but . . . well . . . you know . . . magic . . .'

His voice trailed off.

'Yeah,' said Brother Plasterer uncomfortably.

'It's, er, the wizards, see,' said Brother Fingers. 'You prob'ly dint know this, when you was banged up with them venerable herberts on their mountain, but the wizards round here come down on you like a ton of bricks if they catches you doin' anything like that.'

'Demarcation, they call it,' said Brother Plasterer. 'Like, I don't go around fiddling with the mystic interleaved wossnames of causality, and they don't do any plastering.'

'I fail to see the problem,' said the Supreme Grand Master. In fact, he saw it all too clearly. This was the last hurdle. Help their tiny little minds over this, and he held the world in the palm of his hand. Their stupefyingly unintelligent self-interest hadn't let him down so far, surely it couldn't fail him now . . .

The Brethren shuffled uneasily. Then Brother Dunnykin spoke.

'Huh. *Wizards*. What do they know about a day's work?'

The Supreme Grand Master breathed deeply. *Ah* . . .

The air of mean-minded resentfulness thickened noticeably.

'Nothing, and that's a fact,' said Brother Fingers. 'Goin' around with their noses in the air, too good for the likes a'us. I used to see 'em when I worked up the University. Backsides a mile wide, I'm telling you. Catch 'em doing a job of honest toil?'

'Like thieving, you mean?' said Brother Watchtower, who had never liked Brother Fingers much.

'O'course, they *tell* you,' Brother Fingers went on, pointedly ignoring the comment, 'that you shouldn't go round doin' magic on account of only them knowin' about not disturbin' the universal harmony and whatnot. Load of rubbish, in my opinion.'

'We-ell,' said Brother Plasterer, 'I dunno, really. I mean, you get the mix wrong, you just got a lot of damp plaster round your ankles. But you get a bit of magic wrong, and they say ghastly things comes out the woodwork and stitches you *right* up.'

'Yeah, but it's the wizards that say that,' said Brother Watchtower thoughtfully. 'Never could stand them myself, to tell you the truth. Could be they're on to a good thing and don't want the rest of us to find out. It's only waving your arms and chanting, when all's said and done.'

The Brethren considered this. It sounded plausible. If *they* were on to a good thing, *they* certainly wouldn't want anyone else muscling in.

The Supreme Grand Master decided that the time was ripe.

'Then we are agreed, Brethren? You are prepared to practise magic?'

'Oh, *practise*,' said Brother Plasterer, relieved. 'I don't mind *practising*. So long as we don't have to do it for real—'

The Supreme Grand Master thumped the book.

'I mean carry out real spells! Put the city back on the right lines! Summon a dragon!' he shouted.

They took a step back. Then Brother Doorkeeper said, 'And then, if we get this dragon, the rightful king'll turn up, just like that?'

'Yes!' said the Supreme Grand Master.

'I can see that,' said Brother Watchtower supportively. 'Stands to reason. Because of destiny and the gnomic workings of fate.'

There was a moment's hesitation, and then a general nodding of cowls. Only Brother Plasterer looked vaguely unhappy.

'We-ell,' he said. 'It won't get out of hand, will it?'

'I assure you, Brother Plasterer, that you can give it up any time you like,' said the Supreme Grand Master smoothly.

'Well . . . all right,' said the reluctant Brother. 'Just for a bit, then. Could we get it to stay here long enough to burn down, for example, any oppressive vegetable shops?'

Ah . . .

He'd won. There'd be dragons again. And a king again. Not like the old kings. A king who would do what he was told.

'That,' said the Supreme Grand Master, 'depends on how much help you can be. We shall need, initially, any items of magic you can bring . . .'

It might not be a good idea to let them see that the last half of de Malachite's book was a charred lump. The man was clearly not up to it.

He could do a lot better. And absolutely no-one would be able to stop him.

Thunder rolled . . .

It is said that the gods play games with the lives of men. But what games, and why, and the identities of the actual pawns, and what the game is, and what the rules are – who knows?

Best not to speculate.

Thunder rolled . .

It rolled a six.

Now pull back briefly from the dripping streets of Ankh-Morpork, pan across the morning mists of the Disc, and focus in again on a young man heading for the city with all the openness, sincerity and innocence of purpose of an iceberg drifting into a major shipping lane.

The young man is called Carrot. This is not because of his hair, which his father has always clipped short for reasons of Hygiene. It is because of his shape.

It is the kind of tapering shape a boy gets through clean living, healthy eating, and good mountain air in huge lungfuls. When he flexes his shoulder muscles, other muscles have to move out of the way first.

He is also bearing a sword presented to him in mysterious circumstances. Very mysterious circumstances. Surprisingly, therefore, there is something very unexpected about this sword. It isn't magical. It hasn't got a name. When you wield it you don't get a feeling of power, you just get blisters; you could believe it was a sword that had been used so much that it had ceased to be anything other than a quintessential sword, a long piece of metal with very sharp edges. And it hasn't got destiny written all over it.

It's practically unique, in fact.

Thunder rolled.

The gutters of the city gurgled softly as the detritus of the night was carried along, in some cases protesting feebly.

When it came to the recumbent figure of Captain Vimes, the water diverted and flowed around him in two streams. Vimes opened his eyes. There was a moment of empty peace before memory hit him like a shovel.

It had been a bad day for the Watch. There had been the funeral of Herbert Gaskin, for one thing. Poor old Gaskin. He had broken one of the fundamental rules of being a guard. It wasn't the sort of rule that someone like Gaskin could break twice.

And so he'd been lowered into the sodden ground with the rain drumming on his coffin and no-one present to mourn him but the three surviving members of the Night Watch, the most despised group of men in the entire city. Sergeant Colon had been in tears. Poor old Gaskin.

Poor old Vimes, Vimes thought.

Poor old Vimes, here in gutter. But that's where he started. Poor old Vimes, with the water swirling in under breastplate. Poor old Vimes, watching rest of gutter's contents ooze by. Prob'ly even poor old Gaskin has got better view now, he thought.

Lessee . . . he'd gone off after the funeral and got drunk. No, not drunk, another word, ended with 'er'. Drunker, that was it. Because world all twisted up and wrong, like distorted glass, only came back into focus if you looked at it through bottom of bottle.

Something else now, what was it.

Oh, yes. Night-time. Time for duty. Not for Gaskin, though. Have to get new fellow. New fellow coming anyway, wasn't that it? Some stick from the hicks. Written letter. Some tick from the shicks . . .

Vimes gave up, and slumped back. The gutter continued to swirl.

Overhead, the lighted letters fizzed and flickered in the rain.

It wasn't only the fresh mountain air that had given Carrot his huge physique. Being brought up in a gold mine run by dwarfs and working a twelve-hour day hauling wagons to the surface must have helped.

He walked with a stoop. What will do *that* is being brought up in a gold mine run by dwarfs who thought that five feet was a good height for a ceiling.

He'd always known he was different. More bruised for one thing. And then one day his father had come up to him or, rather, come up to his waist, and told him that he was not, in fact, as he had always believed, a dwarf.

It's a terrible thing to be nearly sixteen and the wrong species.

'We didn't like to say so before, son,' said his father. 'We thought you'd grow out of it, see.'

'Grow out of what?' said Carrot.

'Growing. But now your mother thinks, that is, we *both* think, it's time you went out among your own kind. I mean, it's not fair, keeping you cooped up here without company of your own height.' His father twiddled a loose rivet on his helmet, a sure sign that he was worried. 'Er,' he added.

'But *you're* my kind!' said Carrot desperately.

'In a manner of speaking, yes,' said his father. 'In another manner of speaking, which is a rather more precise and accurate manner of speaking, no. It's all this genetics business, you see. So it might be a very good idea if you were to go out and see something of the world.'

'What, for good?'

'Oh, no! No. Of course not. Come back and visit whenever you like. But, well, a lad your age, stuck down here . . . It's not right. You know. I mean. Not a child any more. Having to shuffle around on your knees most of the time, and everything. It's not right.'

'What is my own kind, then?' said Carrot, bewildered.

The old dwarf took a deep breath. 'You're human,' he said.

'What, like Mr Varneshi?' Mr Varneshi drove an ox-cart up the mountain trails once a week, to trade things for gold. 'One of the Big People?'

'You're six foot six, lad. He's only five foot.' The dwarf twiddled the loose rivet again. 'You see how it is.'

'Yes, but – but maybe I'm just tall for my height,' said Carrot desperately. 'After all, if you can have short humans, can't you have tall dwarfs?'

His father patted him companionably on the back of the knees.

'You've got to face facts, boy. You'd be much more at home up on the surface. It's in your blood. The roof isn't so low, either.' You can't keep knocking yourself out on the sky, he told himself.

'Hold on,' said Carrot, his honest brow wrinkling with the effort of calculation. 'You're a dwarf, right? And mam's a dwarf. So I should be a dwarf, too. Fact of life.'

The dwarf sighed. He'd hoped to creep up on this, over a period of months maybe, sort of break it to him gently, but there wasn't any time any more.

'Sit down, lad,' he said. Carrot sat.

'The thing is,' he said wretchedly, when the boy's big honest face was a little nearer his own, 'we found you in the woods one day. Toddling about near one of the tracks . . . um.' The loose rivet squeaked. The dwarf plunged on.

'Thing is, you see . . . there were these carts. On fire, as you might say. And dead people. Um yes. Extremely dead people. Because of bandits. It was a bad winter that winter, there were all sorts coming into the hills . . . so we took you in, of course, and then, well, it was a long winter, like I said, and your mam got used to you, and, well, we never got around to asking Varneshi to make enquiries. That's the long and the short of it.'

Carrot took this fairly calmly, mostly because he didn't understand nearly all of it. Besides, as far as he was aware, being found toddling in the woods was the normal method of childbirth. A dwarf is not considered old enough to have the technical processes explained to him* until he has reached puberty.**

'All right, dad,' he said, and leaned down so as to be level with the dwarf's ear. 'But you know, me and – you know Minty Rocksmacker? She's really beautiful, dad, got a beard as soft as a, a, a very soft thing – we've got an understanding, and—'

'Yes,' said the dwarf, coldly. 'I know. Her father's had a word with me.' So did her mother with your mother, he added silently, and then *she* had a word with me. Lots of words.

'It's not that they don't like you, you're a steady

---

*The pronoun is used by dwarfs to indicate both sexes. All dwarfs have beards and wear up to twelve layers of clothing. Gender is more or less optional.
**i.e., about 55.

lad and a fine worker, you'd make a good son-in-
law. *Four* good sons-in-law. That's the trouble. And
she's only sixty, anyway. It's not proper. It's not
right.'

He'd heard about children being reared by wolves.
He wondered whether the leader of the pack ever had
to sort out something tricky like this. Perhaps he'd
have to take him into a quiet clearing somewhere and
say, Look, son, you might have wondered why you're
not as hairy as everyone else . . .

He'd discussed it with Varneshi. A good solid
man, Varneshi. Of course, he'd known the man's
father. And his grandfather, now he came to think
about it. Humans didn't seem to last long, it was
probably all the effort of pumping blood up that
high.

'Got a problem there, king.* Right enough,' the
old man had said, as they shared a nip of spirits on a
bench outside Shaft #2.

'He's a good lad, mind you,' said the king. 'Sound
character. Honest. Not exactly brilliant, but you tell
him to do something, he don't rest until he's done it.
Obedient.'

'You could chop his legs off,' said Varneshi.

'It's not his legs that's going to be the problem,'
said the king darkly.

'Ah. Yes. Well, in *that* case you could—'

'No.'

'No,' agreed Varneshi, thoughtfully. 'Hmm. Well,
then what you should do is, you should send him

*Lit. *dezka-knik*, 'mine supervisor'.

away for a bit. Let him mix a bit with humans.' He sat back. 'What you've got here, king, is a duck,' he added, in knowledgeable tones.

'I don't think I should tell him that. He's refusing to believe he's a human as it is.'

'What I mean is, a duck brought up among chickens. Well-known farmyard phenomenon. Finds it can't bloody well peck and doesn't know what swimming is.' The king listened politely. Dwarfs don't go in much for agriculture. 'But you send him off to see a lot of other ducks, let him get his feet wet, and he won't go running around after bantams any more. And Bob's your uncle.'

Varneshi sat back and looked rather pleased with himself.

When you spend a large part of your life underground, you develop a very literal mind. Dwarfs have no use for metaphor and simile. Rocks are hard, the darkness is dark. Start messing around with descriptions like that and you're in big trouble, is their motto. But after two hundred years of talking to humans the king had, as it were, developed a painstaking mental toolkit which was nearly adequate for the job of understanding them.

'Surely Bjorn Stronginthearm is my uncle,' he pointed out, slowly.

'Same thing.'

There was a pause while the king subjected this to careful analysis.

'You're saying,' he said, weighing each word, 'that we should send Carrot away to be a duck among humans because Bjorn Stronginthearm is my uncle.'

41

'He's a fine lad. Plenty of openings for a big strong lad like him,' said Varneshi.

'I have heard that dwarfs go off to work in the Big City,' said the king uncertainly. 'And they send back money to their families, which is very commendable and proper.'

'There you are then. Get him a job in, in—' Varneshi sought for inspiration – 'in the Watch, or something. My great-grandfather was in the Watch, you know. Fine job for a big lad, my grandad said.'

'What is a Watch?' said the king.

'Oh,' said Varneshi, with the vagueness of someone whose family for the last three generations hadn't travelled more than twenty miles, 'they goes about making sure people keep the laws and do what they're told.'

'That is a very proper concern,' said the king who, since he was usually the one doing the telling, had very solid views about people doing what they were told.

'Of course, they don't take just anyone,' said Varneshi, dredging the depths of his recollection.

'I should think not, for such an important task. I shall write to their king.'

'I don't think they have a king there,' said Varneshi. 'Just some man who tells them what to do.'

The king of the dwarfs took this calmly. This seemed to be about ninety-seven per cent of the definition of kingship, as far as he was concerned.

Carrot took the news without fuss, just as he took instructions about re-opening Shaft #4 or cutting timber for shoring props. All dwarfs are by nature dutiful, serious, literate, obedient and thoughtful people whose only minor failing is a tendency, after one drink, to rush at enemies screaming 'Arrrrrrgh!' and axing their legs off at the knee. Carrot saw no reason to be any different. He would go to this city – whatever *that* was – and have a man made of him.

They took only the finest, Varneshi had said. A watchman had to be a skilled fighter and clean in thought, word and deed. From the depths of his ancestral anecdotage the old man had dragged tales of moonlight chases across rooftops, and tremendous battles with miscreants which, of course, his great-grandad had won despite being heavily outnumbered.

Carrot had to admit it sounded better than mining.

After some thought, the king wrote to the ruler of Ankh-Morpork, respectfully asking if Carrot could be considered for a place amongst the city's finest.

Letters rarely got written in that mine. Work stopped and the whole clan had sat around in respectful silence as his pen scrittered across the parchment. His aunt had been sent up to Varneshi's to beg his pardon but could he see his way clear to sparing a smidgen of wax. His sister had been sent down to the village to ask Mistress Garlick the witch how you stopped spelling recommendation.

Months had gone by.

And then there'd been the reply. It was fairly grubby, since mail in the Ramtops was generally handed to whoever was going in more or less the right direction, and it was also fairly short. It said, baldly, that his application was accepted, and would he present himself for duty immediately.

'Just like that?' he said. 'I thought there'd be tests and things. To see if I was suitable.'

'You're my son,' said the king. 'I told them that, see. Stands to reason you'll be suitable. Probably officer material.'

He'd pulled a sack from under his chair, rummaged around in it and presented Carrot with a length of metal, more a sword than a saw but only just.

'This might rightly belong to you,' he said. 'When we found the . . . carts, this was the only thing left. The bandits, you see. Just between you and me—' he beckoned Carrot closer – 'we had a witch look at it. In case it was magic. But it isn't. Quite the most unmagical sword she'd ever seen, she said. They normally have a bit, see, on account of it's like magnetism, I suppose. Got quite a nice balance, though.'

He handed it over.

He rummaged around some more. 'And then there's this.' He held up a shirt. 'It'll protect you.'

Carrot fingered it carefully. It was made from the wool of Ramtop sheep, which had all the warmth and softness of hog bristles. It was one of the legendary woolly dwarf vests, the kind of vest that needs hinges.

'Protect me from what?' he said.

'Colds, and so on,' said the king. 'Your mother says you've got to wear it. And, er . . . that reminds me. Mr Varneshi says he'd like you to drop in on the way down the mountain. He's got something for you.'

His father and mother had waved him out of sight. Minty didn't. Funny, that. She seemed to have been avoiding him lately.

He'd taken the sword, slung on his back, sandwiches and clean underwear in his pack, and the world, more or less, at his feet. In his pocket was the famous letter from the Patrician, the man who ruled the great fine city of Ankh-Morpork.

At least, that's how his mother had referred to it. It certainly had an important-looking crest at the top, but the signature was something like 'Lupin Squiggle, Sec'y, pp'.

Still, if it wasn't actually *signed* by the Patrician then it had certainly been written by someone who worked for him. Or in the same building. Probably the Patrician had at least *known* about the letter. In general terms. Not *this* letter, perhaps, but probably he knew about the existence of letters in general.

Carrot walked steadfastly down the mountain paths, disturbing clouds of bumblebees. After a while he unsheathed the sword and made experimental stabs at felonious tree stumps and unlawful assemblies of stinging nettles.

Varneshi was sitting outside his hut, threading dried mushrooms on a string.

'Hallo, Carrot,' he said, leading the way inside. 'Looking forward to the city?'

Carrot gave this due consideration.

'No,' he said.

'Having second thoughts, are you?'

'No. I was just walking along,' said Carrot honestly. 'I wasn't thinking about anything much.'

'Your dad give you the sword, did he?' said Varneshi, rummaging on a fetid shelf.

'Yes. And a woolly vest to protect me against chills.'

'Ah. Yes, it can be very damp down there, so I've heard. Protection. Very important.' He turned around and added, dramatically, '*This* belonged to my great-grandfather.'

It was a strange, vaguely hemispherical device surrounded by straps.

'It's some sort of sling?' said Carrot, after examining it in polite silence.

Varneshi told him what it was.

'Codpiece like in fish?' said Carrot, mystified.

'No. It's for the fighting,' mumbled Varneshi. 'You should wear it all the time. Protects your vitals, like.'

Carrot tried it on.

'It's a bit small, Mr Varneshi.'

'That's because you don't wear it on your head, you see.'

Varneshi explained some more, to Carrot's mounting bewilderment and, subsequently, horror. 'My great-grandad used to say,' Varneshi finished, 'that but for this I wouldn't be here today.'

'What did he mean by that?'

Varneshi's mouth opened and shut a few times. 'I've no idea,' he said, spinelessly.

Anyway, the shameful thing was now at the very

bottom of Carrot's pack. Dwarfs didn't have much truck with things like that. The ghastly preventative represented a glimpse into a world as alien as the backside of the moon.

There had been another gift from Mr Varneshi. It was a small but very thick book, bound in a leather that had become like wood over the years.

It was called: *The Laws And Ordinances of The Cities of Ankh And Morpork.*

'This belonged to my great-grandad as well,' he said. 'This is what the Watch has to know. You have to know all the laws,' he said virtuously, 'to be a good officer.'

Perhaps Varneshi should have recalled that, in the whole of Carrot's life, no-one had ever really lied to him or given him an instruction that he wasn't meant to take quite literally. Carrot solemnly took the book. It would never have occurred to him, if he was going to be an officer of the Watch, to be less than a good one.

It was a five hundred mile journey and, surprisingly, quite uneventful. People who are rather more than six feet tall and nearly as broad across the shoulders often have uneventful journeys. People jump out at them from behind rocks then say things like, 'Oh. Sorry. I thought you were someone else.'

He'd spent most of the journey reading.

And now Ankh-Morpork was before him.

It was a little disappointing. He'd expected high white towers rearing over the landscape, and flags. Ankh-Morpork didn't rear. Rather, it sort of skulked, clinging to the soil as if afraid someone might steal it. There were no flags.

There was a guard on the gate. At least, he was wearing chainmail and the thing he was propped up against was a spear. He had to be a guard.

Carrot saluted him and presented the letter. The man looked at it for some time.

'Mm?' he said, eventually.

'I think I've got to see Lupin Squiggle Sec'y pp,' said Carrot.

'What's the pp for?' said the guard suspiciously.

'Could it be Pretty Promptly?' said Carrot, who had wondered about this himself.

'Well, I don't know about any Sec'y,' said the guard. 'You want Captain Vimes of the Night Watch.'

'And where is he based?' said Carrot, politely.

'At this time of day I'd try The Bunch of Grapes in Easy Street,' said the guard. He looked Carrot up and down. 'Joining the Watch, are you?'

'I hope to prove worthy, yes,' said Carrot.

The guard gave him what could loosely be called an old-fashioned look. It was practically neolithic.

'What was it you done?' he said.

'I'm sorry?' said Carrot.

'You must of done something,' said the guard.

'My father wrote a letter,' said Carrot proudly. 'I've been volunteered.'

'Bloody hellfire,' said the guard.

Now it was night again, and beyond the dread portal:

'Are the Wheels of Torment duly spun?' said the Supreme Grand Master.

The Elucidated Brethren shuffled around their circle.

'Brother Watchtower?' said the Supreme Grand Master.

'Not my job to spin the Wheels of Torment,' muttered Brother Watchtower. ''s Brother Plasterer's job, spinning the Wheels of Torment—'

'No it bloody well isn't, it's my job to oil the Axles of the Universal Lemon,' said Brother Plasterer hotly. 'You always say it's *my* job—'

The Supreme Grand Master sighed in the depths of his cowl as yet another row began. From this dross he was going to forge an Age of Rationality?

'Just shut up, will you?' he snapped. 'We don't really need the Wheels of Torment tonight. Stop it, the pair of you. Now, Brethren – you have all brought the items as instructed?'

There was a general murmuring.

'Place them in the Circle of Conjuration,' said the Supreme Grand Master.

It was a sorry collection. Bring magical things, he'd said. Only Brother Fingers had produced anything worthwhile. It looked like some sort of altar ornament, best not to ask from where. The Supreme Grand Master stepped forward and prodded one of the other things with his toe.

'What,' he said, 'is this?'

''s a amulet,' muttered Brother Dunnykin. ''s very powerful. Bought it off a man. Guaranteed. Protects you against crocodile bites.'

'Are you sure you can spare it?' said the Supreme

Grand Master. There was a dutiful titter from the rest of the Brethren.

'Less of that, brothers,' said the Grand Master, spinning around. 'Bring magical things, I said. Not cheap jewellery and rubbish! Good grief, this city is lousy with magic!' He reached down. 'What are these things, for heaven's sake?'

'They're stones,' said Brother Plasterer uncertainly.

'I can see that. Why're they magical?'

Brother Plasterer began to tremble. 'They've got holes in them, Supreme Grand Master. Everyone knows that stones with holes in them are magical.'

The Supreme Grand Master walked back to his place on the circle. He threw his arms up.

'Right, fine, OK,' he said wearily. 'If that's how we're going to do it, that's how we're going to do it. If we get a dragon six inches long we'll *all* know the reason why. Won't we, Brother Plasterer. Brother Plasterer? Sorry. I didn't hear what you said? Brother Plasterer?'

'I said yes, Supreme Grand Master,' whispered Brother Plasterer.

'Very well. So long as that's *quite* understood.' The Supreme Grand Master turned and picked up the book.

'And now,' he said, 'if we are all quite ready . . .'

'Um.' Brother Watchtower meekly raised his hand.

'Ready for what, Supreme Grand Master?' he said.

'For the summoning, of course. Good grief, I should have thought—'

'But you haven't told us what we're supposed to *do*, Supreme Grand Master,' whined Brother Watchtower.

The Grand Master hesitated. This was quite true, but he wasn't going to admit it.

'Well, of course,' he said. 'It's obvious. You have to focus your concentration. Think hard about dragons,' he translated. 'All of you.'

'That's all, is it?' said Brother Doorkeeper.

'Yes.'

'Don't we have to chant a mystic prune or something?'

The Supreme Grand Master stared at him. Brother Doorkeeper managed to look as defiant in the face of oppression as an anonymous shadow in a black cowl could look. He hadn't joined a secret society not to chant mystic runes. He'd been looking forward to it.

'You can if you like,' said the Supreme Grand Master. 'Now, I want you – *yes, what is it, Brother Dunnykin?*'

The little Brother lowered his hand. 'Don't know any mystic prunes, Grand Master. Not to what you might call chant . . .'

'*Hum!*'

He opened the book.

He'd been rather surprised to find, after pages and pages of pious ramblings, that the actual Summoning itself was one short sentence. Not a chant, not a brief piece of poetry, but a mere assemblage of meaningless syllables. De Malachite said they caused interference patterns in the waves of reality, but the daft old fool

was probably making it up as he went along. That was
the trouble with wizards, they had to make everything
look difficult. All you really needed was willpower.
And the Brethren had a lot of that. Small-minded and
vitriolic willpower, yes, lousy with malignity maybe,
but still powerful enough in its way . . .

They'd try nothing fancy this time round. Somewhere inconspicuous . . .

Around him the Brethren were chanting what
each man considered, according to his lights, to be
something mystical. The general effect was actually
quite good, if you didn't listen to the words.

The words. Oh, yes . . .

He looked down, and spoke them aloud.

Nothing happened.

He blinked.

When he opened his eyes again he was in a dark
alley, his stomach was full of fire, and he was very
angry.

It was about to be the worst night of his life for
Zebbo Mooty, Thief Third Class, and it wouldn't
have made him any happier to know that it was also
going to be the last one. The rain was keeping people
indoors, and he was way behind on his quota. He
was, therefore, a little less cautious than he might
otherwise have been.

In the night time streets of Ankh-Morpork
caution is an absolute. There is no such thing as
moderately cautious. You are either very cautious, or
you are dead. You might be walking around and
breathing, but you're dead, just the same.

He heard the muffled sounds coming from the nearby alley, slid his leather-bound cosh from his sleeve, waited until the victim was almost turning the corner, sprang out, said 'Oh, shi—' and died.

It was a most unusual death. No-one else had died like that for hundreds of years.

The stone wall behind him glowed cherry red with heat, which gradually faded into darkness.

He was the first to see the Ankh-Morpork dragon. He derived little comfort from knowing this, however, because he was dead.

'—t,' he said, and his disembodied self looked down at the small heap of charcoal which, he knew with an unfamiliar sort of certainty, was what he had just been disembodied from. It was a strange sensation, seeing your own mortal remains. He didn't find it as horrifying as he would have imagined if you'd asked him, say, ten minutes ago. Finding that you are dead is mitigated by also finding that there really is a *you* who can find you dead.

The alley opposite was empty again.

'That was really strange,' said Mooty.

EXTREMELY UNUSUAL, CERTAINLY.

'Did you see that? What was it?' Mooty looked up at the dark figure emerging from the shadows. 'Who're you, anyway?' he added suspiciously.

GUESS, said the voice.

Mooty peered at the hooded figure.

'Cor!' he said. 'I thought you dint turn up for the likes o' me.'

I TURN UP FOR *EVERYONE*.

'I mean in . . . person, sort of thing.'

SOMETIMES. ON SPECIAL OCCASIONS.

'Yeah, well,' said Mooty, 'this is one of them, all right! I mean, it looked like a bloody dragon! What's a man to do? You don't expect to find a dragon around the corner!'

AND NOW, IF YOU WOULD CARE TO STEP THIS WAY . . . said Death, laying a skeletal hand on Mooty's shoulder.

'Do you know, a fortune teller once told me I'd die in my bed, surrounded by grieving great-grand-children,' said Mooty, following the stately figure. 'What do you think of that, eh?'

I THINK SHE WAS WRONG.

'A bloody dragon,' said Mooty. 'Fire breathing, too. Did I suffer much?'

NO. IT WAS PRACTICALLY INSTANTANEOUS.

'That's good. I wouldn't like to think I'd suffered much.' Mooty looked around him. 'What happens now?' he said.

Behind them, the rain washed the little heap of black ash into the mud.

The Supreme Grand Master opened his eyes. He was lying on his back. Brother Dunnykin was preparing to give him the kiss of life. The mere thought was enough to jerk anyone from the borders of consciousness.

He sat up, trying to shed the feeling that he weighed several tons and was covered in scales.

'We did it,' he whispered. 'The dragon! It came! I felt it!'

The Brethren glanced at one another.

'We never saw nothing,' said Brother Plasterer.

'I might of seen something,' said Brother Watchtower loyally.

'No, not *here*,' snapped the Supreme Grand Master. 'You hardly want it to materialize *here*, do you? It was out there, in the city. Just for a few seconds . . .'

He pointed. 'Look!'

The Brethren turned around guiltily, expecting at any moment the hot flame of retribution.

In the centre of the circle the magic items were gently crumbling to dust. Even as they watched, Brother Dunnykin's amulet collapsed.

'Sucked dry,' whispered Brother Fingers. 'I'll be damned!'

'Three dollars that amulet cost me,' muttered Brother Dunnykin.

'But it proves it works,' said the Supreme Grand Master. 'Don't you see, you fools? It works! We *can* summon dragons!'

'Could be a bit expensive in magical items,' said Brother Fingers doubtfully.

'—*three dollars, it was. No rubbish*—'

'Power,' growled the Supreme Grand Master, 'does not come cheap.'

'Very true,' nodded Brother Watchtower. 'Not cheap. Very true.' He looked at the little heap of exhausted magic again. 'Cor,' he said. 'We did it, though, dint we! We only went and bloody well did some magic, right?'

'See?' said Brother Fingers. 'I *tole* you there was nothin' to it.'

'You all did exceptionally well,' said the Supreme Grand Master encouragingly.

'—*should've been six dollars, but he said he'd cut his own throat and sell it me for three dollars*—'

'Yeah,' said Brother Watchtower. 'We got the hang of it all right! Dint hurt a bit. We done real magic! And dint get et by tooth fairies from out of the woodwork either, Brother Plasterer, I couldn't help noticing.'

The other Brethren nodded. Real magic. Nothing to it. Everyone had just better *watch out*.

'Hang on, though,' said Brother Plasterer. 'Where's this dragon *gone*? I mean, did we really summon it or not?'

'Fancy you asking a silly question like that,' said Brother Watchtower doubtfully.

The Supreme Grand Master brushed the dust off his mystic robe.

'We summoned it,' he said, 'and it came. But only as long as the magic lasted. Then it went back. If we want it to stay longer, we need more magic. Understand? And that is what we must get.'

'—*three dollars I shan't see again in a hurry*—'

'Shut up!'

Dearest Father [wrote Carrot] Well, here I am in Ankh-Morpork. It is not like at home. I think it must have changed a bit since Mr Varneshi's great-grandfather was here. I don't think people here know Right from Wrong.

I found Captain Vimes in a common ale-house. I remembered what you said about a good dwarf not going into such places, but since he did not come out, I went in. He was lying with his head on the table. When I spoke to him, he said, pull the other one, kid, it has got bells on. I believe he was the worse for drink. He told me to find a place to stay and report to Sgt Colon at the Watch House tonight. He said, anyone wanting to join the guard needed their head examined.

Mr Varneshi did not mention this. Perhaps it is done for reasons of Hygiene.

I went for a walk. There are many people here. I found a place, it is called The Shades. Then I saw some men trying to rob a young Lady. I set about them. They did not know how to fight properly and one of them tried to kick me in the Vitals, but I was wearing the Protective as instructed and he hurt himself. Then the Lady came up to me and said, Was I Interested in Bed. I said yes. She took me to where she lived, a boarding house, I think it is called. It is run by a Mrs Palm. The Lady whose purse it was, she is called Reet, said, You should of seen him, there were 3 of them, it was amazing. Mrs Palm said, It is on the house. She said, what a big Protective. So I went upstairs and fell asleep, although it is a very noisy place. Reet woke me up once or twice to say, Do you want anything, but they had no apples. So I have fallen on my Feet, as they say here but, I don't see how that is possible because, if you fall you fall off your Feet, it is Common Sense.

There is certainly a lot to do. When I went to see the Sgt I saw a place called, The Thieves' Guild!! I asked Mrs Palm and she said, Of course. She said the leaders of the Thieves in the City meet there. I went to the Watch House and met Sgt Colon, a very fat man, and when I told him about the Thieves' Guild he said, Don't be A Idiot. I do not think he is serious. He says, Don't you worry about Thieves' Guilds, This is all what you have to do, you walk along the Streets at Night, shouting, It's Twelve O'clock and All's Well. I said, What if it is not all well, and he said, You bloody well find another street.

This is not Leadership.

I have been given some chain mail. It is rusty and not well made.

They give you money for being a guard. It is, 20 dollars a month. When I get it I will send you it.

I hope you are all well and that Shaft #5 is now open. This afternoon I will go and look at the Thieves' Guild. It is disgraceful. If I do something about it, it will be a Feather in my Cap. I am getting the Hang of how they talk here already. Your loving son, Carrot.

PS. Please give all my love to Minty. I really miss her.

Lord Vetinari, the Patrician of Ankh-Morpork, put his hand over his eyes.

'He did what?'

'I was *marched* through the streets,' said Urdo van Pew, currently President of the Guild of Thieves, Burglars and Allied Trades. 'In broad daylight!

With my hands tied together!' He took a few steps towards the Patrician's severe chair of office, waving a finger.

'You know very well that we have kept within the Budget,' he said. 'To be *humiliated* like that! Like a common criminal! There had better be a *full* apology,' he said, 'or you will have another strike on your hands. We will be driven to it, despite our natural civic responsibilities,' he added.

It was the finger. The finger was a mistake. The Patrician was staring coldly at the finger. Van Pew followed his gaze, and quickly lowered the digit. The Patrician was not a man you shook a finger at unless you wanted to end up being able to count only to nine.

'And you say this was one person?' said Lord Vetinari.

'Yes! That is—' Van Pew hesitated.

It did sound weird, now he came to tell someone.

'But there are hundreds of you in there,' said the Patrician calmly. 'Thick as, you should excuse the expression, thieves.'

Van Pew opened and shut his mouth a few times. The honest answer would have been: yes, and if anyone had come sidling in and skulking around the corridors it would have been the worse for them. It was the way he strode in as if he owned the place that fooled everyone. That and the fact that he kept hitting people and telling them to Mend their Ways.

The Patrician nodded.

'I shall deal with the matter momentarily,' he said. It was a good word. It always made people hesitate. They were never quite sure whether he meant he'd deal with it *now*, or just deal with it *briefly*. And no-one ever dared ask.

Van Pew backed down.

'A full apology, mark you. I have a position to maintain,' he added.

'Thank you. Do not let me detain you,' said the Patrician, once again giving the language his own individual spin.

'Right. Good. Thank you. Very well,' said the thief.

'After all, you have such a lot of work to do,' Lord Vetinari went on.

'Well, of course this is the case.' The thief hesitated. The Patrician's last remark had barbs on it. You found yourself waiting for him to strike.

'Er,' he said, hoping for a clue.

'With so much business being conducted, that is.'

Panic took over the thief's features. Randomized guilt flooded his mind. It wasn't a case of what had he done, it was a question of what the Patrician had found out about. The man had eyes everywhere, none of them so terrifying as the icy blue ones just above his nose.

'I, er, don't quite follow . . .' he began.

'Curious choice of targets.' The Patrician picked up a sheet of paper. 'For example, a crystal ball belonging to a fortune teller in Sheer Street. A small ornament from the temple of Offler the Crocodile God. And so on. Gewgaws.'

'I am afraid I really don't know—' said the head thief. The Patrician leaned forward.

'No *unlicensed* thieving, surely?' he said.*

'I shall look into it directly!' stuttered the head thief. 'Depend upon it!'

The Patrician gave him a sweet smile. 'I'm sure I can,' he said. 'Thank you for coming to see me. Don't hesitate to leave.'

The thief shuffled out. It was always like this with the Patrician, he reflected bitterly. You came to him with a perfectly reasonable complaint. Next thing you knew, you were shuffling out backwards, bowing and scraping, relieved simply to be getting away. You had to hand it to the Patrician, he admitted grudgingly. If you didn't, he sent men to come and take it away.

When he'd gone Lord Vetinari rang the little bronze bell that summoned his secretary. The man's name, despite his handwriting, was Lupine Wonse. He appeared, pen poised.

You could say this about Lupine Wonse. He was neat. He always gave the impression of just being completed. Even his hair was so smoothed-down and oiled it looked as though it had been painted on.

'The Watch appears to be having some difficulty with the Thieves' Guild,' said the Patrician. 'Van Pew has been in here claiming that a member of the Watch arrested him.'

---

*One of the remarkable innovations introduced by the Patrician was to make the Thieves' Guild *responsible* for theft, with annual budgets, forward planning and, above all, rigid job protection. Thus, in return for an agreed average level of crime per annum, the thieves themselves saw to it that unauthorized crime was met with the full force of Injustice, which was generally a stick with nails in it.

'What for, sir?'

'Being a thief, apparently.'

'A member of the *Watch*?' said the secretary.

'I know. But just sort it out, will you?'

The Patrician smiled to himself.

It was always hard to fathom Lord Vetinari's idiosyncratic sense of humour, but a vision of the red-faced, irate head thief kept coming back to him.

One of the Patrician's greatest contributions to the reliable operation of Ankh-Morpork had been, very early in his administration, the legalizing of the ancient Guild of Thieves. Crime was always with us, he reasoned, and therefore, if you were going to have crime, it at least should be *organized* crime.

And so the Guild had been encouraged to come out of the shadows and build a big Guildhouse, take their place at civic banquets, and set up their training college with day-release courses and City and Guilds certificates and everything. In exchange for the winding down of the Watch, they agreed, while trying to keep their faces straight, to keep crime levels to a level to be determined annually. That way, everyone could plan ahead, said Lord Vetinari, and part of the uncertainty had been removed from the chaos that is life.

And then, a little while later, the Patrician summoned the leading thieves again and said, oh, by the way, there was something else. What was it, now? Oh, yes . . .

I know who you are, he said. I know where you live. I know what kind of horse you ride. I know where your wife has her hair done. I know where your lovely children, how old are they now, my, doesn't time fly, I know where they play. So you won't forget about what we agreed, will you? And he smiled.

So did they, after a fashion.

And in fact it had turned out very satisfactorily from everyone's point of view. It took the head thieves a very little time to grow paunches and start having coats-of-arms made and meet in a proper building rather than smoky dens, which no-one had liked much. A complicated arrangement of receipts and vouchers saw to it that, while everyone was eligible for the attentions of the Guild, no-one had too much, and this was very acceptable – at least to those citizens who were rich enough to afford the quite reasonable premiums the Guild charged for an uninterrupted life. There was a strange foreign word for this: *inn-sewer-ants*. No-one knew exactly what it had originally meant, but Ankh-Morpork had made it its own.

The Watch hadn't liked it, but the plain fact was that the thieves were far better at controlling crime than the Watch had ever been. After all, the Watch had to work twice as hard to cut crime just a little, whereas all the Guild had to do was to work less.

And so the city prospered, while the Watch had dwindled away, like a useless appendix, into a handful of unemployables who no-one in their right mind could ever take seriously.

The last thing anyone wanted them to do was get it into their heads to fight crime. But seeing the head thief discommoded was always worth the trouble, the Patrician felt.

Captain Vimes knocked very hesitantly at the door, because each tap echoed around his skull.

'Enter.'

Vimes removed his helmet, tucked it under his arm and pushed the door open. Its creak was a blunt saw across the front of his brain.

He always felt uneasy in the presence of Lupine Wonse. Come to that, he felt uneasy in the presence of Lord Vetinari – but that was different, that was down to *breeding*. And ordinary fear, of course. Whereas he'd known Wonse since their childhood in the Shades. The boy had shown promise even then. He was never a gang leader. Never a gang leader. Hadn't got the strength or stamina for that. And, after all, what was the point in being the gang leader? Behind every gang leader were a couple of lieutenants bucking for promotion. Being a gang leader is not a job with long-term prospects. But in every gang there is a pale youth who's allowed to stay because he's the one who comes up with all the clever ideas, usually to do with old women and un-locked shops; this was Wonse's natural place in the order of things.

Vimes had been one of the middle rankers, the falsetto equivalent of a yes-man. He remembered Wonse as a skinny little kid, always tagging along behind in hand-me-down pants with the kind of odd skipping run he'd invented to keep up with the bigger boys, and forever coming up with fresh ideas to stop them idly ganging up on him, which was the usual recreation if nothing more interesting presented itself. It was superb training for the rigours of adulthood, and Wonse became good at it.

Yes, they'd both started in the gutter. But Wonse had worked his way up whereas, as he himself would be the first to admit, Vimes had merely worked his way *along*. Every time he seemed to be getting anywhere he spoke his mind, or said the wrong thing. Usually both at once.

That was what made him uncomfortable around Wonse. It was the ticking of the bright clockwork of ambition.

Vimes had never mastered ambition. It was something that happened to other people.

'Ah, Vimes.'

'Sir,' said Vimes woodenly. He didn't try to salute in case he fell over. He wished he'd had time to drink dinner.

Wonse rummaged in the papers of his desk.

'Strange things afoot, Vimes. Serious complaint about you, I'm afraid,' he said. Wonse didn't wear glasses. If he *had* worn glasses, he'd have peered at Vimes over the top of them.

'Sir?'

'One of your Night Watch men. Seems he arrested the head of the Thieves' Guild.'

Vimes swayed a little and tried hard to focus. He wasn't ready for this sort of thing.

'Sorry, sir,' he said. 'Seem to have lost you there.'

'I *said*, Vimes, that one of your men arrested the head of the Thieves' Guild.'

'One of my men?'

'*Yes.*'

Vimes's scattered brain cells tried valiantly to regroup. 'A member of the *Watch*?' he said.

Wonse grinned mirthlessly. 'Tied him up and left him in front of the palace. There's a bit of a stink about it, I'm afraid. There was a note . . . ah . . . here it is . . . "This man is charged with, Conspiracy to commit Crime, under Section 14 (iii) of the General Felonies Act, 1678, by me, Carrot Ironfoundersson." '

Vimes squinted at him.

'Fourteen eye-eye-eye?'

'Apparently,' said Wonse.

'What does that mean?'

'I really haven't the faintest notion,' said Wonse drily. 'And what about the name . . . Carrot?'

'But we don't do things like that!' said Vimes. 'You can't go around arresting the Thieves' Guild. I mean, we'd be at it all day!'

'Apparently this Carrot thinks otherwise.'

The captain shook his head, and winced. 'Carrot? Doesn't ring a bell.' The tone of blurred conviction was enough even for Wonse, who was momentarily taken aback.

'He was quite—' The secretary hesitated. 'Carrot, Carrot,' he said. '*I've* heard the name before. Seen it written down.' His face went blank. 'The volunteer, that was it! Remember me showing you?'

Vimes stared at him. 'Wasn't there a letter from, I don't know, some dwarf—?'

'All about serving the community and keeping

the streets safe, that's right. Begging that his son would be found suitable for a humble position in the Watch.' The secretary was rummaging among his files.

'What'd he done?' said Vimes.

'Nothing. That was it. Not a blessed thing.'

Vimes's brow creased as his thoughts shaped themselves around a new concept.

'A *volunteer*?' he said.

'Yes.'

'He didn't have to join?'

'He *wanted* to join. And you said it must be a joke, and I said we ought to try and get more ethnic minorities into the Watch. You remember?'

Vimes tried to. It wasn't easy. He was vaguely aware that he drank to forget. What made it rather pointless was that he couldn't remember what it was he was forgetting any more. In the end he just drank to forget about drinking.

A trawl of the chaotic assortment of recollections that he didn't even try to dignify any more by the name of memory produced no clue.

'Do I?' he said helplessly.

Wonse folded his hands on the desk and leaned forward.

'Now look, Captain,' he said. 'Lordship wants an explanation. I don't want to have to tell him the captain of the Night Watch hasn't the faintest idea what goes on among the men under, if I may use the term loosely, his command. That sort of thing only leads to trouble, questions asked, that sort of thing. We don't want that, do we. Do we?'

'No, sir,' Vimes muttered. A vague recollection of someone earnestly talking to him in the Bunch of Grapes was bobbing guiltily at the back of his mind. Surely that hadn't been a dwarf? Not unless the qualification had been radically altered, at any rate.

'Of course we don't,' said Wonse. 'For old times' sake. And so on. So I'll think of something to tell him and you, Captain, will make a point of finding out what's going on and putting a stop to it. Give this dwarf a short lesson in what it means to be a guard, all right?'

'Haha,' said Vimes dutifully.

'I'm sorry?' said Wonse.

'Oh. Thought you made an ethnic joke, there. Sir.'

'Look, Vimes, I'm being very understanding. In the circumstances. Now, I want you to get out there and sort this out. Do *you* understand?'

Vimes saluted. The black depression that always lurked ready to take advantage of his sobriety moved in on his tongue.

'Right you are, Mr Secretary,' he said. 'I'll see to it that he learns that arresting thieves is against the law.'

He wished he hadn't said that. If he didn't say things like that he'd have been better off now, Captain of the *Palace* Guard, a big man. Giving him the Watch had been the Patrician's little joke. But Wonse was already reading a new document on his desk. If he noticed the sarcasm, he didn't show it.

'Very good,' he said.

*   *   *

Dearest Mother [Carrot wrote] It has been a much better day. I went into the Thieves' Guild and arrested the chief Miscreant and dragged him to the Patrician's Palace. No more trouble from him, I fancy. And Mrs Palm says I can stay in the attic because, it is always useful to have a man around the place. This was because, in the night, there were men the Worse for Drink making a Fuss in one of the Girl's Rooms, and I had to speak to them and they Showed Fight and one of them tried to hurt me with his knee but I had the Protective and Mrs Palm says he has broken his Patella but I needn't pay for a new one.

I do not understand some of the Watch duties. I have a partner, his name is Nobby. He says I am too keen. He says I have got a lot to learn. I think this is true, because, I have only got up to Page 326 in The Laws and Ordinances of the Cities of Ankh and Morpork. Love to all, Your Son, Carrot.

PS. Love to Minty.

It wasn't just the loneliness, it was the back-to-front way of living. That was it, thought Vimes.

The Night Watch got up when the rest of the world was going to bed, and went to bed when dawn drifted over the landscape. You spent your whole time in the damp, dark streets, in a world of shadows. The Night Watch attracted the kind of people who for one reason or another were inclined to that kind of life.

He reached the Watch House. It was an ancient

and surprisingly large building, wedged between a tannery and a tailor who made suspicious leather goods. It must have been quite imposing once, but quite a lot of it was now uninhabitable and patrolled only by owls and rats. Over the door a motto in the ancient tongue of the city was now almost eroded by time and grime and lichen, but could just be made out:

FABRICATI DIEM, PVNC

It translated – according to Sergeant Colon, who had served in foreign parts and considered himself an expert on languages – as 'To Protect and to Serve'.

Yes. Being a guard must have meant something, once.

Sergeant Colon, he thought, as he stumbled into the musty gloom. Now there was a man who liked the dark. Sergeant Colon owed thirty years of happy marriage to the fact that Mrs Colon worked all day and Sergeant Colon worked all night. They communicated by means of notes. He got her tea ready before he left at night, she left his breakfast nice and hot in the oven in the mornings. They had three grown-up children, all born, Vimes had assumed, as a result of extremely persuasive handwriting.

And Corporal Nobbs . . . well, anyone like Nobby had unlimited reasons for not wishing to be seen by other people. You didn't have to think hard about *that*. The only reason you couldn't say that Nobby was close to the animal kingdom was that the animal kingdom would get up and walk away.

And then, of course, there was himself. Just a skinny, unshaven collection of bad habits marinated in alcohol. And that was the Night Watch. Just the three of them. Once there had been dozens, hundreds. And now – just three.

Vimes fumbled his way up the stairs, groped his way into his office, slumped into the primeval leather chair with its prolapsed stuffing, scrabbled at the bottom drawer, grabbed bottle, bit cork, tugged, spat out cork, drank. Began his day.

The world swam into focus.

Life is just chemicals. A drop here, a drip there, everything's changed. A mere dribble of fermented juices and suddenly you're going to live another few hours.

Once, in the days when this had been a respectable district, some hopeful owner of the tavern next door had paid a wizard a considerable sum of money for an illuminated sign, every letter a different colour. Now it worked erratically and sometimes short-circuited in the damp. At the moment the E was a garish pink and flashed on and off at random.

Vimes had grown accustomed to it. It seemed like part of life.

He stared at the flickering play of light on the crumbling plaster for a while, and then raised one sandalled foot and thumped heavily on the floorboards, twice.

After a few minutes a distant wheezing indicated that Sergeant Colon was climbing the stairs.

Vimes counted silently. Colon always paused for six seconds at the top of the flight to get some of his breath back.

On the seventh second the door opened. The

sergeant's face appeared around it like a harvest moon.

You could describe Sergeant Colon like this: he was the sort of man who, if he took up a military career, would automatically gravitate to the post of sergeant. You couldn't imagine him ever being a corporal. Or, for that matter, a captain. If he didn't take up a military career, then he looked cut out for something like, perhaps, a sausage butcher; some job where a big red face and a tendency to sweat even in frosty weather were practically part of the specification.

He saluted and, with considerable care, placed a scruffy piece of paper on Vimes's desk and smoothed it out.

'Evenin', Captain,' he said. 'Yesterday's incident reports, and that. Also, you owe fourpence to the Tea Club.'

'What's this about a dwarf, Sergeant?' said Vimes abruptly.

Colon's brow wrinkled. 'What dwarf?'

'The one who's just joined the Watch. Name of—' Vimes hesitated – 'Carrot, or something.'

'Him?' Colon's mouth dropped open. 'He's a *dwarf*? I always said you couldn't trust them little buggers! He fooled me all right, Captain, the little sod must of lied about his height!' Colon was a sizeist, at least when it came to people smaller than himself.

'Do you know he arrested the President of the Thieves' Guild this morning?'

'What for?'

'For being president of the Thieves' Guild, it seems.'

The sergeant looked puzzled. 'Where's the crime in that?'

'I think perhaps I had better have a word with this Carrot,' said Vimes.

'Didn't you see him, sir?' said Colon. 'He said he'd reported to you, sir.'

'I, uh, must have been busy at the time. Lot on my mind,' said Vimes.

'Yes, sir,' said Colon, politely. Vimes had just enough self-respect left to look away and shuffle the strata of paperwork on his desk.

'We've got to get him off the streets as soon as possible,' he muttered. 'Next thing you know he'll be bringing in the chief of the Assassins' Guild for bloody well killing people! Where is he?'

'I sent him out with Corporal Nobbs, Captain. I said he'd show him the ropes, sort of thing.'

'You sent a raw recruit out with *Nobby*?' said Vimes wearily.

Colon stuttered. 'Well, sir, experienced man, I thought, Corporal Nobbs could teach him a lot—'

'Let's just hope he's a slow learner,' said Vimes, ramming his brown iron helmet on his head. 'Come on.'

When they stepped out of the Watch House there was a ladder against the tavern wall. A bulky man at the top of it swore under his breath as he wrestled with the illuminated sign.

'It's the E that doesn't work properly,' Vimes called up.

'What?'

'The E. And the T sizzles when it rains. It's about time it was fixed.'

'Fixed? Oh. Yes. Fixed. That's what I'm doing all right. Fixing.'

The Watch men splashed off through the puddles. Brother Watchtower shook his head slowly, and turned his attention once again to his screwdriver.

Men like Corporal Nobbs can be found in every armed force. Although their grasp of the minutiae of the Regulations is usually encyclopedic, they take good care never to be promoted beyond, perhaps, corporal. He tended to speak out of the corner of his mouth. He smoked incessantly but the weird thing, Carrot noticed, was that any cigarette smoked by Nobby became a dog-end almost instantly but *remained* a dog-end indefinitely or until lodged behind his ear, which was a sort of nicotine Elephant's Graveyard. On the rare occasions he took one out of his mouth he held it cupped in his hand.

He was a small, bandy-legged man, with a certain resemblance to a chimpanzee who never got invited to tea parties.

His age was indeterminate. But in cynicism and general world weariness, which is a sort of carbon dating of the personality, he was about seven thousand years old.

'A cushy number, this route,' he said, as they strolled along a damp street in the merchants' quarter. He tried a doorhandle. It was locked. 'You stick with me,' he added, 'and I'll see you're all right. Now, you try the handles on the other side of the street.'

'Ah. I understand, Corporal Nobbs. We've got to see if anyone's left their store unlocked,' said Carrot.

'You catch on fast, son.'

'I hope I can apprehend a miscreant in the act,' said Carrot zealously.

'Er, yeah,' said Nobby, uncertainly.

'But if we find a door unlocked I suppose we must summon the owner,' Carrot went on. 'And one of us would have to stay to guard things, right?'

'Yeah?' Nobby brightened. 'I'll do that,' he said. 'Don't you worry about it. Then you could go and find the victim. Owner, I mean.'

He tried another doorknob. It turned under his grip.

'Back in the mountains,' said Carrot, 'if a thief was caught, he was hung up by the—'

He paused, idly rattling a doorknob.

Nobby froze.

'By the what?' he said, in horrified fascination.

'Can't remember now,' said Carrot. 'My mother said it was too good for them, anyway. Stealing is Wrong.'

Nobby had survived any number of famous massacres by not being there. He let go of the door-knob, and gave it a friendly pat.

'Got it!' said Carrot. Nobby jumped.

'Got what?' he shouted.

'I remember what we hang them up by,' said Carrot.

'Oh,' said Nobby weakly. 'Where?'

'We hang them up by the town hall,' said Carrot. 'Sometimes for days. They don't do it again, I can tell you. And Bjorn Stronginthearm's your uncle.'

Nobby leaned his pike against the wall and fumbled a fag-end from the recesses of his ear. One or two things, he decided, needed to be sorted out.

'Why did you have to become a guard, lad?' he said.

'Everyone keeps on asking me that,' said Carrot. 'I didn't have to. I wanted to. It will make a Man of me.'

Nobby never looked anyone directly in the eye. He stared at Carrot's right ear in amazement.

'You mean you ain't running away from anything?' he said.

'What would I want to run away from anything for?'

Nobby floundered a bit. 'Ah. There's always something. Maybe – maybe you was wrongly accused of something. Like, maybe,' he grinned, 'maybe the stores was mysteriously short on certain items and you was unjustly blamed. Or certain items was found in your kit and you never knew how they got there. That sort of thing. You can tell old Nobby. Or,' he nudged Carrot, 'p'raps it was something else, eh? *Shershay la fem*, eh? Got a girl into trouble?'

'I—' Carrot began, and then remembered that, yes, one should tell the truth, even to odd people like Nobby who didn't seem to know what it was. And the truth was that he was always getting Minty in trouble, although exactly how and why was a bit of a mystery. Just about every time he left after paying calls on her at the Rocksmacker cave, he could hear her father and mother shouting at her. They were always very polite to him, but somehow merely being seen with him was enough to get Minty into trouble.

'Yes,' he said.

'Ah. Often the case,' said Nobby wisely.

'All the time,' said Carrot. 'Just about every night, really.'

'Blimey,' said Nobby, impressed. He looked down at the Protective. 'Is that why they make you wear that, then?'

'What do you mean?'

'Well, don't worry about it,' said Nobby. 'Everyone's got their little secret. Or big secret, as it might be. Even the captain. He's only with us because he was Brung Low by a Woman. That's what the sergeant says. Brung low.'

'Goodness,' said Carrot. It sounded painful.

'But I reckon it's 'cos he speaks his mind. Spoke it once too often to the Patrician, I heard. Said the Thieves' Guild was nothing but a pack of thieves, or something. That's why he's with us. Dunno, really.' He looked speculatively at the pavement and then said: 'So where're you staying, lad?'

'There's a lady called Mrs Palm—' Carrot began.

Nobby choked on some smoke that went the wrong way.

'In the Shades?' he wheezed. 'You're staying *there*?'

'Oh, yes.'

'Every *night*?'

'Well, every day, really. Yes.'

'And you've come here to have a man made of you?'

'Yes!'

'I don't think I should like to live where you come from,' said Nobby.

'Look,' said Carrot, thoroughly lost, 'I came because Mr Varneshi said it was the finest job in the world, upholding the law and everything. That's right, isn't it?'

'Well, er,' said Nobby. 'As to that . . . I mean, upholding the Law . . . I mean, *once*, yes, before we had all the Guilds and stuff . . . the law, sort of thing, ain't really, I mean, these days, everything's more . . . oh, I dunno. Basically you just ring your bell and keep your head down.'

Nobby sighed. Then he grunted, snatched his hourglass from his belt, and peered in at the rapidly-draining sand grains. He put it back, pulled the leather muffler off his bell's clapper, and shook it once or twice, not very loudly.

'Twelve of the clock,' he muttered, 'and all's well.'

'And that's it, is it?' said Carrot, as the tiny echoes died away.

'More or less. More or less.' Nobby took a quick drag on his dog-end.

'Just that? No moonlight chases across rooftops? No swinging on chandeliers? Nothing like that?' said Carrot.

'Shouldn't think so,' said Nobby fervently. 'I never done anything like that. No-one ever said any-thing to me about that.' He snatched a puff on the cigarette. 'A man could catch his death of cold, chasing around on rooftops. I reckon I'll stick to the bell, if it's all the same to you.'

'Can I have a go?' said Carrot.

Nobby was feeling unbalanced. It can be the only reason why he made the mistake of wordlessly handing Carrot the bell.

Carrot examined it for a few seconds. Then he waved it vigorously over his head.

'*Twelve o'clock!*' he bellowed. '*And all's weeeeelllll!*'

The echoes bounced back and forth across the street and finally were overwhelmed by a horrible, thick silence. Several dogs barked somewhere in the night. A baby started crying.

'Ssshh!' hissed Nobby.

'Well, it *is* all well, isn't it?' said Carrot.

'It won't be if you keep on ringing that bloody bell! Give it here.'

'I don't understand!' said Carrot. 'Look, I've got this book Mr Varneshi gave me—' he fumbled for the *Laws and Ordinances.*

Nobby glanced at them, and shrugged. 'Never heard of 'em,' he said. 'Now just shut up your row. You don't want to go making a din like that. You could attract all sorts. Come on, this way.'

He grabbed Carrot's arm and bustled him along the street.

'What sorts?' protested Carrot as he was pushed determinedly forward.

'Bad sorts,' muttered Nobby.

'But we're the *Watch*!'

'Damn right! And we don't want to go tangling

with people like that! Remember what happened to Gaskin!'

'I don't remember what happened to Gaskin!' said Carrot, totally bewildered. 'Who's Gaskin?'

'Before your time,' mumbled Nobby. He deflated a bit. 'Poor bugger. Could of happened to any of us.' He looked up and glared at Carrot. 'Now stop all this, you hear? It's getting on my nerves. Moonlight bloody chases, my bum!'

He stalked along the street. Nobby's normal method of locomotion was a kind of sidle, and the combination of stalking and sidling at the same time created a strange effect, like a crab limping.

'But, but,' said Carrot, 'in this book it says—'

'I don't want to know from no book,' growled Nobby.

Carrot looked utterly crestfallen.

'But it's the Law—' he began.

He was nearly terminally interrupted by an axe that whirred out of a low doorway beside him and bounced off the opposite wall. It was followed by sounds of splintering timber and breaking glass.

'Hey, Nobby!' said Carrot urgently. 'There's a fight going on!'

Nobby glanced at the doorway. 'O'*course* there is,' he said. 'It's a dwarf bar. Worst kind. You keep out of there, kid. Them little buggers like to trip you up and then kick twelve kinds of shit out of you. You come along o'Nobby and he'll—'

He grabbed Carrot's treetrunk arm. It was like trying to tow a building.

Carrot had gone pale.

'Dwarfs *drinking*? And *fighting*?' he said.

'You bet,' said Nobby. 'All the time. And they use the kind of language I wouldn't even use to my own dear mother. You don't want to mix it with them, they're a poisonous bunch of – *don't go in there!*'

No-one knows why dwarfs, who at home in the mountains lead quiet, orderly lives, forget it all when they move to the big city. Something comes over even the most blameless iron-ore miner and prompts him to wear chain-mail all the time, carry an axe, change his name to something like Grabthroat Shinkicker and drink himself into surly oblivion.

It's probably because they *do* live such quiet and orderly lives back home. After all, probably the first thing a young dwarf wants to do when he hits the big city after seventy years of working for his father at the bottom of a pit is have a big drink and then hit someone.

The fight was one of those enjoyable dwarfish fights with about a hundred participants and one hundred and fifty alliances. The screams, oaths and the ringing of axes on iron helmets mingled with the sounds of a drunken group by the fireplace who – another dwarfish custom – were singing about gold.

Nobby bumped into the back of Carrot, who was watching the scene with horror.

'Look, it's like this every night in here,' said Nobby. 'Don't interfere, that's what the sergeant says. It's their ethnic folkways, or somethin'. You don't go messin' with ethnic folkways.'

'But, but,' Carrot stuttered, 'these are my *people*. Sort of. It's shameful, acting like this. What must everyone think?'

'We think they're mean little buggers,' said Nobby. 'Now, *come on*!'

But Carrot had waded into the scuffling mass. He cupped his hands around his mouth and bellowed something in a language Nobby didn't understand. Practically any language including his native one would have fitted that description, but in this case it was Dwarfish.

'Gr-duzk! Gr'duzk! aaK'zt ezem ke bur'k tze tzim?'*

The fighting stopped. A hundred bearded faces glared up at Carrot's stooped figure, their annoyance mingled with surprise.

A battered tankard bounced off his breastplate. Carrot reached down and picked up a struggling figure, without apparent effort.

'J'uk, ydtruz-t'rud-eztuza, hudr'zd dezek drez'huk, huzu-kruk't b'tduz g'ke'k me'ek b'tduz t' be'tk kce'drutk ke'hkt'd. aaDb'thuk?'**

No dwarf had ever heard so many Old Tongue words from the mouth of anyone over four feet high. They were astonished.

---

*Lit: 'Good day! Good day! What is all of this that is going on here (in this place)?'

'Listen, sunshine [lit: 'the stare of the great hot eye in the sky whose fiery gaze penetrates the mouth of the cavern'] I don't want to have to give anyone a smacking, so if you play B'tduz* with me, I'll play B'tduz with you. OK?'****

***A popular dwarfish game which consists of standing a few feet apart and throwing large rocks at one another's head.

****Lit: 'All correctly beamed and propped?'

Carrot lowered the offending dwarf to the floor. There were tears in his eyes.

'You're dwarfs!' he said. 'Dwarfs shouldn't be acting like this! Look at you all. Aren't you ashamed?'

One hundred bone-hard jaws dropped.

'I mean, *look* at you!' Carrot shook his head. 'Can you imagine what your poor, white-bearded old mother, slaving away back in her little hole, wondering how her son is getting on tonight, can you imagine what she'd think if she saw you now? Your own dear mothers, who first showed you how to use a pickaxe—'

Nobby, standing by the doorway in terror and amazement, was aware of a growing chorus of nose-blowings and muffled sobs as Carrot went on: '—she's probably thinking, I expect he's having a quiet game of dominoes or something—'

A nearby dwarf, wearing a helmet encrusted with six-inch spikes, started to cry gently into his beer.

'And I bet it's a *long time* since any of you wrote her a letter, too, and you promised to write every week—'

Nobby absent-mindedly took out a grubby hand-kerchief and passed it to a dwarf who was leaning against the wall, shaking with grief.

'Now, then,' said Carrot kindly. 'I don't want to be hard on anyone, but I shall be coming past here every night from now on and I shall expect to see proper standards of dwarf behaviour. I know what it's like when you're far from home, but there's no excuse for this sort of thing.' He touched his helmet. '*G'hruk, t'uk.*'*

He gave them all a bright smile and half-walked, half-crouched out of the bar. As he emerged into the street Nobby tapped him on the arm.

'Don't you ever do anything like that to me again,' he fumed. 'You're in the City Watch! Don't give me any more of this law business!'

'But it is very important,' said Carrot seriously, trotting after Nobby as he sidled into a narrower street.

'Not as important as stayin' in one piece,' said Nobby. 'Dwarf bars! If you've got any sense, my lad, you'll come in here. And shut up.'

Carrot stared up at the building they had reached. It was set back a little from the mud of the street. The sounds of considerable drinking were coming from inside. A battered sign hung over the door. It showed a drum.

'A tavern, is it?' said Carrot, thoughtfully. 'Open at this hour?'

'Don't see why not,' said Nobby, pushing open the door. 'Damn useful idea. The Mended Drum.'

'And more drinking?' Carrot thumbed hastily through the book.

'I hope so,' said Nobby. He nodded to the troll which was employed by the Drum as a splatter.** 'Evenin', Detritus. Just showing the new lad the ropes.'

---

*'Evening, all.' (Lit: 'Felicitations to all present at the closing of the day'.)
**Like a bouncer, but trolls use more force.

The troll grunted, and waved a crusted arm.

The inside of the Mended Drum is now legendary as the most famous disreputable tavern on the Discworld, and such a feature of the city that, after recent unavoidable redecorations, the new owner spent days recreating the original patina of dirt, soot and less identifiable substances on the walls and imported a ton of pre-rotted rushes for the floor. The drinkers were the usual bunch of heroes, cut throats, mercenaries, desperadoes and villains, and only microscopic analysis could have told which was which. Thick coils of smoke hung in the air, perhaps to avoid touching the walls.

The conversation dipped fractionally as the two guards wandered in, and then rose to its former level. A couple of cronies waved to Nobby.

He realized that Carrot was busy.

'What you doin'?' he said. 'And no talkin' about mothers, right?'

'I'm taking notes,' said Carrot, grimly. 'I've got a notebook.'

'That's the ticket,' said Nobby. 'You'll like this place. I comes here every night for my supper.'

'How do you spell "contravention"?' said Carrot, turning over a page.

'I don't,' said Nobby, pushing through the crowds. A rare impulse to generosity lodged in his mind. 'What d'you want to drink?'

'I don't think that would be very appropriate,' said Carrot. 'Anyway, Strong Drink is a Mocker.'

He was aware of a penetrating stare in the back of his neck, and turned and looked into the big, bland and gentle face of an orangutan.

It was seated at the bar with a pint mug and a bowl of peanuts in front of it. It tilted its glass amicably towards Carrot and then drank deeply and noisily by apparently forming its lower lip into a sort of prehensile funnel and making a noise like a canal being drained.

Carrot nudged Nobby.

'There's a monk—' he began.

'Don't say it!' said Nobby urgently. 'Don't say the word! It's the Librarian. Works up at the University. Always comes down here for a nightcap of an evening.'

'And people don't object?'

'Why should they?' said Nobby. 'He always stands his round, just like everyone else.'

Carrot turned and looked at the ape again. A number of questions pressed for attention, such as: where does it keep its money? The Librarian caught his gaze, misinterpreted it, and gently pushed the bowl of peanuts towards him.

Carrot pulled himself to his full impressive height and consulted his notebook. The afternoon spent reading *The Laws and Ordinances* had been well spent.

'Who is the owner, proprietor, lessee, or landlord of these premises?' he said to Nobby.

'Wassat?' said the small guard. 'Landlord? Well, I suppose Charley here is in charge tonight. Why?' He indicated a large, heavy-set man whose face was a net of scars; its owner paused in the act of spreading the dirt more evenly around some glasses by means of a damp cloth, and gave Carrot a conspiratorial wink.

'Charley, this is Carrot,' said Nobby. 'He's stopping along of Rosie Palm's.'

'What, every night?' said Charley.

Carrot cleared his throat.

'If you are in charge,' he intoned, 'then it is my duty to inform you that you are under arrest.'

'A rest of what, friend?' said Charley, still polishing.

'Under *arrest*,' said Carrot, 'with a view to the presentation of charges to whit 1)(i) that on or about 18th Grune, at a place called the Mended Drum, Filigree Street, you did a) serve or b) did cause to serve alcoholic beverages after the hours of 12 (twelve) midnight, contrary to the provisions of the Public Ale Houses (Opening) Act of 1678, and 1)(ii) on or about 18th Grune, at a place called the Mended Drum, Filigree Street, you did serve or did cause to serve alcoholic beverages in containers other than of a size and capacity laid down by aforesaid Act, and 2)(i) that on or about 18th Grune, at a place called the Mended Drum, Filigree Street, you did allow customers to carry unsheathed edge weapons of a length greater than 7 (seven) inches, contrary to Section Three of said Act and 2)(ii) that on or about 18th Grune, at a place called the Mended Drum, Filigree Street, you did serve alcoholic beverages in premises apparently unlicensed for the sale and/or consumption of said beverages, contrary to Section Three of the aforesaid Act.'

There was dead silence as Carrot turned over another page, and went on: 'It is also my duty to inform you that it is my intention to lay evidence before the Justices with a view to the consideration of charges under the Public Foregatherings (Gambling) Act, 1567, the Licensed Premises (Hygiene) Acts of 1433, 1456, 1463, 1465, er, and 1470 through 1690, and also—' he glanced sideways at the Librarian, who knew trouble when he heard it coming and was hurriedly trying to finish his drink – 'the Domestic and Domesticated Animals (Care and Protection) Act, 1673.'

The silence that followed held a rare quality of breathless anticipation as the assembled company waited to see what would happen next.

Charley carefully put down the glass, whose smears had been buffed up to a brilliant shine, and looked down at Nobby.

Nobby was endeavouring to pretend that he was totally alone and had no connection whatsoever with anyone who might be standing next to him and coincidentally wearing an identical uniform.

'What'd he mean, Justices?' he said to Nobby. 'There ain't no Justices.'

Nobby gave a terrified shrug.

'New, is he?' said Charley.

'Make it easy on yourself,' said Carrot.

'This is nothing personal, you understand,' said Charley to Nobby. 'It's just a wossname. Had a wizard in here the other night talking about it. Sort of bendy educational thing, you know?' He appeared to think for a moment. '*Learning curve*. That was it.

It's a learning curve. Detritus, get your big stony arse over here a moment.'

Generally, about this time in the Mended Drum, someone throws a glass. And, in fact, this now happened.

Captain Vimes ran up Short Street – the longest in the city, which shows the famous Morpork subtle sense of humour in a nutshell – with Sergeant Colon stumbling along behind, protesting.

Nobby was outside the Drum, hopping from one foot to another. In times of danger he had a way of propelling himself from place to place without apparently moving through the intervening space which could put any ordinary matter transporter to shame.

''E's fighting in there!' he stuttered, grabbing the captain's arm.

'All by himself?' said the captain.

'No, with everyone!' shouted Nobby, hopping from one foot to the other.

'Oh.'

Conscience said: There's three of you. He's wearing the same uniform. He's one of your *men*. Remember poor old Gaskin.

Another part of his brain, the hated, despicable part which had nevertheless enabled him to survive in the Guards these past ten years, said: It's rude to butt in. We'll wait until he's finished, and then ask him if he wants any assistance. Besides, it isn't Watch policy to interfere in fights. It's a lot simpler to go in afterwards and arrest anyone recumbent.

There was a crash as a nearby window burst outwards and deposited a stunned fighter on the opposite side of the street.

'I think,' said the captain carefully, 'that we'd better take prompt action.'

'That's right,' said Sergeant Colon, 'a man could get hurt standing here.'

They sidled cautiously a little way down the street, where the sound of splintering wood and breaking glass wasn't so overpowering, and carefully avoided one another's eyes. There was the occasional scream from within the tavern, and every now and again a mysterious ringing noise, as though someone was hitting a gong with their knee.

They stood in a little pool of embarrassed silence.

'You had your holidays this year, Sergeant?' said Captain Vimes eventually, rocking back and forth on his heels.

'Yessir. Sent the wife to Quirm last month, sir, to see her aunt.'

'Very nice at this time of year, I'm told.'

'Yessir.'

'All the geraniums and whatnot.'

A figure tumbled out of an upper window and crumpled on the cobbles.

'That's where they've got the floral sundial, isn't it?' said the captain desperately.

'Yessir. Very nice, sir. All done with little flowers, sir.'

There was a sound like something hitting something else repeatedly with something heavy and wooden. Vimes winced.

'I don't think he'd of been *happy* in the Watch, sir,' said the sergeant, in a kindly voice.

The door of the Mended Drum had been torn off during riots so often that specially-tempered hinges had recently been installed, and the fact that the next tremendous crash tore the whole door and door-frame out of the wall only showed that quite a lot of money had been wasted. A figure in the midst of the wreckage tried to raise itself on its elbows, groaned, and slumped back.

'Well, it would seem that it's all—' the captain began, and Nobby said: 'It's that bloody troll!'

'What?' said Vimes.

'It's the troll! The one they have on the door!'

They advanced with extreme caution.

It was, indeed, Detritus the splatter.

It is very difficult to hurt a creature that is, to all intents and purposes, a mobile stone. Someone seemed to have managed it, though. The fallen figure was groaning like a couple of bricks being crushed together.

'That's a turnup for the books,' said the sergeant vaguely. All three of them turned and peered at the brightly-lit rectangle where the doorway had been. Things had definitely quietened down a bit in there.

'You don't think,' said the sergeant, 'that he's *winning*, do you?'

The captain thrust out his jaw. 'We owe it to our colleague and fellow officer,' he said, 'to find out.'

There was a whimper from behind them. They turned and saw Nobby hopping on one leg and clutching a foot.

'What's up with you, man?' said Vimes.

Nobby made agonized noises.

Sergeant Colon began to understand. Although cautious obsequiousness was the general tenor of Watch behaviour, there wasn't one member of the entire squad who hadn't, at some time, been at the wrong end of Detritus's fists. Nobby had merely tried to play catch-up in the very best traditions of policemen everywhere.

'He went and kicked him inna rocks, sir,' he said.

'Disgraceful,' said the captain vaguely. He hesitated. 'Do trolls *have* rocks?' he said.

'Take it from me, sir.'

'Good grief,' Vimes said. 'Dame Nature moves in strange ways, doesn't she.'

'Right you are, sir,' said the sergeant obediently.

'And now,' said the captain, drawing his sword, 'forward!'

'Yessir.'

'This means you too, Sergeant,' the captain added.

'Yessir.'

It was possibly the most circumspect advance in the history of military manoeuvres, right down at the bottom end of the scale that things like the Charge of the Light Brigade are at the top of.

They peered cautiously around the ravished doorway.

There were a number of people sprawled across the tables, or what remained of the tables. Those who were still conscious looked unhappy about it.

Carrot stood in the middle of the floor. His rusty

chain mail was torn, his helmet was missing, he was swaying a little from side to side and one eye was already starting to swell, but he recognized the captain, dropped the feebly-protesting customer he was holding, and threw a salute.

'Beg to report thirty-one offences of Making an Affray, sir, and fifty-six cases of Riotous Behaviour, forty-one offences of Obstructing an Officer of the Watch in the Execution of his Duty, thirteen offences of Assault with a Deadly Weapon, six cases of Malicious Lingering, and – and – Corporal Nobby hasn't even shown me one rope yet—'

He fell backwards, breaking a table.

Captain Vimes coughed. He wasn't at all sure what you were supposed to do next. As far as he knew, the Watch had never been in this position before.

'I think you should get him a drink, Sergeant,' he said.

'Yessir.'

'And get me one, too.'

'Yessir.'

'Have one yourself, why don't you.'

'Yessir.'

'And you, Corporal, will you please – *what* are you doing?'

'Searchingthebodiesir,' said Nobby quickly, straightening up. 'For incriminating evidence, and that.'

'In their money pouches?'

Nobby thrust his hands behind his back. 'You never know, sir,' he said.

The sergeant had located a miraculously un-broken bottle of spirits in the wreckage and forced a lot of its contents between Carrot's lips.

'What we going to do with all this lot, Captain?' he said over his shoulder.

'I haven't the faintest idea,' said Vimes, sitting down. The Watch jail was just about big enough for six very small people, which were usually the only sort to be put in it. Whereas these—

He looked around him desperately. There was Nork the Impaler, lying under a table and making bubbling noises. There was Big Henri. There was Grabber Simmons, one of the most feared bar-room fighters in the city. All in all, there were a lot of people it wouldn't pay to be near when they woke up.

'We could cut their froats, sir,' said Nobby, veteran of a score of residual battlefields. He had found an unconscious fighter who was about the right size and was speculatively removing his boots, which looked quite new and about the right size.

'That would be entirely wrong,' said Vimes. He wasn't sure how you actually went about cutting a throat. It had never hitherto been an option.

'No,' he said, 'I think perhaps we'll let them off with a caution.'

There was a groan from under the bench.

'Besides,' he went on quickly, 'we should get our fallen comrade to a place of safety as soon as possible.'

'Good point,' said the sergeant. He took a swig of the spirits, for the sake of his nerves.

The two of them managed to sling Carrot between them and guide his wobbling legs up the steps. Vimes, collapsing under the weight, looked around for Nobby.

'Corporal Nobbs,' he rasped, 'why are you kicking people when they're down?'

'Safest way, sir,' said Nobby.

Nobby had long ago been told about fighting fair and not striking a fallen opponent, and had then given some creative thought to how these rules applied to someone four feet tall with the muscle tone of an elastic band.

'Well, stop it. I want you to caution the felons,' said the captain.

'How, sir?'

'Well, you—' Captain Vimes stopped. He was blowed if he knew. He'd never done it.

'Just do it,' he snapped. 'Surely I don't have to tell you everything?'

Nobby was left alone at the top of the stairs. A general muttering and groaning from the floor indicated that people were waking up. Nobby thought quickly. He shook an admonitory cheese-straw of a finger.

'Let that be a lesson to you,' he said. '*Don't do it again.*'

And ran for it.

Up in the darkness of the rafters the Librarian scratched himself reflectively. Life was certainly full of surprises. He was going to watch developments with interest. He shelled a thoughtful peanut with his feet, and swung away into the darkness.

*　　*　　*

The Supreme Grand Master raised his hands.

'Are the Thuribles of Destiny ritually chastised, that Evil and Loose Thinking may be banished from this Sanctified Circle?'

'Yep.'

The Supreme Grand Master lowered his hands.

'Yep?' he said.

'Yep,' said Brother Dunnykin happily. 'Done it myself.'

'You are *supposed* to say "Yea, O Supreme One",' said the Supreme Grand Master. 'Honestly, I've told you enough times, if you're not all going to enter into the spirit of the thing—'

'Yes, you listen to what the Supreme Grand Master tells you,' said Brother Watchtower, glaring at the errant Brother.

'I spent hours chastising them thuribles,' muttered Brother Dunnykin.

'Carry on, O Supreme Grand Master,' said Brother Watchtower.

'Very well, then,' said the Grand Master. 'Tonight we'll try another experimental summoning. I trust you have obtained suitable raw material, brothers?'

'*—scrubbed and scrubbed, not that you get any thanks—*'

'All sorted out, Supreme Grand Master,' said Brother Watchtower.

It was, the Grand Master conceded, a slightly better collection. The Brothers had certainly been busy. Pride of place was given to an illuminated tavern sign whose removal, the Grand Master thought, should have merited some sort of civic award. At the moment the E was a ghastly pink and flashed on and off at random.

'*I* got that,' said Brother Watchtower proudly. 'They thought I was mending it or something, but I took my screwdriver and I—'

'Yes, well done,' said the Supreme Grand Master. 'Shows initiative.'

'*Thank* you, Supreme Grand Master,' beamed Brother Watchtower.

'*—knuckles rubbed raw, all red and cracked. Never even got my three dollars back, either, no-one as much as says—*'

'And now,' said the Supreme Grand Master, taking up the book, 'we will begin to commence. Shut up, Brother Dunnykin.'

Every town in the multiverse has a part that is something like Ankh-Morpork's Shades. It's usually the oldest part, its lanes faithfully following the original tracks of medieval cows going down to the river, and they have names like the Shambles, the Rookery, Sniggs Alley . . .

Most of Ankh-Morpork is like that in any case. But the Shades was even more so, a sort of black hole of bred-in-the-brickwork lawlessness. Put it like this: even the *criminals* were afraid to walk the streets. The Watch didn't set foot in it.

They were accidentally setting foot in it now. Not very reliably. It had been a trying night, and they had been steadying their nerves. They were now so steady that all four were relying on the other three to keep them upright and steer.

Captain Vimes passed the bottle back to the sergeant.

'Shame on, on, on,' he thought for a bit, 'you,' he said. 'Drun' in fron' of a super, super, superererer ofisiler.'

The sergeant tried to speak, but could only come out with a series of esses.

'Put yoursel' onna charge,' said Captain Vimes, rebounding off a wall. He glared at the brickwork. 'This wall assaulted me,' he declared. 'Hah! Think you're tough, eh! Well, 'm a ofisler of, of, of the Lawe I'llhaveyouknow, and we don' take any, any, any.'

He blinked slowly, once or twice.

'What's it we don' take any of, Sar'nt?' he said.

'Chances, sir?' said Colon.

'No, no, no. S'other stuff. Never mind. Anyway, we don' take any of, of, of *it* from anyone.' Vague visions were trotting through his mind, of a room full of criminal types, people that had jeered at him, people whose very existence had offended and taunted him for years, lying around and groaning. He was a little unclear how it had happened, but some almost forgotten part of him, some much younger Vimes with a bright shining breastplate and big hopes, a Vimes he thought the alcohol had long ago drowned, was suddenly restless.

'Shallie, shallie, shallie tell you something, Sarn't?' he said.

'Sir?' The four of them bounced gently off another wall and began another slow crabwise waltz across the alley.

'This city. This city. This city, Sarn't. This city is a, is a, is a Woman, Sarn't. So t'is. A Woman, Sarn't. Ancient raddled old beauty, Sarn't. Butifyoufallinlovewithher, then, then, then shekicksyouinnateeth—'

''s woman?' said Colon.

He screwed up his sweating face with the effort of thought.

''s eight miles wide, sir. ''s gotta river in it. Lots of, of houses and stuff, sir,' he reasoned.

'Ah. Ah. Ah.' Vimes waggled an unsteady finger at him. 'Never, never, never said it wasa *small* woman, did I. Be fair.' He waved the bottle. Another random thought exploded in the froth of his mind.

'We showed 'em anyway,' he said excitedly, as the four of them began an oblique shuffle back to the opposite wall. 'Showed them, dint we? Taught thema forget they won't lesson inna hurry, eh?'

'S'right,' said the sergeant, but not very enthusiastically. He was still wondering about his superior officer's sex life.

But Vimes was in the kind of mood that didn't need encouragement.

'Hah!' he shouted, at the dark alleyways. 'Don' like it, eh? Taste of your, your, your own medicine thingy. Well, now you can bootle in your trems!' He threw the empty bottle into the air.

'Two o'clock!' he yelled. 'And all's weeeellll!'

Which was astonishing news to the various shadowy figures who had been silently shadowing the four of them for some time. Only sheer puzzlement had prevented them making their attentions sharp and plain. These people are clearly guards, they were thinking, they've got the right helmets and everything, and yet here they are in the Shades. So they were being watched with the fascination that a pack of wolves might focus on a handful of sheep who had not only trotted into the clearing, but were making playful butts and baa-ing noises; the outcome was, of course, going to be mutton but in the meantime inquisitiveness gave a stay of execution.

Carrot raised his muzzy head.

'Where're we?' he groaned.

'On our way home,' said the sergeant. He looked up at the pitted, worm-eaten and knife-scored sign above them. 'We're jus' goin' down, goin' down, goin' down—' he squinted – 'Sweetheart Lane.'

'Sweetheart Lane s'not on the way home,' slurred Nobby. 'We wouldn't wanta go down Sweetheart Lane, it's in the Shades. Catch us goin' down Sweetheart Lane—'

There was a crowded moment in which realization did the icy work of a good night's sleep and several pints of black coffee. The three of them, by unspoken agreement, clustered up towards Carrot.

'What we gonna *do*, Captain?' said Colon.

'Er. We could call for help,' said the captain uncertainly.

'What, *here*?'

'You've got a point.'

'I reckon we must of turned left out of Silver Street instead of right,' quavered Nobby.

'Well, that's one mistake we won't make again in a hurry,' said the captain. Then he wished he hadn't.

They could hear footsteps. Somewhere off to their left, there was a snigger.

'We must form a square,' said the captain. They all tried to form a point.

'Hey! What was that?' said Sergeant Colon.

'What?'

'There it was again. Sort of a leathery sound.'

Captain Vimes tried not to think about hoods and garrotting.

There were, he knew, many gods. There was a god for every trade. There was a beggars' god, a whores' goddess, a thieves' god, probably even an assassins' god.

He wondered whether there was, somewhere in that vast pantheon, a god who would look kindly on hard-pressed and fairly innocent law-enforcement officers who were quite definitely about to die.

There probably wasn't, he thought bitterly. Something like that wasn't *stylish* enough for gods. Catch any god worrying about any poor sod trying to do his best for a handful of dollars a month. Not them. Gods went overboard for smart bastards whose idea of a day's work was prising the Ruby Eye of the Earwig King out of its socket, not for some unimaginative sap who just pounded the pavement every night . . .

'More sort of slithery,' said the sergeant, who liked to get things right.

And then there was a sound—

—perhaps a volcanic sound, or the sound of a boiling geyser, but at any rate a long, dry *roar* of a sound, like the bellows in the forges of the Titans—

—but it was not so bad as the light, which was blue-white and the sort of light to print the pattern of your eyeballs' blood vessels on the back of the inside of your skull.

They both went on for hundreds of years and then, instantly, stopped.

The dark aftermath was filled with purple images and, once the ears regained an ability to hear, a faint, clinkery sound.

The guards remained perfectly still for some time.

'Well, well,' said the captain weakly.

After a further pause he said, very clearly, every consonant slotting perfectly into place, 'Sergeant, take some men and investigate that, will you?'

'Investigate what, sir?' said Colon, but it had already dawned on the captain that if the sergeant took some men it would leave him, Captain Vimes, all alone.

'No, I've a better idea. We'll all go,' he said firmly. They all went.

Now that their eyes were used to the darkness they could see an indistinct red glow ahead of them.

It turned out to be a wall, cooling rapidly. Bits of calcined brickwork were falling off as they contracted, making little pinging noises.

That wasn't the worst bit. The worst bit was what was on the wall.

They stared at it.

They stared at it for a long time.

It was only an hour or two till dawn, and no-one even suggested trying to find their way back in the dark. They waited by the wall. At least it was warm.

They tried not to look at it.

Eventually Colon stretched uneasily and said, 'Chin up, Captain. It could have been worse.'

Vimes finished the bottle. It didn't have any effect. There were some types of sobriety that you just couldn't budge.

'Yes,' he said. 'It could have been us.'

The Supreme Grand Master opened his eyes.

'Once again,' he said, 'we have achieved success.'

The Brethren burst into a ragged cheer. The Brothers Watchtower and Fingers linked arms and danced an enthusiastic jig in their magic circle.

The Supreme Grand Master took a deep breath.

First the carrot, he thought, and now the stick. He *liked* the stick.

'Silence!' he screamed.

'Brother Fingers, Brother Watchtower, cease this shameful display!' he screeched. 'The rest of you, be silent!'

They quietened down, like rowdy children who have just seen the teacher come into the room. Then they quietened down a lot more, like children who have just seen the teacher's *expression*.

The Supreme Grand Master let this sink in, and then stalked along their ragged ranks.

'I suppose,' he said, 'that we think we've done some magic, do we? *Hmm*? Brother Watchtower?'

Brother Watchtower swallowed. 'Well, er, you *said* we were, er, I mean—'

'*You haven't done ANYTHING yet!*'

'Well, er, no, er—' Brother Watchtower trembled.

'Do *real* wizards leap about after a tiny spell and start chanting "Here we go, here we go, here we go", Brother Watchtower? *Hmm?*'

'Well, we were sort of—'

The Supreme Grand Master spun on his heel.

'And do they keep looking apprehensively at the woodwork, Brother Plasterer?'

Brother Plasterer hung his head. He hadn't realized anyone had noticed.

When the tension was twanging satisfactorily, like a bow-string, the Supreme Grand Master stood back.

'Why do I bother?' he said, shaking his head. 'I could have chosen *anyone*. I could have picked the *best*. But I've got a bunch of *children*.'

'Er, honest,' said Brother Watchtower, 'we was making an effort, I mean, we was really concentrating. Weren't we, lads?'

'Yes,' they chorused. The Supreme Grand Master glared at them.

'There's no room in this Brotherhood for Brothers who are not behind us all the way,' he warned.

With almost visible relief the Brethren, like panicked sheep who see that a hurdle has been opened in the fold, galloped towards the opening.

'No worries about that, your supremity,' said Brother Watchtower fervently.

'Commitment must be our watchword!' said the Supreme Grand Master.

'Watchword. Yeah,' said Brother Watchtower. He nudged Brother Plasterer, whose eyes had strayed to the skirting board again.

'Wha? Oh. Yeah. Watchword. Yeah,' said Brother Plasterer.

'And trust and fraternity,' said the Supreme Grand Master.

'Yeah. And them, too,' said Brother Fingers.

'*So,*' said the Supreme Grand Master, 'if there be any one here not anxious, yea, *eager* to continue in this great work, let him step forward now.'

No-one moved.

They're hooked. Ye gods, I'm good at this, thought the Supreme Grand Master. I can play on their horrible little minds like a xylophone. It's amazing, the sheer power of mundanity. Who'd have thought that weakness could be a greater force than strength? But you have to know how to direct it. And I do.

'Very well, then,' he said. 'And now, we will repeat the Oath.'

He led their stumbling, terrified voices through it, noting with approval the strangled way they said 'figgin'. And he kept one eye on Brother Fingers, too.

He's slightly brighter than the others, he thought. Slightly less gullible, at least. Better make sure I'm always the last to leave. Don't want any clever ideas about following me home.

You need a special kind of mind to rule a city like Ankh-Morpork, and Lord Vetinari had it. But then, he was a special kind of person.

105

He baffled and infuriated the lesser merchant princes, to the extent that they had long ago given up trying to assassinate him and now merely jockeyed for position amongst themselves. Anyway, any assassin who tried to attack the Patrician would be hard put to it to find enough flesh to insert the dagger.

While other lords dined on larks stuffed with peacocks' tongues, Lord Vetinari considered that a glass of boiled water and half a slice of dry bread was an elegant sufficiency.

It was exasperating. He appeared to have no vice that anyone could discover. You'd have thought, with that pale, equine face, that he'd incline towards stuff with whips, needles, and young women in dungeons. The other lords could have accepted that. Nothing wrong with whips and needles, in moderation. But the Patrician apparently spent his evenings studying reports and, on special occasions, if he could stand the excitement, playing chess.

He wore black a lot. It wasn't particularly impressive black, such as the best assassins wore, but the sober, slightly shabby black of a man who doesn't want to waste time in the mornings wondering what to wear. And you had to get up very early in the morning to get the better of the Patrician; in fact, it was wiser not to go to bed at all.

But he was popular, in a way. Under his hand, for the first time in a thousand years, Ankh-Morpork *operated*. It might not be fair or just or particularly democratic, but it worked. He tended it as one tends a topiary bush, encouraging a growth here, pruning an errant twig there. It was said that he would tolerate absolutely anything apart from anything that threatened the city,* and here it was . . .

He stared at the stricken wall for a long time, while the rain dripped off his chin and soaked his clothes. Behind him, Wonse hovered nervously.

Then one long, thin, blue-veined hand reached out and the fingertips traced the shadows.

Well, not so much shadows, more a series of silhouettes. The outline was very distinct. Inside, there was the familiar pattern of brickwork. Outside, though, something had fused the wall in a rather nice ceramic substance, giving the ancient flettons a melted, mirror-like finish.

The shapes outlined in brickwork showed a tableau of six men frozen in an attitude of surprise. Various upraised hands had quite clearly been holding knives and cutlasses.

The Patrician looked down silently on the pile of ash at his feet. A few streaks of molten metal might once have been the very same weapons that were now so decisively etched into the wall.

'Hmm,' he said.

Captain Vimes respectfully led him across the lane and into Fast Luck Alley, where he pointed out Exhibit A, to whit . . .

'Footprints,' he said. 'Which is stretching it a bit,

---

*And mime artists. It was a strange aversion, but there you are. Anyone in baggy trousers and a white face who tried to ply their art anywhere within Ankh's crumbling walls would very quickly find themselves in a scorpion pit, on one wall of which was painted the advice: Learn The Words.

sir. They're more what you'd call claws. One might go so far as to say talons.'

The Patrician stared at the prints in the mud. His expression was quite unreadable.

'I see,' he said eventually. 'And do you have an opinion about all this, Captain?'

The captain did. In the hours until dawn he'd had all sorts of opinions, starting with a conviction that it had been a big mistake to be born.

And then the grey light had filtered even into the Shades, and he was still alive and uncooked, and had looked around him with an expression of idiot relief and seen, not a yard away, these footprints. That had not been a good moment to be sober.

'Well, sir,' he said, 'I know that dragons have been extinct for thousands of years, sir—'

'Yes?' The Patrician's eyes narrowed.

Vimes plunged on. 'But, sir, the thing is, do *they* know? Sergeant Colon said he heard a leathery sound just before, just before, just before the, er . . . offence.'

'So you think an extinct, and indeed a possibly entirely mythical, dragon flew into the city, landed in this narrow alley, incinerated a group of criminals, and then flew away?' said the Patrician. 'One might say, it was a very public-spirited creature.'

'Well, when you put it like that—'

'If I recall, the dragons of legend were solitary and rural creatures who shunned people and dwelt in forsaken, out of the way places,' said the Patrician. 'They were hardly *urban* creatures.'

'No, sir,' said the captain, repressing a comment

that if you wanted to find a really forsaken, out of the way place then the Shades would fit the bill pretty well.

'Besides,' said Lord Vetinari, 'one would imagine that someone would have noticed, wouldn't you agree?'

The captain nodded at the wall and its dreadful frieze. 'Apart from them, you mean, sir?'

'In my opinion,' said Lord Vetinari, 'it's some kind of warfare. Possibly a rival gang has hired a wizard. A little local difficulty.'

'Could be linked to all this strange thieving, sir,' volunteered Wonse.

'But there's the footprints, sir,' said Vimes doggedly.

'We're close to the river,' said the Patrician. 'Possibly it was, perhaps, a wading bird of some sort. A mere coincidence,' he added, 'but I should cover them over, if I were you. We don't want people getting the wrong idea and jumping to silly conclusions, do we?' he added sharply.

Vimes gave in.

'As you wish, sir,' he said, looking at his sandals.

The Patrician patted him on the shoulder.

'Never mind,' he said. 'Carry on. Good show of initiative, that man. Patrolling in the Shades, too. Well done.'

He turned, and almost walked into the wall of chain mail that was Carrot.

To his horror, Captain Vimes saw his newest recruit point politely to the Patrician's coach. Around it, fully armed and wary, were six members of the Palace Guard, who straightened up and took a wary interest. Vimes disliked them intensely. They had plumes on their helmets. He hated plumes on a guard.

He heard Carrot say, 'Excuse me, sir, is this your coach, sir?' and the Patrician looked him blankly up and down and said, 'It is. Who are you, young man?'

Carrot saluted. 'Lance-constable Carrot, sir.'

'Carrot, Carrot. That name rings a bell.'

Lupine Wonse, who had been hovering behind him, whispered in the Patrician's ear. His face brightened. 'Ah, the young thief-taker. A little error there, I think, but commendable. No person is above the law, eh?'

'No, sir,' said Carrot.

'Commendable, commendable,' said the Patrician. 'And now, gentlemen—'

'About your coach, sir,' said Carrot doggedly, 'I couldn't help noticing that the front offside wheel, contrary to the—'

He's going to arrest the Patrician, Vimes told himself, the thought trickling through his brain like an icy rivulet. He's actually going to arrest the Patrician. The supreme ruler. He's going to arrest him. This is what he's actually going to do. The boy doesn't know the meaning of the word 'fear'. Oh, wouldn't it be a good idea if he knew the meaning of the word 'survival' . . .

And I can't get my jaw muscles to move.

We're all dead. Or worse, we're all detained at the Patrician's pleasure. And as we all know, he's seldom that pleased.

It was at this precise moment that Sergeant Colon earned himself a metaphorical medal.

'Lance-constable Carrot!' he shouted. 'Attention! Lance-constable Carrot, abou-uta turna! Lance-constable Carrot, qui-uck marcha!'

Carrot brought himself to attention like a barn being raised and stared straight ahead with a ferocious expression of acute obedience.

'Well done, that man,' said the Patrician thoughtfully, as Carrot strode stiffly away. 'Carry on, Captain. And do come down heavily on any silly rumours about dragons, right?'

'Yes, sir,' said Captain Vimes.

'Good man.'

The coach rattled off, the bodyguard running alongside.

Behind him, Captain Vimes was only vaguely aware of the sergeant yelling at the retreating Carrot to stop.

He was thinking.

He looked at the prints in the mud. He used his regulation pike, which he knew was exactly seven feet long, to measure their size and the distance between them. He whistled under his breath. Then, with considerable caution, he followed the alley around the corner; it led to a small, padlocked and dirt-encrusted door in the back of a timber warehouse.

There was something very wrong, he thought.

The prints come out of the alley, but they don't go in. And we don't often get any wading birds in the Ankh, mainly because the pollution would eat their legs away and anyway, it's easier for them to walk on the surface.

He looked up. A myriad washing lines criss-crossed the narrow rectangle of the sky as efficiently as a net.

So, he thought, something big and fiery came out of this alley but didn't come into it.

And the Patrician is very worried about it.

I've been told to forget about it.

He noticed something else at the side of the alley, and bent down and picked up a fresh, empty peanut shell.

He tossed it from hand to hand, staring at nothing.

Right now, he needed a drink. But perhaps it ought to wait.

The Librarian knuckled his way urgently along the dark aisles between the slumbering bookshelves.

The rooftops of the city belonged to him. Oh, assassins and thieves might make use of them, but he'd long ago found the forest of chimneys, buttresses, gargoyles and weathervanes a convenient and somehow comforting alternative to the streets.

At least, up until now.

It had seemed amusing and instructive to follow the Watch into the Shades, an urban jungle which held no fears for a 300-lb ape. But now the nightmare he had seen while brachiating across a dark alley would, if he had been human, have made him doubt the evidence of his own eyes.

As an ape, he had no doubts whatsoever about his eyes and believed them all the time.

Right now he wanted to concentrate them urgently on a book that might hold a clue. It was in a section no-one bothered with much these days; the books in there were not really magical. Dust lay accusingly on the floor.

Dust with footprints in it.

'Oook?' said the Librarian, in the warm gloom.

He proceeded cautiously now, realizing with a sense of inevitability that the footprints seemed to have the same destination in mind as he did.

He turned a corner and there it was.

The section.

The bookcase.

The shelf.

The gap.

There are many horrible sights in the multiverse. Somehow, though, to a soul attuned to the subtle rhythms of a library, there are few worse sights than a hole where a book ought to be.

Someone had stolen a book.

In the privacy of the Oblong Office, his personal sanctum, the Patrician paced up and down. He was dictating a stream of instructions.

'And send some men to paint that wall,' he finished.

Lupine Wonse raised an eyebrow.

'Is that wise, sir?' he said.

'You don't think a frieze of ghastly shadows will cause comment and speculation?' said the Patrician sourly.

'Not as much as fresh paint in the Shades,' said Wonse evenly.

The Patrician hesitated a moment. 'Good point,' he snapped. 'Have some men demolish it.'

He reached the end of the room, spun on his heel, and stalked up it again. Dragons! As if there were not enough important, enough *real* things to take up his time.

'Do you believe in dragons?' he said.

Wonse shook his head. 'They're impossible, sir.'

'So I've heard,' said Lord Vetinari. He reached the opposite wall, turned.

'Would you like me to investigate further?' said Wonse.

'Yes. Do so.'

'And I shall ensure the Watch take great care,' said Wonse.

The Patrician stopped his pacing. 'The Watch? The Watch? My dear chap, the Watch are a bunch of incompetents commanded by a drunkard. It's taken me years to achieve it. The last thing we need to concern ourselves with is the Watch.'

He thought for a moment. 'Ever seen a dragon, Wonse? One of the big ones, I mean? Oh, they're impossible. You said.'

'They're just legend, really. Superstition,' said Wonse.

'Hmm,' said the Patrician. 'And the thing about legends, of course, is that they are legendary.'

'Exactly, sir.'

'Even so—' The Patrician paused, and stared at Wonse for some time. 'Oh, well,' he said. 'Sort it out. I'm not having any of this dragon business. It's the type of thing that makes people restless. Put a stop to it.'

When he was alone he stood and looked out gloomily over the twin city. It was drizzling again.

Ankh-Morpork! Brawling city of a hundred thousand souls! And, as the Patrician privately observed, ten times that number of actual people. The fresh rain glistened on the panorama of towers and rooftops, all unaware of the teeming, rancorous world it was dropping into. Luckier rain fell on upland sheep, or whispered gently over forests, or pattered somewhat incestuously into the sea. Rain that fell on Ankh-Morpork, though, was rain that was in trouble. They did terrible things to water, in Ankh-Morpork. Being drunk was only the start of its problems.

The Patrician liked to feel that he was looking out over a city that worked. Not a beautiful city, or a renowned city, or a well-drained city, and certainly not an architecturally favoured city; even its most enthusiastic citizens would agree that, from a high point of vantage, Ankh-Morpork looked as though someone had tried to achieve in stone and wood an effect normally associated with the pavements outside all-night takeaways.

But it worked. It spun along cheerfully like a gyroscope on the lip of a catastrophe curve. And this, the Patrician firmly believed, was because no one group was ever powerful enough to push it over. Merchants, thieves, assassins, wizards – all competed energetically in the race without really realizing that it needn't be a race at all, and certainly not trusting one another enough to stop and wonder who had marked out the course and was holding the starting flag.

The Patrician disliked the word 'dictator'. It affronted him. He never told anyone what to do. He didn't have to, that was the wonderful part. A large part of his life consisted of arranging matters so that this state of affairs continued.

Of course, there were various groups seeking his overthrow, and this was right and proper and the sign of a vigorous and healthy society. No-one could call him unreasonable about the matter. Why, hadn't he founded most of them himself? And what was so beautiful was the way in which they spent nearly all their time bickering with one another.

Human nature, the Patrician always said, was a marvellous thing. Once you understood where its levers were.

He had an unpleasant premonition about this dragon business. If ever there was a creature that didn't have any obvious levers, it was a dragon. It would have to be sorted out.

The Patrician didn't believe in unnecessary cruelty.* He did not believe in pointless revenge. But he was a great believer in the need for things to be sorted out.

Funnily enough, Captain Vimes was thinking the same thing. He found he didn't like the idea of

---

*While being bang alongside the idea of necessary cruelty, of course.

citizens, even of the Shades, being turned into a mere ceramic tint.

And it had been done in front of the Watch, more or less. As if the Watch didn't matter, as if the Watch was just an irrelevant detail. That was what rankled.

Of course, it was true. That only made it worse.

What was making him even angrier was that he had disobeyed orders. He had scuffed up the tracks, certainly. But in the bottom drawer of his ancient desk, hidden under a pile of empty bottles, was a plaster cast. He could feel it staring at him through three layers of wood.

He couldn't imagine what had got into him. And now he was going even further out on to the limb.

He reviewed his, for want of a better word, troops. He'd asked the senior pair to turn up in plain clothes. This meant that Sergeant Colon, who'd worn uniform all his life, was looking red-faced and uncomfortable in the suit he wore for funerals. Whereas Nobby—

'I wonder if I made the word "plain" clear enough?' said Captain Vimes.

'It's what I wear outside work, guv,' said Nobby reproachfully.

'Sir,' corrected Sergeant Colon.

'My voice is in plain clothes too,' said Nobby. 'Initiative, that is.'

Vimes walked slowly around the corporal.

'And your plain clothes do not cause old women to faint and small boys to run after you in the street?' he said.

Nobby shifted uneasily. He wasn't at home with irony.

'No, sir, guv,' he said. 'It's all the go, this style.'

This was broadly true. There was a current fad in Ankh for big, feathered hats, ruffs, slashed doublets with gold frogging, flared pantaloons and boots with ornamental spurs. The trouble was, Vimes reflected, that most of the fashion-conscious had more body to go between these component bits, whereas all that could be said of Corporal Nobbs was that he was in there somewhere.

It might be advantageous. After all, absolutely no-one would ever believe, when they saw him coming down the street, that here was a member of the Watch trying to look inconspicuous.

It occurred to Vimes that he knew absolutely nothing about Nobbs outside working hours. He couldn't even remember where the man lived. All these years he'd known the man and he'd never realized that, in his secret private life, Corporal Nobbs was a bit of a peacock. A very *short* peacock, it was true, a peacock that had been hit repeatedly with something heavy, perhaps, but a peacock nonetheless. It just went to show, you never could tell.

He brought his attention back to the business in hand.

'I want you two,' he said to Nobbs and Colon, 'to mingle unobtrusively, or obtrusively in your case, Corporal Nobbs, with people tonight and, er, see if you can detect anything unusual.'

'Unusual like what?' said the sergeant.

Vimes hesitated. He wasn't exactly sure himself. 'Anything,' he said, 'pertinent.'

'Ah.' The sergeant nodded wisely. 'Pertinent. Right.'

There was an awkward silence.

'Maybe people have seen weird things,' said Captain Vimes. 'Or perhaps there have been unexplained fires. Or footprints. You know,' he finished, desperately, 'signs of dragons.'

'You mean, like, piles of gold what have been slept on,' said the sergeant.

'And virgins being chained to rocks,' said Nobbs, knowingly.

'I can see you're experts,' sighed Vimes. 'Just do the best you can.'

'This mingling,' said Sergeant Colon delicately, 'it would involve going into taverns and drinking and similar, would it?'

'To a certain extent,' said Vimes.

'Ah,' said the sergeant, happily.

'In moderation.'

'Right you are, sir.'

'And at your own expense.'

'Oh.'

'But before you go,' said the captain, 'do either of you know anyone who might *know* anything about dragons? Apart from sleeping on gold and the bit with the young women, I mean.'

'Wizards would,' volunteered Nobby.

'Apart from wizards,' said Vimes firmly. You couldn't trust wizards. Every guard knew you couldn't trust wizards. They were even worse than civilians.

Colon thought about it. 'There's always Lady Ramkin,' he said. 'Lives in Scoone Avenue. Breeds swamp dragons. You know, the little buggers people keep as pets?'

'Oh, her,' said Vimes gloomily. 'I think I've seen her around. The one with the "Whinny If You Love Dragons" sticker on the back of her carriage?'

'That's her. She's mental,' said Sergeant Colon.

'What do you want *me* to do, sir?' said Carrot.

'Er. You have the most important job,' said Vimes hurriedly. 'I want you to stay here and watch the office.'

Carrot's face broadened in a slow, unbelieving grin.

'You mean I'm left in *charge*, sir?' he said.

'In a manner of speaking,' said Vimes. 'But you're not allowed to arrest anyone, understand?' he added quickly.

'Not even if they're breaking the law, sir?'

'Not even then. Just make a note of it.'

'I'll read my book, then,' said Carrot. 'And polish my helmet.'

'Good boy,' said the captain. It should be safe enough, he thought. No-one ever comes in here, not even to report a lost dog. No-one ever thinks about the Watch. You'd have to be really out of touch to go to the Watch for help, he thought bitterly.

Scoone Avenue was a wide, tree-lined, and incredibly select part of Ankh, high enough above the river to be away from its all-pervading smell. People in Scoone Avenue had old money, which was supposed to be much better than new money, although Captain Vimes had never had enough of either to spot the difference. People in Scoone Avenue had their own personal bodyguards. People in Scoone Avenue were said to be so aloof they wouldn't even talk to the gods. This was a slight slander. They *would* talk to gods, if they were well-bred gods of decent family.

Lady Ramkin's house was not hard to find. It commanded an outcrop that gave it a magnificent view of the city, if that was your idea of a good time. There were stone dragons on the gatepost, and the gardens had an unkempt overgrown look. Statues of Ramkins long gone loomed up out of the greenery. Most of them had swords and were covered in ivy up to the neck.

Vimes sensed that this was not because the garden's owner was too poor to do anything about it, but rather that the garden's owner thought there were much more important things than ancestors, which was a pretty unusual point of view for an aristocrat.

They also apparently thought that there were more important things than property repair. When he rang the bell of the rather pleasant old house itself, in the middle of a flourishing rhododendron forest, several bits of the plaster facade fell off.

That seemed to be the only effect, except that something round the back of the house started to howl. Some *things*.

It started to rain again. After a while Vimes felt the dignity of his position and cautiously edged around the building, keeping well back in case anything else collapsed.

He reached a heavy wooden gate in a heavy wooden wall. In contrast with the general decrepitude of the rest of the place, it seemed comparatively new and very solid.

He knocked. This caused another fusillade of strange whistling noises.

The door opened. Something dreadful loomed over him.

'Ah, good man. Do you know anything about mating?' it boomed.

It was quiet and warm in the Watch House. Carrot listened to the hissing of sand in the hourglass and concentrated on buffing up his breastplate. Centuries of tarnish had given up under his cheerful onslaught. It gleamed.

You knew where you were with a shiny breastplate. The strangeness of the city, where they had all these laws and concentrated on ignoring them, was too much for him. But a shiny breastplate was a breastplate well shined.

The door opened. He peered across the top of the ancient desk. There was no-one there.

He tried a few more industrious rubs.

There was the vague sound of someone who had got fed up with waiting. Two purple-fingernailed hands grasped the edge of the desk, and the Librarian's face rose slowly into view like an early-morning coconut.

'Oook,' he said.

Carrot stared. It had been explained to him carefully that, contrary to appearances, laws governing the animal kingdom did not apply to the Librarian. On the other hand, the Librarian himself was never very interested in obeying the laws governing the human kingdom, either. He was one of those little anomalies you have to build around.

'Hallo,' said Carrot uncertainly. ('Don't call him "boy" or pat him, that always gets him annoyed.')

'Oook.'

The Librarian prodded the desk with a long, many-jointed finger.

'What?'

'*Oook.*'

'Sorry?'

The Librarian rolled his eyes. It was strange, he felt, that so-called intelligent dogs, horses and dolphins never had any difficulty indicating to humans the vital news of the moment, e.g., that the three children were lost in the cave, or the train was about to take the line leading to the bridge that had been washed away or similar, while he, only a handful of chromosomes away from wearing a vest, found it difficult to persuade the average human to come in out of the rain. You just couldn't talk to some people.

'*Oook!*' he said, and beckoned.

'I can't leave the office,' said Carrot. 'I've had Orders.'

The Librarian's upper lip rolled back like a blind.

'Is that a smile?' said Carrot. The Librarian shook his head.

'Someone hasn't committed a crime, have they?' said Carrot.

'Oook.'

'A bad crime?'

'Oook!'

'Like murder?'

'Eeek.'

'Worse than murder?'

'*Eeek!*' The Librarian knuckled over to the door and bounced up and down urgently.

Carrot gulped. Orders were orders, yes, but this was something else. The people in this city were capable of anything.

He buckled on his breastplate, screwed his sparkling helmet on to his head, and strode towards the door.

Then he remembered his responsibilities. He went back to the desk, found a scrap of paper, and painstakingly wrote: *Out Fighting Crime. Please Call Again Later. Thankyou.*

And *then* he went out on to the streets, untarnished and unafraid.

The Supreme Grand Master raised his arms.

'Brethren,' he said, 'let us begin . . .'

It was so easy. All you had to do was channel that great septic reservoir of jealousy and cringing resentment that the Brothers had in such abundance, harness their dreadful mundane unpleasantness which had a force greater in its way than roaring evil, and then open your own mind . . .

. . . into the place where the dragons went.

*   *   *

Vimes found himself grabbed by the arm and pulled inside. The heavy door shut behind him with a definite click.

'It's Lord Mountjoy Gayscale Talonthrust III of Ankh,' said the apparition, which was dressed in huge and fearsomely-padded armour. 'You know, I really don't think he can cut the mustard.'

'He can't?' said Vimes, backing away.

'It really needs two of you.'

'It does, doesn't it,' whispered Vimes, his shoulder blades trying to carve their way out through the fence.

'Could you oblige?' boomed the thing.

'What?'

'Oh, don't be squeamish, man. You just have to help him up into the air. It's me who has the tricky part. I know it's cruel, but if he can't manage it tonight then he's for the choppy-chop. Survival of the fittest and all that, don't you know.'

Captain Vimes managed to get a grip on himself. He was clearly in the presence of some sex-crazed would-be murderess, insofar as any gender could be determined under the strange lumpy garments. If it wasn't female, then references to 'it's me who has the tricky part' gave rise to mental images that would haunt him for some time to come. He knew the rich did things differently, but this was going too far.

'Madam,' he said coldly, 'I am an officer of the Watch and I must warn you that the course of action you are suggesting breaks the laws of the city—' and also of several of the more strait-laced gods, he added silently – 'and I must advise you that his Lordship should be released unharmed immediately—'

The figure stared at him in astonishment.

'Why?' it said. 'It's *my* bloody dragon.'

'Have another drink, not-Corporal Nobby?' said Sergeant Colon unsteadily.

'I do not mind if I do, not-Sergeant Colon,' said Nobby.

They were taking inconspicuosity seriously. That ruled out most of the taverns on the Morpork side of the river, where they were very well known. Now they were in a rather elegant one in downtown Ankh, where they were being as unobtrusive as they knew how. The other drinkers thought they were some kind of cabaret.

'I was thinking,' said Sergeant Colon.

'What?'

'If we bought a bottle or two, we could go home and then we'd be really inconspicuous.'

Nobby gave this some thought.

'But he said we've got to keep our ears open,' he said. 'We're supposed to, what he said, detect anything.'

'We can do that at my house,' said Sergeant Colon. 'We could listen all night, really hard.'

'Tha's a good point,' said Nobby. In fact, it sounded better and better the more he thought about it.

'But first,' he announced, 'I got to pay a visit.'

'Me too,' said the sergeant. 'This detecting business gets to you after a while, doesn't it.'

They stumbled out into the alley behind the tavern. There was a full moon up, but a few rags of scruffy cloud were drifting across it. The pair inconspicuously bumped into one another in the darkness.

'Is that you, Detector Sergeant Colon?' said Nobby.

'Tha's right! Now, can you detect the door to the privy, Detector Corporal Nobbs? We're looking for a short, dark door of mean appearance, ahahaha.'

There were a couple of clanks and a muffled swear-word from Nobby as he staggered across the alley, followed by a yowl when one of Ankh-Morpork's enormous population of feral cats fled between his legs.

'Who loves you, pussycat?' said Nobby under his breath.

'Needs must, then,' said Sergeant Colon, and faced a handy corner.

His private musings were interrupted by a grunt from the corporal.

'You there, Sergeant?'

'*Detector* Sergeant to you, Nobby,' said Sergeant Colon pleasantly.

Nobby's tone was urgent and suddenly very sober. 'Don't piss about, Sergeant, I just saw a dragon fly over!'

'I've seen a horsefly,' said Sergeant Colon, hiccuping gently. 'And I've seen a housefly. I've even seen a greenfly. But I ain't never seen a dragon fly.'

'Of course you have, you pillock,' said Nobby urgently. 'Look, I'm not messing about! He had wings on him like, like, like great big wings!'

Sergeant Colon turned majestically. The corporal's face had gone so white that it showed up in the darkness.

'Honest, Sergeant!'

Sergeant Colon turned his eyes to the damp sky and the rain-washed moon.

'All right,' he said, 'show me.'

There was a slithering noise behind him, and a couple of roof tiles smashed on to the street.

He turned. And there, on the roof, was the dragon.

'There's a dragon on the roof!' he warbled. 'Nobby, it's a *dragon* on the roof! What shall I do, Nobby? There's a dragon on the roof! It's looking right at me, Nobby!'

'For a start, you could do your trousers up,' said Nobby, from behind the nearest wall.

Even shorn of her layers of protective clothing, Lady Sybil Ramkin was still toweringly big. Vimes knew that the barbarian hublander folk had legends about great chain-mailed, armour-bra'd, carthorse-riding maidens who swooped down on battlefields and carried off dead warriors on their cropper to a glorious roistering afterlife, while singing in a pleasing mezzo-soprano. Lady Ramkin could have been one of them. She could have led them. She could have carried off a *battalion*. When she spoke, every word was like a hearty slap on the back and clanged with the aristocratic self-assurance of the totally well-bred. The vowel sounds alone would have cut teak.

Vimes's ragged forebears were used to voices like that, usually from heavily-armoured people on the back of a war charger telling them why it would be a jolly good idea, don'tcherknow, to charge the enemy and hit them for six. His legs wanted to stand to attention.

Prehistoric men would have worshipped her, and in fact had amazingly managed to carve lifelike statues of her thousands of years ago. She had a mass of chestnut hair; a wig, Vimes learned later. No-one who had much to do with dragons kept their own hair for long.

She also had a dragon on her shoulder. It had been introduced as Talonthrust Vincent Wonder-kind of Quirm, referred to as Vinny, and seemed to be making a large contribution to the unusual chemical smell that pervaded the house. This smell permeated everything. Even the generous slice of cake she offered him tasted of it.

'The, er, shoulder . . . it looks . . . very nice,' he said, desperate to make conversation.

'Rubbish,' said her ladyship. 'I'm just training him up because shoulder-sitters fetch twice the price.'

Vimes murmured that he had occasionally seen society ladies with small, colourful dragons on their shoulders, and thought it looked very, er, nice.

'Oh, it *sounds* nice,' she said. 'I'll grant you. Then they realize it means sootburns, frizzled hair and crap all down their back. Those talons dig in, too. And then they think the thing's getting too big and smelly and next thing you know it's either down to the Morpork Sunshine Sanctuary for Lost Dragons or the old heave-ho into the river with a rope round your neck, poor little buggers.' She sat down, arranging a skirt that could have made sails for a small fleet. 'Now then. *Captain* Vimes, was it?'

Vimes was at a loss. Ramkins long-dead stared down at him from ornate frames high on the shadowy walls. Between, around and under the portraits were the weapons they'd presumably used, and had used well and often by the look of them. Suits of armour stood in dented ranks along the walls. Quite a number, he couldn't help noticing, had large holes in them. The ceiling was a faded riot of moth-eaten banners. You did not need forensic examination to understand that Lady Ramkin's ancestors had never shirked a fight.

It was amazing that she was capable of doing something so unwarlike as having a cup of tea.

'My forebears,' she said, following his hypnotized gaze. 'You know, not one Ramkin in the last thousand years has died in his bed.'

'Yes, ma'am?'

'Source of family pride, that.'

'Yes, ma'am.'

'*Quite* a few of them have died in other people's, of course.'

Captain Vimes's teacup rattled in its saucer. 'Yes, ma'am,' he said.

'Captain is *such* a dashing title, I've always thought.' She gave him a bright, brittle smile. 'I mean, colonels and so on are always so stuffy, majors are pompous, but one always feels somehow that there is something delightfully *dangerous* about a captain. What was it you had to show me?'

Vimes gripped his parcel like a chastity belt.

'I wondered,' he faltered, 'how big swamp . . . er . . .' He stopped. Something dreadful was happening to his lower regions.

Lady Ramkin followed his gaze. 'Oh, take no notice of him,' she said cheerfully. 'Hit him with a cushion if he's a bother.'

A small elderly dragon had crawled out from under his chair and placed its jowly muzzle in Vimes's lap. It stared up at him soulfully with big brown eyes and gently dribbled something quite corrosive, by the feel of it, over his knees. And it stank like the ring around an acid bath.

'That's Dewdrop Mabelline Talonthrust the First,' said her ladyship. 'Champion and sire of champions. No fire left now, poor soppy old thing. He likes his belly rubbed.'

Vimes made surreptitiously vicious jerking motions to dislodge the old dragon. It blinked mournfully at him with rheumy eyes and rolled back the corner of its mouth, exposing a picket fence of soot-blackened teeth.

'Just push him off if he's a nuisance,' said Lady Ramkin cheerfully. 'Now then, what was it you were asking?'

'I was wondering how big swamp dragons grow?' said Vimes, trying to shift position. There was a faint growling noise.

'You came all the way up here to ask me that? Well . . . I seem to recall Gayheart Talonthrust of

Ankh stood fourteen thumbs high, toe to matlock,' mused Lady Ramkin.

'Er . . .'

'About three foot six inches,' she added kindly.

'No bigger than that?' said Vimes hopefully. In his lap the old dragon began to snore gently.

'Golly, no. He was a bit of a freak, actually. Mostly they don't get much bigger than eight thumbs.'

Captain Vimes's lips moved in hurried calculation. 'Two feet?' he ventured.

'Well done. That's the cobbs, of course. The hens are a bit smaller.'

Captain Vimes wasn't going to give in. 'A cobb would be a male dragon?' he said.

'Only after the age of two years,' said Lady Ramkin triumphantly. 'Up to the age of eight months he's a pewmet, then he's a cock until fourteen months, and then he's a snood—'

Captain Vimes sat entranced, eating the horrible cake, britches gradually dissolving, as the stream of information flooded over him; how the males fought with flame but in the laying season only the hens* breathed fire, from the combustion of complex intestinal gases, to incubate the eggs which needed such a fierce temperature, while the males gathered firewood; a group of swamp dragons was a *slump* or an *embarrassment*; a female was capable of laying up to three clutches of four eggs every year, most of which were trodden on by absent-minded males; and

---

*Only until their third clutch, of course. After that they're dams.

that dragons of both sexes were vaguely uninterested in one another, and indeed everything except firewood, except for about once every two months when they became as single-minded as a buzzsaw.

He was helpless to prevent himself being taken out to the kennels at the back, outfitted from neck to ankle in leather armour faced with steel plates, and ushered into the long low building where the whistling had come from.

The temperature was terrible, but not as bad as the cocktail of smells. He staggered aimlessly from one metal-lined pen to another, while pear-shaped, squeaking little horrors with red eyes were introduced as 'Moonpenny Duchess Marchpaine, who's gravid at the moment' and 'Moonmist Talon-thrust II, who was Best of Breed at Pseudopolis last year'. Jets of pale green flame played across his knees.

Many of the stalls had rosettes and certificates pinned over them.

'And this one, I'm afraid, is Goodboy Bindle Featherstone of Quirm,' said Lady Ramkin relentlessly.

Vimes stared groggily over the charred barrier at the small creature curled up in the middle of the floor. It bore about the same resemblance to the rest of them as Nobby did to the average human being. Something in its ancestry had given it a pair of eyebrows that were about the same size as its stubby wings, which could never have supported it in the air. Its head was the wrong shape, like an anteater. It had nostrils like jet intakes. If it ever managed to get airborne the things would have the drag of twin parachutes.

It was also turning on Captain Vimes the most silently intelligent look he'd ever had from any animal, including Corporal Nobbs.

'It happens,' said Lady Ramkin sadly. 'It's all down to genes, you know.'

'It is?' said Vimes. Somehow, the creature seemed to be concentrating all the power its siblings wasted in flame and noise into a stare like a thermic lance. He couldn't help remembering how much he'd wanted a puppy when he was a little boy. Mind you, they'd been starving – anything with meat on it would have done.

He heard the dragon lady say, 'One tries to breed for a good flame, depth of scale, correct colour and so on. One just has to put up with the occasional total whittle.'

The little dragon turned on Vimes a gaze that would be guaranteed to win it the award for Dragon the Judges would Most Like to Take Home and Use as A Portable Gas Lighter.

Total whittle, Vimes thought. He wasn't sure of the precise meaning of the word, but he could hazard a shrewd guess. It sounded like whatever it was you had left when you had extracted everything of any value whatsoever. Like the Watch, he thought. Total whittles, every one of them. And just like him. It was the saga of his life.

'That's Nature for you,' said her ladyship. 'Of course I wouldn't *dream* of breeding from him, but he wouldn't be able to anyway.'

'Why not?' said Vimes.

'Because dragons have to mate in the air and he'll never be able to fly with those wings, I'm afraid. I'll be sorry to lose the bloodline, naturally. His sire was Brenda Rodley's Treebite Brightscale. Do you know Brenda?'

'Er, no,' said Vimes. Lady Ramkin was one of those people who assumed that everyone else knew everyone one knew.

'Charming gel. Anyway, his brothers and sisters are shaping up very well.'

Poor little bastard, thought Vimes. That's Nature for you in a nutshell. Always dealing off the bottom of the pack.

No wonder they call her a *mother* . . .

'You said you had something to show me,' Lady Ramkin prompted.

Vimes wordlessly handed her the parcel. She slipped off her heavy mittens and unwrapped it.

'Plaster cast of a footprint,' she said, baldly. 'Well?'

'Does it remind you of anything?' said Vimes.

'Could be a wading bird.'

'Oh.' Vimes was crestfallen.

Lady Ramkin laughed. 'Or a really big dragon. Got it out of a museum, did you?'

'No. I got it off the street this morning.'

'Ha? Someone's been playing tricks on you, old chap.'

'Er. There was, er, circumstantial evidence.'

He told her. She stared at him.

'*Draco nobilis*,' she said hoarsely.

'Pardon?' said Vimes.

135

'*Draco nobilis*. The Noble dragon. As opposed to
these fellows—' she waved a hand in the direction
of the massed ranks of whistling lizards – '*Draco
vulgaris*, the lot of them. But the big ones are all
gone, you know. This really is a nonsense. No two
ways about it. All gone. Beautiful things, they were.
Weighed tons. Biggest things ever to fly. No-one
knows how they did it.'

And then they realized.

It was suddenly very quiet.

All along the rows of kennels, the dragons were
silent, bright-eyed and watchful. They were staring at
the roof.

Carrot looked around him. Shelves stretched away in
every direction. On those shelves, books. He made a
calculated guess.

'This is the Library, isn't it?' he said.

The Librarian maintained his gentle but firm grip
on the boy's hand and led him along the maze of
aisles.

'Is there a body?' said Carrot. There'd have to be.
Worse than murder! A body in a library. It could
lead to anything.

The ape eventually padded to a halt in front of a
shelf no different than, it seemed, a hundred others.
Some of the books were chained up. There was a gap.
The Librarian pointed to it.

'Oook.'

'Well, what about it? A hole where a book should
be.'

'Oook.'

'A book has been taken. A book has been taken? You summoned the Watch,' Carrot drew himself up proudly, 'because someone's taken a *book*? You think that's worse than murder?'

The Librarian gave him the kind of look other people would reserve for people who said things like 'What's so bad about genocide?'

'This is practically a criminal offence, wasting Watch time,' said Carrot. 'Why don't you just tell the head wizards, or whoever they are?'

'Oook.' The Librarian indicated with some surprisingly economical gestures that most wizards would not find their own bottoms with both hands.

'Well, I don't see what we can do about it,' said Carrot. 'What's the book called?'

The Librarian scratched his head. This one was going to be tricky. He faced Carrot, put his leather-glove hands together, then folded them open.

'I *know* it's a book. What's its name?'

The Librarian sighed, and held up a hand.

'Four words?' said Carrot. 'First word.' The ape pinched two wrinkled fingers together. 'Small word? A. The. Fo—'

'Oook!'

'The? The. Second word . . . third word? Small word. The? A? To? Of? Fro – Of? Of. The something Of something. Second word. What? Oh. First syllable. Fingers? Touching your fingers. Thumbs.'

The orangutan growled and tugged theatrically at one large hairy ear.

'Oh, *sounds* like. Fingers? Hand? Adding up. Sums. Cut off. Smaller word . . . Sum. Sum! Second syllable. Small. Very small syllable. A. In. Un. On. On! Sum. On. Sum On? Summon! Summon-*er*? Summon-*ing*? Summoning. Summoning. The Summoning of Something. This is fun, isn't it! Fourth word. Whole word—'

He peered intently as the Librarian gyrated mysteriously.

'Big thing. Huge big thing. Flapping. Great big flapping leaping thing. Teeth. Huffing. Blowing. Great big huge blowing flapping thing.' Sweat broke out on Carrot's forehead as he tried obediently to understand. 'Sucking fingers. Sucking fingers thing. Burnt. Hot. Great big hot blowing flapping thing . . .'

The Librarian rolled his eyes. Homo sapiens? You could keep it.

The great dragon danced and spun and trod the air over the city. Its colour was moonlight, gleaming off its scales. Sometimes it would twist and glide with deceptive speed over the rooftops for the sheer joy of existing.

And it was all wrong, Vimes thought. Part of him was marvelling at the sheer beauty of the sight, but an insistent, weaselly little group of brain cells from the wrong side of the synapses was scrawling its graffiti on the walls of wonderment.

It's a bloody great lizard, they jeered. Must weigh tons. Nothing that big can fly, not even on beautiful wings. And what is a flying lizard doing with great big scales on its back?

Five hundred feet above him a lance of blue-white flame roared into the sky.

It can't *do* something like that! It'd burn its own lips off!

Beside him Lady Ramkin stood with her mouth open. Behind her, the little caged dragons yammered and howled.

The great beast turned in the air and swooped over the rooftops. The flame darted out again. Below it, yellow flames sprang up. It was done so quietly and stylishly that it took Vimes several seconds to realize that several buildings had in fact been set on fire.

'Golly!' said Lady Ramkin. 'Look! It's using the thermals! That's what the fire is for!' She turned to Vimes, her eyes hopelessly aglow. 'Do you realize we're very probably seeing something that no-one has seen for centuries?'

'Yes, it's a bloody flying alligator setting fire to my city!' shouted Vimes.

She wasn't listening to him. 'There must be a breeding colony somewhere,' she said. 'After all this time! Where do you think it lives?'

Vimes didn't know. But he swore to himself that he would find out, and ask it some very serious questions.

'One egg,' breathed the breeder. 'Just let me get my hands on one egg . . .'

Vimes stared at her in genuine astonishment. It dawned on him that he was very probably a flawed character.

Below them, another building exploded into flame.

'How far exactly,' he said, speaking very slowly and carefully, as to a child, 'did these things fly?'

'They're very territorial animals,' murmured her ladyship. 'According to legend, they—'

Vimes realized he was in for another dose of dragon lore. 'Just give me the facts, m'lady,' he said impatiently.

'Not very far, really,' she said, slightly taken aback.

'Thank you very much, ma'am, you've been very helpful,' muttered Vimes, and broke into a run.

Somewhere in the city. There was nothing outside for miles except low fields and swamp. It had to be living somewhere in the city.

His sandals flapped on the cobbles as he hurtled down the streets. Somewhere in the city! Which was totally ridiculous, of course. Totally ridiculous and impossible.

He didn't deserve this. Of all the cities in all the world it could have flown into, he thought, it's flown into mine . . .

By the time he reached the river the dragon had vanished. But a pall of smoke was hanging over the streets and several human bucket chains had been formed to pass lumps of the river to the stricken buildings.* The job was considerably hampered by

---

*The Guild of Fire Fighters had been outlawed by the Patrician the previous year after many complaints. The point was that, if you bought a contract from the Guild, your house would be protected against fire. Unfortunately, the general Ankh-Morpork ethos quickly came to the fore and fire fighters would tend to go to prospective clients' houses in groups, making loud comments like 'Very inflammable looking place, this' and 'Probably go up like a firework with just one carelessly-dropped match, know what I mean?'

140

the droves of people streaming out of the streets, carrying their possessions. Most of the city was wood and thatch, and they weren't taking any chances.

In fact the danger was surprisingly small. Mysteriously small, when you came to think about it.

Vimes had surreptitiously taken to carrying a notebook these days, and he had noted the damage as if the mere act of writing it down somehow made the world a more understandable place.

Itym: Ae Coache House (belonging to an inoffensive businessman, who'd seen his new carriage go up in flames).

Itym: Ae smalle vegettable shope (with pin-point accuracy).

Vimes wondered about that. He'd bought some apples in there once, and there didn't appear to be anything about it that a dragon could possibly take offence at.

Still, very considerate of the dragon, he thought as he made his way to the Watch House. When you think of all the timber yards, hayricks, thatched roofs and oil stores it could have hit by chance, it's managed to really frighten everyone without actually harming the city.

Rays of early morning sunlight were piercing the drifts of smoke as he pushed open the door. This was home. Not the bare little room over the candle-maker's shop in Wixon's Alley, where he slept, but this nasty brown room that smelt of unswept chimneys, Sergeant Colon's pipe, Nobby's mysterious personal problem and, latterly, Carrot's armour polish. It was almost like home.

No-one else was there. He wasn't entirely surprised. He clumped up to his office and leaned back in his chair, whose cushion would have been thrown out of its basket in disgust by an incontinent dog, pulled his helmet over his eyes, and tried to think.

No good rushing about. The dragon had vanished in all the smoke and confusion, as suddenly as it had come. Time for rushing about soon enough. The important thing was working out where to rush to . . .

He'd been right. Wading bird! But where did you start looking for a bloody great dragon in a city of a million people?

He was aware that his right hand, entirely unbidden, had pulled open the bottom drawer, and three of his fingers, acting on sealed orders from his hindbrain, had lifted out a bottle. It was one of those bottles that emptied themselves. Reason told him that sometimes he must occasionally start one, break the seal, see amber liquid glistening all the way up to the neck. It was just that he couldn't remember the sensation. It was as if the bottles arrived two-thirds empty . . .

He stared at the label. It seemed to be Jimkin Bearhugger's Old Selected Dragon's Blood Whiskey. Cheap and powerful, you could light fires with it, you could clean spoons. You didn't have to drink much of it to be drunk, which was just as well.

It was Nobby who shook him awake with the news that there was a dragon in the city, and also that Sergeant Colon had had a nasty turn. Vimes sat and blinked owlishly while the words washed around him. Apparently having a fire-breathing lizard focusing interestedly on one's nether regions from a distance of a few feet can upset the strongest constitution. An experience like that could leave a lasting mark on a person.

Vimes was still digesting this when Carrot turned up with the Librarian swinging along behind him.

'Did you see it? Did you see it?' he said.

'We all saw it,' said Vimes.

'I know all about it!' said Carrot triumphantly. 'Someone's brought it here with magic. Someone's stolen a book out of the Library and guess what it's called?'

'Can't even begin to,' said Vimes weakly.

'It's called *The Summoning of Dragons*!'

'Oook,' confirmed the Librarian.

'Oh? What's it about?' said Vimes. The Librarian rolled his eyes.

'It's about how to summon dragons. By magic!'

'Oook.'

'And that's illegal, that is!' said Carrot happily. 'Releasing Feral Creatures upon the Streets, contrary to the Wild Animals (Public—'

Vimes groaned. That meant wizards. You got nothing but trouble with wizards.

'I suppose,' he said, 'there wouldn't be another copy of this book around, would there?'

'Oook.' The Librarian shook his head.

'And you wouldn't happen to know what's in it?' Vimes sighed. 'What? Oh. Four words,' he said

143

wearily. 'First word. Sounds like. Bend. Bough? Sow, cow, how . . . How. Second word. Small word. The, a, to . . . To. Yes *understood*, but I meant in any kind of detail? No. I see.'

'What're we going to do now, sir?' said Carrot anxiously.

'It's out there,' intoned Nobby. 'Gone to ground, like, during the hours of daylight. Coiled up in its secret lair, on top of a great hoard of gold, dreamin' ancient reptilian dreams fromma dawna time, waitin' for the secret curtains of the night, when once more it will sally forth—' He hesitated and added sullenly, 'What're you all looking at me like that for?'

'Very poetic,' said Carrot.

'Well, everyone knows the real old dragons used to go to sleep on a hoard of gold,' said Nobby. 'Well known folk myth.'

Vimes looked blankly into the immediate future. Vile though Nobby was, he was also a good indication of what was going through the mind of the average citizen. You could use him as a sort of laboratory rat to forecast what was going to happen next.

'I expect you'd be really interested in finding out where that hoard is, wouldn't you?' said Vimes experimentally.

Nobby looked even more shifty than usual. 'Well, Cap'n, I was thinking of having a bit of a look around. You know. When I'm off duty, of course,' he added virtuously.

'Oh, dear,' said Captain Vimes.

He lifted up the empty bottle and, with great care, put it back in the drawer.

The Elucidated Brethren were nervous. A kind of fear crackled from brother to brother. It was the fear of someone who, having cheerfully experimented with pouring the powder and wadding the ball, has found that pulling the trigger had led to a godawful bang and pretty soon someone is bound to come and see who's making all the noise.

The Supreme Grand Master knew that he had them, though. Sheep and lamb, sheep and lamb. Since they couldn't do anything much worse than they had already done they might as well press on and damn the world, and pretend they'd wanted it like this all along. Oh, the joy of it . . .

Only Brother Plasterer was actually happy.

'Let that be a lesson to all oppressive vegetable sellers,' he kept saying.

'Yes, er,' said Brother Doorkeeper. 'Only, the thing is, there's no chance of us sort of accidentally summoning the dragon *here*, is there?'

'I – that is, *we* – have it under perfect control,' said the Supreme Grand Master smoothly. 'The power is ours. I can assure you.'

The Brothers cheered up a little bit.

'And now,' the Supreme Grand Master continued, 'there is the matter of the king.'

The Brothers looked solemn, except for Brother Plasterer.

'Have we found him, then?' he said. 'That's a stroke of luck.'

'You never listen, do you?' snapped Brother Watchtower. 'It was all explained last week, we don't go around *finding* anyone, we *make* a king.'

'I thought he was supposed to turn up. 'Cos of destiny.'

Brother Watchtower sniggered. 'We sort of help Destiny along a bit.'

The Supreme Grand Master smiled in the depths of his robe. It was amazing, this mystic business. You tell them a lie, and then when you don't need it any more you tell them another lie and tell them they're progressing along the road to wisdom. Then instead of laughing they follow you even more, hoping that at the heart of all the lies they'll find the truth. And bit by bit they accept the unacceptable. Amazing.

'Bloody hell, that's clever,' said Brother Doorkeeper. 'How do we do that, then?'

'Look, the Supreme Grand Master said what we do, we find some handsome lad who's good at taking orders, he kills the dragon, and Bob's your uncle. Simple. Much more *intelligent* than waitin' for a so-called real king.'

'But—' Brother Plasterer seemed deep in the toils of cerebration, 'if *we* control the dragon, and we *do* control the dragon, right? Then we don't need anyone killing it, we just stop summoning it, and everyone'll be happy, right?'

'Ho yes,' said Brother Watchtower nastily, 'I can just see it, can you? We just trot out, say "Hallo, we won't set fire to your houses any more, aren't we nice", do we? The whole point about the thing with the king is that he'll be a, a sort of—'

'Undeniably potent and romantic symbol of absolute authority,' said the Supreme Grand Master smoothly.

'That's it,' said Brother Watchtower. 'A potent authority.'

'Oh, I *see*,' said Brother Plasterer. 'Right. OK. That's what the king'll be.'

'That's it,' said Brother Watchtower.

'No-one going to argue with a potent authority, are they?'

'Too right,' said Brother Watchtower.

'Stroke of luck, then, finding the true king right now,' said Brother Plasterer. 'Million to one chance, really.'

'We *haven't* found the right king. We don't *need* the right king,' said the Supreme Grand Master wearily. 'For the last time! I've just found us a likely lad who looks good in a crown and can take orders and knows how to flourish a sword. Now just *listen . . .*'

Flourishing, of course, was important. It didn't have much to do with wielding. Wielding a sword, the Supreme Grand Master considered, was simply the messy business of dynastic surgery. It was just a matter of thrust and cut. Whereas a king had to flourish one. It had to catch the light in just the right way, leaving watchers in no doubt that here was Destiny's chosen. He'd taken a long time preparing the sword and shield. It had been very expensive. The shield shone like a dollar in a sweep's earhole but the sword, the sword was magnificent . . .

It was long and shiny. It looked like something

147

some genius of metalwork – one of those little Zen guys who works only by the light of dawn and can beat a club sandwich of folded steels into something with the cutting edge of a scalpel and the stopping-power of a sex-crazed rhinoceros on bad acid – had made and then retired in tears because he'd never, ever, do anything so good again. There were so many jewels on the hilt it had to be sheathed in velvet, you had to look at it through smoked glass. Just laying a hand on it practically conferred kingship.

As for the lad . . . he was a distant cousin, keen and vain, and stupid in a passably aristocratic way. Currently he was under guard in a distant farm-house, with an adequate supply of drink and several young ladies, although what the boy seemed most interested in was mirrors. Probably hero material, the Supreme Grand Master thought glumly.

'I suppose,' said Brother Watchtower, 'that he *isn't* the real air to the throne?'

'What do you mean?' said the Supreme Grand Master.

'Well, you know how it is. Fate plays funny tricks. Haha. It'd be a laugh, wouldn't it,' said Brother Watchtower, 'if this lad turned out to be the real king. After all this trouble—'

'*There is no real king any more!*' snapped the Supreme Grand Master. 'What do you expect? Some people wandering in the wilderness for hundreds and hundreds of years, patiently handing down a sword and a birthmark? Some sort of *magic*?' He spat the word. He'd make use of magic, means to an end, end justifies means and so forth, but to go around believing it, believing it had some sort of moral force, like logic, made him wince. 'Good grief, man, be logical! Be rational. Even if any of the old royal family survived, the blood line'd be so watered down by now that there must be thousands of people who lay claim to the throne. Even—' he tried to think of the least likely claimant – 'even someone like Brother Dunnykin.' He stared at the assembled Brethren. 'Don't see him here tonight, by the way.'

'Funny thing, that,' said Brother Watchtower thoughtfully. 'Didn't you hear?'

'What?'

'He got bitten by a crocodile on his way home last night. Poor little bugger.'

'*What?*'

'Million-to-one chance. It'd escaped from a menagerie, or something, and was lying low in his back yard. He went to feel under his doormat for his doorkey and it had him by the funes.'* Brother Watchtower fumbled under his robe and produced a grubby brown envelope. 'We're having a whipround to buy him some grapes and that, I don't know whether you'd like to, er . . .'

'Put me down for three dollars,' said the Supreme Grand Master.

Brother Watchtower nodded. 'Funny thing,' he said, 'I already have.'

Just a few more nights, thought the Supreme Grand Master. By tomorrow the people'll be so desperate, they'd crown even a one-legged troll if he

---

*A species of geranium.

got rid of the dragon. And we'll have a king, and he'll have an advisor, a trusted man, of course, and this stupid rabble can go back to the gutter. No more dressing up, no more ritual.

No more summoning the dragon.

I can give it up, he thought. I can give it up any time I like.

The streets outside the Patrician's palace were thronged. There was a manic air of carnival. Vimes ran a practised eye over the assortment before him. It was the usual Ankh-Morpork mob in times of crisis; half of them were here to complain, a quarter of them were here to watch the other half, and the remainder were here to rob, importune or sell hot-dogs to the rest. There were a few new faces, though. There were a number of grim men with big swords slung over their shoulders and whips slung on their belts, striding through the crowds.

'News spreads quick, don't it,' observed a familiar voice by his ear. 'Morning, Captain.'

Vimes looked into the grinning, cadaverous face of Cut-me-own-Throat Dibbler, purveyor of absolutely anything that could be sold hurriedly from an open suitcase in a busy street and was guaranteed to have fallen off the back of an oxcart.

'Morning, Throat,' said Vimes absently. 'What're you selling?'

'Genuine article, Captain.' Throat leaned closer. He was the sort of person who could make 'Good morning' sound like a once-in-a-lifetime, never-to-be-repeated offer. His eyes swivelled back and forth in their sockets, like two rodents trying to find a way out. 'Can't afford to be without it,' he hissed. 'Anti-dragon cream. Personal guarantee: if you're incinerated you get your money back, no quibble.'

'What you're saying,' said Vimes slowly, 'if I understand the wording correctly, is that if I am baked alive by the dragon you'll return the money?'

'Upon personal application,' said Cut-me-own-Throat. He unscrewed the lid from a jar of vivid green ointment and thrust it under Vimes's nose. 'Made from over fifty different rare spices and herbs to a recipe known only to a bunch of ancient monks what live on some mountain somewhere. One dollar a jar, and I'm cutting my own throat. It's a public service, really,' he added piously.

'You've got to hand it to those ancient monks, brewing it up so quickly,' said Vimes.

'Clever buggers,' agreed Cut-me-own-Throat. 'It must be all that meditation and yak yogurt.'

'So what's happening, Throat?' said Vimes. 'Who're all the guys with the big swords?'

'Dragon hunters, Cap'n. The Patrician announced a reward of fifty thousand dollars to anyone who brings him the dragon's head. Not attached to the dragon, either; he's no fool, that man.'

'What?'

'That's what he said. It's all written on posters.'

'Fifty thousand dollars!'

'Not chicken feed, eh?'

'More like dragon fodder,' said Vimes. It'd bring trouble, you mark his words. 'I'm amazed you're not grabbing a sword and joining in.'

'I'm more in what you might call the service sector, Cap'n.' Throat looked both ways conspiratorially, and then passed Vimes a slip of parchment.

It said:

> Anti-dragon mirror shields A$500
> Portable lair detectors A$250
> Dragon-piercing arrows A$100 per each
> Shovels A$5 Picks A$5 Sacks A$1

Vimes handed it back. 'Why the sacks?' he said.

'On account of the hoard,' said Throat.

'Oh, yes,' said Vimes gloomily. 'Of course.'

'Tell you what,' said Throat, 'tell you what. For our boys in brown, ten percent off.'

'And you're cutting your own throat, Throat?'

'Fifteen percent for officers!' urged Throat, as Vimes walked away. The cause of the slight panic in his voice was soon apparent. He had plenty of competition.

The people of Ankh-Morpork were not by nature heroic but were, by nature, salesmen. In the space of a few feet Vimes could have bought any number of magical weapons *Genuine certyfycate of orthenticity with everyone*, a cloak of invisibility – a good touch, he thought, and he was really impressed by the way the stallowner was using a mirror with no glass in it – and, by way of lighter relief, dragon biscuits, balloons and windmills on sticks. Copper bracelets guaranteed to bring relief from dragons were a nice thought.

There seemed to be as many sacks and shovels about as there were swords.

Gold, that was it. The hoard. Hah!

Fifty thousand dollars! An officer of the Watch earned thirty dollars a month and had to pay to have his own dents beaten out.

What he couldn't do with fifty thousand dollars . . .

Vimes thought about this for a while and then thought of the things he *could* do with fifty thousand dollars. There were so many more of them, for a start.

He almost walked into a group of men clustered around a poster nailed to the wall. It declared, indeed, that the head of the dragon that had terrorized the city would be worth A\$50,000 to the brave hero that delivered it to the palace.

One of the cluster, who from his size, weaponry and that way he was slowly tracing the lettering with his finger Vimes decided was a leading hero, was doing the reading for the others.

'—to ter-her pal-ack-ee,' he concluded.

'Fifty thousand,' said one of them reflectively, rubbing his chin.

'Cheap job,' said the intellectual. 'Well below the rate. Should be half the kingdom and his daughter's hand in marriage.'

'Yes, but he ain't a king. He's a Patrician.'

'Well, half his Patrimony or whatever. What's his daughter like?'

The assembled hunters didn't know.

'He's not married,' Vimes volunteered. 'And he hasn't got a daughter.'

They turned and looked him up and down. He could see the disdain in their eyes. They probably got through dozens like him every day. 'Not got a daughter?' said one of them. 'Wants people to kill dragons and he hasn't got a daughter?'

Vimes felt, in an odd way, that he ought to support the lord of the city. 'He's got a little dog that he's very fond of,' he said helpfully.

'Bleeding disgusting, not even having a daughter,' said one of the hunters. 'And what's fifty thousand dollars these days? You spend that much in nets.'

'S'right,' said another. 'People think it's a fortune, but they don't reckon on, well, it's not pensionable, there's all the medical expenses, you've got to buy and maintain your own gear—'

'—wear and tear on virgins—' nodded a small fat hunter.

'Yeah, and then there's . . . what?'

'My speciality is unicorns,' the hunter explained, with an embarrassed smile.

'Oh, right.' The first speaker looked like someone who'd always been dying to ask the question. 'I thought they were very rare these days.'

'You're right there. You don't see many unicorns, either,' said the unicorn hunter. Vimes got the impression that, in his whole life, this was his only joke.

'Yeah, well. Times are hard,' said the first speaker sharply.

'Monsters are getting more uppity, too,' said another. 'I heard where this guy, he killed this monster, in this lake, no problem, stuck its arm up over the door—'

'Pour encourjay lays ortras,' said one of the listeners.

'Right, and you know what? Its mum come and complained. Its actual mum come right down to the hall next day and *complained*. Actually *complained*. That's the respect you get.'

'The females are always the worst,' said another hunter gloomily. 'I knew this cross-eyed gorgon once, oh, she was a terror. Kept turning her own nose to stone.'

'It's *our* arses on the line every time,' said the intellectual. 'I mean, I wish I had a dollar for every horse I've had eaten out from underneath me.'

'Right. Fifty thousand dollars? He can stuff it.'

'Yeah.'

'Right. Cheapskate.'

'Let's go and have a drink.'

'Right.'

They nodded in righteous agreement and strode off towards the Mended Drum, except for the intellectual, who sidled uneasily back to Vimes.

'What sort of dog?' he said.

'What?' said Vimes.

'I said, what sort of dog?'

'A small wire-haired terrier, I think,' said Vimes.

The hunter thought about this for some time. 'Nah,' he said eventually, and hurried off after the others.

'He's got an aunt in Pseudopolis, I believe,' Vimes called after him.

There was no response. The captain of the Watch shrugged, and carried on through the throng to the Patrician's palace . . .

*　　*　　*

155

. . . where the Patrician was having a difficult lunchtime.

'Gentlemen!' he snapped. 'I really don't see what else there is to do!'

The assembled civic leaders muttered amongst themselves.

'At times like this it's traditional that a hero comes forth,' said the President of the Guild of Assassins. 'A dragon slayer. Where is he, that's what I want to know? Why aren't our schools turning out young people with the kind of skills society needs?'

'Fifty thousand dollars doesn't sound much,' said the Chairman of the Guild of Thieves.

'It may not be much to you, my dear sir, but it is all the city can afford,' said the Patrician firmly.

'If it doesn't afford any more than that I don't think there'll *be* a city for long,' said the thief.

'And what about trade?' said the representative of the Guild of Merchants. 'People aren't going to sail here with a cargo of rare comestibles just to have it incinerated, are they?'

'Gentlemen! Gentlemen!' The Patrician raised his hands in a conciliatory fashion. 'It seems to me,' he went on, taking advantage of the brief pause, 'that what we have here is a strictly *magical* phenomenon. I would like to hear from our learned friend on this point. Hmm?'

Someone nudged the Archchancellor of Unseen University, who had nodded off.

'Eh? What?' said the wizard, startled into wakefulness.

'We were wondering,' said the Patrician loudly,

'what you were intending to do about this dragon of yours?'

The Archchancellor was old, but a lifetime of survival in the world of competitive wizardry and the byzantine politics of Unseen University meant that he could whip up a defensive argument in a split second. You didn't remain Archchancellor for long if you let *that* sort of ingenuous remark whizz past your ear.

'*My* dragon?' he said.

'It's well known that the great dragons are extinct,' said the Patrician brusquely. 'And, besides, their natural habitat was definitely rural. So it seems to me that this one must be mag—'

'With respect, Lord Vetinari,' said the Archchancellor, 'it has often been *claimed* that dragons are extinct, but the current evidence, if I may make so bold, tends to cast a certain doubt on the theory. As to habitat, what we are seeing here is simply a change of behaviour pattern, occasioned by the spread of urban areas into the countryside which has led many hitherto rural creatures to adopt, nay in many cases to positively embrace, a more municipal mode of existence, and many of them thrive on the new opportunities thereby opened to them. For example, foxes are always knocking over my dustbins.'

He beamed. He'd managed to get all the way through it without actually needing to engage his brain.

'Are you saying,' said the assassin slowly, 'that what we've got here is the first *civic* dragon?'

'That's evolution for you,' said the wizard, happily. 'It should do well, too,' he added. 'Plenty of nesting sites, and a more than adequate food supply.'

Silence greeted this statement, until the merchant said, 'What exactly is it that they *do* eat?'

The thief shrugged. 'I seem to recall stories about virgins chained to huge rocks,' he volunteered.

'It'll starve round here, then,' said the assassin. 'We're on loam.'

'They used to go around ravening,' said the thief. 'Dunno if that's any help . . .'

'Anyway,' said the leader of the merchants, 'it seems to be your problem again, my lord.'

Five minutes later the Patrician was striding the length of the Oblong Office, fuming.

'They were laughing at me,' said the Patrician. 'I could tell!'

'Did you suggest a working party?' said Wonse.

'Of course I did! It didn't do the trick this time. You know, I really am inclined to increase the reward money.'

'I don't think that would work, my lord. Any proficient monster slayer knows the rate for the job.'

'Ha! Half the kingdom,' muttered the Patrician.

'And your daughter's hand in marriage,' said Wonse.

'I suppose an aunt isn't acceptable?' the Patrician said hopefully.

'Tradition demands a daughter, my lord.'

The Patrician nodded gloomily.

'Perhaps we can buy it off,' he said aloud. 'Are dragons intelligent?'

'I believe the word traditionally is "cunning", my lord,' said Wonse. 'I understand they have a liking for gold.'

'Really? What do they spend it on?'

'They sleep on it, my lord.'

'What, do you mean in a mattress?'

'No, my lord. On *it*.'

The Patrician turned this fact over in his mind. 'Don't they find it rather knobbly?' he said.

'So I would imagine, sir. I don't suppose anyone has ever asked.'

'Hmm. Can they talk?'

'They're apparently good at it, my lord.'

'Ah. Interesting.'

The Patrician was thinking: if it can talk, it can negotiate. If it can negotiate, then I have it by the short – by the small scales, or whatever it is they have.

'And they are said to be silver tongued,' said Wonse. The Patrician leaned back in his chair.

'Only silver?' he said.

There was the sound of muted voices in the passageway outside and Vimes was ushered in.

'Ah, Captain,' said the Patrician, 'what progress?'

'I'm sorry, my lord?' said Vimes, as the rain dripped off his cape.

'Towards apprehending this dragon,' said the Patrician firmly.

'The wading bird?' said Vimes.

'You know very well what I mean,' said Vetinari sharply.

'Investigations are in hand,' said Vimes automatically.

The Patrician snorted. 'All you have to do is find its lair,' he said. 'Once you have the lair, you have the dragon. That's obvious. Half the city seems to be looking for it.'

'If there is a lair,' said Vimes.

Wonse looked up sharply.

'Why do you say that?'

'We are considering a number of possibilities,' said Vimes woodenly.

'If it has no lair, where does it spend its days?' said the Patrician.

'Enquiries are being pursued,' said Vimes.

'Then pursue them with alacrity. And find the lair,' said the Patrician sourly.

'Yes, sir. Permission to leave, sir?'

'Very well. But I shall expect progress by tonight, do you understand?'

Now why did I wonder if it has a lair? Vimes thought, as he stepped out into the daylight and the crowded square. *Because it didn't look real, that's why. If it isn't real, it doesn't need to do anything we expect. How can it walk out of an alley it didn't go into?*

Once you've ruled out the impossible then whatever is left, however improbable, must be the truth. The problem lay in working out what was impossible, of course. That was the trick, all right.

There was also the curious incident of the orangutan in the night-time . . .

*   *   *

By day the Library buzzed with activity. Vimes moved through it diffidently. Strictly speaking, he could go anywhere in the city, but the University had always held that it fell under thaumaturgical law and he felt it wouldn't be wise to make the kind of enemies where you were lucky to end up the same temperature, let alone the same shape.

He found the Librarian hunched over his desk. The ape gave him an expectant look.

'Haven't found it yet. Sorry,' said Vimes. 'Enquiries are continuing. But there is a little help you can give me.'

'Oook?'

'Well, this is a magical library, right? I mean, these books are sort of intelligent, isn't that so? So I've been thinking: I bet if I got in here at night, they'd soon kick up a fuss. Because they don't know me. But if they *did* know me, they'd probably not mind. So whoever took the book would have to be a wizard, wouldn't they? Or someone who works for the University, at any rate.'

The Librarian glanced from side to side, then grasped Vimes's hand and led him into the seclusion of a couple of bookshelves. Only then did he nod his head.

'Someone they know?'

A shrug, and then another nod.

'That's why you told us, is it?'

'Oook.'

'And not the University Council?'

'Oook.'

'Any idea who it is?'

The Librarian shrugged, a decidedly expressive gesture for a body which was basically a sack between a pair of shoulderblades.

'Well, it's something. Let me know if any other strange things happen, won't you?' Vimes looked up at the banks of shelves. 'Stranger than usual, I mean.'

'Oook.'

'Thank you. It's a pleasure to meet a citizen who regards it as their duty to assist the Watch.'

The Librarian gave him a banana.

Vimes felt curiously elated as he stepped out into the city's throbbing streets again. He was definitely detecting things. They were little bits of things, like a jigsaw. No one of them made any real sense, but they all hinted at a bigger picture. All he needed to do was find a corner, or a bit of an edge . . .

He was pretty certain it wasn't a wizard, whatever the Librarian might think. Not a proper, paid-up wizard. This sort of thing wasn't their style.

And there was, of course, this business about the lair. The most sensible course would be to wait and see if the dragon turned up tonight, and try and see *where*. That meant a high place. Was there some way of detecting dragons themselves? He'd had a look at Cut-me-own-Throat Dibbler's dragon detectors, which consisted solely of a piece of wood on a metal stick. When the stick was burned through, you'd found your dragon. Like a lot of Cut-me-own-Throat's devices, it was completely efficient in its own special way while at the same time being totally useless.

There had to be a better way of finding the thing than waiting until your fingers were burned off.

The setting sun spread out on the horizon like a lightly-poached egg.

The rooftops of Ankh-Morpork sprouted a fine array of gargoyles even in normal times, but now they were alive with as ghastly an array of faces as ever were seen outside a woodcut about the evils of gin-drinking among the non-woodcut-buying classes. Many of the faces were attached to bodies holding a fearsome array of homely weapons that had been handed down from generation to generation for centuries, often with some force.

From his perch on the roof of the Watch House Vimes could see the wizards lining the rooftops of the University, and the gangs of opportunist hoard-researchers waiting in the streets, shovels at the ready. If the dragon really did have a bed somewhere in the city, then it would be sleeping on the floor tomorrow.

From somewhere below came the cry of Cut-me-own-Throat Dibbler, or one of his colleagues, selling hot sausages. Vimes felt a sudden surge of civic pride. There had to be something right about a citizenry which, when faced with catastrophe, thought about selling sausages to the participants.

The city waited. A few stars came out.

Colon, Nobby and Carrot were also on the roof. Colon was sulking because Vimes had forbidden him to use his bow and arrow.

These weren't encouraged in the city, since the

heft and throw of a longbow's arrow could send it through an innocent bystander a hundred yards away rather than the innocent bystander at whom it was aimed.

'That's right,' said Carrot, 'the Projectile Weapons (Civic Safety) Act, 1634.'

'Don't you keep on quoting all that sort of stuff,' snapped Colon. 'We don't *have* any of them laws any more! That's all old stuff! It's all more wossname now. Pragmatic.'

'Law or no law,' said Vimes, '*I* say put it away.'

'But Captain, I was a dab hand at this!' protested Colon. 'Anyway,' he added peevishly, 'a lot of other people have got them.'

That was true enough. Neighbouring rooftops bristled like hedgehogs. If the wretched thing turned up, it was going to think it was flying through solid wood with slots in it. You could almost feel sorry for it.

'I said put it away,' said Vimes. 'I'm not having my guards shooting citizens. So put it away.'

'That's very true,' said Carrot. 'We're here to protect and to serve, aren't we, Captain.'

Vimes gave him a sidelong look. 'Er,' he said. 'Yeah. Yes. That's right.'

On the roof of her house on the hill, Lady Ramkin adjusted a rather inadequate folding chair on the roof, arranged the telescope, coffee flask and sandwiches on the parapet in front of her, and settled down to wait. She had a notebook on her knee.

Half an hour went by. Hails of arrows greeted

a passing cloud, several unfortunate bats, and the rising moon.

'Bugger this for a game of soldiers,' said Nobby, eventually. 'It's been scared off.'

Sergeant Colon lowered his pike. 'Looks like it,' he conceded.

'And it's getting chilly up here,' said Carrot. He politely nudged Captain Vimes, who was slumped against the chimney, staring moodily into space.

'Maybe we ought to be getting down, sir?' he said. 'Lots of people are.'

'Hmm?' said Vimes, without moving his head.

'Could be coming on to rain, too,' said Carrot.

Vimes said nothing. For some minutes he had been watching the Tower of Art, which was the centre of Unseen University and reputedly the oldest building in the city. It was certainly the tallest. Time, weather and indifferent repairs had given it a gnarled appearance, like a tree that has seen too many thunderstorms.

He was trying to remember its shape. As is the case with many things that are totally familiar, he hadn't really looked at it for years. Now he was trying to convince himself that the forest of little turrets and crenellations at its top looked just the same tonight as they had done yesterday.

It was giving him some difficulty.

Without taking his eyes off it, he grabbed Sergeant Colon's shoulder and gently pointed him in the right direction.

He said, 'Can you see anything odd about the top of the tower?'

Colon stared up for a while, and then laughed nervously. 'Well, it looks like there's a dragon sitting on it, doesn't it?'

'Yes. That's what I thought.'

'Only, only, only when you sort of look properly, you can see it's just made up out of shadows and clumps of ivy and that. I mean, if you half-close one eye, it looks like two old women and a wheelbarrow.'

Vimes tried this. 'Nope,' he said. 'It still looks like a dragon. A huge one. Sort of hunched up, and looking down. Look, you can see its wings folded up.'

'Beg pardon, sir. That's just a broken turret giving the effect.'

They watched it for a while.

Then Vimes said, 'Tell me, Sergeant – I ask in a spirit of pure enquiry – what do you think's causing the effect of a pair of huge wings unfurling?'

Colon swallowed.

'I think that's caused by a pair of huge wings, sir,' he said.

'Spot on, Sergeant.'

The dragon dropped. It wasn't a swoop. It simply kicked away from the top of the tower and half-fell, half-flew straight downwards, disappearing from view behind the University buildings.

Vimes caught himself listening for the thump.

And then the dragon was in view again, moving like an arrow, moving like a shooting star, moving like something that has somehow turned a thirty-two feet per second per second plummet into an

unstoppable upward swoop. It glided over the rooftops at little more than head height, all the more
horrible because of the sound. It was as though the
air was slowly and carefully being torn in half.

The Watch threw themselves flat. Vimes caught a
glimpse of huge, vaguely horse-like features before it
slid past.

'Sodding arseholes,' said Nobby, from somewhere in the guttering.

Vimes redoubled his grip on the chimney and
pulled himself upright. 'You are in uniform,
Corporal Nobbs,' he said, his voice hardly shaking at
all.

'Sorry, Captain. Sodding arseholes, *sir*.'

'Where's Sergeant Colon?'

'Down here, sir. Holding on to this drainpipe,
sir.'

'Oh, for goodness sake. Help him up, Carrot.'

'Gosh,' said Carrot, 'look at it go!'

You could tell the position of the dragon by the
rattle of arrows across the city, and by the screams
and gurgles of all those hit by the misses and
ricochets.

'He hasn't even flapped his wings yet!' shouted
Carrot, trying to stand on the chimney pot. 'Look at
him *go*!'

It shouldn't be that *big*, Vimes told himself,
watching the huge shape wheel over the river. It's as
long as a street!

There was a puff of flame above the docks, and
for a moment the creature passed in front of the
moon. *Then* it flapped its wings, once, with a sound

like the damp hides of a pedigree herd being slapped across a cliff.

It turned in a tight circle, pounded the air a few times to build up speed, and came back.

When it passed over the Watch House it coughed a column of spitting white fire. Tiles under it didn't just melt, they erupted in red-hot droplets. The chimney stack exploded and rained bricks across the street.

Vast wings hammered at the air as the creature hovered over the burning building, fire spearing down on what rapidly became a glowing heap. Then, when all that was left was a spreading puddle of melted rock with interesting streaks and bubbles in it, the dragon raised itself with a contemptuous flick of its wings and soared away and upwards, over the city.

Lady Ramkin lowered her telescope and shook her head slowly.

'That's not right,' she whispered. 'That's not right at *all*. Shouldn't be able to do anything like *that*.'

She raised the lens again and squinted, trying to see what was on fire. Down below, in their long kennels, the little dragons howled.

Traditionally, upon waking from blissfully uneventful insensibility, you ask: 'Where am I?' It's probably part of the racial consciousness or something.

Vimes said it.

Tradition allows a choice of second lines. A key point in the selection process is an audit to see that the body has all the bits it remembers having yesterday.

Vimes checked.

Then comes the tantalizing bit. Now that the snowball of consciousness is starting to roll, is it going to find that it's waking up inside a body lying in a gutter with something multiple, the noun doesn't matter after an adjective like 'multiple', nothing good ever follows 'multiple', or is it going to be a case of crisp sheets, a soothing hand, and a businesslike figure in white pulling open the curtains on a bright new day? Is it all over, with nothing worse to look forward to now than weak tea, nourishing gruel, short, strengthening walks in the garden and possibly a brief platonic love affair with a ministering angel, or was this all just a moment's blackout and some looming bastard is now about to get down to real business with the thick end of a pickaxe helve? Are there, the consciousness wants to know, going to be grapes?

At this point some outside stimulus is helpful. 'It's going to be all right' is favourite, whereas 'Did anyone get his number?' is definitely a bad sign; either, however, is better than 'You two hold his hands behind his back.'

In fact someone said, 'You were nearly a goner there, Captain.'

The pain sensations, which had taken advantage of Vimes's unconscious state to bunk off for a metaphorical quick cigarette, rushed back.

Vimes said, 'Arrgh.' Then he opened his eyes.

There was a ceiling. This ruled out one particular range of unpleasant options and was very welcome. His blurred vision also revealed Corporal Nobbs, which was less so. Corporal Nobbs proved nothing; you could be *dead* and see something like Corporal Nobbs.

Ankh-Morpork did not have many hospitals. All the Guilds maintained their own sanitariums, and there were a few public ones run by the odder religious organizations, like the Balancing Monks, but by and large medical assistance was non-existent and people had to die inefficiently, without the aid of doctors. It was generally thought that the existence of cures encouraged slackness and was in any case probably against Nature's way.

'Have I already said "Where am I?" ' said Vimes faintly.

'Yes.'

'Did I get an answer?'

'Dunno where this place is, Captain. It belongs to some posh bint. She said to bring you up here.'

Even though Vimes's mind appeared to be full of pink treacle he nevertheless grabbed two clues and wrestled them together. The combination of 'rich' and 'up here' meant something. So did the strange chemical smell in the room, which even over-powered Nobby's more everyday odours.

'We're not talking about Lady Ramkin, are we?' he said cautiously.

'You could be right. Great big biddy. Mad for dragons.' Nobby's rodent face broke into the most horribly knowing grin Vimes had ever seen. 'You're in her bed,' he said.

Vimes peered around him, feeling the first over-tures of a vague panic. Because now that he could halfway focus, he could see a certain lack of bachelor sockness about the place. There was a faint hint of talcum powder.

'Bit of a boodwah,' said Nobby, with the air of a connoisseur.

'Hang on, hang on a minute,' said Vimes. 'There was this dragon. It was right over us . . .'

The memory rose up and hit him like a zombie with a grudge.

'You all right, Captain?'

—the talons, outspread, wide as a man's reach; the boom and thump of the wings, bigger than sails; the stink of chemicals, the gods alone knew what sort . . .

It had been so close he could see the tiny scales on its legs and the red gleam in its eyes. They were more than just reptile eyes. They were eyes you could drown in.

And the breath, so hot that it wasn't like fire at all, but something almost solid, not burning things but smashing them apart . . .

On the other hand, he was here and alive. His left side felt as though it had been hit with an iron bar, but he was quite definitely alive.

'What happened?' he said.

'It was young Carrot,' said Nobby. 'He grabbed you and the sergeant and jumped off the roof just before it got us.'

171

'My side hurts. It must have got me,' said Vimes.

'No, I reckon that was where you hit the privy roof,' said Nobby. 'And then you rolled off and hit the water butt.'

'What about Colon? Is he hurt?'

'Not hurt. Not exactly *hurt*. He landed more sort of softly. Him being so heavy, he went *through* the roof. Talk about a short sharp shower of—'

'And then what happened?'

'Well, we sort of made you comfy, and then everyone went blundering about and shouting for the sergeant. Until they found out where he was, o'course, then they just stood where they were and shouted. And then this woman come running up yelling,' said Nobby.

'This is Lady Ramkin you're referring to?' said Vimes coldly. His ribs were aching really magnificently now.

'Yeah. Big fat party,' said Nobby, unmoved. 'Cor, she can't half boss people about! "Oh, the poor dear man, you must bring him up to my house this instant." So we did. Best place, too. Everyone's running around down in the city like chickens with their heads cut off.'

'How much damage did it do?'

'Well, after you were out of it the wizards hit it with fireballs. It didn't like that at all. Just seemed to make it stronger and angrier. Took out the University's entire Widdershins wing.'

'And—?'

'That's about it, really. It flamed a few more

things, and then it must of flown away in all the smoke.'

'No-one saw where it went?'

'If they did, they ain't saying.' Nobby sat back and leered. 'Disgusting, really, her livin' in a room like this. She's got pots of money, sarge says, she's got no call livin' in ordinary rooms. What's the good of not wanting to be poor if the rich are allowed to go round livin' in ordinary rooms? Should be marble.' He sniffed. 'Anyway, she said I was to fetch her when you woke up. She's feeding her dragons now. Odd little buggers, aren't they. It's amazing she's allowed to keep 'em.'

'What do you mean?'

'You know. Tarred with the same brush, and that.'

When Nobby had shambled out Vimes took another look around the room. It did, indeed, lack the gold leaf and marble that Nobby felt was compulsory for people of a high station in life. All the furniture was old, and the pictures on the wall, though doubtless valuable, looked the sort of pictures that are hung on bedroom walls because people can't think of anywhere else to put them. There were also a few amateurish watercolours of dragons. All in all, it had the look about it of a room that is only ever occupied by one person, and has been absent-mindedly moulded around them over the years, like a suit of clothes with a ceiling.

It was clearly the room of a woman, but one who had cheerfully and without any silly moping been getting on with her life while all that soppy romance stuff had been happening to other people somewhere else, and been jolly grateful that she had her health.

Such clothing as was visible had been chosen for sensible hardwearing qualities, possibly by a previous generation by the look of it, rather than its use as light artillery in the war between the sexes. There were bottles and jars neatly arranged on the dressing table, but a certain severity of line suggested that their labels would say things like 'Rub on nightly' rather than 'Just a dab behind the ears'. You could imagine that the occupant of this room had slept in it all her life and had been called 'my little girl' by her father until she was forty.

There was a big sensible blue dressing gown hanging behind the door. Vimes knew, without even looking, that it would have a rabbit on the pocket.

In short, it was the room of a woman who never expected that a man would ever see the inside of it.

The bedside table was piled high with papers. Feeling guilty, but doing it anyway, Vimes squinted at them.

Dragons was the theme. There were letters from the Cavern Club Exhibitions Committee and the Friendly Flamethrowers League. There were pamphlets and appeals from the Sunshine Sanctuary for Sick Dragons – 'Poor little VINNY's fires were nearly Damped after Five years' Cruel Use as a Paint-Stripper, but now—' And there were requests for donations, and talks, and things that added up to a heart big enough for the whole world, or at least that part of it that had wings and breathed fire.

If you let your mind dwell on rooms like this, you

could end up being oddly sad and full of a strange, diffuse compassion which would lead you to believe that it might be a good idea to wipe out the whole human race and start again with amoebas.

Beside the drift of paperwork was a book. Vimes twisted painfully and looked at the spine. It said: *Diseases of the Dragon*, by Sybil Deidre Olgivanna Ramkin.

He turned the stiff pages in horrified fascination. They opened into another world, a world of quite stupefying problems. Slab Throat. The Black Tups. Dry Lung. Storge. Staggers, Heaves, Weeps, Stones. It was amazing, he decided after reading a few pages, that a swamp dragon ever survived to see a second sunrise. Even walking across a room must be reckoned a biological triumph.

The painstakingly-drawn illustrations he looked away from hurriedly. You could only take so much innards.

There was a knock at the door.

'I say? Are you decent?' Lady Ramkin boomed cheerfully.

'Er—'

'I've brought you something jolly nourishing.'

Somehow Vimes imagined it would be soup. Instead it was a plate stacked high with bacon, fried potatoes and eggs. He could hear his arteries panic just by looking at it.

'I've made a bread pudding, too,' said Lady Ramkin, slightly sheepishly. 'I don't normally cook much, just for myself. You know how it is, catering for one.'

Vimes thought about the meals at his lodgings. Somehow the meat was always grey, with mysterious tubes in it.

'Er,' he began, not used to addressing ladies from a recumbent position in their own beds. 'Corporal Nobbs tells me—'

'And what a colourful little man Nobby is!' said Lady Ramkin.

Vimes wasn't certain he could cope with this.

'Colourful?' he said weakly.

'A real character. We've been getting along famously.'

'You have?'

'Oh, yes. What a great fund of anecdotes he has.'

'Oh, yes. He's got that all right.' It always amazed Vimes how Nobby got along with practically everyone. It must, he'd decided, have something to do with the common denominator. In the entire world of mathematics there could be no denominator as common as Nobby.

'Er,' he said, and then found he couldn't leave this strange new byway, 'you don't find his language a bit, er, ripe?'

'Salty,' corrected Lady Ramkin cheerfully. 'You should have heard my father when he was annoyed. Anyway, we found we've got a lot in common. It's an amazing coincidence, but my grandfather once had his grandfather whipped for malicious lingering.'

That must make them practically family, Vimes thought. Another stab of pain from his stricken side made him wince.

'You've got some very bad bruising and probably a cracked rib or two,' she said. 'If you roll over I'll put some more of this on.' Lady Ramkin flourished a jar of yellow ointment.

Panic crossed Vimes's face. Instinctively, he raised the sheets up around his neck.

'Don't play silly buggers, man,' she said. 'I shan't see anything I haven't seen before. One backside is pretty much like another. It's just that the ones I see generally have tails on. Now roll over and up with the nightshirt. It belonged to my grandfather, you know.'

There was no resisting that tone of voice. Vimes thought about demanding that Nobby be brought in as a chaperon, and then decided that would be even worse.

The cream burned like ice.

'What *is* it?'

'All kinds of stuff. It'll reduce the bruising and promote the growth of healthy scale.'

'What?'

'Sorry. Probably not scale. Don't look so worried. I'm almost positive about that. OK, all done.' She gave him a slap on the rump.

'Madam, I am Captain of the Night Watch,' said Vimes, knowing it was a bloody daft thing to say even as he said it.

'Half naked in a lady's bed, too,' said Lady Ramkin, unmoved. 'Now sit up and eat your tea. We've got to get you good and strong.'

Vimes's eyes filled with panic.

'Why?' he said.

Lady Ramkin reached into the pocket of her grubby jacket.

'I made some notes last night,' she said. 'About the dragon.'

'Oh, the dragon.' Vimes relaxed a bit. Right now the dragon seemed a much safer prospect.

'And I did a bit of working out, too. I'll tell you this: it's a very odd beast. It shouldn't be able to get airborne.'

'You're right there.'

'If it's built like swamp dragons, it should weigh about twenty tons. Twenty tons! It's impossible. It's all down to weight and wingspan ratios, you see.'

'I saw it drop off the tower like a swallow.'

'I know. It should have torn its wings off and left a bloody great hole in the ground,' said Lady Ramkin firmly. 'You can't muck about with aerodynamics. You can't just scale up from small to big and leave it at that, you see. It's all a matter of muscle power and lifting surfaces.'

'I *knew* there was something wrong,' said Vimes, brightening up. 'And the flame, too. Nothing goes around with that kind of heat inside it. How do swamp dragons manage it?'

'Oh, that's just chemicals,' said Lady Ramkin dismissively. 'They just distill something flammable from whatever they've eaten and ignite the flame just as it comes out of the ducts. They never actually have fire inside them, unless they get a case of blow-back.'

'What happens then?'

'You're scraping dragon off the scenery,' said

Lady Ramkin cheerfully. 'I'm afraid they're not very well-designed creatures, dragons.'

Vimes listened.

They would never have survived at all except that their home swamps were isolated and short of predators. Not that a dragon made good eating, anyway – once you'd taken away the leathery skin and the enormous flight muscles, what was left must have been like biting into a badly-run chemical factory. No wonder dragons were always ill. They relied on permanent stomach trouble for supplies of fuel. Most of their brain power was taken up with controlling the complexities of their digestion, which could distill flame-producing fuels from the most unlikely ingredients. They could even rearrange their internal plumbing overnight to deal with difficult processes. They lived on a chemical knife-edge the whole time. One misplaced hiccup and they were geography.

And when it came to choosing nesting sites, the females had all the common sense and mothering instinct of a brick.

Vimes wondered why people had been so worried about dragons in the olden days. If there was one in a cave near you, all you had to do was wait until it self-ignited, blew itself up, or died of acute indigestion.

'You've really studied them, haven't you,' he said.

'Someone ought to.'

'But what about the big ones?'

'Golly, yes. They're a great mystery, you know,' she said, her expression becoming extremely serious.

179

'Yes, you said.'

'There are legends, you know. It seems as though one species of dragon started to get bigger and bigger and then . . . just vanished.'

'Died out, you mean?'

'No . . . they turned up, sometimes. From somewhere. Full of vim and vigour. And then, one day, they stopped coming at all.' She gave Vimes a triumphant look. '*I* think they found somewhere where they could really *be*.'

'Really be what?'

'Dragons. Where they could really fulfil their potential. Some other dimension or something. Where the gravity isn't so strong, or something.'

'I thought when I saw it,' said Vimes, 'I thought, you can't have something that flies *and* has scales like that.'

They looked at each other.

'We've got to find it in its lair,' said Lady Ramkin.

'No bloody flying newt sets fire to *my* city,' said Vimes.

'Just think of the contribution to dragon lore,' said Lady Ramkin.

'Listen, if anyone ever sets fire to this city, it's going to be *me*.'

'It's an amazing opportunity. There's so many questions . . .'

'You're right there.' A phrase of Carrot's crossed Vimes's mind. 'It can help us with our enquiries,' he suggested.

'But in the morning,' said Lady Ramkin firmly.

Vimes's look of bitter determination faded.

'I shall sleep downstairs, in the kitchen,' said Lady Ramkin cheerfully. 'I usually have a camp bed made up down there when it's egg-laying time. Some of the females always need assistance. Don't you worry about me.'

'You're being very helpful,' Vimes muttered.

'I've sent Nobby down to the city to help the others set up your headquarters,' said Lady Ramkin.

Vimes had completely forgotten the Watch House. 'It must have been badly damaged,' he ventured.

'Totally destroyed,' said Lady Ramkin. 'Just a patch of melted rock. So I'm letting you have a place in Pseudopolis Yard.'

'Sorry?'

'Oh, my father had property all over the city,' she said. 'Quite useless to me, really. So I told my agent to give Sergeant Colon the keys to the old house in Pseudopolis Yard. It'll do it good to be aired.'

'But that area – I mean, there's real cobbles on the streets – the rent alone, I mean, Lord Vetinari won't—'

'Don't you worry about it,' she said, giving him a friendly pat. 'Now, you really ought to get some sleep.'

Vimes lay in bed, his mind racing. Pseudopolis Yard was on the Ankh side of the river, in quite a high-rent district. The sight of Nobby or Sergeant Colon walking down the street in daylight would probably have the same effect on the area as the opening of a plague hospital.

He dozed, gliding in and out of a sleep where

giant dragons pursued him waving jars of ointment . . .

And awoke to the sound of a mob.

Lady Ramkin drawing herself up haughtily was not a
sight to forget, although you could try. It was like
watching continental drift in reverse as various sub-
continents and islands pulled themselves together to
form one massive, angry protowoman.

The broken door of the dragon house swung on
its hinges. The inmates, already as highly strung as
a harp on amphetamines, were going mad. Little
gouts of flame burst against the metal plates as they
stampeded back and forth in their pens.

'Hwhat,' she said, 'is the meaning of this?'

If a Ramkin had ever been given to introspection
she'd have admitted that it wasn't a very original
line. But it was handy. It did the job. The reason that
cliches become cliches is that they are the hammers
and screwdrivers in the toolbox of communi-
cation.

The mob filled the broken doorway. Some of it
was waving various sharp implements with the up-
and-down motion proper to rioters.

'Worl,' said the leader, 'it's the dragon, innit?'

There was a chorus of muttered agreement.

'Hwhat about it?' said Lady Ramkin.

'Worl. It's been burning the city. They don't fly
far. You got dragons here. Could be one of them,
couldn't it?'

'Yeah.'

'S'right.'

'*QED*.'*

'So what we're going to do is, we're going to put 'em down.'

'S'right.'

'Yeah.'

'*Pro bono publico.*'

Lady Ramkin's bosom rose and fell like an empire. She reached out and grabbed the dunging fork from its hook on the wall.

'One step nearer, I warn you, and you'll be sorry,' she said.

The leader looked beyond her to the frantic dragons.

'Yeah?' he said, nastily. 'And what'll you do, eh?'

Her mouth opened and shut once or twice. 'I shall summon the Watch!' she said at last.

The threat did not have the effect she had expected. Lady Ramkin had never paid much attention to those bits of the city that didn't have scales on.

'Well, that's too bad,' said the leader. 'That's really worrying you know that? Makes me go all weak at the knees, that does.'

He extracted a lengthy cleaver from his belt. 'And now you just stand aside, lady, because—'

A streak of green fire blasted out of the back of the shed, passed a foot over the heads of the mob, and burned a charred rosette in the woodwork over the door.

*Some rioters can be quite well-educated.

183

Then came a voice that was a honeyed purr of sheer deadly menace.

'*This is Lord Mountjoy Quickfang Winterforth IV, the hottest dragon in the city. It could burn your head clean off.*'

Captain Vimes limped forward from the shadows.

A small and extremely frightened golden dragon was clamped firmly under one arm. His other hand held it by the tail.

The rioters watched it, hypnotized.

'Now I know what you're thinking,' Vimes went on, softly. 'You're wondering, after all this excitement, has it got enough flame left? And, y'know, I ain't so sure myself . . .'

He leaned forward, sighting between the dragon's ears, and his voice buzzed like a knife blade:

'What you've got to ask yourself is: Am I feeling lucky?'

They swayed backwards as he advanced.

'Well?' he said. '*Are* you feeling lucky?'

For a few moments the only sound was Lord Mountjoy Quickfang Winterforth IV's stomach rumbling ominously as fuel sloshed into his flame chambers.

'Now look, er,' said the leader, his eyes fixed hypnotically on the dragon's head, 'there's no call for anything like that—'

'In fact he might just decide to flare off all by himself,' said Vimes. 'They have to do it to stop the gas building up. It builds up when they get nervous. And, y'know, I reckon you've made them all pretty nervous now.'

The leader made what he hoped was a vaguely conciliatory gesture, but unfortunately did it with the hand that was still holding a knife.

'Drop it,' said Vimes sharply, 'or you're history.'

The knife clanged on the flagstones. There was a scuffle at the back of the crowd as a number of people, metaphorically speaking, were a long way away and knew nothing about it.

'*But before the rest of you good citizens disperse quietly and go about your business,*' said Vimes meaningfully, 'I suggest you look hard at these dragons. Do any of them look sixty feet long? Would you say they've got an eighty-foot wing-span? How hot do they flame, would you say?'

'Dunno,' said the leader.

Vimes raised the dragon's head slightly. The leader rolled his eyes.

'Dunno, sir,' he corrected.

'Do you want to find out?'

The leader shook his head. But he did manage to find his voice.

'Who are you, anyway?' he said.

Vimes drew himself up. 'Captain Vimes, City Watch,' he said.

This met with almost complete silence. The exception was the cheerful voice, somewhere in the back of the crowd, which said: 'Night shift, is it?'

Vimes looked down at his nightshirt. In his hurry to get off his sickbed he'd shuffled hastily into a pair of Lady Ramkin's slippers. For the first time he saw they had pink pompoms on them.

And it was at this moment that Lord Mountjoy Quickfang Winterforth IV chose to belch.

It wasn't another stab of roaring fire. It was just a near-invisible ball of damp flame which rolled over the mob and singed a few eyebrows. But it definitely made an impression.

Vimes rallied magnificently. They couldn't have noticed his brief moment of sheer horror.

'That one was just to get your attention,' he said, poker-faced. 'The next one will be a little lower.'

'Er,' said the leader. 'Right you are. No problem. We were just going anyhow. No big dragons here, right enough. Sorry you've been troubled.'

'Oh, no,' said Lady Ramkin triumphantly. 'You don't get away *that* easily!' She reached up on to a shelf and produced a tin box. It had a slot in the lid. It rattled. On the side was the legend: *The Sunshine Sanctuary for Sick Dragons.*

The initial whip-round produced four dollars and thirty-one pence. After Captain Vimes gestured pointedly with the dragon, a further twenty-five dollars and sixteen pence were miraculously forthcoming. Then the mob fled.

'We made a profit on the day, anyway,' said Vimes, when they were alone again.

'That was jolly brave of you!'

'Let's just hope it doesn't catch on,' said Vimes, gingerly putting the exhausted dragon back in its pen. He felt quite lightheaded.

Once again he was aware of eyes staring fixedly at him. He glanced sideways into the long, pointed face of Goodboy Bindle Featherstone, rearing up in a pose best described as The Last Puppy in the Shop.

To his astonishment, he found himself reaching over and scratching it behind its ears, or at least behind the two spiky things at the sides of its head which were presumably its ears. It responded with a strange noise that sounded like a complicated blockage in a brewery. He took his hand away hurriedly.

'It's all right,' said Lady Ramkin. 'It's his stomachs rumbling. That means he likes you.'

To his amazement, Vimes found that he was rather pleased about this. As far as he could recall, nothing in his life before had thought him worth a burp.

'I thought you were, er, going to get rid of him,' he said.

'I suppose I shall have to,' she said. 'You know how it is, though. They look up at you with those big, soulful eyes—'

There was a brief, mutual, awkward silence.

'How would it be if I—'

'You don't think you might like—'

They stopped.

'It'd be the least I could do,' said Lady Ramkin.

'But you're already giving us the new head-quarters and everything!'

'That was simply my duty as a good citizen,' said Lady Ramkin. 'Please accept Goodboy as, as a *friend*.'

Vimes felt that he was being inched out over a very deep chasm on a very thin plank.

'I don't even know what they eat,' he said.

'They're omnivores, actually,' she said. 'They eat everything except metal and igneous rocks. You can't be finicky, you see, when you evolve in a swamp.'

'But doesn't he need to be taken for walks? Or flights, or whatever?'

'He seems to sleep most of the time.' She scratched the ugly thing on top of its scaly head. 'He's the most relaxed dragon I've ever bred, I must say.'

'What about, er, you know?' He indicated the dunging fork.

'Well, it's mainly gas. Just keep him somewhere well ventilated. You haven't got any valuable carpets, have you? It's best not to let them lick your face, but they can be trained to control their flame. They're very helpful for lighting fires.'

Goodboy Bindle Featherstone curled up amidst a barrage of plumbing noises.

They've got eight stomachs, Vimes remembered; the drawings in the book had been very detailed. And there's lots of other stuff like fractional-distillation tubes and mad alchemy sets in there.

No swamp dragon could ever terrorize a kingdom, except by accident. Vimes wondered how many had been killed by enterprising heroes. It was terribly cruel to do something like that to creatures whose only crime was to blow themselves absent-mindedly to pieces in mid-air, which was not something any individual dragon made a habit of. It made him quite angry to think about it. A race of, of *whittles*, that's what dragons were. Born to lose. Live fast, die wide. Omnivores or not, what they must *really* live on was their nerves, flapping apologetically through the world in mortal fear of their own digestive system. The family would be just getting over father's explosion, and some twerp in a suit of armour would come plodding into the swamp to stick a sword into a bag of guts that was only one step away from self-destruction in any case.

Huh. It'd be interesting to see how the great dragon slayers of the past stood up to the *big* dragon. Armour? Best not to wear it. It'd all be the same in any case, and at least your ashes wouldn't come prepackaged in their own foil.

He stared and stared at the malformed little thing, and the idea that had been knocking for attention for the last few minutes finally gained entrance. Everyone in Ankh-Morpork wanted to find the dragon's lair. At least, wanted to find it empty. Bits of wood on a stick wouldn't do it, he was certain. But, as they said, set a thief . . .*

He said, 'Could one dragon sniff out another? I mean, follow a scent?'

Dearest Mother [wrote Carrot] Talk about a Turn Up for the Books. Last night the dragon burned up our Headquarters and Lo and Behold we have been given a better one, it is in a place called Pseudopolis

---

*The phrase 'Set a thief to catch a thief' had by this time (after strong representations from the Thieves' Guild) replaced a much older and quintessentially Ankh-Morporkian proverb, which was 'Set a deep hole with spring-loaded sides, trip-wires, whirling knife blades driven by water power, broken glass and scorpions, to catch a thief.'

Yard, opposite the Opera House. Sgt Colon said we have gone Up in the World and has told Nobby not to try to sell the furnishings. Going Up in the World is a metaphor, which I am learning about, it is like Lying but more decorative. There are proper carpets to spit on. Twice today groups of people have tried to search the cellars here for the dragon, it is amazing. And digging up people's privies and poking into attics, it is like a Fever. One thing is, people haven't got time for much else, and Sgt Colon says, when you go out on your Rounds and shout Twelve of the Clock and All's Well while a dragon is melting the street you feel a bit of a Burke.

I have moved out of Mrs Palm's because, there are dozens of bedrooms here. It was sad and they made me a cake but I think it is for the best, although Mrs Palm never charged me rent which was very nice of her considering she is a widow with so many fine daughters to bring up plus dowries ekcetra.

Also I have made friends with this ape who keeps coming round to see if we have found his book. Nobby says it is a flea-ridden moron because it won 18d off him playing Cripple Mr Onion, which is a game of chance with cards which I do not play, I have told Nobby about the Gambling (Regulation) Acts, and he said Piss off, which I think is in violation of the Decency Ordinances of 1389 but I have decided to use my Discretion.

Capt Vimes is ill and is being looked after by a Lady. Nobby says it is well known she is Mental, but Sgt Colon says it's just because of living in a big house with a lot of dragons but she is worth a Fortune and well done to the Capt for getting his feet under the table. I do not see what the furniture has to do with it. This morning I went for a walk with Reet and showed her many interesting examples of the ironwork to be found in the city. She said it was very interesting. She said I was quite different to anyone she's ever met. Your loving son, Carrot. X.

PS. I hope Minty is keeping well.

He folded the paper carefully and shoved it into the envelope.

'Sun's going down,' said Sergeant Colon.

Carrot looked up from his sealing wax.

'That means it will be night soon,' Colon went on, accurately.

'Yes, Sergeant.'

Colon ran a finger round his collar. His skin was impressively pink, the result of a morning's scrubbing, but people were still staying at a respectful distance.

Some people are born to command. Some people achieve command. And others have command thrust upon them, and the sergeant was now included in this category and wasn't very happy about it.

Any minute now, he knew, he was going to have to say that it was time they went out on patrol. He didn't want to go out on patrol. He wanted to find a nice sub-basement somewhere. But *nobblyess obligay* – if he was in charge, he had to do it.

It wasn't the loneliness of command that was bothering him. It was the being-fried-alive of command that was giving him problems.

He was also pretty sure that unless they came up with something about this dragon very soon then the Patrician was going to be unhappy. And when the Patrician was unhappy, he became very democratic. He found intricate and painful ways of spreading that unhappiness as far as possible. Responsibility, the sergeant thought, was a terrible thing. So was being horribly tortured. As far as he could see, the two facts were rapidly heading towards one another.

And thus he was terribly relieved when a small coach pulled up outside the Yard. It was very old, and battered. There was a faded coat of arms on the door. Painted on the back, and rather newer, was the little message: *Whinny If You Love Dragons.*

Out of it, wincing as he got down, stepped Captain Vimes. Following him was the woman known to the sergeant as Mad Sybil Ramkin. And finally, hopping down obediently on the end of its lead, was a small—

The sergeant was too nervous to take account of actual size.

'Well, I'll be mogadored! They've only gone and caught it!'

Nobby looked up from the table in the corner where he was continually failing to learn that it is almost impossible to play a game of skill and bluff against an opponent who smiles all the time. The Librarian took advantage of the diversion to help himself to a couple of cards off the bottom of the pack.

'Don't be daft. That's just a swamp dragon,' said Nobby. 'She's all right, is Lady Sybil. A real lady.'

The other two guards turned and stared at him. This was Nobby talking.

'You two can bloody well stop that,' he said. 'Why shouldn't I know a lady when I sees one? She give me a cup of tea in a cup fin as paper and a silver spoon in it,' he said, speaking as one who had peeped over the plateau of social distinction. '*And* I give it back to her, so you can stop looking at me like that!'

'What is it you actually *do* on your evenings off?' said Colon.

'No business of yourn.'

'Did you really give the spoon back?' said Carrot.

'Yes I bloody well did!' said Nobby hotly.

'Attention, lads,' said the sergeant, flooded with relief.

The other two entered the room. Vimes gave his men his usual look of resigned dismay.

'My squad,' he mumbled.

'Fine body of men,' said Lady Ramkin. 'The good old rank and file, eh?'

'The rank, anyway,' said Vimes.

Lady Ramkin beamed encouragingly. This led to a strange shuffling among the men. Sergeant Colon, by dint of some effort, managed to make his chest stick out more than his stomach. Carrot straightened up from his habitual stoop. Nobby vibrated with soldierly bearing, hands thrust straight down by his sides, thumbs pointing sharply forward, pigeon chest inflated so much that his feet were in danger of leaving the ground.

'I always think we can all sleep safer in my bed knowing that these brave men are watching over us,' said Lady Ramkin, walking sedately along the rank, like a treasure galleon running ahead of a mild breeze. 'And who is this?'

It is difficult for an orangutan to stand to attention. Its body can master the general idea, but its skin can't. The Librarian was doing his best, however, standing in a sort of respectful heap at the end of the line and maintaining the kind of complex salute you can only achieve with a four-foot arm.

''E's plain clothes, ma'am,' said Nobby smartly. 'Special Ape Services.'

'Very enterprising. Very enterprising indeed,' said Lady Ramkin. 'How long have you been an ape, my man?'

'Oook.'

'Well done.' She turned to Vimes, who was definitely looking incredulous.

'A credit to you,' she said. 'A fine body of men—'

'Oook.'

'—anthropoids,' corrected Lady Ramkin, with barely a break in the flow.

For a moment the rank felt as though they had just returned from single-handedly conquering a distant province. They felt, in fact, tremendously bucked-up, which was how Lady Ramkin would almost certainly have put it and which was definitely several letters of the alphabet away from how they normally felt. Even the Librarian felt favoured, and for once had let the phrase 'my man' pass without comment.

A trickling noise and a strong chemical smell prompted them to look around.

Goodboy Bindle Featherstone was squatting with an air of sheepish innocence alongside what was not so much a stain on the carpet as a hole in the floor. A few wisps of smoke were curling up from the edges.

Lady Ramkin sighed.

'Don't you worry, ma'am,' volunteered Nobby cheerfully. 'Soon have that cleaned up.'

'I'm afraid they're often like that when they're excited,' she said.

'Fine specimen you got there, ma'am,' Nobby went on, revelling in the new-found experience of social intercourse.

'It's not mine,' she said. 'It belongs to the captain now. Or all of you, perhaps. A sort of mascot. His name is Goodboy Bindle Featherstone.'

Goodboy Bindle Featherstone bore up stoically under the weight of the name, and sniffed a table leg.

'He looks more like my brother Errol,' said Nobby, playing the cheeky chirpy lovable city sparrow card for all it was worth. 'Got the same pointed nose, excuse me for saying so, milady.'

Vimes looked at the creature, which was investigating its new environment, and knew that it was now, irrevocably, an Errol. The little dragon took an experimental bite out of the table, chewed it for a few seconds, spat it out, curled up and went to sleep.

'He ain't going to set fire to anything, is he?' said the sergeant anxiously.

'I don't think so. He doesn't seem to have worked

195

out what his flame ducts are for yet,' said Lady Ramkin.

'You can't teach him anything about relaxing, though,' said Vimes. 'Anyway, men . . .'

'Oook.'

'I wasn't talking to you, sir. What's this doing here?'

'Er,' said Sergeant Colon hurriedly, 'I, er . . . with you being away and all, and us likely to be short-handed . . . Carrot here says it's all according to the law and that . . . I swore him in, sir. The ape, sir.'

'Swore him in what, Sergeant?' said Vimes.

'As Special Constable, sir,' said Colon, blushing. 'You know, sir. Sort of citizens' Watch.'

Vimes threw up his hands. 'Special? Bloody *unique*!'

The Librarian gave Vimes a big smile.

'Just temporarily, sir. For the duration, like,' said Colon pleadingly. 'We could do with the help, sir, and . . . well, he's the only one who seems to like us . . .'

'I think it's a *frightfully* good idea,' said Lady Ramkin. 'Well done, that ape.'

Vimes shrugged. The world was mad enough already, what could make it worse?

'OK,' he said. 'OK! I give in. Fine! Give him a badge, although I'm damned if I know where he'll wear it! Fine! Yes! Why not?'

'You all right, Captain?' said Colon, all concern.

'Fine! Fine! Welcome to the new Watch!' snapped Vimes, striding vaguely around the room. 'Great! After all, we pay peanuts, don't we, so we might as well employ mon—'

The sergeant's hand slapped respectfully across Vimes's mouth.

'Er, just one thing, Captain,' said Colon urgently, to Vimes's astonished eyes. 'You don't use the "M" word. Gets right up his nose, sir. He can't help it, he loses all self-control. Like a red rag to a wossname, sir. "Ape" is all right, sir, but not the "M" word. Because, sir, when he gets angry he doesn't just go and sulk, sir, if you get my drift. He's no trouble at all apart from that, sir. All right? Just don't say monkey. Ohshit.'

The Brethren were nervous.

He'd heard them talking. Things were moving too fast for them. He thought he'd led them into the conspiracy a bit at a time, never giving them more truth than their little brains could cope with, but he'd still overestimated them. A firm hand was needed. Firm but fair.

'Brothers,' said the Supreme Grand Master, 'are the Cuffs of Veracity duly enhanced?'

'What?' said Brother Watchtower vaguely. 'Oh. The Cuffs. Yeah. Enhanced. Right.'

'And the Martlets of Beckoning, are they fittingly divested?'

Brother Plasterer gave a guilty start. 'Me? What? Oh. Fine, no problem. Divested. Yes.'

The Supreme Grand Master paused.

'Brothers,' he said softly. 'We are so *near*. Just once more. Just a few *hours*. Once more and the world is *ours*. Do you *understand*, Brothers?'

Brother Plasterer shuffled a foot.

'Well,' he said. 'I mean, of course. Yes. No fears about that. Behind you one hundred and ten percent—'

He's going to say *only*, thought the Supreme Grand Master.

'—only—'

Ah.

'—we, that is, all of us, we've been . . . odd, really, you feel so different, don't you, after summoning the dragon, sort of—'

'Cleaned out,' said Brother Plasterer helpfully.

'—yes, like it's sort of—' Brother Watchtower struggled with the serpents of self-expression – 'taking something out of you . . .'

'Sucked dry,' said Brother Plasterer.

'Yes, like he said, and we . . . well, it's maybe it's a bit risky . . .'

'Like stuff's been dragged from your actual living brain by eldritch creatures from the Beyond,' said Brother Plasterer.

'I'd have said more like a bit of a sick headache, myself,' said Brother Watchtower helplessly. 'And we was wondering, you know, about all this stuff about cosmic balance and that, because, well, look what happened to poor old Dunnykin. Could be a bit of a judgement. Er.'

'It was just a maddened crocodile hidden in a flower bed,' said the Supreme Grand Master. 'It could have happened to anyone. I understand your feelings, however.'

'You do?' said Brother Watchtower.

'Oh, yes. They're only natural. All the greatest

wizards feel a little ill-at-ease before undertaking a great work such as this.' The Brethren preened themselves. Great wizards. That's us. Yeah. 'But in a few hours it'll be over, and I am sure that the king will reward you handsomely. The future will be glorious.'

This normally did the trick. It didn't appear to be working this time.

'But the dragon—' Brother Watchtower began.

'There won't *be* any dragon! We won't need it. Look,' said the Supreme Grand Master, 'it's quite simple. The lad will have a marvellous sword. Everyone *knows* kings have marvellous swords—'

'This'd be the marvellous sword you've been telling us about, would it?' said Brother Plasterer.

'And when it touches the dragon,' said the Supreme Grand Master, 'it'll be . . . *foom!*'

'Yeah, they do that,' said Brother Doorkeeper. 'My uncle kicked a swamp dragon once. He found it eating his pumpkins. Damn thing nearly took his leg off.'

The Supreme Grand Master sighed. A few more hours, yes, and then no more of this. The only thing he hadn't decided was whether to let them alone – who'd believe them, after all? – or send the Guard to arrest them for being terminally stupid.

'No,' he said patiently, 'I mean the dragon will vanish. We'll have sent it back. End of dragon.'

'Won't people be a bit suspicious?' said Brother Plasterer. 'Won't they expect lumps of dragon all over the place?'

'No,' said the Supreme Grand Master triumphantly, 'because one touch from the Sword of

Truth and Justice will totally destroy the Spawn of Evil!'

The Brethren stared at him.

'That's what they'll believe, anyway,' he added. 'We can provide a bit of mystic smoke at the time.'

'Dead easy, mystic smoke,' said Brother Fingers.

'No bits, then?' said Brother Plasterer, a shade disappointed.

Brother Watchtower coughed. 'Dunno if people will accept that,' he said. 'Sounds a bit too neat, like.'

'Listen,' snapped the Supreme Grand Master, 'they'll accept anything! They'll see it *happen*! People will be so keen to see the boy win, they won't think twice about it! Depend upon it! Now . . . let us commence . . .'

He concentrated.

Yes, it was easier. Easier every time. He could feel the scales, feel the rage of the dragon as he reached into *the place where the dragons went* and took control.

This was power, and it was his.

Sergeant Colon winced. 'Ow.'

'Don't be a big softy,' said Lady Ramkin cheerfully, tightening the bandage with a well-practised skill handed down through many generations of Ramkin womenfolk. 'He hardly touched you.'

'And he's *very sorry*,' said Carrot sharply. 'Show the sergeant how sorry you are. Go on.'

'Oook,' said the Librarian, sheepishly.

'Don't let him kiss me!' squeaked Colon.

'Do you think picking someone up by their

200

ankles and bouncing their head on the floor comes under the heading of Striking a Superior Officer?' said Carrot.

'I'm not pressing charges, me,' said the sergeant hurriedly.

'Can we get on?' said Vimes impatiently. 'We're going to see if Errol can sniff out the dragon's lair. Lady Ramkin thinks it's got to be worth a try.'

'You mean set a deep hole with spring-loaded sides, trip-wires, whirling knife blades driven by water power, broken glass and scorpions, to catch a thief, Captain?' said the sergeant doubtfully. 'Ow!'

'Yes, we don't want to lose the scent,' said Lady Ramkin. 'Stop being a big baby, Sergeant.'

'Brilliant idea about using Errol, ma'am, if I may make so bold,' said Nobby, while the sergeant blushed under his bandage.

Vimes was not certain how long he would be able to put up with Nobby the social mountaineer.

Carrot said nothing. He was gradually coming to terms with the fact that he probably wasn't a dwarf, but dwarf blood flowed in his veins in accordance with the famous principle of morphic resonance, and his borrowed genes were telling him that nothing was going to be that simple. Finding a hoard even when the dragon wasn't at home was pretty risky. Anyway, he was certain he'd know if there was one around. The presence of large amounts of gold always made a dwarf's palms itch, and his weren't itching.

'We'll start by that wall in the Shades,' said the captain.

Sergeant Colon glanced sideways at Lady Ramkin, and found it impossible to show cowardice in the face of the supportive. He contented himself with, 'Is that wise, Captain?'

'Of course it isn't. If we were wise, we wouldn't be in the Watch.'

'I say! All this is tremendously exciting,' said Lady Ramkin.

'Oh, I don't think you should come, m'lady—' Vimes began.

'—*Sybil*, please!—'

'—it's a very disreputable area, you see.'

'But I'm sure I shall be perfectly safe with your men,' she said. 'I'm sure vagabonds just *melt* away when they see you.'

That's dragons, thought Vimes. They melt away when they see dragons, and just leave their shadows on the wall. Whenever he felt that he was slowing down, or that he was losing interest, he remembered those shadows, and it was like having dull fire poured down his backbone. Things like that shouldn't be allowed to happen. Not in my city.

In fact the Shades were not a problem. Many of its denizens were out hoard-hunting anyway, and those that remained were far less inclined than hitherto to lurk in dark alleys. Besides, the more sensible of them recognized that Lady Ramkin, if waylaid, would probably tell them to pull up their socks and not be silly, in a voice so used to command that they would probably find themselves doing it.

The wall hadn't been knocked down yet and still

bore its grisly fresco. Errol sniffed around it, trotted up the alley once or twice, and went to sleep.

'Dint work,' said Sergeant Colon.

'Good idea, though,' said Nobby loyally.

'It could be all the rain and people walking about, I suppose,' said Lady Ramkin.

Vimes scooped up the dragon. It had been a vain hope anyway. It was just better to be doing something than nothing.

'We'd better get back,' he said. 'The sun's gone down.'

They walked back in silence. The dragon's even tamed the Shades, Vimes thought. It's taken over the whole city, even when it isn't here. People'll start tying virgins to rocks any day now.

It's a metaphor of human bloody existence, a dragon. And if that wasn't bad enough, it's also a bloody great hot flying thing.

He pulled out the key to the new headquarters. While he was fumbling in the lock, Errol woke up and started to yammer.

'Not now,' Vimes said. His side twinged. The night had barely started and already he felt too tired.

A slate slid down the roof and smashed on the cobbles beside him.

'Captain,' hissed Sergeant Colon.

'What?'

'It's on the roof, Captain.'

Something about the sergeant's voice got through to Vimes. It wasn't excited. It wasn't frightened. It just had a tone of dull, leaden terror.

He looked up. Errol started to bounce up and down under his arm.

The dragon – *the* dragon – was peering down interestedly over the guttering. Its face alone was taller than a man. Its eyes were the size of very large eyes, coloured a smouldering red and filled with an intelligence that had nothing to do with human beings. It was far older, for one thing. It was an intelligence that had already been long basted in guile and marinated in cunning by the time a group of almost-monkeys were wondering whether standing on two legs was a good career move. It wasn't an intelligence that had any truck with, or even understood, the arts of diplomacy.

It wouldn't play with you, or ask you riddles. But it understood all about arrogance and power and cruelty and if it could possibly manage it, it would burn your head off. Because it liked to.

It was even more angry than usual at the moment. It could sense something behind its eyes. A tiny, weak, *alien* mind, bloated with self-satisfaction. It was infuriating, like an unscratchable itch. It was making it do things it didn't want to do . . . and stopping it from doing things it wanted to do very much.

Those eyes were, for the moment, focused on Errol, who was going frantic. Vimes realized that all that stood between him and a million degrees of heat was the dragon's vague interest in why Vimes had a smaller dragon under his arm.

'Don't make any sudden moves,' said Lady Ramkin's voice behind him. 'And don't show fear. They can always tell when you're afraid.'

'Is there any other advice you can offer at this time?' said Vimes slowly, trying to speak without moving his lips.

'Well, tickling them behind their ears often works.'

'Oh,' said Vimes weakly.

'And a good sharp "no!" and taking away their food bowl.'

'Ah?'

'And hitting them on the nose with a roll of paper is what I do in *extreme* cases.'

In the slow, brightly-outlined, desperate world Vimes was now inhabiting, which seemed to revolve around the craggy nostrils a few metres away from him, he became aware of a gentle hissing sound.

The dragon was taking a deep beath.

The intake of air stopped. Vimes looked into the darkness of the flame ducts and wondered whether he'd see anything, whether there'd be some tiny white glow or something, before fiery oblivion swept over him.

At that moment a horn rang out.

The dragon raised its head in a puzzled way and made a noise that sounded vaguely interrogative without being in any way a word.

The horn rang out again. The noise seemed to have a number of echoes that lived a life of their own. It sounded like a challenge. If that wasn't what it was, then the horn blower was soon going to be in trouble, because the dragon gave Vimes a smouldering look, unfolded its enormous wings, leapt heavily into the air and, against all the rules of aeronautics, flew slowly away in the direction of the sound.

Nothing in the world should have been able to fly like that. The wings thumped up and down with a noise like potted thunder, but the dragon moved as though it was idly sculling through the air. If it stopped flapping, the movement suggested, it would simply glide to a halt. It floated, not flew. For something the size of a barn with an armour-plated hide, it was a pretty good trick.

It passed over their heads like a barge, heading for the Plaza of Broken Moons.

'Follow it!' shouted Lady Ramkin.

'That's not right, it flying like that. I'm pretty sure there's something in one of the Witchcraft Laws,' said Carrot, taking out his notebook. '*And* it's damaged the roof. It's really piling up the offences, you know.'

'You all right, Captain?' said Sergeant Colon.

'I could see right up its nose,' said Captain Vimes dreamily. His eyes focused on the worried face of the sergeant. 'Where's it gone?' he demanded. Colon pointed along the street.

Vimes glowered at the shape disappearing over the rooftops.

'Follow it!' he said.

The horn sounded again.

Other people were hurrying towards the plaza. The dragon drifted ahead of them like a shark heading towards a wayward airbed, its tail flicking slowly from side to side.

'Some loony is going to fight it!' said Nobby.

'I thought someone would have a go,' said Colon. 'Poor bugger'll be baked in his own armour.'

This seemed to be the opinion of the crowds lining the plaza. The people of Ankh-Morpork had a straightforward, no-nonsense approach to entertainment, and while they were looking forward to seeing a dragon slain, they'd be happy to settle instead for seeing someone being baked alive in his own armour. You didn't get the chance every day to see someone baked alive in their own armour. It would be something for the children to remember.

Vimes was jostled and bounced around by the crowd as more people flooded into the plaza behind them.

The horn sounded a third challenge.

'That's a slug-horn, that is,' said Colon knowledgeably. 'Like a tocsin, only deeper.'

'You sure?' said Nobby.

'Yep.'

'It must have been a bloody big slug.'

'Peanuts! Figgins! Hot sausages!' whined a voice behind them. 'Hallo, lads. Hallo, Captain Vimes! In at the death, eh? Have a sausage. On the house.'

'What's going on, Throat?' said Vimes, clinging to the vendor's tray as more people spilled around them.

'Some kid's ridden into the city and said he'd kill the dragon,' said Cut-me-own-Throat. 'Got a magic sword, he says.'

'Has he got a magic skin?'

'You've got no romance in your soul, Captain,'

said Throat, removing a very hot toasting fork from the tiny frying pan on his tray and applying it gently to the buttock of a large woman in front of him. 'Stand aside, madam, commerce *is* the lifeblood of the city, thank you very much. O'course,' he continued, 'by rights there should be a maiden chained to a rock. Only the aunt said no. That's the trouble with some people. No sense of tradition. This lad says he's the rightful air, too.'

Vimes shook his head. The world was definitely going mad around him. 'You've lost me there,' he said.

'Air,' said Throat patiently. 'You know Air to the throne.'

'What throne?'

'The throne of Ankh.'

'*What throne of Ankh?*'

'You know. Kings and that.' Throat looked reflective. 'Wish I knew what his bloody name is,' he said. 'I put an order in to Igneous the Troll's all-night wholesale pottery for three gross of coronation mugs and it's going to be a right pain, painting all the names in afterwards. Shall I put you down for a couple, Cap'n? To you ninety pence, and that's cutting me own throat.'

Vimes gave up, and shoved his way back through the throng using Carrot as a lighthouse. The lance-constable loomed over the crowd, and the rest of the rank had anchored themselves to him.

'It's all gone mad,' he shouted. 'What's going on, Carrot?'

'There's a lad on a horse in the middle of the

plaza,' said Carrot. 'He's got a glittery sword, you know. Doesn't seem to be doing much at the moment, though.'

Vimes fought his way into the lee of Lady Ramkin.

'Kings,' he panted. 'Of Ankh. And Thrones. Are there?'

'What? Oh, yes. There used to be,' said Lady Ramkin. 'Hundreds of years ago. Why?'

'Some kid says he's heir to the throne!'

'That's right,' said Throat, who'd followed Vimes in the hope of clinching a sale. 'He made a big speech about how he was going to kill the dragon, overthrow the usurpers and right all wrongs. Everyone cheered. Hot sausages, two for a dollar, made of genuine pig, why not buy one for the lady?'

'Don't you mean pork, sir?' said Carrot warily, eyeing the glistening tubes.

'Manner of speaking, manner of speaking,' said Throat quickly. 'Certainly your actual pig products. Genuine pig.'

'Everyone cheers any speech in this city,' growled Vimes. 'It doesn't mean anything!'

'Get your pig sausages, five for two dollars!' said Throat, who never let a conversation stand in the way of trade. 'Could be good for business, could monarchy. Pig sausages! Pig sausages! Inna bun! And righting all wrongs, too. Sounds like a solid idea to me. With onions!'

'Can I press you to a hot sausage, ma'am?' said Nobby.

Lady Ramkin looked at the tray around Throat's

neck. Thousands of years of good breeding came to her aid and there was only the faintest suggestion of horror in her voice when she said, 'My, they look good. What splendid foodstuffs.'

'Are they made by monks on some mystic mountain?' said Carrot.

Throat gave him an odd look. 'No,' he said patiently, 'by pigs.'

'What wrongs?' said Vimes urgently. 'Come on, tell me. What wrongs is he going to right?'

'We-ell,' said Throat, 'there's, well, taxes. That's wrong, for a start.' He had the grace to look slightly embarrassed. Paying taxes was something that, in Throat's world, happened only to other people.

'That's right,' said an old woman next to him. 'And the gutter of my house leaks something dreadful and the landlord won't do nothing. That's wrong.'

'And premature baldness,' said the man in front of her. 'That's wrong, too.' Vimes's mouth dropped open.

'Ah. Kings can cure that, you know,' said another protomonarchist knowingly.

'As a matter of fact,' said Throat, rummaging in his pack, 'I've got one bottle left of this astonishing ointment what is made—' he glared at Carrot – 'by some ancient monks who live on a mountain—'

'And they can't answer back, you know,' the monarchist went on. 'That's how you can tell they're royal. Completely incapable of it. It's to do with being gracious.'

'Fancy,' said the leaky-guttering woman.

'Money, too,' said the monarchist, enjoying the

attention. 'They don't carry it. That's how you can always tell a king.'

'Why? It's not that heavy,' said the man whose remaining hair was spread across the dome of his head like the remnant of a defeated army. '*I* can carry hundreds of dollars, no problem.'

'You probably get weak arms, being a king,' said the woman wisely. 'Probably with the waving.'

'I've always thought,' said the monarchist, pulling out a pipe and beginning to fill it with the ponderous air of one who is going to deliver a lecture, 'that one of the major problems of being a king is the risk of your daughter getting a prick.'

There was a thoughtful pause.

'And falling asleep for a hundred years,' the monarchist went on stolidly.

'Ah,' said the others, unaccountably relieved.

'And then there's wear and tear on peas,' he added.

'Well, there would be,' said the woman, uncertainly.

'Having to sleep on them all the time,' said the monarchist.

'Not to mention hundreds of mattresses.'

'Right.'

'Is that so? I think I could get 'em for him wholesale,' said Throat. He turned to Vimes, who had been listening to all this with leaden depression. 'See, Captain? And you'd be in the *royal* guard, I expect. Get some plumes in your helmet.'

'Ah, pageantry,' said the monarchist, pointing with his pipe. 'Very important. Lots of spectacles.'

'What, free?' said Throat.

'We-ell, I think maybe you have to pay for the frames,' said the monarchist.

'You're all bloody mad!' shouted Vimes. 'You don't know anything about him and he hasn't even won yet!'

'Bit of a formality, I expect,' said the woman.

'It's a fire-breathing dragon!' screamed Vimes, remembering those nostrils. 'And he's just a guy on a horse, for heaven's sake!'

Throat prodded him gently in the breastplate. 'You got no soul, Cap'n,' he said. 'When a stranger comes into the city under the thrall of the dragon and challenges it with a glittery sword, weeell, there's only one outcome, ain't there? It's probably destiny.'

'Thrall?' shouted Vimes. '*Thrall?* You thieving bugger, Throat, you were flogging cuddly dragon dolls yesterday!'

'That was just business, Cap'n. No need to get excited about it,' said Throat pleasantly.

Vimes went back to the rank in a gloomy rage. Say what you liked about the people of Ankh-Morpork, they had always been staunchly independent, yielding to no man their right to rob, defraud, embezzle and murder on an equal basis. This seemed absolutely right, to Vimes's way of thinking. There was no difference at all between the richest man and the poorest beggar, apart from the fact that the former had lots of money, food, power, fine clothes, and good health. But at least he wasn't any *better*. Just richer, fatter, more powerful, better dressed and healthier. It had been like that for hundreds of years.

'And now they get one sniff of an ermine robe and they go all gooey,' he muttered.

The dragon was circling the plaza slowly and warily. Vimes craned to see over the heads in front of him.

In the same way that various predators have the silhouette of their prey almost programmed into their genes, it was possible that the shape of someone on a horse holding a sword clicked a few tumblers in a dragon's brain. It was showing keen but wary interest.

Back in the crowd, Vimes shrugged. 'I didn't even know we were a kingdom.'

'Well, we haven't been for ages,' said Lady Ramkin. 'The kings got thrown out, and jolly good job too. They could be quite frightful.'

'But you're, well, from a pos – from a high-born family,' he said. 'I should have thought you'd be all for kings.'

'Some of them were fearful oiks, you know,' she said airily. 'Wives all over the place, and chopping people's heads off, fighting pointless wars, eating with their knife, chucking half-eaten chicken legs over their shoulders, that sort of thing. Not *our* sort of people at all.'

The plaza went quiet. The dragon had flapped slowly to the far end and was almost stationary in the air, apart from the slow beating of its wings.

Vimes felt something claw gently at his back, and then Errol was on his shoulder, gripping with his hind claws. His stubby wings were beating in time with those of the bigger specimen. He was hissing. His eyes were fixed on the hovering bulk.

The boy's horse jigged nervously on the plaza's flagstones as he dismounted, flourished the sword and turned to face the distant enemy.

He certainly looks confident, Vimes told himself. On the other hand, how does the ability to slay dragons fit you for kingship in this day and age?

It was certainly a very *shiny* sword. You had to admit that.

And now it was two of the clock the following morning. And all was well, apart from the rain. It was drizzling again.

There are some towns in the multiverse which think they know how to have a good time. Places like New Orleans and Rio reckon they not only know how to push the boat out but set fire to the harbour as well; but compared to Ankh-Morpork with its hair down they're a Welsh village at 2 p.m. on a wet Sunday afternoon.

Fireworks banged and sparkled in the damp air over the turbid mud of the river Ankh. Various domesticated animals were being roasted in the streets. Dancers conga'd from house to house, often managing to pick up any loose ornaments while doing so. There was a lot of quaffing going on. People who in normal circumstances would never think of doing it were shouting 'Hurrah'.

Vimes stalked gloomily through the crowded streets, feeling like the only pickled onion in a fruit salad. He'd given the rank the evening off.

He wasn't feeling at all royalist. He didn't

think he had anything against kings as such, but the sight of *Ankh-Morporkians* waving flags was mysteriously upsetting. That was something only silly subject people did, in other countries. Besides, the idea of royal plumes in his hat revolted him. He'd always had a thing about plumes. Plumes sort of, well, bought you off, told everyone that you didn't belong to yourself. And he'd feel like a bird. It'd be the last straw.

His errant feet led him back to the Yard. After all, where else was there? His lodgings were depressing and his landlady had complained about the holes which, despite much shouting, Errol kept making in the carpet. And the smell Errol made. And Vimes couldn't drink in a tavern tonight without seeing things that would upset him even more than the things he normally saw when he was drunk.

It was nice and quiet, although the distant sounds of revelry could be heard through the window.

Errol scrambled down from his shoulder and started to eat the coke in the fireplace.

Vimes sat back and put his feet up.

What a day! And what a fight! The dodging, the weaving, the shouts of the crowd, the young man standing there looking tiny and unprotected, the dragon taking a deep breath in a way now very familiar to Vimes . . .

And not flaming. That had surprised Vimes. It had surprised the crowd. It had certainly surprised the dragon, which had tried to squint at its own nose and clawed desperately at its flame ducts. It had remained surprised right up to the moment when the lad ducked in under one claw and thrust the sword home.

And then a thunderclap.

You'd have thought there'd have been some bits of dragon left, really.

Vimes pulled a scrap of paper towards him. He looked at the notes he'd made yesterday:

Itym: Heavy draggon, but yet it can flye right welle;

Itym: The fyre be main hot, yet issueth from ane living Thinge;

Itym: The Swamp draggons be right Poor Thinges, yet this monstrous Form waxeth full mightily;

Itym: From whence it cometh none knowe, nor wither it goeth, nor where it bideth betweentimes;

Itym: Whyfore did it burneth so neatlie?

He pulled the pen and ink towards him and, in a slow round hand, added:

Itym: Can a draggon be destroyed into utterlye noethinge?

He thought for a while, and continued:

Itym: Whyfore did it Explode that noone may find It, search they greatly?

A puzzler, that. Lady Ramkin said that when a swamp dragon exploded there was dragon everywhere. And this one had been a damn great thing.

Admittedly its insides must have been an alchemical nightmare, but the citizens of Ankh-Morpork should still have been spending the night shovelling dragon off the streets. No-one seemed to have bothered about this. The purple smoke was quite impressive, though.

Errol finished off the coke and started on the fire irons. So far this evening he had eaten three cobblestones, a door-knob, something unidentifiable he'd found in the gutter and, to general astonishment, three of Cut-me-own-Throat's sausages made of genuine pork organs. The crunching of the poker going down mingled with the patter of rain on the windows.

Vimes stared at the paper again and then wrote:

Itym: How can Kinges come of noethinge?

He hadn't even seen the lad close to. He looked personable enough, not exactly a great thinker, but definitely the kind of profile you wouldn't mind seeing on your small change. Mind you, after killing the dragon he could have been a cross-eyed goblin for all that it mattered. The mob had borne him in triumph to the Patrician's palace.

Lord Vetinari had been locked up in his own dungeons. He hadn't put up much fight, apparently. Just smiled at everyone and went quietly.

What a happy coincidence for the city that, just when it needed a champion to kill the dragon, a king came forth.

Vimes turned this thought over for a while. Then

he turned it back to front. He picked up the quill and wrote:

Itym: What a happy chance it be, for a lad that would be Kinge, that there be a Draggon to slae to prove beyond doubt his boney fiddes.

It was a lot better than birthmarks and swords, that was for sure.

He twiddled the quill for a while, and then doodled:

Itym: The draggon was not a Mechanical devise, yette surely no wizzard has the power to create a beaste of that mag. magg. maggnyt. Size.
Itym: Whye, in the Pinche, could it not Flame?
Itym: Where did it come from?
Itym: Where did it goe?

The rain pounded harder on the window. The sounds of celebration became distinctly damp, and then faded completely. There was a murmur of thunder.

Vimes underlined *goe* several times. After further consideration he added two more question marks: ??

After staring at the effect for some time he rolled the paper into a ball and threw it into the fireplace, where it was fielded and swallowed by Errol.

There had been a crime. Senses Vimes didn't know he possessed, ancient policeman's senses, prickled the hairs on his neck and told him there had been a crime. It was probably such an odd crime that it didn't figure anywhere in Carrot's book, but it had been committed all right. A handful of high-temperature murders was only the start of it. He'd find it, and give it a name.

Then he stood up, took his leather rain cape from its hook behind the door, and stepped out into the naked city.

This is where the dragons went.

They lie . . .

Not dead, not asleep. Not waiting, because waiting implies expectation. Possibly the word we're looking for here is . . .

. . . *angry.*

It could remember the feel of real air under its wings, and the sheer pleasure of the flame. There had been empty skies above and an interesting world below, full of strange running creatures. Existence had a different texture there. A better texture.

And just when it was beginning to enjoy it, it had been crippled, stopped from flaming and whipped back, like some hairy canine mammal.

The world had been taken away from it.

In the reptilian synapses of the dragon's mind the suggestion was kindled that, just possibly, it could get the world back. It had been summoned, and disdainfully banished again. But perhaps there was a trail, a scent, a thread which would lead it to the sky . . .

Perhaps there was a pathway of thought itself . . .

It recalled a mind. The peevish voice, so full of its own diminutive importance, a mind almost like that of a dragon, but on a tiny, tiny scale.

Aha.

It stretched its wings.

Lady Ramkin made herself a cup of cocoa and listened to the rain gurgling in the pipes outside.

She slipped off the hated dancing shoes, which even she was prepared to concede were like a pair of pink canoes. But *nobbyless obligay*, as the funny little sergeant would say, and as the last representative of one of Ankh-Morpork's oldest families she'd had to go to the victory ball to show willing.

Lord Vetinari seldom had balls. There was a popular song about it, in fact. But now it was going to be balls all the way.

She couldn't stand balls. For sheer enjoyment it wasn't a patch on mucking out dragons. You knew where you were, mucking out dragons. You didn't get hot and pink and have to eat silly things on sticks, or wear a dress that made you look like a cloud full of cherubs. Little dragons didn't give a damn what you looked like so long as there was a feeding bowl in your hands.

Funny, really. She'd always thought it took weeks, *months*, to organize a ball. Invitations, decorations, sausages on poles, ghastly chickeny mixture to force into those little pastry cases. But it had all been done in a matter of hours, as if someone had been expecting it. One of the miracles of catering, obviously. She'd even danced with the, for want of a better word, new king, who had said some polite words to her although they had been rather muffled.

And a coronation tomorrow. You'd have thought it'd take months to sort out.

She was still musing on that as she mixed the dragons' late night feed of rock oil and peat, spiked with flowers of sulphur. She didn't bother to change out of the ballgown but slipped the heavy apron over the top, donned the gloves and helmet, pulled the visor down over her face and ran, clutching the feed buckets, through the driving rain to the shed.

She knew it as soon as she opened the door. Normally the arrival of food would be greeted with hoots and whistles and brief bursts of flame.

The dragons, each in its pen, were sitting up in attentive silence and staring up through the roof.

It was somehow scary. She clanged the buckets together.

'No need to be afraid, nasty big dragon all gone!' she said brightly. 'Get stuck in to this, you people!'

One or two of them gave her a brief glance, and then went back to their—

What? They didn't seem to be frightened. Just very, very attentive. It was like a vigil. They were waiting for something to happen.

The thunder muttered again.

A couple of minutes later she was on her way down into the damp city.

There are some songs which are never sung sober. 'Nellie Dean' is one. So is any song beginning 'As I was a walking . . .' In the area around Ankh-Morpork, the favoured air is 'A Wizard's Staff Has A Knob On The End'.

The rank were drunk. At least, two out of three of the rank were drunk. Carrot had been persuaded to try a shandy and hadn't liked it much. He didn't know all the words, either, and many of the ones he did know he didn't understand.

'Oh, I *see*,' he said eventually. 'It's a sort of humorous play on words, is it?'

'You know,' said Colon wistfully, peering into the thickening mists rolling in off the Ankh, 's'at times like this I wish old—'

'You're not to say it,' said Nobby, swaying a little. 'You agreed, we wouldn't say nothing, it's no good talking about it.'

'It was his favourite song,' said Colon sadly. 'He was a good light tenor.'

'Now, *Sarge*—'

'He was a righteous man, our Gaskin,' said Colon.

'We couldn't of helped it,' said Nobby sulkily.

'We could have,' said Colon. 'We could have run faster.'

'What happened, then?' said Carrot.

'He died,' said Nobby, 'in the hexecution of his duty.'

'I *told* him,' said Colon, taking a swig at the bottle they had brought along to see them through the night, 'I *told* him. Slow down, I said. You'll do yourself a mischief, I said. I don't know what got into him, running ahead like that.'

'I blame the Thieves' Guild,' said Nobby. 'Allowing people like that on the streets—'

'There was this bloke we saw done a robbery one

night,' said Colon miserably. 'Right in front of us! And Captain Vimes, he said Come On, and we run, only the point is you shouldn't run too fast, see. Else you might catch them. Leads to all sorts of problems, catching people—'

'They don't like it,' said Nobby. There was a mutter of thunder, and a flurry of rain.

'They don't like it,' agreed Colon. 'But Gaskin went and forgot, he ran on, went round the corner and, well, this bloke had a couple of mates waiting—'

'It was his heart really,' said Nobby.

'Well. Anyway. And there he was,' said Colon. 'Captain Vimes was very upset about it. You shouldn't run fast in the Watch, lad,' he said solemnly. 'You can be a fast guard or you can be an old guard, but you can't be a fast old guard. Poor old Gaskin.'

'It didn't ought to be like that,' said Carrot.

Colon took a pull at the bottle.

'Well, it is,' he said. Rain bounced on his helmet and trickled down his face.

'But it didn't ought to be,' said Carrot flatly.

'But it is,' said Colon.

Someone else in the city was also ill at ease. He was the Librarian.

Sergeant Colon had given him a badge. The Librarian turned it round and round in his big gentle hands, nibbling at it.

It wasn't that the city suddenly had a king. Orangs are traditionalists, and you couldn't get more traditional than a king. But they also liked things neat, and things weren't neat. Or, rather, they were *too* neat. Truth and reality were never as neat as this. Sudden heirs to ancient thrones didn't grow on trees, and he should know.

Besides, no-one was looking for his book. That was human priorities for you.

The book was the key to it. He was sure of that. Well, there was one way to find out what was in the book. It was a perilous way, but the Librarian ambled along perilous ways all day.

In the silence of the sleeping library he opened his desk and removed from its deepest recesses a small lantern carefully built to prevent any naked flame being exposed. You couldn't be too careful with all this paper around . . .

He also took a bag of peanuts and, after some thought, a large ball of string. He bit off a short length of the string and used it to tie the badge around his neck, like a talisman. Then he tied one end of the ball to the desk and, after a moment's contemplation, knuckled off between the bookshelves, paying out the string behind him.

Knowledge equals power . . .

The string was important. After a while the Librarian stopped. He concentrated all his powers of librarianship.

Power equals energy . . .

People were stupid, sometimes. They thought the Library was a dangerous place because of all the magical books, which was true enough, but what made it really one of the most dangerous places there could ever be was the simple fact that it was a library.

Energy equals matter . . .

He swung into an avenue of shelving that was apparently a few feet long and walked along it briskly for half an hour.

Matter equals mass.

And mass distorts space. It distorts it into poly-fractal L-space.

So, while the Dewey system has its fine points, when you're setting out to look something up in the multidimensional folds of L-space what you really need is a ball of string.

Now the rain was trying hard. It glistened off the flagstones in the Plaza of Broken Moons, littered here and there with torn bunting, flags, broken bottles and the occasional regurgitated supper. There was still plenty of thunder about, and a green, fresh smell in the air. A few shreds of mist from the Ankh hovered over the stones. It would be dawn soon.

Vimes's footsteps echoed wetly from the surrounding buildings as he picked his way across the plaza. The boy had stood *here*.

He peered through the mist shreds at the surrounding buildings, getting his bearings. So the dragon had been hovering – he paced forward – *here*.

'And,' said Vimes, 'this is where it was killed.'

He fumbled in his pockets. There were all sorts of things in there – keys, bits of string, corks. His finger closed on a stub end of chalk.

He knelt down. Errol jumped off his shoulder and waddled away to inspect the detritus of the celebration. He always sniffed everything before he ate it, Vimes noticed. It was a bit of a puzzle why he bothered, because he always ate it anyway.

Its head had been about, let's see, *here.*

He walked backwards, dragging the chalk over the stones, progressing slowly over the damp, empty square like an ancient worshipper treading a maze. Here a wing, curving away towards a tail which stretched out to *here*, change hands, now head for the other wing . . .

When he finished he walked to the centre of the outline and ran his hands over the stones. He realized he was half-expecting them to be warm.

Surely there should be something. Some, oh, he didn't know, some grease or something, some crispy fried dragon lumps.

Errol started eating a broken bottle with every sign of enjoyment.

'You know what I think?' said Vimes. 'I think it went somewhere.'

Thunder rolled again.

'All right, all right,' muttered Vimes. 'It was just a thought. It wasn't that dramatic.'

Errol stopped in mid-crunch.

Very slowly, as though it was mounted on very smooth, well-oiled bearings, the dragon's head turned to face upwards.

What it was staring at intently was a patch of empty air. There wasn't much else you could say about it.

Vimes shivered under his cape. This was daft.

'Look, don't muck about,' he said. 'There's nothing there.'

Errol started to tremble.

'It's just the rain,' said Vimes. 'Go on, finish your bottle. *Nice* bottle.'

A thin, worried keening noise broke from the dragon's mouth.

'I'll show you,' said Vimes. He cast around and spotted one of Throat's sausages, cast aside by a hungry reveller who had decided he was never going to be *that* hungry. He picked it up.

'Look,' he said, and threw it upwards.

He felt sure, watching its trajectory, that it ought to have fallen back to the ground. It shouldn't have fallen *away*, as if he'd dropped it neatly into a tunnel in the sky. And the tunnel shouldn't have been looking back at him.

Vivid purple lightning lashed from the empty air and struck the houses on the near side of the plaza, skittering across the walls for several yards before winking out with a suddenness that almost denied that it had ever happened at all.

Then it erupted again, this time hitting the rimward wall. The light broke where it hit into a network of searching tendrils spreading across the stones.

The third attempt went upwards, forming an actinic column that eventually rose fifty or sixty feet in the air, appeared to stabilize, and started to spin slowly.

Vimes felt that a comment was called for. He said: 'Arrgh.'

As the light revolved it sent out thin zigzag streamers that jittered away across the rooftops, sometimes dipping, sometimes doubling back. *Searching.*

Errol ran up Vimes's back in a flurry of claws and fastened himself firmly on his shoulder. The excruciating agony recalled to Vimes that there was something he should be doing. Was it time to scream again? He tried another 'Arrgh.' No, probably not.

The air started to smell like burning tin.

Lady Ramkin's coach rattled into the plaza making a noise like a roulette wheel and pounded straight for Vimes, stopping in a skid that sent it juddering around in a semi-circle and forced the horses either to face the other way or plait their legs. A furious vision in padded leather, gauntlets, tiara and thirty yards of damp pink tulle leaned down towards him and screamed: 'Come on, you bloody idiot!'

One glove caught him under his unresisting shoulder and hauled him bodily on to the box.

'And stop screaming!' the phantom ordered, focusing generations of natural authority into four syllables. Another shout spurred the horses from a bewildered standing start to a full gallop.

The coach bounced away over the flagstones. An exploratory tendril of flickering light brushed the reins for a moment and then lost interest.

'I suppose you haven't got any idea what's happening?' shouted Vimes, against the crackling of the spinning fire.

'Not the foggiest!'

The crawling lines spread like a web over the city, growing fainter with distance. Vimes imagined them creeping through windows and sneaking under doors.

'It looks as though it's searching for something!' he shouted.

'Then getting away before it finds it is a first-class idea, don't you think?'

A tongue of fire hit the dark Tower of Art, slid blindly down its ivy-grown flanks, and disappeared through the dome of Unseen University's Library.

The other lines blinked out.

Lady Ramkin brought the coach to a halt at the far side of the square.

'What does it want the Library for?' she said, frowning.

'Maybe it wants to look something up?'

'Don't be silly,' she said breezily. 'There's just a lot of books in there. What would a flash of lightning want to read?'

'Something very short?'

'I really think you could try to be a bit more help.'

The line of light exploded into an arc between the Library's dome and the centre of the plaza and hung in the air, a band of brilliance several feet across.

Then, in a sudden rush, it became a sphere of fire which grew swiftly to encompass almost all the plaza, vanished suddenly, and left the night full of ringing, violet shadows.

And the plaza full of dragon.

*　　*　　*

Who would have thought it? So much power, so close at hand. The dragon could feel the magic flowing into it, renewing it from second to second, in defiance of all boring physical laws. This wasn't the poor fare it had been given before. This was the right stuff. There was no end to what it could do, with power like this.

But first it had to pay its respects to certain people . . .

It sniffed the dawn air. It was searching for the stink of minds.

Noble dragons don't have friends. The nearest they can get to the idea is an enemy who is still alive.

The air became very still, so still that you could almost hear the slow fall of dust. The Librarian swung on his knuckles between the endless bookshelves. The dome of the Library was still overhead but then, it always was.

It seemed quite logical to the Librarian that, since there were aisles where the shelves were on the outside then there should be other aisles in the space between the books themselves, created out of quantum ripples by the sheer weight of words. There were certainly some odd sounds coming from the other side of some shelving, and the Librarian knew that if he gently pulled out a book or two he would be peeking into different libraries under different skies.

Books bend space and time. One reason the owners of those aforesaid little rambling, poky second-hand bookshops always seem slightly unearthly is that many of them really *are*, having strayed into this world after taking a wrong turning in their own bookshops in worlds where it is considered commendable business practice to wear carpet slippers all the time and open your shop only when you feel like it. You stray into L-space at your peril.

Very senior librarians, however, once they have proved themselves worthy by performing some valiant act of librarianship, are accepted into a secret order and are taught the raw arts of survival beyond the Shelves We Know. The Librarian was highly skilled in all of them, but what he was attempting now wouldn't just get him thrown out of the Order but probably out of life itself.

All libraries everywhere are connected in L-space. All libraries. Everywhere. And the Librarian, navigating by booksign carved on shelves by past explorers, navigating by smell, navigating even by the siren whisperings of nostalgia, was heading purposely for one very special one.

There was one consolation. If he got it wrong, he'd never know it.

Somehow the dragon was worse on the ground. In the air it was an elemental thing, graceful even when it was trying to burn you to your boots. On the ground it was just a damn great animal.

Its huge head reared against the grey of dawn, turning slowly.

Lady Ramkin and Vimes peered cautiously from behind a watertrough. Vimes had his hand clamped over Errol's muzzle. The little dragon was whimpering like a kicked puppy, and fighting to get away.

'It's a magnificent brute,' said Lady Ramkin, in what she probably thought was a whisper.

'I do wish you wouldn't keep saying that,' said Vimes.

There was a scraping noise as the dragon dragged itself over the stones.

'I *knew* it wasn't killed,' growled Vimes. 'There were no bits. It was too neat. It was sent somewhere by some sort of magic, I bet. Look at it. It's bloody impossible! It needs magic to keep it alive!'

'What do you mean?' said Lady Ramkin, not tearing her gaze from its armoured flanks.

What did he mean? What *did* he mean? He thought fast.

'It's just not physically possible, that's what I mean,' he said. 'Nothing that heavy should be able to fly, or breathe fire like that. I told you.'

'But it looks real enough. I mean, you'd expect a magical creature to be, well, gauzy.'

'Oh, it's real. It's real all right,' said Vimes bitterly. 'But supposing it needs magic like we need, like we need . . . sunlight? Or food.'

'It's a thaumivore, you mean?'

'I just think it eats magic, that's all,' said Vimes, who had not had a classical education. 'I mean, all these little swamp dragons, always on the point of extinction, suppose one day back in prehistoric times some of them found out how to use magic?'

'There used to be a lot of natural magic around once,' said Lady Ramkin thoughtfully.

'There you are, then. After all, creatures use the air and the sea. I mean, if there's a natural resource around, something's going to use it, aren't they? Then it wouldn't matter about bad digestion and weight and wing size and so on, because the magic would take care of it. Wow!'

But you'd need a *lot*, he thought. He wasn't certain how much magic you'd need to change the world enough to let tons of armoured carcass flit around the sky like a swallow, but he'd bet it was lots.

All those thefts. Someone'd been feeding the dragon.

He looked at the bulk of the Unseen University Library of magic books, the greatest accumulation of distilled magical power on the Discworld.

And now the dragon had learned how to feed itself.

He became terribly aware that Lady Ramkin had moved, and saw to his horror that she was striding towards the dragon, chin stuck out like an anvil.

'What the hell are you doing?' he whispered loudly.

'If it's descended from the swamp dragons then *I* can probably control it,' she called back. 'You have to look them in the eye and use a no-nonsense tone of voice. They can't resist a stern human voice. They don't have the willpower, you know. They're just big softies.'

To his shame, Vimes realized that his legs were going to have nothing to do with any mad dash to drag her back. His pride didn't like that, but his body pointed out that it wasn't his pride that stood a very reasonable chance of being thinly laminated to the nearest building. Through ears burning with embarrassment he heard her say: 'Bad boy!'

The echoes of that stern injunction rang out across the plaza.

Oh gods, he thought, is that how you train a dragon? Point them at the melted patch on the floor and threaten to rub their nose in it?

He risked a peep over the horsetrough.

The dragon's head was swinging around slowly, like a crane jib. It had some difficulty focusing on her, right below it. Vimes could see the great red eyes narrow as the creature tried to squint down the length of its own nose. It looked puzzled. He wasn't surprised.

'Sit!' bellowed Lady Ramkin, in a tone so undisobeyable that even Vimes felt his legs involuntarily sag. 'Good boy! I think I may have a lump of coke somewhere—' She patted her pockets.

Eye contact. That was the important thing. She really, Vimes thought, shouldn't have looked down even for a moment.

The dragon raised one talon in a leisurely fashion and pinned her to the ground.

As Vimes half-rose in horror Errol escaped from his grip and cleared the trough in one leap. He bounced across the plaza in a series of wing-whirring arcs, mouth gaping, emitting wheezing burps, trying to flame.

He was answered with a tongue of blue-white fire that melted a streak of bubbling rock several yards long but failed to strike the challenger. It was hard to pick him out of the air because, quite clearly, even Errol didn't know where he was going to be, or what way up he was going to be when he got there. His only hope at this point lay in movement, and he vaulted and spun between the increasingly furious bursts of fire like a scared but determined random particle.

The great dragon reared up with the sound of a dozen anchor chains being thrown into a corner, and tried to bat the tormenter out of the air.

Vimes's legs gave in at that point and decided that they might allow themselves to be heroic legs for a while. He scurried across the intervening space, sword at the ready for what good it might do, grabbed Lady Ramkin by an arm and a handful of bedraggled ballgown, and swung her on to his shoulder.

He got several yards before the essential bad judgement of this move dawned on him.

He went 'Gngh'. His vertebrae and knees were trying to fuse into one lump. Purple spots flashed on and off in front of his eyes. On top of it all, something unfamiliar but apparently made of whalebone was poking sharply into the back of his neck.

He managed a few more steps by sheer momentum, knowing that when he stopped he was going to be utterly crushed. The Ramkins hadn't bred for beauty, they'd bred for healthy solidity and big bones, and they'd got very good at it over the centuries.

A gout of livid dragonfire crackled into the flagstones a few feet away.

Afterwards he wondered if he'd only imagined leaping several inches into the air and covering the rest of the distance to the horsetrough at a respectable run. Perhaps, in extremis, everyone learned the kind of instant movement that was second nature to Nobby. Anyway, the horsetrough was behind him and Lady Ramkin was in his arms, or at least was pinning his arms to the ground. He managed to free them and tried to massage a bit of life back. What did you do next? She didn't seem to be injured. He recalled something about loosening a person's clothing, but in Lady Ramkin's case that might be dangerous without special tools.

She solved the immediate problem by grabbing the edge of the trough and hauling herself upright.

'*Right*,' she said, 'it's the slipper for you—' Her eyes focused on Vimes for the first time.

'What the hell's going on—' she began again, and then caught the scene over his shoulder.

'Oh *sod*,' she said. 'Pardon my Klatchian.'

Errol was running out of energy. The stubby wings were indeed incapable of real flight, and he was remaining airborne solely by flapping madly, like a chicken. The great talons swished through the air. One of them caught one of the plaza's fountains, and demolished it.

The next one swatted Errol neatly.

He shot over Vimes's head in a straight rising line, hit a roof behind him, and slid down it.

'You've got to catch him!' shouted Lady Ramkin. 'You must! It's vital!'

Vimes stared at her, and then dived forward as

Errol's pear-shaped body slithered over the edge of the roof and dropped. He was surprisingly heavy.

'Thank goodness,' said Lady Ramkin, struggling to her feet. 'They explode so easily, you know. It could have been very dangerous.'

They remembered the other dragon. It wasn't the exploding sort. It was the killing-people kind. They turned, slowly.

The creature loomed over them, sniffed and then, as if they were of no importance at all, turned away. It sprang ponderously into the air and, with one slow flap of its wings, began to scull leisurely away down the plaza and up and into the mists that were rolling over the city.

Vimes was currently more concerned with the smaller dragon in his hands. Its stomach was rumbling alarmingly. He wished he'd paid more attention to the book on dragons. Was a stomach noise like this a sign they were about to explode, or was the point you had to watch out for the point when the rumbling stopped?

'We've got to follow it!' said Lady Ramkin. 'What happened to the carriage?'

Vimes waved a hand vaguely in the direction that, as far as he could tell, the horses had taken in their panic.

Errol sneezed a cloud of warm gas that smelled worse than something walled up in a cellar, pawed the air weakly, licked Vimes's face with a tongue like a hot cheese-grater, struggled out of his arms and trotted away.

'Where's he off to?' boomed Lady Ramkin,

emerging from the mists dragging the horses behind her. They didn't want to come, their hooves were scraping up sparks, but they were fighting a losing battle.

'He's still trying to challenge it!' said Vimes. 'You'd think he'd give in, wouldn't you?'

'They fight like blazes,' said Lady Ramkin, as he climbed on to the coach. 'It's a matter of making your opponent explode, you see.'

'I thought, in Nature, the defeated animal just rolls on its back in submission and that's an end of it,' said Vimes, as they clattered after the disappearing swamp dragon.

'Wouldn't work with dragons,' said Lady Ramkin. 'Some daft creature rolls on its back, you disembowel it. That's how they look at it. Almost human, really.'

The clouds were clustered thickly over Ankh-Morpork. Above them, the slow golden sunlight of the Discworld unrolled.

The dragon sparkled in the dawn as it trod the air joyously, doing impossible turns and rolls for the sheer delight of it. Then it remembered the business of the day.

They'd had the *presumption* to summon it . . .

Below it, the rank wandered from side to side up the Street of Small Gods. Despite the thick fog it was beginning to get busy.

'What d'you call them things, like thin stairs?' said Sergeant Colon.

'Ladders,' said Carrot.

'Lot of 'em about,' said Nobby. He mooched over to the nearest one, and kicked it.

'Oi!' A figure struggled down, half buried in a string of flags.

'What's going on?' said Nobby.

The flag bearer looked him up and down.

'Who wants to know, tiddler?' he said.

'Excuse me, we do,' said Carrot, looming out of the fog like an iceberg. The man gave a sickly grin.

'Well, it's the coronation, isn't it,' he said. 'Got to get the streets ready for the coronation. Got to have the flags up. Got to get the old bunting out, haven't we?'

Nobby gave the dripping finery a jaundiced look. 'Doesn't look that old to me,' he said. 'It looks new. What're them fat saggy things on that shield?'

'Those are the royal hippos of Ankh,' said the man proudly. 'Reminders of our noble heritage.'

'How long have we had a noble heritage, then?' said Nobby.

'Since yesterday, of course.'

'You can't have a heritage in a day,' said Carrot. 'It has to last a long time.'

'If we haven't got one,' said Sergeant Colon, 'I bet we'll soon have had one. My wife left me a note about it. All these years, and she turned out to be a monarchist.' He kicked the pavement viciously. 'Huh!' he said. 'A man knocks his pipes out for thirty years to put a bit of meat on the table, but all she's talking about is some boy who gets to be king for five minutes' work. Know what was for my tea last night? Beef dripping sandwiches!'

This did not have the expected response from the two bachelors.

'Cor!' said Nobby.

'*Real* beef dripping?' said Carrot. 'The kind with the little crunchy bits on top? And shiny blobs of fat?'

'Can't remember when I last addressed the crust on a bowl of dripping,' mused Nobby, in a gastronomic heaven. 'With just a bit of salt and pepper, you've got a meal fit for a k—'

'Don't even say it,' warned Colon.

'The best bit is when you stick the knife in and crack the fat and all the browny gold stuff bubbles up,' said Carrot dreamily. 'A moment like that is worth a ki—'

'Shutup! Shutup!' shouted Colon. 'You're just – *what the hell was that?*'

They felt the sudden downdraught, saw the mist above them roll into coils that broke against the house walls. A blast of colder air swept along the street, and was gone.

'It was like something gliding past, up there somewhere,' said the sergeant. He froze. 'Here, you don't think—?'

'We saw it killed, didn't we?' said Nobby urgently.

'We saw it *vanish*,' said Carrot.

They looked at one another, alone and damp in the mist-shrouded street. There could be anything up there. The imagination peopled the dank air with terrible apparitions. And what was worse was the knowledge that Nature might have done an even better job.

'Nah,' said Colon. 'It was probably just some . . . some big wading bird. Or something.'

'Isn't there anything we should do?' said Carrot.

'Yes,' said Nobby. 'We should go away quickly. Remember Gaskin.'

'Maybe it's another dragon,' said Carrot. 'We should warn people and—'

'No,' said Sergeant Colon vehemently, 'because, Ae, they wouldn't believe us and Bee, we've got a king now. 'S his job, dragons.'

'S'right,' said Nobby. 'He'd probably be really angry. Dragons are probably, you know, royal animals. Like deer. A man could probably have his tridlins plucked just for thinking about killing one, when there's a king around.'*

'Makes you glad you're common,' said Colon.

'Commoner,' corrected Nobby.

'That's not a very civic attitude—' Carrot began. He was interrupted by Errol.

The little dragon came trotting up the middle of the street, stumpy tail high, his eyes fixed on the clouds above him. He went right by the rank without giving them any attention at all.

'What's up with him?' said Nobby.

A clatter behind them introduced the Ramkin coach.

*Tridlins: A short and unnecessary religious observance performed daily by the Holy Balancing Dervishes of Otherz, according to the *Dictionary of Eye-Watering Words*.

'Men?' said Vimes hesitantly, peering through the fog.

'Definitely,' said Sergeant Colon.

'Did you see a dragon go past? Apart from Errol?'

'Well, er,' said the sergeant, looking at the other two. 'Sort of, sir. Possibly. It might of been.'

'Then don't stand there like a lot of boobies,' said Lady Ramkin. 'Get in! Plenty of room inside!'

There was. When it was built, the coach had probably been the marvel of the day, all plush and gilt and tasselled hangings. Time, neglect and the ripping out of the seats to allow its frequent use to transport dragons to shows had taken their toll, but it still reeked of privilege, style and, of course, dragons.

'What do you think you're doing?' said Colon, as it rattled off through the fog.

'Wavin',' said Nobby, gesturing graciously to the billows around them.

'Disgusting, this sort of thing, really,' mused Sergeant Colon. 'People goin' around in coaches like this when there's people with no roof to their heads.'

'It's Lady Ramkin's coach,' said Nobby. 'She's all right.'

'Well, yes, but what about her ancestors, eh? You don't get big houses and carriages without grindin' the faces of the poor a bit.'

'You're just annoyed because your missus has been embroidering crowns on her undies,' said Nobby.

'That's got nothing to do with it,' said Sergeant

Colon indignantly. 'I've always been very firm on the rights of man.'

'And dwarf,' said Carrot.

'Yeah, right,' said the sergeant uncertainly. 'But all this business about kings and lords, it's against basic human dignity. We're all born equal. It makes me sick.'

'Never heard you talk like this before, Frederick,' said Nobby.

'It's Sergeant Colon to you, Nobby.'

'Sorry, Sergeant.'

The fog itself was shaping up to be a real Ankh-Morpork autumn gumbo.* Vimes squinted through it as the droplets buckled down to a good day's work soaking him to the skin.

'I can just make him out,' he said. 'Turn left here.'

'Any ideas where we are?' said Lady Ramkin.

'Business district somewhere,' said Vimes shortly. Errol's progress was slowing a bit. He kept looking up and whining.

'Can't see a damn thing above us in this fog,' he said. 'I wonder if—'

The fog, as if in acknowledgement, lit up. Ahead of them it blossomed, like a chrysanthemum, and made a noise like 'whoomph'.

'Oh, no,' moaned Vimes. 'Not again!'

* * *

---

*Like a pea-souper, only much thicker, fishier, and with things in it you'd probably rather not know about.

'Are the Cups of Integrity well and truly suffused?' intoned Brother Watchtower.

'Aye, suffused full well.'

'The Waters of the World, are they Abjured?'

'Yea, abjured full mightily.'

'Have the Demons of Infinity been bound with many chains?'

'Damn,' said Brother Plasterer, 'there's always something.'

Brother Watchtower sagged. 'Just once it would be nice if we could get the ancient and timeless rituals right, wouldn't it. You'd better get on with it.'

'Wouldn't it be quicker, Brother Watchtower, if I just did it twice next time?' said Brother Plasterer.

Brother Watchtower gave this some grudging consideration. It seemed reasonable.

'All right,' he said. 'Now get back down there with the others. And you should call me Acting Supreme Grand Master, understand?'

This did not meet with what he considered to be a proper and dignified reception among the brethren.

'No-one said anything to us about you being Acting Supreme Grand Master,' muttered Brother Doorkeeper.

'Well, that's all you know because I bloody well am because Supreme Grand Master asked me to open the Lodge on account of him being delayed with all this coronation work,' said Brother Watch-tower haughtily. 'If that doesn't make me Acting Supreme Grand bloody Master I'd like to know what does, all right?'

'I don't see why,' muttered Brother Doorkeeper. 'You don't have to have a grand title like that. You could just be called something like, well . . . Rituals Monitor.'

'Yeah,' said Brother Plasterer. 'Don't see why you should give yourself airs. You ain't even been taught the ancient and mystic mysteries by monks, or anything.'

'We've been hanging around for hours, too,' said Brother Doorkeeper. 'That's not right. I thought we'd get rewarded—'

Brother Watchtower realized that he was losing control. He tried wheedling diplomacy.

'I'm sure Supreme Grand Master will be along directly,' he said. 'Let's not spoil it all now, eh? Lads? Arranging that fight with the dragon and everything, getting it all off right, that was something, wasn't it? We've been through a lot, right? It's worth waiting just a bit longer, OK?'

The circle of robed and cowled figures shuffled in grudging agreement.

'OK.'

'Fair enough.'

'Yeah.'

CERTAINLY.

'OK.'

'If you say so.'

It began to creep over Brother Watchtower that something wasn't right, but he couldn't quite put a name to it.

'Uh,' he said. 'Brothers?'

They, too, shifted uneasily. Something in the

room was setting their teeth on edge. There was an atmosphere.

'Brothers,' repeated Brother Watchtower, trying to reassert himself, 'we are *all* here, aren't we?'

There was a worried chorus of agreement.

'Of course we are.'

'What's the matter?'

'Yes!'

YES.

'Yes.'

There it was again, a subtle wrongness about things that you couldn't quite put your finger on because your finger was too scared. But Brother Watchtower's troublesome thoughts were interrupted by a scrabbling sound on the roof. A few nubs of plaster dropped into the circle.

'Brothers?' repeated Brother Watchtower nervously.

Now there was one of those silent sounds, a long, buzzing silence of extreme concentration and just possibly the indrawing of breath into lungs the size of haystacks. The last rats of Brother Watchtower's self-confidence fled the sinking ship of courage.

'Brother Doorkeeper, if you could just unbolt the dread portal—' he quavered.

And then there was light.

There was no pain. There was no time.

Death strips away many things, especially when it arrives at a temperature hot enough to vaporize iron, and among them are your illusions. The immortal remains of Brother Watchtower watched the dragon flap away into the fog, and then looked down at the congealing puddle of stone, metal and miscellaneous trace elements that was all that remained of the secret headquarters. And of its occupants, he realized in the dispassionate way that is part of being dead. You go through your whole life and end up a smear swirling around like cream in a coffee cup. Whatever the gods' games were, they played them in a damn mysterious way.

He looked up at the hooded figure beside him.

'We never intended this,' he said weakly. 'Honestly. No offence. We just wanted what was due to us.'

A skeletal hand patted him on the shoulder, not unkindly.

And Death said, CONGRATULATIONS.

Apart from the Supreme Grand Master, the only Elucidated Brother to be away at the time of the dragon was Brother Fingers. He'd been sent out for some pizzas. Brother Fingers was always the one sent out for takeaway food. It was cheaper. He'd never bothered to master the art of paying for things.

When the guards rolled up just behind Errol, Brother Fingers was standing with a stack of cardboard boxes in his hands and his mouth open.

Where the dread portal should have been was a warm melted patch of assorted substances.

'Oh, my goodness,' said Lady Ramkin.

Vimes slid down from the coach and tapped Brother Fingers on the shoulder.

'Excuse me, sir,' he said, 'did you by any chance see what—'

When Brother Fingers turned towards him his face was the face of a man who has hang-glided over the entrance to Hell. He kept opening and shutting his mouth but no words were coming out.

Vimes tried again. The sheer terror frozen in Brother Fingers's expression was getting to him.

'If you would be so kind to accompany me to the Yard,' said Vimes, 'I have reason to believe that you—' He hesitated. He wasn't entirely certain what it was that he had reason to believe. But the man was clearly guilty. You could tell just by looking at him. Not, perhaps, guilty of anything specific. Just guilty in general terms.

'Mmmmmuh,' said Brother Fingers.

Sergeant Colon gently lifted the lid of the top box.

'What do you make of it, Sergeant?' said Vimes, stepping back.

'Er. It looks like a Klatchian Hots with anchovies, sir,' said Sergeant Colon knowledgeably.

'I mean the man,' said Vimes wearily.

'Nnnnn,' said Brother Fingers.

Colon peered under the hood. 'Oh, I know him, sir,' he said. 'Bengy "Lightfoot" Boggis, sir. He's a capo de monty in the Thieves' Guild. I know him of old, sir. Sly little bugger. Used to work at the University.'

'What, as a wizard?' said Vimes.

'Odd job man, sir. Gardening and carpentry and that.'

'Oh. *Did* he?'

'Can't we do something for the poor man?' said Lady Ramkin.

Nobby saluted smartly. 'I could kick him in the bollocks for you if you like, m'lady.'

'Dddrrr,' said Brother Fingers, beginning to shake uncontrollably, while Lady Ramkin smiled the iron-hard blank smile of a high-born lady who is determined not to show that she has understood what has just been said to her.

'Put him in the coach, you two,' said Vimes. 'If it's all right with you, Lady Ramkin—'

'—Sybil—' corrected Lady Ramkin. Vimes blushed, and plunged on – 'it might be a good idea to get him indoors. Charge him with the theft of one book, to whit, *The Summoning of Dragons*.'

'Right you are, sir,' said Sergeant Colon. 'The pizzas're getting cold, too. You know how the cheese goes all manky when it gets cold.'

'And no kicking him, either,' Vimes warned. 'Not *even* where it doesn't show. Carrot, you come with me.'

'DDddrrraa,' Brother Fingers volunteered.

'And take Errol,' added Vimes. 'He's driving himself mad here. Game little devil, I'll give him that.'

'Marvellous, when you come to think about it,' said Colon.

Errol was trotting up and down in front of the ravaged building, whining.

'Look at him,' said Vimes. 'Can't wait to get to grips.' His gaze found itself drawn, as though by wires, up to the rolling clouds of fog.

It's in there somewhere, he thought.

'What we going to do now, sir?' said Carrot, as the carriage rattled off.

'Not nervous, are you?' said Vimes.

'No, sir.'

The way he said it jogged something in Vimes's mind.

'No,' he said, 'you're not, are you? I suppose it's being brought up by the dwarfs that did it. You've got no imagination.'

'I'm sure I try to do my best, sir,' said Carrot firmly.

'Still sending all your pay home to your mother?'

'Yes, sir.'

'You're a good boy.'

'Yessir. So what are we going to do, Captain Vimes?' Carrot repeated.

Vimes looked around him. He walked a few aimless, exasperated steps. He spread his arms wide and then flopped them down by his sides.

'How should I know?' he said. 'Warn people, I guess. We'd better get over to the Patrician's palace. And then—'

There were footsteps in the fog. Vimes stiffened, put his finger to his lips and pulled Carrot into the shelter of a doorway.

A figure loomed out of the billows.

Another one of 'em, thought Vimes. Well, there's no law about wearing long black robes and deep cowls. There could be dozens of perfectly innocent reasons why this person is wearing long black robes and a deep cowl and standing in front of a melted-down house at dawn.

Perhaps I should ask him to name just one.

He stepped out.

'Excuse me, sir—' he began.

The cowl swung around. There was a hiss of indrawn breath.

'I just wonder if you would mind – *after him, Lance-constable!*'

The figure had a good start. It scuttled along the street and had reached the corner before Vimes was halfway there. He skidded around it in time to see a shape vanish down an alley.

Vimes realized he was running alone. He panted to a halt and looked back just in time to see Carrot jog gently around the corner.

'What's wrong?' he wheezed.

'Sergeant Colon said I wasn't to run,' said Carrot.

Vimes looked at him vaguely. Then slow comprehension dawned.

'Oh,' he said. 'I, er, see. I don't think he meant in *every* circumstance, lad.' He stared back into the fog. 'Not that we had much of a chance in this fog and these streets.'

'Might have been just an innocent bystander, sir,' said Carrot.

'What, in Ankh-Morpork?'

'Yes, sir.'

'We should have grabbed him, then, just for the rarity value,' said Vimes.

He patted Carrot on the shoulder. 'Come on. We'd better get along to the Patrician's palace.'

'The King's palace,' corrected Carrot.

'What?' said Vimes, his train of thought temporarily shunted.

'It's the King's palace now,' said Carrot. Vimes squinted sideways at him.

He gave a short, mirthless laugh.

'Yeah, that's right,' he conceded. 'Our dragon-killing king. Well done that man.' He sighed. 'They're not going to like this.'

They didn't. None of them did.

The first problem was the palace guard.

Vimes had never liked them. They'd never liked *him*. OK, so maybe the rank were only one step away from petty scofflaws, but in Vimes's professional opinion the palace guard these days were only one step away from being the worst criminal scum the city had ever produced. A step further *down*. They'd have to *reform* a bit before they could even be considered for inclusion in the Ten Most Unwanted list.

They were rough. They were tough. They weren't the sweepings off the gutter, they were what you still found sticking to the gutter when the gutter sweepers had given up in exhaustion. They had been extremely well-paid by the Patrician, and presumably were extremely well-paid by someone else now, because when Vimes walked up to the gates a couple of them stopped lounging against the walls and straightened up while still maintaining just the right amount of psychological slouch to cause maximum offence.

'Captain Vimes,' said Vimes, staring straight

ahead. 'To see the king. It's of the utmost importance.'

'Yeah? Well, it'd have to be,' said a guard. 'Captain Slimes, was it?'

'Vimes,' said Vimes evenly. 'With a Vee.'

One of the guards nodded to his companion.

'Vimes,' he said. 'With a Vee.'

'Fancy,' said the other guard.

'It's most urgent,' said Vimes, maintaining a
wooden expression. He tried to move forward.

The first guard sidestepped neatly and pushed
him sharply in the chest.

'No-one is going nowhere,' he said. 'Orders of
the king, see? So you can push off back to your pit,
Captain Vimes with a Vee.'

It wasn't the words which made up Vimes's
mind. It was the way the other man sniggered.

'Stand aside,' he said.

The guard leaned down. 'Who's going to make
me,' he rapped on Vimes's helmet, 'copper?'

There are times when it is a veritable pleasure to
drop the bomb right away.

'Lance-constable Carrot, I want you to charge
these men,' said Vimes.

Carrot saluted. 'Very good, sir,' he said, and
turned and trotted smartly back the way they had
come.

'Hey!' shouted Vimes, as the boy disappeared
around a corner.

'That's what I like to see,' said the first guard,
leaning on his spear. 'That's a young man with initiative, that young man. A bright lad. He doesn't want

to stop along here and have his ears twisted off. That's a young man who's going to go a long way, if he's got any sense.'

'Very sensible,' said the other guard.

He leaned the spear against the wall.

'You Watch men make me want to throw up,' he said conversationally. 'Poncing around all the time, never doing a proper job of work. Throwing your weight about as if you counted for something. So me and Clarence are going to show you what *real* guarding is all about, isn't that right?'

I could just about manage one of them, Vimes thought as he took a few steps backward. If he was facing the other way, at least.

Clarence propped his spear against the gateway and spat on his hands.

There was a long, terrifying ululation. Vimes was amazed to realize it wasn't coming from him.

Carrot appeared around the corner at a dead run. He had a felling axe in either hand.

His huge leather sandals flapped on the cobblestones as he bounded closer, accelerating all the time. And all the time there was this cry, *deedahdeedahdeedah*, like something caught in a trap at the bottom of a two-tone echo canyon.

The two palace guards stood rigid with astonishment.

'I should duck, if I was you,' said Vimes from near ground level.

The two axes left Carrot's hands and whirred through the air making a noise like a brace of partridges. One of them hit the palace gate, burying half the head in the woodwork. The other one hit the shaft of the first one, and split it. Then Carrot arrived.

Vimes went and sat down on a nearby bench for a while, and rolled himself a cigarette.

Eventually he said, 'I think that's about enough, constable. I think they'd like to come quietly now.'

'Yes, sir. What are they accused of, sir?' said Carrot, holding one limp body in either hand.

'Assaulting an officer of the Watch in the execution of his duty and . . . oh, yes. Resisting arrest.'

'Under Section (vii) of the Public Order Act of 1457?' said Carrot.

'Yes,' said Vimes solemnly. 'Yes. Yes, I suppose so.'

'But they didn't resist very much, sir,' Carrot pointed out.

'Well, *attempting* to resist arrest. I should just leave them over by the wall until we come back. I don't expect they'll want to go anywhere.'

'Right you are, sir.'

'Don't hurt them, mind,' said Vimes. 'You mustn't hurt prisoners.'

'That's right, sir,' said Carrot, conscientiously. 'Prisoners once Charged have Rights, sir. It says so in the Dignity of Man (Civic Rights) Act of 1341. I keep telling Corporal Nobbs. They have Rights, I tell him. This means you do not Put the Boot in.'

'Very well put, constable.'

Carrot looked down. 'You have the right to remain silent,' he said. 'You have the right not to injure yourself falling down the steps on the way to the cells. You have the right not to jump out of high windows. You do not have to say anything, you see, but anything you do say, well, I have to take it down and it might be used in evidence.' He pulled out his notebook and licked his pencil. He leaned down further.

'Pardon?' he said. He looked up at Vimes.

'How do you spell "groan", sir?' he said.

'G-R-O-N-E, I think.'

'Very good, sir.'

'Oh, and constable?'

'Yes, sir?'

'Why the axes?'

'They *were* armed, sir. I got them from the blacksmith in Market Street, sir. I said you'd be along later to pay for them.'

'And the cry?' said Vimes weakly.

'Dwarfish war yodel, sir,' said Carrot proudly.

'It's a *good* cry,' said Vimes, picking his words with care. 'But I'd be grateful if you'd warn me first another time, all right?'

'Certainly, sir.'

'In writing, I think.'

The Librarian swung on. It was slow progress, because there were things he wasn't keen on meeting. Creatures evolve to fill every niche in the environment, and some of those in the dusty immensity of L-space were best avoided. They were much more unusual than ordinary unusual creatures.

Usually he could forewarn himself by keeping a careful eye on the kickstool crabs that grazed harmlessly on the dust. When they were spooked, it was time to hide. Several times he had to flatten himself against the shelves as a thesaurus thundered by. He waited patiently as a herd of Critters crawled past, grazing on the contents of the choicer books and leaving behind them piles of small slim volumes of literary criticism. And there were other things, things which he hurried away from and tried not to look hard at . . .

And you had to avoid cliches at all costs.

He finished the last of his peanuts atop a stepladder, which was browsing mindlessly off the high shelves.

The territory definitely had a familiar feel, or at least he got the feeling that it would eventually be familiar. Time had a different meaning in L-space.

There were shelves whose outline he felt he knew. The book titles, while still unreadable, held a tantalizing hint of legibility. Even the musty air had a smell he thought he recognized.

He shambled quickly along a side passage, turned the corner and, with only the slightest twinge of disorientation, shuffled into that set of dimensions that people, because they don't know any better, think of as normal.

He just felt extremely hot and his fur stood straight out from his body as temporal energy gradually discharged.

He was in the dark.

He extended one arm and explored the spines of the books by his side. Ah. *Now* he knew where he was.

He was home.

He was home a week ago.

It was essential that he didn't leave footprints. But that wasn't a problem. He shinned up the side of the nearest bookcase and, under the starlight of the dome, hurried onwards.

Lupine Wonse glared up, red-eyed, from the heap of paperwork on his desk. No-one in the city knew anything about coronations. He'd had to make it up as he went along. There should be plenty of things to wave, he knew that.

'Yes?' he said, abruptly.

'Er, there's a Captain Vimes to see you,' said the flunkey.

'Vimes of the Watch?'

'Yes, sir. Says it's of the utmost importance.'

Wonse looked down his list of other things that were also of the utmost importance. Crowning the king, for one thing. The high priests of fifty-three religions were all claiming the honour. It was going to be a scrum. And then there were the crown jewels.

Or rather, there *weren't* the crown jewels. Somewhere in the preceding generations the crown jewels had disappeared. A jeweller in the Street of Cunning Artificers was doing the best he could in the time with gilt and glass.

Vimes could wait.

'Tell him to come back another day,' said Wonse.

'Good of you to see us,' said Vimes, appearing in the doorway.

Wonse glared at him.

'Since you're here . . .' he said. Vimes dropped his helmet on Wonse's desk in what the secretary thought was an offensive manner, and sat down.

'Take a seat,' said Wonse.

'Have you had breakfast yet?' said Vimes.

'Now really—' Wonse began.

'Don't worry,' said Vimes cheerfully. 'Constable Carrot will go and see what's in the kitchens. This chap will show him the way.'

When they had gone Wonse leaned across the drifts of paperwork.

'There had better,' he said, 'be a very good reason for—'

'The dragon is back,' said Vimes.

Wonse stared at him for a while.

Vimes stared back.

Wonse's senses came back from whatever corners they'd bounced into.

'You've been drinking, haven't you,' he said.

'No. The dragon is *back*.'

'Now, look—' Wonse began.

'I saw it,' said Vimes flatly.

'A dragon? You're sure?'

Vimes leaned across the desk. 'No! I could be bloody mistaken!' he shouted. 'It may have been something else with sodding great big claws, huge leathery wings and hot, fiery breath! There must be masses of things like that!'

'But we all saw it killed!' said Wonse.

'I don't know what *we* saw!' said Vimes, 'But I know what *I* saw!'

He leaned back, shaking. He was suddenly feeling extremely tired.

'Anyway,' he said, in a more normal voice, 'it's flamed a house in Bitwash Street. Just like the other ones.'

'Any of them get out?'

Vimes put his head in his hands. He wondered how long it was since he'd last had any sleep, proper sleep, the sort with sheets. Or food, come to that. Was it last night, or the night before? Had he ever, come to think of it, ever slept at all in all his life? It didn't seem like it. The arms of Morpheus had rolled up their sleeves and were giving the back of his brain a right pummelling, but bits were fighting back. Any of them get . . . ?

'Any of who?' he said.

'The people in the house, of course,' said Wonse. 'I assume there were people in it. At night, I mean.'

'Oh? Oh. Yes. It wasn't like a normal house. I think it was some sort of secret society thing,' Vimes managed. Something was clicking in his mind, but he was too tired to examine it.

'Magic, you mean?'

'Dunno,' said Vimes. 'Could be. Guys in robes.'

He's going to tell me I've been overdoing it, he said. He'll be right, too.

'Look,' said Wonse, kindly. 'People who mess around with magic and don't know how to control it, well, they can blow themselves up and—'

'Blow themselves up?'

'And you've had a busy few days,' said Wonse soothingly. 'If I'd been knocked down and almost burned alive by a dragon I expect *I'd* be seeing them all the time.'

Vimes stared at him with his mouth open. He couldn't think of anything to say. Whatever stretched and knotted elastic had been driving him along these last few days had gone entirely limp.

'You don't think you've been overdoing it, do you?' said Wonse.

Ah, thought Vimes. Jolly good.

He slumped forward.

The Librarian leaned cautiously over the top of the bookcase and unfolded an arm into the darkness.

There it was.

His thick fingernails grasped the spine of the book, pulled it gently from its shelf and hoisted it up. He raised the lantern carefully.

No doubt about it. *The Summoning of Dragons.* Single copy, first edition, slightly foxed and extremely dragoned.

He set the lamp down beside him, and began to read the first page.

'Mmm?' said Vimes, waking up.

'Brung you a nice cup of tea, Cap'n,' said Sergeant Colon. 'And a figgin.'

Vimes looked at him blankly.

'You've been asleep,' said Sergeant Colon helpfully. 'You was spark out when Carrot brought you back.'

Vimes looked around at the now-familiar surroundings of the Yard. 'Oh,' he said.

'Me and Nobby have been doing some *detectoring*,' said Colon. 'You know that house that got melted? Well, no-one lives there. It's just rooms that get hired out. So we found out who hired them. There's a caretaker who goes along every night to put the chairs away and lock up. He wasn't half creating about it being burned down. You know what caretakers are like.'

He stood back, waiting for the applause.

'Well done,' said Vimes dutifully, dunking the figgin into the tea.

'There's three societies use it,' said Colon. He extracted his notebook. 'To wit, viz, The Ankh-Morpork Fine Art Appreciation Society, hem hem, the Morpork Folk-Dance and Song Club, and the Elucidated Brethren of the Ebon Night.'

'Why hem hem?' said Vimes.

'Well, you know. Fine *Art*. It's just men paintin' pictures of young wimmin in the nudd. The altogether,' explained Colon the connoisseur. 'The caretaker told me. Some of them don't even have any paint on their brushes, you know. Shameful.'

There must be a million stories in the naked city, thought Vimes. So why do I always have to listen to ones like these?

'When do they meet?' he said.

'Mondays, 7.30, admission ten pence,' said Colon, promptly. 'As for the folk-dance people – well, no problem there. You know you always wondered what Corporal Nobbs does on his evenings off?'

Colon's face split into a watermelon grin.

'No!' said Vimes incredulously. 'Not Nobby?'

'Yep!' said Colon, delighted at the result.

'What, jumping about with bells on and waving his hanky in the air?'

'He says it is important to preserve old folkways,' said Colon.

'Nobby? Mr Steel-toecaps-in-the-groin, I-was-just-checking-the-doorhandle-and-it-opened-all-by-itself?'

'Yeah! Funny old world, ain't it? He was very bashful about it.'

'Good grief,' said Vimes.

'It just goes to show, you never can tell,' said Colon. 'Anyway, the caretaker said the Elucidated Brethren always leave the place in a mess. Scuffed chalk marks on the floor, he said. And they never put the chairs back properly or wash out the tea urn. They've been meeting a lot lately, he said. The nuddy wimmin painters had to meet somewhere else last week.'

'What did you do with our suspect?' said Vimes.

'Him? Oh, he done a runner, Captain,' said the sergeant, looking embarrassed.

'Why? He didn't look in any shape to run anywhere.'

'Well, when we got back here, we sat him down by the fire and wrapped him up because he kept on shivering,' said Sergeant Colon, as Vimes buckled his armour on.

'I hope you didn't eat his pizzas.'

'Errol et 'em. It's the cheese, see, it goes all—'

'Go on.'

'Well,' said Colon awkwardly, 'he kept on

shivering, sort of thing, and groaning on about dragons and that. We felt sorry for him, to tell the truth. And then he jumps up and runs out of the door for no reason at all.'

Vimes glanced at the sergeant's big, open, dishonest face.

'No reason?' he prompted.

'*Well*, we decided to have a bite, so I sent Nobby out to the baker's, see, and, well, we fought the prisoner ought to have something to eat . . .'

'Yes?' said Vimes encouragingly.

'*Well*, when Nobby asked him if he wanted his figgin toasted, he just give a scream and ran off.'

'Just that?' said Vimes. 'You didn't threaten him in any way?'

'Straight up, Captain. Bit of a mystery, if you ask me. He kept going on about someone called Supreme Grand Master.'

'Hmm.' Vimes glanced out of the window. Grey fog lagged the world with dim light. 'What time is it?' he said.

'Five of the clock, sir.'

'Right. Well, before it gets dark—'

Colon gave a cough. 'In the morning, sir. This is tomorrow, sir.'

'You let me sleep all *day*?'

'Didn't have the heart to wake you up, sir. No dragon activity, if that's what you're thinking. Dead quiet all round, in fact.'

Vimes glared at him and threw the window open.

The fog rolled in, in a slow, yellow-edged waterfall.

'We reckon it must of flown away,' said Colon's voice, behind him.

Vimes stared up into the heavy, rolling clouds.

'Hope it clears up for the coronation,' Colon went on, in a worried voice. 'You all right, sir?'

It hasn't flown away, Vimes thought. Why should it fly away? We can't hurt it, and it's got everything it wants right here. It's up there somewhere.

'You all right, sir?' Colon repeated.

It's got to be up high somewhere, in the fog. There's all kinds of towers and things.

'What time's the coronation, Sergeant?' he said.

'Noon, sir. And Mr Wonse has sent a message about how you're to be in your best armour among all the civic leaders, sir.'

'Oh, has he?'

'And Sergeant Hummock and the day squad will be lining the route, sir.'

'What with?' said Vimes vaguely, watching the skies.

'Sorry, sir?'

Vimes squinted upwards to get a better view of the roof. 'Hmm?' he said.

'I said they'll be lining the route, sir,' said Sergeant Colon.

'It's up there, Sergeant,' said Vimes. 'I can practically smell it.'

'Yes, sir,' said Colon obediently.

'It's deciding what to do next.'

'Yes, sir?'

'They're not unintelligent, you know. They just don't think like us.'

'Yes, sir.'

'So be damned to any lining of the route. I want you three up on roofs, understand?'

'Yes, si – what?'

'Up on the roofs. Up high. When it makes its move, I want us to be the first to know.'

Colon tried to indicate by his expression that *he* didn't.

'Do you think that's a good idea, sir?' he ventured.

Vimes gave him a blank look. 'Yes, Sergeant, I do. It was one of mine,' he said coldly. 'Now go and see to it.'

When he was left to himself Vimes washed and shaved in cold water, and then rummaged in his campaign chest until he unearthed his ceremonial breastplate and red cloak. Well, the cloak had been red *once*, and still was, here and there, although more of it resembled a small net used very successfully for catching moths. There was also a helmet, defiantly without plumes, from which the molecule-thick gold leaf had long ago peeled.

He'd started saving up for a new cloak, once. Whatever had happened to the money?

There was no-one in the guardroom. Errol lay in the wreckage of the fourth fruit box Nobby had scrounged for him. The rest had all been eaten, or had dissolved.

In the warm silence the everlasting rumbling of his stomach sounded especially loud. Occasionally he whimpered.

Vimes scratched him vaguely behind the ears.

'What's up with you, boy?' he said.

The door creaked open. Carrot came in, saw Vimes hunkered down by the ravaged box, and saluted.

'We're a bit worried about him, Captain,' he volunteered. 'He hasn't eaten his coal. Just lies there twitching and whining all the time. You don't think something's wrong with him, do you?'

'Possibly,' said Vimes. 'But having something wrong with them is quite normal for a dragon. They always get over it. One way or another.'

Errol gave him a mournful look and closed his eyes again. Vimes pulled his scrap of blanket over him.

There was a squeak. He fished around beside the dragon's shivering body, pulled out a small rubber hippo, stared at it in surprise and then gave it one or two experimental squeezes.

'I thought it would be something for him to play with,' said Carrot, slightly shamefaced.

'You bought him a little toy?'

'Yes, sir.'

'What a kind thought.'

Vimes hoped Carrot hadn't noticed the fluffy ball tucked into the back of the box. It had been quite expensive.

He left the two of them and stepped into the outside world.

There was even more bunting now. People were beginning to line the main streets, even though there were hours to wait. It was still very depressing.

He felt an appetite for once, one that it'd

take more than a drink or two to satisfy. He strolled along for breakfast at Harga's House of Ribs, the habit of years, and got another unpleasant surprise. Normally the only decoration in there was on Sham Harga's vest and the food was good solid stuff for a cold morning, all calories and fat and protein and maybe a vitamin crying softly because it was all alone. Now laboriously-made paper streamers crisscrossed the room and he was confronted with a crayonned menu in which the words 'Coronasion' and 'Royall' figured somewhere on every crooked line.

Vimes pointed wearily at the top of the menu.

'What's this?' he said.

Harga peered at it. They were alone in the grease-walled cafe.

'It says "Bye Royarl Appointmente", Captain,' he said proudly.

'What's it mean?'

Harga scratched his head with a ladle. 'What it means is,' he said, 'if the king comes in here, he'll like it.'

'Have you got anything that isn't too aristocratic for me to eat, then?' said Vimes sourly, and settled for a slice of plebeian fried bread and a proletarian steak cooked so rare you could still hear it bray. Vimes ate it at the counter.

A vague scraping noise disturbed his thoughts. 'What're you doing?' he said.

Harga looked up guiltily from his work behind the counter.

'Nothing, Cap'n,' he said. He tried to hide the

evidence behind him when Vimes glared over the knife-chewed woodwork.

'Come on, Sham. You can show me.'

Harga's beefy hands came reluctantly into view.

'I was only scraping the old fat out of the pan,' he mumbled.

'I see. And how long have we known each other, Sham?' said Vimes, with terrible kindness.

'Years, Cap'n,' said Harga. 'You bin coming in here nearly every day, reg'lar. One of my best customers.'

Vimes leaned over the counter until his nose was level with the squashy pink thing in the middle of Harga's face.

'And in all that time, have you *ever* changed the fat?' he demanded.

Harga tried to back away. 'Well—'

'It's been like a friend to me, that old fat,' said Vimes. 'There's little black bits in there I've grown to know and love. It's a meal in itself. And you've cleaned out the coffee jug, haven't you. I can tell. This is love-in-a-canoe coffee if ever I tasted it. The other stuff had *flavour*.'

'Well, I thought it was time—'

'*Why?*'

Harga let the pan fall from his pudgy fingers. 'Well, I thought, if the king should happen to come in—'

'You're all *mad*!'

'But, Cap'n—'

Vimes's accusing finger buried itself up to the second joint in Harga's expensive vest.

'You don't even know the wretched fellow's name!' he shouted.

Harga rallied. 'I do, Cap'n,' he stuttered. 'Course I do. Seen it on the decorations and everything. He's called Rex Vivat.'

Very gently, shaking his head in despair, crying in his heart for the essential servility of mankind, Vimes let him go.

In another time and place, the Librarian finished reading. He'd reached the end of the text. Not the end of the book – there was plenty more book. It had been scorched beyond the point of legibility, though.

Not that the last few unburned pages were very easy to read. The author's hand had been shaking, he'd been writing fast, and he'd blotted a lot. But the Librarian had wrestled with many a terrifying text in some of the worst books ever bound, words that tried to read you as you read them, words that writhed on the page. At least these weren't words like that. These were just the words of a man frightened for his life. A man writing a dreadful warning.

It was a page a little back from the burned section that drew the Librarian's eye. He sat and stared at it for some time.

Then he stared at the darkness.

It was *his* darkness. He was asleep out there somewhere. Somewhere out there a thief was heading for this place, to steal this book. And then someone would read this book, read these words, and do it anyway.

His hands itched.

All he had to do was hide the book, or drop on to the thief's head and unscrew it by the ears.

He stared into the darkness again . . .

But that would be interfering with the course of history. Horrible things could happen. The Librarian knew all about this sort of thing, it was part of what you had to know before you were allowed into L-space. He'd seen pictures in ancient books. Time could bifurcate, like a pair of trousers. You could end up in the wrong leg, living a life that was actually happening in the *other* leg, talking to people who weren't in your leg, walking into walls that weren't there any more. Life could be horrible in the wrong trouser of Time.

Besides, it was against Library rules.* The assembled Librarians of Time and Space would certainly have something to say about it if he started to tinker with causality.

He closed the book carefully and tucked it back into the shelf. Then he swung gently from bookcase to bookcase until he reached the doorway. For a moment he stopped and looked down at his own sleeping body. Perhaps he wondered, briefly, whether to wake himself up, have a little chat, tell himself that he had friends and not to worry. If so, he must have decided against it. You could get your-self into a lot of trouble that way.

Instead he slipped out of the door, and lurked in

---

*The three rules of the Librarians of Time and Space are: 1) Silence; 2) Books must be returned no later than the last date shown; and 3) Do not interfere with the nature of causality.

the shadows, and followed the hooded thief when it came out clutching the book, and waited near the dread portal in the rain until the Elucidated Brethren had met and, when the last one left, followed him to his home, and murmured to himself in anthropoid surprise . . .

And then ran back to his Library and the treacherous pathways of L-space.

By mid-morning the streets were packed, Vimes had docked Nobby a day's salary for waving a flag, and an air of barbed gloom settled over the Yard, like a big black cloud with occasional flashes of lightning in it.

' "Get up in a high place",' muttered Nobby. 'That's all very well to say.'

'I was looking forward to lining the streets,' said Colon. 'I'd have got a good view.'

'You were going on about privilege and the rights of man the other night,' said Nobby accusingly.

'Yes, well, one of the privileges and rights of this man is getting a good view,' said the sergeant. 'That's all I'm saying.'

'I've never seen the captain in such a filthy temper,' said Nobby. 'I liked it better when he was on the drink. I reckon he's—'

'You know, I think Errol is really ill,' said Carrot. They turned towards the fruit basket.

'He's very hot. And his skin looks all shiny.'

'What's the right temperature for a dragon?' said Colon.

'Yeah. How do you take it?' said Nobby.

'I think we ought to ask Lady Ramkin to have a look at him,' said Carrot. 'She knows about these things.'

'No, she'll be getting ready for the coronation. We shouldn't go disturbing her,' said Colon. He stretched out his hand to Errol's quivering flanks. 'I used to have a dog that – arrgh! That's not hot, that's boiling!'

'I've offered him lots of water and he just won't touch it. What are you *doing* with that kettle, Nobby?'

Nobby looked innocent. 'Well, I thought we might as well make a cup of tea before we go out. It's a shame to waste—'

'Take it off him!'

Noon came. The fog didn't lift but it did thin a bit, to allow a pale yellow haze where the sun should have been.

Although the passage of years had turned the post of Captain of the Watch into something rather shabby, it still meant that Vimes was entitled to a seat at official occasions. The pecking order had moved it, though, so that now he was in the lowest tier on the rickety bleachers between the Master of the Fellowship of Beggars and the head of the Teachers' Guild. He didn't mind that. Anything was better than the top row, among the Assassins, Thieves, Merchants and all the other things that had floated to the top of society. He never knew what to talk about. Anyway, the teacher was restful company since he didn't do much but clench and unclench his hands occasionally, and whimper.

'Something wrong with your neck, Captain?' said the chief beggar politely, as they waited for the coaches.

'What?' said Vimes distractedly.

'You keep on staring upwards,' said the beggar.

'Hmm? Oh. No. Nothing wrong,' said Vimes.

The beggar wrapped his velvet cloak around him.

'You couldn't by any chance spare—' he paused, calculating a sum in accordance with his station – 'about three hundred dollars for a twelve-course civic banquet, could you?'

'No.'

'Fair enough. Fair enough,' said the chief beggar amiably. He sighed. It wasn't a rewarding job, being chief beggar. It was the differentials that did for you. Low-grade beggars made a reasonable enough living on pennies, but people tended to look the other way when you asked them for a sixteen-bedroom mansion for the night.

Vimes resumed his study of the sky.

Up on the dais the High Priest of Blind Io, who last night by dint of elaborate ecumenical argument and eventually by a club with nails in it had won the right to crown the king, fussed over his preparations. By the small portable sacrificial altar a tethered billy goat was peacefully chewing the cud and possibly thinking, in Goat: What a lucky billy goat I am, to be given such a good view of the proceedings. This is going to be something to tell the kids.

Vimes scanned the diffused outlines of the nearest buildings.

A distant cheering suggested that the ceremonial procession was on its way.

There was a scuffle of activity around the dais as Lupine Wonse chivvied a scramble of servants who rolled a purple carpet down the steps.

Across the square, amongst the ranks of Ankh-Morpork's faded aristocracy, Lady Ramkin's face tilted upwards.

Around the throne, which had been hastily created out of wood and gold foil, a number of lesser priests, some of them with slight head wounds, shuffled into position.

Vimes shifted in his seat, aware of the sound of his own heartbeat, and glared at the haze over the river.

. . . and saw the wings.

Dear Mother and Father [wrote Carrot, in between staring dutifully into the fog] Well, the town is *On Fate* for the coronation, which is more complicated than at home, and now I am on Day duty as well. This is a shame because, I was going to watch the Coronation with Reet, but it does not do to complain. I must go now because we are expecting a dragon any minute although it does not exist really. Your loving son, Carrot.

PS. Have you seen anything of Minty lately?

'You idiot!'

'Sorry,' said Vimes. 'Sorry.'

People were climbing back into their seats, many of them giving him furious looks. Wonse was white with fury.

'How could you have been so *stupid*?' he raged.

Vimes stared at his own fingers.

'I thought I saw——' he began.

'It was a *raven*! You know what ravens are? There must be hundreds of them in the city!'

'In the fog, you see, the size wasn't easy to—' Vimes mumbled.

'And poor Master Greetling, you ought to have known what loud noises do to him!' The head of the Teachers' Guild had to be led away by some kind people.

'Shouting out like that!' Wonse went on.

'Look, I said I'm sorry! It was an honest mistake!'

'I've had to hold up the procession and everything!'

Vimes said nothing. He could feel hundreds of amused or unsympathetic eyes on him.

'Well,' he muttered, 'I'd better be getting back to the Yard—'

Wonse's eyes narrowed. 'No,' he snapped. 'But you can go home, if you like. Or anywhere your *fancies* take you. Give me your badge.'

'Huh?'

Wonse held out his hand.

'Your badge,' he repeated.

'My badge?'

'That's what I said. I want to keep you out of trouble.'

Vimes looked at him in astonishment. 'But it's my *badge*!'

'And you're going to give it to me,' said Wonse grimly. 'By order of the king.'

'What d'you mean? He doesn't even know!' Vimes heard the wailing in his own voice.

Wonse scowled. 'But he will,' he said. 'And I don't expect he'll even bother to appoint a successor.'

Vimes slowly unclipped the verdigrised disc of copper, weighed it in his hand, and then tossed it to Wonse without a word.

For a moment he considered pleading, but something rebelled. He turned, and stalked off through the crowd.

So that was it.

As simple as that. After half a lifetime of service. No more City Watch. Huh. Vimes kicked at the pavement. It'd be some sort of Royal Guard now.

With plumes in their damn helmets.

Well, he'd had enough. It wasn't a proper life anyway, in the Watch. You didn't meet people in the best of circumstances. There must be hundreds of other things he could do, and if he thought for long enough he could probably remember what some of them were.

Pseudopolis Yard was off the route of the procession, and as he stumbled into the Watch House he could hear the distant cheering beyond the rooftops. Across the city the temple gongs were being sounded.

Now they are ringing the gongs, thought Vimes, but soon they will – they will – they will *not* be ringing the gongs. Not much of an aphorism, he thought, but he could work on it. He had the time, now.

Vimes noticed the mess.

Errol had started eating again. He'd eaten most of the table, the grate, the coal scuttle, several lamps and the squeaky rubber hippo. Now he lay in his box again, skin twitching, whimpering in his sleep.

'A right mess you've made,' said Vimes enigmatically. Still at least *he* wouldn't have to tidy it up.

He opened his desk drawer.

Someone had eaten into that, too. All that was left was a few shards of glass.

Sergeant Colon hauled himself on to the parapet around the Temple of Small Gods. He was too old for this sort of thing. He'd joined for the bell ringing, not sitting around on high places waiting for dragons to find him.

He got his breath back, and peered through the fog.

'Anyone human still up here?' he whispered.

Carrot's voice sounded dead and featureless in the dull air.

'Here I am, Sergeant,' he said.

'I was just checking if you were still here,' said Colon.

'I'm still here, Sergeant,' said Carrot, obediently.

Colon joined him.

'Just checking you were not et,' he said, trying to grin.

'I haven't been et,' said Carrot.

'Oh,' said Colon. 'Good, then.' He tapped his fingers on the damp stonework, feeling he ought to make his position absolutely clear.

'Just checking,' he repeated. 'Part of my duty, see.

Going around, sort of thing. It's not that I'm fright-ened of being up on the roofs by myself, you understand. Thick up here, isn't it.'

'Yes, Sergeant.'

'Everything all OK?' Nobby's muffled voice sidled its way through the thick air, quickly followed by its owner.

'Yes, Corporal,' said Carrot.

'What you doing up here?' Colon demanded.

'I was just coming up to check Lance-constable Carrot was all right,' said Nobby innocently. 'What were *you* doing, Sergeant?'

'We're all all right,' said Carrot, beaming. 'That's good, isn't it.'

The two NCOs shifted uneasily and avoided looking at one another. It seemed like a long way back to their posts, across the damp, cloudy and, above all, *exposed* rooftops.

Colon made an executive decision.

'Sod this,' he said, and found a piece of fallen statuary to sit on. Nobby leaned on the parapet and winkled a damp dogend from the unspeakable ash-tray behind his ear.

'Heard the procession go by,' he observed. Colon filled his pipe, and struck a match on the stone beside him.

'If that dragon's alive,' he said, blowing out a plume of smoke and turning a small patch of fog into smog, 'then it'll have got the hell away from here, I'm telling you. Not the right sort of place for dragons, a city,' he added, in the tones of someone doing a great job of convincing himself. 'It'll have gone off to somewhere where there's high places and plenty to eat, you mark my words.'

'Somewhere like the city, you mean?' said Carrot.

'Shut up,' said the other two in unison.

'Chuck us the matches, Sergeant,' said Nobby.

Colon tossed the bundle of evil yellow-headed lucifers across the leads. Nobby struck one, which was immediately blown out. Shreds of fog drifted past him.

'Wind's getting up,' he observed.

'Good. Can't stand this fog,' said Colon. 'What was I saying?'

'You were saying the dragon'll be miles away,' prompted Nobby.

'Oh. Right. Well, it stands to reason, doesn't it? I mean, *I* wouldn't hang around here if I could fly away. If I could fly, I wouldn't be sitting on a roof on some manky old statue. If I could fly, I'd—'

'What statue?' said Nobby, cigarette halfway to his mouth.

'This one,' said Colon, thumping the stone. 'And don't try to give me the willies, Nobby. You know there's hundreds of mouldy old statues up on Small Gods.'

'No I don't,' said Nobby. 'What I do know is, they were all taken down last month when they releaded the roof. There's just the roof and the dome and that's it. You have to take notice of little things like that,' he added, 'when you're detectoring.'

In the damp silence that followed Sergeant Colon looked down at the stone he was sitting on. It had a taper, and a scaly pattern, and a sort of indefinable tail-like quality. Then he followed its length up and into the rapidly-thinning fog.

On the dome of Small Gods the dragon raised its head, yawned, and unfolded its wings.

The unfolding wasn't a simple operation. It seemed to go on for some time, as the complex biological machinery of ribs and pleats slid apart. Then, with wings outstretched, the dragon yawned, took a few steps to the edge of the roof, and launched itself into the air.

After a while a hand appeared over the edge of the parapet. It flailed around for a moment until it got a decent grip.

There was a grunt. Carrot hauled himself back on to the roof and pulled the other two up behind him. They lay flat out on the leads, panting. Carrot observed the way that the dragon's talons had scored deep grooves in the metal. You couldn't help noticing things like that.

'Hadn't,' he panted, 'hadn't we better warn people?'

Colon dragged himself forward until he could look across the city.

'I don't think we need bother,' he said. 'I think they'll soon find out.'

The High Priest of Blind Io was stumbling over his words. There had never been an official coronation service in Ankh-Morpork, as far as he could find out. The old kings had managed quite well with something on the lines of: 'We hath got the crown, i'faith, and we will kill any whoreson who tries to take it away, by the Lord Harry.' Apart from anything else, this was rather short. He'd spent a long time drafting something longer and more in keeping with the spirit of the times, and was having some trouble remembering it.

He was also being put off by the goat, which was watching him with loyal interest.

'Get *on* with it!' Wonse hissed, from his position behind the throne.

'All in good time,' the high priest hissed back. 'This is a coronation, I'll have you know. You might try to show a little respect.'

'Of course I'm showing respect! Now get on—'

There was a shout, off to the right. Wonse glared into the crowd.

'It's that Ramkin woman,' he said. 'What's she up to?'

People around her were chattering excitedly now. Fingers pointed all the same way, like a small fallen forest. There were one or two screams, and then the crowd moved like a tide.

Wonse looked along the wide Street of Small Gods.

It wasn't a raven out there. Not this time.

The dragon flew slowly, only a few feet above the ground, wings sculling gracefully through the air.

The flags that crisscrossed the street were caught up and snapped like so much cobweb, piling up on the creature's spine plates and flapping back along the length of its tail.

It flew with head and neck fully extended, as if the great body was being towed like a barge. The people on the street yelled and fought one another for the safety of doorways. It paid them no attention.

It should have come roaring, but the only sounds were the creaking of wings and the snapping of banners.

It *should* have come roaring. Not like this, not slowly and deliberately, giving terror time to mature. It should have come threatening. Not promising.

It should have come roaring, not flying gently to the accompaniment of the zip and zing of merry bunting.

Vimes pulled open the other drawer of his desk and glared at the paperwork, such as there was of it. There wasn't really much in there that he could call his own. A scrap of sugar bag reminded him that he now owed the Tea Kitty six pence.

Odd. He wasn't angry yet. He would be later on, of course. By evening he'd be furious. Drunk and furious. But not yet. Not yet. It hadn't really sunk in, and he knew he was just going through the motions as a preventative against thinking.

Errol stirred sluggishly in his box, raised his head and whined.

'What's the matter, boy?' said Vimes, reaching down. 'Upset stomach?'

The little dragon's skin was moving as though heavy industry was being carried on inside. Nothing in *Diseases of the Dragon* said anything about *this*.

From the swollen stomach came sounds like a distant and complicated war in an earthquake zone.

That surely wasn't right. Sybil Ramkin said you had to pay great attention to a dragon's diet, since even a minor stomach upset would decorate the walls and ceiling with pathetic bits of scaly skin. But in the past few days . . . well, there had been cold pizzas, and the ash from Nobby's horrible dog-ends, and all-in-all Errol had eaten more or less what he liked. Which was just about everything, to judge by the room. Not to mention the contents of the bottom drawer.

'We really haven't looked after you very well, have we?' said Vimes. 'Treated you like a dog, really.' He wondered what effect squeaky rubber hippos had on the digestion.

Vimes became slowly aware that the distant cheering had turned to screams.

He stared vaguely at Errol, and then smiled an incredibly evil smile and stood up.

There were sounds of panic and the mob on the run.

He placed his battered helmet on his head and gave it a jaunty tap. Then, humming a mad little tune, he sauntered out of the building.

Errol remained quite still for a while and then, with extreme difficulty, half-crawled and half-rolled out of his box. Strange messages were coming from the massive part of his brain that controlled his digestive system. It was demanding certain things that he couldn't put a name to. Fortunately it was able to describe them in minute detail to the complex receptors in his enormous nostrils. They flared, subjecting the air of the room to an intimate examination. His head turned, triangulating.

He pulled himself across the floor and began to eat, with every sign of enjoyment, Carrot's tin of armour polish.

People streamed past Vimes as he strolled up the Street of Small Gods. Smoke rose into the air from the Plaza of Broken Moons.

The dragon squatted in the middle of it, on what remained of the coronation dais. It had a self-satisfied expression.

There was no sign of the throne, or of its occupant, although it was possible that complicated forensic examination of the small pile of charcoal in the wrecked and smouldering woodwork might offer some clue.

Vimes caught hold of an ornamental fountain to steady himself as the crowds stampeded by. Every street out of the plaza was packed with struggling bodies. Not noisy ones, Vimes noticed. People weren't wasting their breath with screaming any more. There was just this solid, deadly determination to be somewhere else.

The dragon spread its wings and flapped them luxuriously. The people at the rear of the crowd took this as a signal to climb up the backs of the people in front of them and run for safety from head to head.

Within a few seconds the square was empty of all save the stupid and the terminally bewildered. Even the badly trampled were making a spirited crawl for the nearest exit.

Vimes looked around him. There seemed to be a lot of fallen flags, some of which were being eaten by an elderly goat which couldn't believe its luck. He could distantly see Cut-me-own-Throat on his hands and knees, trying to restore the contents of his tray.

By Vimes's side a small child waved a flag hesitantly and shouted 'Hurrah'.

Then everything went quiet.

Vimes bent down.

'I think you should be going home,' he said.

The child squinted up at him.

'Are you a Watch man?' it said.

'No,' said Vimes. 'And yes.'

'What happened to the king, Watch man?'

'Er. I think he's gone off for a rest,' said Vimes.

'My auntie said I shouldn't talk to Watch men,' said the child.

'Do you think it might be a good idea to go home and tell her how obedient you've been, then?' said Vimes.

'My auntie said, if I was naughty, she'd put me on the roof and call the dragon,' said the child, conversationally. 'My auntie said it eats you all up starting with the legs, so's you can see what's happening.'

'Why don't you go home and tell your auntie she's acting in the best traditions of Ankh-Morpork child-rearing?' said Vimes. 'Go on. Run along.'

'It crunches up all your bones,' said the child happily. 'And when it gets to your head, it—'

'Look, it's up there!' shouted Vimes. 'The great big dragon that crunches you up! Now go *home*!'

The child looked up at the thing perched on the crippled dais.

'I haven't seen it crunch anyone yet,' it complained.

'Push off or you'll feel the back of my hand,' said Vimes.

This seemed to fit the bill. The child nodded understandingly.

'Right. Can I shout hurrah again?'

'If you like,' said Vimes.

'Hurrah.'

So much for community policing, Vimes thought. He peered out from behind the fountain again.

A voice immediately above him rumbled, 'Say what you like, I still swear it's a magnificent specimen.'

Vimes's gaze travelled upwards until it crested the edge of the fountain's top bowl.

'Have you noticed,' said Sybil Ramkin, hauling herself upright by a piece of eroded statuary and dropping down in front of him, 'how every time we meet, a dragon turns up?' She gave him an arch smile. 'It's a bit like having your own tune. Or something.'

'It's just sitting there,' said Vimes hurriedly. 'Just looking around. As if it's waiting for something to happen.'

The dragon blinked with Jurassic patience.

The roads off the square were packed with people. That's the Ankh-Morpork instinct, Vimes thought. Run away, and then stop and see if anything interesting is going to happen to other people.

There was a movement in the wreckage near the dragon's front talon, and the High Priest of Blind Io staggered to his feet, dust and splinters cascading from his robes. He was still holding the ersatz crown in one hand.

Vimes watched the old man look upwards into a couple of glowing red eyes a few feet away.

'Can dragons read minds?' whispered Vimes.

'I'm sure mine understand every word I say,' hissed Lady Ramkin. 'Oh, no! The silly old fool is giving it the crown!'

'But isn't that a smart move?' said Vimes. 'Dragons like gold. It's like throwing a stick for a dog, isn't it?'

'Oh dear,' said Sybil Ramkin. 'It might not, you know. Dragons have such sensitive mouths.'

The great dragon blinked at the tiny circle of gold. Then, with extreme delicacy, it extended one metre-long claw and hooked the thing out of the priest's trembling fingers.

'What d'you mean, sensitive?' said Vimes, watching the claw travel slowly towards the long, horse-like face.

'A really incredible sense of taste. They're so, well, chemically orientated.'

'You mean it can probably *taste* gold?' whispered Vimes, watching the crown being carefully licked.

'Oh, certainly. And smell it.'

Vimes wondered what the chances were of the crown being made of gold. Not high, he decided.

Gold foil over copper, perhaps. Enough to fool human beings. And then he wondered what some-one's reaction would be if they were offered sugar which turned out, once you'd put three spoonfuls in your coffee, to be salt.

The dragon removed the claw from its mouth in one graceful movement and caught the high priest, who was just sneaking away, a blow which knocked him high into the air. When he was screaming at the top of the arc the great mouth came around and –

'Gosh!' said Lady Ramkin.

There was a groan from the watchers.

'The *temperature* of the thing!' said Vimes. 'I mean, nothing left! Just a wisp of smoke!'

There was another movement in the rubble. Another figure pulled itself upright and leaned dazedly against a broken spar.

It was Lupine Wonse, under a coating of soot.

Vimes watched him look up into a pair of nostrils the size of drain-covers.

Wonse broke into a run. Vimes wondered what it felt like, running away from something like that, expecting any minute your backbone to reach, very briefly, a temperature somewhere beyond the vaporization point of iron. He could guess.

Wonse made it halfway across the square before the dragon darted forward with surprising agility for such a bulk and snatched him up. The talon swept on upward until the struggling figure was being held a few feet from the dragon's face.

It appeared to examine him for some time, turning him this way and that. Then, moving on its three free legs and flapping its wings occasionally to help with its balance, it trotted away across the plaza and headed towards the – what once had *been* the Patrician's palace. To what once had been the king's palace, too.

It ignored the frightened spectators silently pressing themselves against the walls. The arched gateway was shouldered aside with depressing ease. The doors themselves, tall and iron-bound and solid, lasted a surprising ten seconds before collapsing into a heap of glowing ash.

The dragon stepped through.

Lady Ramkin turned in astonishment. Vimes had started to laugh.

There was a manic edge to it and there were tears in his eyes, but it was still laughter. He laughed and laughed until he slid gently down the edge of the fountain, his legs splaying out in front of him.

'Hooray, hooray, hooray!' he giggled, almost choking.

'What on earth d'you mean?' Lady Ramkin demanded.

'Put out more flags! Blow the cymbals, roast the tocsin! We've crowned it! We've got a king after all! What ho!'

'Have you been drinking?' she snapped.

'Not yet!' sniggered Vimes. 'Not yet! But I will be!'

He laughed on, knowing that when he stopped black depression was going to drop on him like a lead soufflé. But he could see the future stretching out ahead of them . . .

. . . after all, it was definitely *noble*. And it didn't carry money, and it couldn't answer back. It could certainly do something for the inner cities, too. Like torching them to the bedrock.

We'll really do it, he thought. That's the Ankh-Morpork way. If you can't beat it or corrupt it, you pretend it was your idea in the first place.

Vivat Draco.

He became aware that the small child had wandered up again. It waved its flag gently at him and said, 'Can I shout hurrah again now?'

'Why not?' said Vimes. 'Everyone else will.'

From the palace came the muffled sounds of complicated destruction . . .

Errol pulled a broomstick across the floor with his mouth and, whimpering with effort, hauled it upright. After a lot more whimpering and several false starts he managed to winkle the end of it between the wall and the big jar of lamp oil.

He paused for a moment, breathing like a bellows, and pushed.

The jar resisted for a moment, rocked back and forth once or twice, and then fell over and smashed on the flagstones. Crude, very badly-refined oil spread out in a black puddle.

Errol's huge nostrils twitched. Somewhere in the back of his brain unfamiliar synapses clicked like telegraph keys. Great balks of information flooded down the thick nerve cord to his nose, carrying inexplicable information about triple bonds, alkanes and geometric isomerism. However, almost all of it missed the small part of Errol's brain that was used for being Errol.

All he knew was that he was suddenly very, very thirsty.

Something major was happening in the palace. There was the occasional crash of a floor or thump of a falling ceiling . . .

In his rat-filled dungeon, behind a door with more locks than a major canal network, the Patrician of Ankh-Morpork lay back and grinned in the darkness.

Outside, bonfires flared in the dusk.

Ankh-Morpork was celebrating. No-one was quite sure why, but they'd worked themselves up for a celebration tonight, barrels had been broached, oxen had been put on spits, one paper hat and celebratory mug had been issued per child, and it seemed a shame to waste all that effort. Anyway, it had been a very interesting day, and the people of Ankh-Morpork set great store by entertainment.

'The way I see it,' said one of the revellers, halfway through a huge greasy lump of half-raw meat, 'a dragon as king mightn't be a bad idea. When you think it through, is what I mean.'

'It definitely looked very gracious,' said the woman to his right, as if testing the idea. 'Sort of, well, sleek. Nice and smart. Not scruffy. Takes a bit of a pride in itself.' She glared at some of the younger revellers further down the table. 'The trouble with people today is they don't take pride in themselves.'

'And there's foreign policy, of course,' said a third, helping himself to a rib. 'When you come to think about it.'

'What d'you mean?'

'Diplomacy,' said the rib-eater, flatly.

They thought about it. And then you could see them turning the idea around and thinking about it the other way, in a polite effort to see what the hell he was getting at.

'Dunno,' said the monarchical expert slowly. 'I mean, your actual dragon, it's got these, basically, two sort of ways of negotiation. Hasn't it? I mean, it's either roasting you alive, or it isn't. Correct me if I'm wrong,' he added.

'That's my point. I mean, let's say the ambassador from Klatch comes along, you know how arrogant that lot are, suppose he says: we want this, we want that, we want the other thing. Well,' he said, beaming at them, 'what *we* say is, shut your face unless you want to go home in a jar.'

They tried out this idea for mental fit. It had that certain something.

'They've got a big fleet, Klatch,' said the monarchist uncertainly. 'Could be a bit risky, roasting diplomats. People see a pile of charcoal come back on the boat, they tend to look a bit askance.'

'Ah, *then* we say, Ho there, Johnny Klatchian, you no like-um, big fella lizard belong-sky bake mud hut belong-you pretty damn chop-chop.'

'We could really say that?'

'Why not? *And* then we say, send plenty tribute toot sweet.'

'I never did like them Klatchians,' said the woman firmly. 'The stuff they eat! It's disgustin'. And gabblin' away all the time in their heathen lingo . . .'

In the shadows, a match flared.

Vimes cupped his hands around the flame, sucked on the foul tobacco, tossed the match into the gutter and slouched off down the damp, puddle-punctuated alley.

If there was anything that depressed him more than his own cynicism, it was that quite often it still wasn't as cynical as real life.

We've got along with the other guys for centuries, he thought. Getting along has practically been all our foreign policy. Now I think I've just heard us declare war on an ancient civilization that we've always got along with, more or less, even if they do talk funny. And after that, the world. What's worse, we'll probably win.

Similar thoughts, although with a different perspective, were going through the minds of the civic leaders of Ankh-Morpork when, next morning, each received a short note bidding them to be at the palace for a working lunch, by order.

It didn't say whose order. Or, they noted, whose lunch.

Now they were assembled in the antechamber.

And there had been changes. It had never been what you might call a select place. The Patrician had always felt that if you made people comfortable they might want to stay. The furniture had been a few very elderly chairs and, around the walls, portraits of earlier city rulers holding scrolls and things.

The chairs were still there. The portraits were not. Or, rather, the stained and cracked canvases were piled in a corner, but the gilt frames were gone.

The councillors tried to avoid one another's faces, and sat tapping their fingers on their knees.

Finally a couple of very worried-looking servants opened the doors to the main hall. Lupine Wonse lurched through.

Most of the councillors had been up all night anyway, trying to formulate some kind of policy *vis-à-vis* dragons, but Wonse looked as though he hadn't been to sleep in years. His face was the colour of a fermented dishcloth. Never particularly well-padded, he now looked like something out of a pyramid.

'Ah,' he intoned. 'Good. Are you all here? Then perhaps you would step this way, gentlemen.'

'Er,' said the head thief, 'the note mentioned lunch?'

'Yes?' said Wonse.

'With a *dragon*?'

'Good grief, you don't think it would eat you, do you?' said Wonse. 'What an idea!'

'Never crossed me mind,' said the head thief, relief blowing from his ears like steam. 'The very idea. Haha.'

'Haha,' said the chief merchant.

'Hoho,' said the head assassin. 'The very idea.'

'No, I expect you're all far too stringy,' said Wonse. 'Haha.'

'Haha.'

'Ahaha.'

'Hoho.' The temperature lowered by several degrees.

'So if you would kindly step this way?'

The great hall had changed. For one thing, it was a great deal greater. Several walls had been knocked into adjoining rooms, and the ceiling and several storeys of upper rooms had been entirely removed. The floor was a mass of rubble except in the middle of the room, which was a heap of gold—

Well, gold*ish*. It looked as though someone had scoured the palace for anything that shone or glittered. There were the picture frames, and the gold thread out of the tapestries, and silver, and the occasional gem. There were also tureens from the kitchens, candlesticks, warming pans, fragments of mirror. Sparkly stuff.

The councillors were not in a position to pay much attention to this, however, because of what was hanging above their heads.

It looked like the biggest badly-rolled cigar in the universe, if the biggest badly-rolled cigar in the universe was in the habit of hanging upside down. Two talons could be dimly seen gripping the dark rafters.

Halfway between the glittering heap and the doorway a small table had been laid. The councillors noted without much surprise that the familiar ancient silverware was missing. There were china plates, and cutlery that looked as though it had very recently been whittled from bits of wood. Wonse took a seat at the head of the table and nodded to the servants.

'Please be seated, gentlemen,' he said. 'I am sorry things are a little . . . different, but the king hopes you will bear with it until matters can be more suitably organized.'

'The, er,' said the head merchant.

'The king,' repeated Wonse. His voice sounded one dribble away from madness.

'Oh. The king. Right,' said the merchant. From where he was sitting he had a good view of the big hanging thing. There seemed to be some movement there, some trembling in the great folds that wrapped it. 'Long life to him, say I,' he added quickly.

The first course was soup with dumplings in it. Wonse didn't have any. The rest of them ate in a terrified silence broken only by the dull chiming of wood on china.

'There are certain matters of decree to which the king feels your assent would be welcome,' said Wonse, eventually. 'A pure formality, of course, and I am sorry to bother you with such petty detail.'

The big bundle appeared to sway in the breeze.

'No trouble at all,' squeaked the head thief.

'The king graciously desires it to be known,' said Wonse, 'that it would be pleased to receive coronation gifts from the population at large. Nothing complex, of course. Simply any precious metals or gems they might have by them and can easily spare. I should stress, by the way, that this is by no means compulsory. Such generosity as he is confident of expecting should be an entirely voluntary act.'

The chief assassin looked sadly at the rings on his fingers, and sighed. The head merchant was already resignedly unclipping his gilt chain of office from around his neck.

'Why, gentlemen!' said Wonse. 'This is most unexpected!'

'Um,' said the Archchancellor of Unseen University. 'You will be – that is, I am sure the king is aware that, traditionally, the University is exempt from all city levies and taxes . . .'

He stifled a yawn. The wizards had spent the night directing their best spells against the dragon. It was like punching fog.

'My dear sir, this is no levy,' protested Wonse. 'I hope that nothing I have said would lead you to expect anything like that. Oh, no! No. Any tribute should be, as I said, entirely voluntary. I hope that is absolutely clear.'

'As crystal,' said the head assassin, glaring at the old wizard. 'And these entirely voluntary tributes we are about to make, they go—?'

'On the hoard,' said Wonse.

'Ah.'

'While I am positive the people of the city will be very generous indeed once they fully understand the situation,' said the head merchant, 'I am sure the king will understand that there is very little gold in Ankh-Morpork?'

'Good point,' said Wonse. 'However, the king intends to pursue a vigorous and dynamic foreign policy which should remedy matters.'

'Ah,' the councillors chorused, rather more enthusiastically this time.

'For example,' Wonse went on, 'the king feels that our legitimate interests in Quirm, Sto Lat, Pseudopolis and Tsort have been seriously compromised in recent centuries. This will be speedily corrected and, gentlemen, I can assure you that treasure will positively flow into the city from those anxious to enjoy the king's protection.'

The head assassin glanced at the hoard. A very definite idea formed in his mind as to where all that treasure would end up. You had to admire the way dragons knew how to put the bite on. It was practically human.

'Oh,' he said.

'Of course, there will probably be other acquisitions in the way of land, property and so forth, and the king wishes it to be fully understood that loyal Privy Councillors will be richly rewarded.'

'And, er,' said the head assassin, who was beginning to feel that he had got a firm grip on the nature of the king's mental processes, 'no doubt the, er—'

'Privy Councillors,' said Wonse.

'No doubt they will respond with even greater generosity in the matter of, for example, treasure?'

'I am sure such considerations haven't crossed the king's mind,' said Wonse, 'but the point is very well made.'

'I thought it would be.'

The next course was fat pork, beans and floury

potatoes. More, as they couldn't help noticing, fattening food.

Wonse had a glass of water.

'Which brings us on to a further matter of some delicacy which I am sure that well-travelled, broad-minded gentlemen such as yourselves will have no difficulty in accepting,' he said. The hand holding the glass was beginning to shake.

'I hope it will also be understood by the population at large, especially since the king will undoubtedly be able to contribute in so many ways to the well-being and defence of the city. For example, I am sure that the people will rest more contentedly in their beds knowing that the dr – the king is tirelessly protecting them from harm. There can, however, be ridiculous ancient . . . prejudices . . . which will only be eradicated by ceaseless work . . . on the part of all men of good will.'

He paused, and looked at them. The head assassin said later that he had looked into the eyes of many men who, obviously, were very near death, but he had never looked into eyes that were so clearly and unmistakably looking back at him from the slopes of Hell. He hoped he would never, he said, ever have to look into eyes like that again.

'I am referring,' said Wonse, each word coming slowly to the surface like bubbles in some quicksand, 'to the matter of . . . the king's . . . diet.'

There was a terrible silence. They heard the faint rustle of wings behind them, and the shadows in the corners of the hall grew darker and seemed to close in.

'Diet,' said the head thief, in a hollow voice.

'Yes,' said Wonse. His voice was almost a squeak. Sweat was dripping down his face. The head assassin had once heard the word 'rictus' and wondered when you should use it correctly to describe someone's expression, and now he knew. That was what Wonse's face had become; it was the ghastly rictus of someone trying not to hear the words his own mouth was saying.

'We, er, we thought,' said the head assassin, very carefully, 'that the dr – the king, well, must have been arranging matters for himself, over the weeks.'

'Ah, but poor stuff, you know. Poor stuff. Stray animals and so forth,' said Wonse, staring hard at the tabletop. 'Obviously, as king, such makeshifts are no longer appropriate.'

The silence grew and took on a texture. The councillors thought hard, especially about the meal they had just eaten. The arrival of a huge trifle with a lot of cream on it only served to concentrate their minds.

'Er,' said the head merchant, 'how often is the king hungry?'

'All the time,' said Wonse, 'but it eats once a month. It is really a ceremonial occasion.'

'Of course,' said the head merchant. 'It would be.'

'And, er,' said the head assassin, 'when did the king last, er, eat?'

'I'm sorry to say it hasn't eaten properly ever since it came here,' said Wonse.

'Oh.'

'You must understand,' said Wonse, fiddling desperately with his wooden cutlery, 'that merely waylaying people like some common assassin—'

'Excuse *me*—' the head assassin began.

'Some common murderer, I mean – there is no . . . satisfaction there. The whole essence of the king's feeding is that it should be, well . . . an act of bonding between king and subjects. It is, it is perhaps a living allegory. Reinforcing the close links between the crown and the community,' he added.

'The precise nature of the meal—' the head thief began, almost choking on the words. 'Are we talking about young maidens here?'

'Sheer prejudice,' said Wonse. 'The age is immaterial. Marital status is, of course, of importance. And social class. Something to do with flavour, I believe.' He leaned forward, and now his voice was pain-filled and urgent and, they felt, genuinely his own for the first time. 'Please consider it!' he hissed. 'After all, just one a month! In exchange for so much! The families of people of use to the king, Privy Councillors such as yourselves, would not, of course, even be considered. And when you think of all the alternatives . . .'

They didn't think about all the alternatives. It was enough to think about just one of them.

The silence purred at them as Wonse talked. They avoided one another's faces, for fear of what they might see mirrored there. Each man thought: one of the others is bound to say something soon, some protest, and then I'll murmur agreement, not actually *say* anything, I'm not as stupid as that, but definitely murmur very firmly, so that the others will be in no doubt that I thoroughly disapprove, because at a time like this it behooves all decent men to nearly stand up and be almost heard . . .

But no-one said anything. The cowards, each man thought.

And no-one touched the pudding, or the brick-thick chocolate mints served afterwards. They just listened in flushed, gloomy horror as Wonse's voice droned on, and when they were dismissed they tried to leave as separately as possible, so that they didn't have to talk to one another.

Except for the head merchant, that is. He found himself leaving the palace with the chief assassin, and they strolled side by side, minds racing. The chief merchant tried to look on the bright side; he was one of those men who organize sing-songs when things go drastically wrong.

'Well, well,' he said. 'So we're privy councillors now. Just fancy.'

'Hmm,' said the assassin.

'I wonder what's the difference between ordinary councillors and privy councillors?' wondered the merchant aloud.

The assassin scowled at him. 'I think,' he said, 'it is because you're expected to eat shit.'

He turned the glare back on his feet again. What kept going through his mind were Wonse's last words, as he shook the secretary's limp hand. He wondered if anyone else had heard them. Unlikely . . .

they'd been a shape rather than a sound. Wonse had simply moved his lips around them while staring fixedly at the assassin's moon-tanned face.

Help. Me.

The assassin shivered. Why him? As far as he could see there was only one kind of help he was qualified to give, and very few people ever asked for it for themselves. In fact, they usually paid large sums for it to be given as a surprise present to other people. He wondered what was happening to Wonse that made any alternative seem better . . .

Wonse sat alone in the dark, ruined hall. Waiting.

He could try running. But it'd find him again. It'd always be able to find him. It could smell his mind.

Or it would flame him. That was worse. Just like the brethren. *Perhaps* it was an instantaneous death, it *looked* an instantaneous death, but Wonse lay awake at night wondering whether those last micro-seconds somehow stretched to a subjective, white-hot eternity, every tiny part of your body a mere smear of plasma and you, there, alive in the middle of it all . . .

Not you. I would not flame you.

It wasn't telepathy. As far as Wonse had always understood it, telepathy was like hearing a voice in your head.

This was like hearing a voice in your body. His whole nervous system twanged to it, like a bow.

Rise.

Wonse jerked to his feet, overturning the chair

and banging his legs on the table. When that voice spoke, he had as much control over his body as water had over gravity.

Come.

Wonse lurched across the floor.

The wings unfolded slowly, with the occasional creak, until they filled the hall from side to side. The tip of one smashed a window, and stuck out into the afternoon air.

The dragon slowly, sensuously, stretched out its neck and yawned. When it had finished, it brought its head around until it was a few inches in front of Wonse's face.

What does voluntary mean?

'It, er, it means doing something of your own free will,' said Wonse.

But they have no free will! They will increase my hoard, or I will flame them!

Wonse gulped. 'Yes,' he said, 'but you mustn't—'

The silent roar of fury spun him around.

There is nothing I mustn't!

'No, no, no!' squeaked Wonse, clutching his head. 'I didn't mean that! Believe me! This way is better, that's all! Better and safer!'

None can defeat me!

'This is certainly the case—'

None can control me!

Wonse flung up his finger-spread hands in a conciliatory fashion. 'Of course, of course,' he said. 'But there are ways and ways, you know. Ways and ways. All the roaring and flaming, you see, you don't need it . . .'

Foolish ape! How else can I make them do my bidding?

Wonse put his hands behind his back.

'They'll do it of their own free will,' he said. 'And in time, they'll come to believe it was their own idea. It'll be a tradition. Take it from me. We humans are adaptable creatures.'

The dragon gave him a long, blank stare.

'In fact,' said Wonse, trying to keep the trembling out of his voice, 'before too long, if someone comes along and tells them that a dragon king is a bad idea, they'll kill him themselves.'

The dragon blinked.

For the first time Wonse could remember, it seemed uncertain.

'I know people, you see,' said Wonse, simply.

The dragon continued to pin him with its gaze.

If you are lying . . . it thought, eventually.

'You know I can't. Not to you.'

And they really act like this?

'Oh, yes. All the time. It's a basic human trait.'

Wonse knew the dragon could read at least the upper levels of his mind. They resonated in terrible harmony. And he could see the mighty thoughts behind the eyes in front of him.

The dragon was horrified.

'I'm sorry,' said Wonse weakly. 'That's just how we are. It's all to do with survival, I think.'

There will be no mighty warriors sent to kill me? it thought, almost plaintively.

'I don't think so.'

No heroes?

'Not any more. They cost too much.'

But I will be eating people!

Wonse whimpered.

He felt the sensation of the dragon rummaging around in his mind, trying to find a clue to understanding. He half-saw, half-sensed the flicker of random images, of dragons, of the mythical age of reptiles and – and here he felt the dragon's genuine astonishment – of some of the less commendable areas of human history, which were most of it. And after the astonishment came the baffled anger. There was practically nothing the dragon could do to people that they had not, sooner or later, tried on one another, often with enthusiasm.

You have the effrontery to be squeamish, it thought at him. *But we were dragons. We were* supposed *to be cruel, cunning, heartless, and terrible. But this much I can tell you, you ape* – the great face pressed even closer, so that Wonse was staring into the pitiless depths of his eyes – *we never burned and tortured and ripped one another apart and called it morality.*

The dragon stretched its wings again, once or twice, and then dropped heavily on to the tawdry assortment of mildly precious things. Its claws scrabbled at the pile. It sneered.

A three-legged lizard wouldn't hoard this lot, it thought.

'There will be better things,' whispered Wonse, temporarily relieved at the change in direction.

There had better be.

'Can I—' Wonse hesitated – 'can I ask you a question?'

Ask.

'You don't *need* to eat people, surely? I think that's the only problem from people's point of view, you see,' he added, his voice speeding up to a gabble. 'The treasure and everything, that doesn't have to be a problem, but if it's just a matter of, well, protein, then perhaps it has occurred to a powerful intellect such as your own that something less controversial, like a cow, might—'

The dragon breathed a horizontal streak of fire that calcined the opposite wall.

Need? Need? it roared, when the sound had died away. *You talk to me of need? Isn't it the tradition that the finest flower of womanhood should be sent to the dragon to ensure peace and prosperity?*

'But, you see, we have always been moderately peaceful and reasonably prosperous—'

DO YOU WANT THIS STATE OF AFFAIRS TO CONTINUE?

The force of the thought drove Wonse to his knees.

'Of course,' he managed.

The dragon stretched its claws luxuriantly.

Then the need is not mine, it is yours, it thought.

Now get out of my sight.

Wonse sagged as it left his mind.

The dragon slithered over the cut-price hoard, leapt up on the ledge of one of the hall's big windows, and smashed the stained glass with its head. The multicoloured image of a city father cascaded into the other debris below.

The long neck stretched out into the early

evening air, and turned like a seeking needle. Lights were coming on across the city. The sound of a million people being alive made a muted, deep thrumming.

The dragon breathed deeply, joyfully.

Then it hauled the rest of its body on to the ledge, shouldered the remains of the window's frame aside, and leapt into the sky.

'What is it?' said Nobby.

It was vaguely round, of a woodish texture, and when struck made a noise like a ruler plucked over the edge of a desk.

Sergeant Colon tapped it again.

'I give in,' he said.

Carrot proudly lifted it out of the battered packaging.

'It's a cake,' he said, shoving both hands under the thing and raising it with some difficulty. 'From my mother.' He managed to put it on the table without trapping his fingers.

'Can you eat it?' said Nobby. 'It's taken months to get here. You'd think it would go stale.'

'Oh, it's to a special dwarfish recipe,' said Carrot. 'Dwarfish cakes don't go stale.'

Sergeant Colon gave it another sharp rap. 'I suppose not,' he conceded.

'It's incredibly sustaining,' said Carrot. 'Practically magical. The secret has been handed down from dwarf to dwarf for centuries. One tiny piece of this and you won't want anything to eat all day.'

'Get away?' said Colon.

'A dwarf can go hundreds of miles with a cake like this in his pack,' Carrot went on.

'I bet he can,' said Colon gloomily. 'I bet all the time he'd be thinking, "Bloody hell, I hope I can find something else to eat soon, otherwise it's the bloody cake again." '

Carrot, to whom the word irony meant something to do with metal, picked up his pike and after a couple of impressive rebounds managed to cut the cake into approximately four slices.

'There we are,' he said cheerfully. 'One for each of us, and one for the captain.' He realized what he had said. 'Oh. Sorry.'

'Yes,' said Colon flatly.

They sat in silence for a moment.

'I *liked* him,' said Carrot. 'I'm sorry he's gone.'

There was some more silence, very similar to the earlier silence but even deeper and more furrowed with depression.

'I expect you'll be made captain now,' said Carrot.

Colon started. 'Me? I don't want to be captain! I can't do the thinking. It's not worth all that thinking, just for another nine dollars a month.'

He drummed his fingers on the table.

'Is that all he got?' said Nobby. 'I thought officers were rolling in it.'

'Nine dollars a month,' said Colon. 'I saw the pay scales once. Nine dollars a month and two dollars plumes allowance. Only he never claimed that bit. Funny, really.'

'He wasn't the plumes type,' said Nobby.

'You're right,' said Colon. 'The thing about the captain, see, I read this book once . . . you know we've all got alcohol in our bodies . . . sort of *natural* alcohol? Even if you never touch a drop in your life, your body sort of makes it anyway . . . but Captain Vimes, see, he's one of those people whose body doesn't do it naturally. Like, he was born two drinks below normal.'

'Gosh,' said Carrot.

'Yes . . . so, when he's sober, he's *really* sober. Knurd, they call it. You know how you feel when you wake up if you've been on the piss all night, Nobby? Well, he feels like that *all the time*.'

'Poor bugger,' said Nobby. 'I never realized. No wonder he's always so gloomy.'

'So he's always trying to catch up, see. It's just that he doesn't always get the dose right. And, of course—' Colon glanced at Carrot – 'he was brung low by a woman. Mind you, just about anything brings him low.'

'So what do *we* do now, Sergeant?' said Nobby.

'And do you think he'd mind if we eat his cake?' said Carrot wistfully. 'It'd be a shame to let it go stale.'

Colon shrugged.

The older men sat in miserable silence as Carrot macerated his way through the cake like a bucket-wheel rockcrusher in a chalk pit. Even if it had been the lightest of soufflés they wouldn't have had any appetite.

They were contemplating life without the

captain. It was going to be bleak, even without dragons. Say what you liked about Captain Vimes, he'd had style. It was cynical, blacknailed style, but he'd had it and they didn't. He could read long words and add up. Even that was style, of a sort. He even got drunk in style.

They'd been trying to drag the minutes out, trying to stretch out the time. But the night had come.

There was no hope for them.

They were going to have to go out on the streets.

It was six of the clock. And all wasn't well.

'I miss Errol, too,' said Carrot.

'He was the captain's, really,' said Nobby. 'Anyway, Lady Ramkin'll know how to look after him.'

'It's not as though we could leave anything around, either,' said Colon. 'I mean, even the lamp oil. He even drank the lamp oil.'

'And mothballs,' said Nobby. 'A whole box of mothballs. Why would anyone want to eat mothballs? And the kettle. And sugar. He was a devil for sugar.'

'He was nice, though,' said Carrot. 'Friendly.'

'Oh, I'll grant you,' said Colon. 'But it's not right, really, a pet where you have to jump behind a table every time it hiccups.'

'I shall miss his little face,' said Carrot.

Nobby blew his nose, loudly.

It was echoed by a hammering on the door. Colon jerked his head. Carrot got up and opened it.

A couple of members of the palace guard were

waiting with arrogant impatience. They stepped back when they saw Carrot, who had to bend a bit to see under the lintel; bad news like Carrot travels fast.

'We've brung you a proclamation,' said one of them. 'You've got to—'

'What's all that fresh paint on your breastplate?' said Carrot politely. Nobby and the sergeant peered around him.

'It's a dragon,' said the younger of the guards.

'*The* dragon,' corrected his superior.

''Ere, I know you,' said Nobby. 'You're Skully Maltoon. Used to live in Mincing Street. Your mum made cough sweets, din't she, and fell in the mixture and died. I never have a cough sweet but I think of your mum.'

'Hallo, Nobby,' said the guard, without enthusiasm.

'I bet your old mum'd be proud of you, you with a *dragon* on your vest,' said Nobby conversationally. The guard gave him a look made of hatred and embarrassment.

'And new plumes on your hat, too,' Nobby added sweetly.

'*This here is a proclamation what you are commanded to read*,' said the guard loudly. 'And post up on street corners also. By order.'

'Whose?' said Nobby.

Sergeant Colon grabbed the scroll in one ham-like fist.

'Where As,' he read slowly, tracing the lettering with a hesitant finger, 'It hathe Pleas-Sed the Der-Rer-Aa-Ger – the dragon, Ker-Ii – king of kings and

313

Aa-Ber-Ess-Uh-Ler—' sweat beaded on the broad pink cliff of his forehead – 'absolute, that is, Rer-Uh-Ler-Eh-Rer, ruler of—'

He lapsed into the tortured silence of academia, his fingertip jerking slowly down the parchment.

'No,' he said at last. 'That's not right, is it? It's not going to eat someone?'

'Consume,' said the older guard.

'It's all part of the social . . . social contract,' said his assistant woodenly. 'A small price to pay, I'm sure you will agree, for the safety and protection of the city.'

'From what?' said Nobby. 'We've never had an enemy we couldn't bribe or corrupt.'

'Until now,' said Colon darkly.

'You catch on fast,' said the guard. 'So you're going to broadcast it. On pain of pain.'

Carrot peered over Colon's shoulder.

'What's a virgin?' he said.

'An unmarried girl,' said Colon quickly.

'What, like my friend Reet?' said Carrot, horrified.

'Well, no,' said Colon.

'She's not married, you know. None of Mrs Palm's girls are married.'

'Well, yes,' said Colon.

'Well, then,' said Carrot, with an air of finality. 'We're not having any of *that* kind of thing, I hope.'

'People won't stand for it,' said Colon. 'You mark my words.'

The guards stepped back, out of range of Carrot's rising wrath.

'They can please themselves,' said the senior guard. 'But if you don't proclaim it, you can try explaining things to His Majesty.'

They hurried off.

Nobby darted out into the street. 'Dragon on your vest!' he shouted. 'If your old mum knew about this she'd turn in her vat, you goin' around with a dragon on your vest!'

Colon wandered back to the table and spread out the scroll.

'Bad business,' he mumbled.

'It's already killed people,' said Carrot. 'Contrary to sixteen separate Acts in Council.'

'Well, yes. But that was just like, you know, the hurly-burly of this and that,' said Colon. 'Not that it wasn't bad, I mean, but people sort of *participating*, just handing over some slip of a girl and standing round watching as if it's all proper and legal, that's much worse.'

'I reckon it all depends on your point of view,' said Nobby thoughtfully.

'What d'you mean?'

'Well, from the point of view of someone being burned alive, it probably doesn't matter much,' said Nobby philosophically.

'People won't stand for it, I said,' said Colon, ignoring this. 'You'll see. They'll march on the palace, and what will the dragon do then, eh?'

'Burn 'em all,' said Nobby promptly.

Colon looked puzzled. 'It wouldn't do that, would it?' he said.

'Don't see what's to prevent it, do you?' said

Nobby. He glanced out of the doorway. 'He was a good lad, that boy. Used to run errands for my grandad. Who'd have thought he'd go around with a dragon on his chest . . .'

'What are we going to *do*, Sergeant?' said Carrot.

'I don't want to be burned alive,' said Sergeant Colon. 'My wife'd give me hell. So I suppose we've got to wossname, proclaim it. But don't worry, lad,' he said, patting Carrot on one muscular arm and repeating, as if he hadn't quite believed himself the first time, 'it won't come to that. People'll never stand for it.'

Lady Ramkin ran her hands over Errol's body.

'Damned if I know what's going on in there,' she said. The little dragon tried to lick her face. 'What's he been eating?'

'The last thing, I think, was a kettle,' said Vimes.

'A kettle of what?'

'No. A kettle. A black thing with a handle and spout. He sniffed it for ages, then he ate it.'

Errol grinned weakly at him, and belched. They both ducked.

'Oh, and then we found him eating soot out of the chimney,' Vimes went on, as their heads rose again over the railings.

They leaned back over the reinforced bunker that was one of Lady Ramkin's sickbay pens. It had to be reinforced. Usually one of the first things a sick dragon did was lose control of its digestive processes.

'He doesn't look sick, exactly,' she said. 'Just fat.'

'He whines a lot. And you can sort of see things

moving under his skin. You know what I think? You know you said they can rearrange their digestive system?'

'Oh, yes. All the stomachs and pancreatic crackers can be hooked up in various ways, you see. To take advantage—'

'Of whatever they can find to make flame with,' said Vimes. 'Yes. I think he's trying to make some sort of very hot flame. He wants to challenge the big dragon. Every time it takes to the air he just sits there whining.'

'And doesn't explode?'

'Not that we've noticed. I mean, I'm sure if he did, we'd spot it.'

'He just eats indiscriminately?'

'Hard to be sure. He sniffs everything, and eats most things. Two gallons of lamp oil, for example. Anyway, I can't leave him down there. We can't look after him properly. It's not as if we need to find out where the dragon is now,' he added bitterly.

'I think you're being a bit silly about all this,' she said, leading the way back to the house.

'Silly? I was sacked in front of all those people!'

'Yes, but it was all a misunderstanding, I'm sure.'

'*I* didn't misunderstand it!'

'Well, I think you're just upset because you're impotent.'

Vimes's eyes bulged. 'Whee?' he said.

'Against the dragon,' Lady Ramkin went on, quite unconcerned. 'You can't do anything about it.'

'I reckon this damn city and the dragon just about deserve one another,' said Vimes.

'People are frightened. You can't expect much of people when they're so frightened.' She touched him gingerly on his arm. It was like watching an industrial robot being expertly manipulated to grasp an egg gently.

'Not everyone's as brave as you,' she added, timidly.

'Me?'

'The other week. When you stopped them killing my dragons.'

'Oh, *that*. That's not bravery. Anyway, that was just people. People are easier. I'll tell you one thing for nothing, I'm not looking up that dragon's nose again. I wake up at days thinking about that.'

'Oh.' She seemed deflated. 'Well, if you're sure . . . I've got a lot of friends, you know. If you need any help, you've only got to say. The Duke of Sto Helit is looking for a guard captain, I'm sure. I'll write you a letter. You'll like them, they're a very nice young couple.'

'I'm not sure what I shall do next,' said Vimes, more gruffly than he intended. 'I'm considering one or two offers.'

'Well, of course. I'm sure you know best.'

Vimes nodded.

Lady Ramkin twisted her handkerchief round and round in her hands.

'Well, then,' she said.

'Well,' said Vimes.

'I, er, expect you'll be wanting to be off, then.'

'Yes, I expect I had better be going.'

There was a pause. Then they both spoke at once.

'It's been very—'

'I'd just like to say—'

'Sorry.'

'Sorry.'

'No, you were speaking.'

'No, sorry, you were saying?'

'Oh.' Vimes hesitated. 'I'll be off, then.'

'Oh. Yes.' Lady Ramkin gave him a washed-out smile. 'Can't keep all these offers waiting, can you,' she said.

She thrust out a hand. Vimes shook it carefully.

'So I'll just be going, then,' he said.

'Do call again,' said Lady Ramkin, more coldly. 'If you are ever in this area. And so on. I'm sure Errol would like to see you.'

'Yes. Well. Goodbye, then.'

'Goodbye, Captain Vimes.'

He stumbled out of the door and walked hurriedly down the dark, overgrown path. He could feel her gaze on the back of his neck as he did so or, at least, he told himself that he could. She'd be standing in the doorway, nearly blocking out the light. Just watching me. But I'm not going to look back, he thought. That would be a really silly thing to do. I mean, she's a lovely person, she's got a lot of common sense and an enormous personality, but really . . .

I'm not going to look back, even if she stands there while I walk all the way down the street. Sometimes you have to be cruel to be kind.

So when he heard the door shut when he was only halfway down the drive he suddenly felt very, very angry, as if he had just been robbed.

He stood still and clasped and unclasped his hands in the darkness. He wasn't Captain Vimes any more, he was Citizen Vimes, which meant that he could do things he'd once never dreamt of doing. Perhaps he could go and smash some windows.

No, that wouldn't be any good. He wanted more than that. To get rid of that bloody dragon, to get his job back, to get his hands on whoever was behind all this, to forget himself just once and hit someone until he was exhausted . . .

He stared at nothing. Down below the city was a mass of smoke and steam. He wasn't thinking of that, though.

He was thinking of a running man. And, further back in the fuddled mists of his life, a boy running to keep up.

And under his breath he said, 'Any of them get out?'

Sergeant Colon finished the proclamation and looked around at the hostile crowd.

'Don't blame me,' he said. 'I just read the things. I don't write 'em.'

'That's a human sacrifice, that is,' said someone.

'There's nothing wrong with human sacrifice,' said a priest.

'Ah, *per say*,' said the first speaker quickly. 'For proper religious reasons. And using condemned criminals and so on.* But that's different from

---

*A number of religions in Ankh-Morpork still practised human sacrifice, except that they didn't really need to practise any more because they had got so good at it. City law said that only condemned criminals should be used, but that was all right because in most of the religions refusing to volunteer for sacrifice was an offence punishable by death.

bunging someone to a dragon just because it's feeling peckish.'

'That's the spirit!' said Sergeant Colon.

'Taxes is one thing, but eating people is another.'

'Well said!'

'If we all say we won't put up with it, what can the dragon do?'

Nobby opened his mouth. Colon clamped a hand over it and raised a triumphant fist in the air.

'It's just what I've always said,' he said. 'The people united can never be ignited!'

There was a ragged cheer.

'Hang on a minute,' said a small man, slowly. 'As far as we know, the dragon's only good at one thing. It flies around the city setting fire to people. I'm not actually certain what is being proposed that would stop it doing this.'

'Yes, but if we *all* protest—' said the first speaker, his voice modulated with uncertainty.

'It can't burn *everybody*,' said Colon. He decided to play his new ace again and added, proudly, 'The people united can never be ignited!' There was rather less of a cheer this time. People were reserving their energy for worrying.

'I'm not exactly sure I understand why not. Why can't it burn everyone and fly off to another city?'

'Because . . .'

'The hoard,' said Colon. 'It needs people to bring it treasure.'

'Yeah.'

'Well, maybe, but how many, exactly?'

'What?'

321

'How many people? Out of the whole city, I mean. Perhaps it won't need to burn the whole city down, just some bits. Do we know what bits?'

'Look, this is getting silly,' said the first speaker. 'If we go around looking at the problems the whole time, we'll never do anything.'

'It just pays to think things through first, that's all I'm saying. Such as, what happens even if we beat the dragon?'

'Oh, come on!' said Sergeant Colon.

'No, seriously. What's the alternative?'

'A human being, for a start!'

'Please yourself,' said the little man primly. 'But I reckon one person a month is pretty good compared to some rulers we've had. Anyone remember Nersh the Lunatic? Or Giggling Lord Smince and his Laugh-A-Minute Dungeon?'

There was a certain amount of mumbling of the 'he's got a point' variety.

'But they got overthrown!' said Colon.

'No they didn't. They were assassinated.'

'Same thing,' said Colon. 'I mean, no-one's going to assassinate the dragon. It'd take more than a dark night and a sharp knife to see it off, I know that.'

I can see what the captain means, he thought. No wonder he always has a drink after he thinks about things. We always beat ourselves before we even start. Give any Ankh-Morpork man a big stick and he'll end up clubbing himself to death.

'Look here, you mealy-mouthed little twerp,' said the first speaker, picking up the little one by his collar and curling his free hand into a fist, 'I happen

322

to have three daughters, and I happen to not want any of them et, thank you very much.'

'Yes, and the people united . . . will . . . never . . . be . . .'

Colon's voice faltered. He realized that the rest of the crowd were all staring upward.

The bugger, he thought, as rationality began to drain away. It must have flannel feet.

The dragon shifted its position on the ridge of the nearest house, flapped its wings once or twice, yawned, and then stretched its neck down into the street.

The man blessed with daughters stood, with his fist upraised, in the centre of a rapidly expanding circle of bare cobbles. The little man wriggled out of his frozen grasp and darted into the shadows.

It suddenly seemed that no man in the entire world was so lonely and without friends.

'I see,' he said quietly. He scowled up at the inquisitive reptile. In fact it didn't seem particularly belligerent. It was looking at him with something approaching interest.

'I don't care!' he shouted, his voice echoing from wall to wall in the silence. 'We defy you! If you kill me, you might as well kill all of us!'

There was some uneasy shuffling of feet amongst those sections of the crowd who didn't feel that this was absolutely axiomatic.

'We can resist you, you know!' growled the man. 'Can't we, everyone. What was that slogan about being united, Sergeant?'

'Er,' said Colon, feeling his spine turn to ice.

'I warn you, dragon, the human spirit is—'

They never found out what it was, or at least what *he* thought it was, although possibly in the dark hours of a sleepless night some of them might have remembered the subsequent events and formed a pretty good and gut-churning insight, to whit, that one of the things sometimes forgotten about the human spirit is that while it is, in the right conditions, noble and brave and wonderful, it is also, when you get right down to it, only human.

The dragon flame caught him full on the chest. For a moment he was visible as a white-hot outline before the neat, black remains spiralled down into a little puddle of melting cobbles.

The flame vanished.

The crowd stood like statues, not knowing if it was staying put or running that would attract more attention.

The dragon stared down, curious to see what they were going to do next.

Colon felt that, as the only civic official present, it was up to him to take charge of the situation. He coughed.

'Right, then,' he said, trying to keep the squeak out of his voice. 'If you would just move along there, ladies and gentlemen. Move along, now. Move along. Let's be having you, please.'

He waved his arms in a vague gesture of authority as the people shuffled nervously away. Out of the corner of his eye he saw red flames behind the rooftops, and sparks spiralling in the sky.

'Haven't you got any homes to go to?' he croaked.

* * *

The Librarian knuckled out into the Library of the here and now. Every hair on his body bristled with rage.

He pushed open the door and swung out into the stricken city.

Someone out there was about to find that their worst nightmare was a maddened Librarian.

With a badge.

The dragon swooped leisurely back and forth over the night-time city, barely flapping its wings. It didn't need to. The thermals were giving it the lift it needed.

There were fires all over Ankh-Morpork. So many bucket chains had formed between the river and various burning buildings that buckets were getting misdirected and hijacked. Not that you really needed a bucket to pick up the turbid waters of the river Ankh – a net was good enough.

Downstream, teams of smoke-stained people worked feverishly to close the huge, corroded gates under the Brass Bridge. They were Ankh-Morpork's last defence against fire, since then the Ankh had no outlet and gradually, oozingly, filled the space between the walls. A man could suffocate under it.

The workers on the bridge were the ones who couldn't or wouldn't run. Many others were teeming through the gates of the city and heading out across the chilly, mist-wreathed plains.

But not for long. The dragon, looping and curving gracefully above the devastation, glided out over the walls. After a few seconds the guards saw actinic fire stab down through the mists. The tide of humanity flowed back, with the dragon hovering over it like a sheepdog. The fires of the stricken city glowed redly off the underside of its wings.

'Got any suggestions about what we do next, Sergeant?' said Nobby.

Colon didn't reply. I wish Captain Vimes were here, he thought. He wouldn't have known what to do either, but he's got a much better vocabulary to be baffled in.

Some of the fires went out as the rising waters and the confused tangle of fire chains did their work. The dragon didn't appear to be inclined to start any more. It had made its point.

'I wonder who it'll be,' said Nobby.

'What?' said Carrot.

'The sacrifice, I mean.'

'Sergeant said people wouldn't put up with it,' said Carrot stoically.

'Yeah, well. Look at it this way: if you say to people, what's it to be, either your house burned down around you or some girl you've probably never met being eaten, well, they might get a bit thoughtful. Human nature, see.'

'I'm sure a hero will turn up in time,' said Carrot. 'With some new sort of weapon, or something. And strike at its voonerable spot.'

There was the silence of sudden intense listening.

'What's one of them?' said Nobby.

'A spot. Where it's voonerable. My grandad used to tell me stories. Hit a dragon in its voonerables, he said, and you've killed it.'

'Like kicking it in the wossnames?' said Nobby, interestedly.

'Dunno. I suppose so. Although, Nobby, I've told you before it is not right to—'

'And where's the spot, like?'

'Oh, a different place on each dragon. You wait till it flies over and then you say, there's the voonerable spot, and then you kill it,' said Carrot. 'Something like that.'

Sergeant Colon stared blankly into space.

'Hmm,' said Nobby.

They watched the panorama of panic for a while. Then Sergeant Colon said, 'You sure about the voonerables?'

'Yes. Oh, yes.'

'I wish you hadn't been, lad.'

They looked at the terrified city again.

'You know,' said Nobby, 'you always told me you used to win prizes for archery in the army, Sergeant. You said you had a lucky arrow, you always made sure you got your lucky arrow back, you said you—'

'All right! All right! But this isn't the same thing, is it? Anyway, I'm not a hero. Why should I do it?'

'Captain Vimes pays us thirty dollars a month,' said Carrot.

'Yes,' said Nobby, grinning, 'and you get five dollars extra responsibility allowance.'

'But Captain Vimes has gone,' said Colon wretchedly.

Carrot looked at him sternly. 'I am sure,' he said, 'that if he were here, he'd be the first to—'

Colon waved him into silence. 'That's all very well,' he said. 'But what if I miss?'

'Look on the bright side,' said Nobby. 'You'll probably never know it.'

Sergeant Colon's expression mutated into an evil, desperate grin. '*We'll* never know it, you mean,' he said.

'What?'

'If you think I'm standing on some rooftop on my tod, you can think again. I order you to accompany me. Anyway,' he added, 'you get one dollar responsibility allowance, too.'

Nobby's face twisted in panic. 'No I don't!' he croaked. 'Captain Vimes said he was docking it for five years for being a disgrace to the species!'

'Well, you might just get it back. Anyway, you know all about voonerables. I've watched you fight.'

Carrot saluted smartly. 'Permission to volunteer, sir,' he said. 'And I only get twenty dollars a month training pay and I don't mind at all, sir.'

Sergeant Colon cleared his throat. Then he straightened the hang of his breastplate. It was one of those with astonishingly impressive pectoral muscles embossed upon it. His chest and stomach fitted into it in the same way that jelly fits into a mould.

What would Captain Vimes do now? Well, he'd have a drink. But if he didn't have a drink, what would he do?

'What we need,' he said slowly, 'is a Plan.'

That sounded good. That sentence alone sounded worth the pay. If you had a Plan, you were halfway there.

And already he thought he could hear the cheering of crowds. They were lining the streets, and they were throwing flowers, and he was being carried triumphantly through the grateful city.

The drawback was, he suspected, that he was being carried in an urn.

Lupine Wonse padded along the draughty corridors to the Patrician's bedroom. It had never been a sumptuous apartment at best, and contained little more than a narrow bed and a few battered cupboards. It looked even worse now, with one wall gone. Sleepwalk at night now and you could step right into the vast cavern that was the Great Hall.

Even so, he shut the door behind him for a semblance of privacy. Then, cautiously and with many nervous glances at the great space beyond, he knelt down in the centre of the floor and pried up a board.

A long black robe was dragged into view. Then Wonse reached further down into the dusty space between the floors and rummaged around. He rummaged still further. Then he lay down and stuck both arms into the gap and flailed desperately.

A book sailed across the room and hit him in the back of the head.

'Looking for this, were you?' said Vimes.

He stepped out of the shadows.

Wonse was on his knees, his mouth opening and shutting.

What's he going to say, Vimes thought. Is it going to be: *I know what this looks like*, or will it be: *How*

329

did you get in here, or maybe it'll be: *Listen, I can explain everything*. I wish I had a loaded dragon in my hands right now.

Wonse said, 'OK. Clever of you to guess.'

Of course, that was always an outside chance, Vimes added.

'Under the floorboards,' he said aloud. 'First place anyone'd look. Rather foolish, that was.'

'I know. I suppose he didn't think anyone would be searching,' said Wonse, standing up and brushing the dust off himself.

'I'm sorry?' said Vimes pleasantly.

'Vetinari. You know how he was for scheming and things. He was involved in most of the plots against himself, that was how he ran things. He enjoyed it. Obviously he called it up and couldn't control it. Something even more cunning than he was.'

'So what were you doing?' said Vimes.

'I wondered if it might be possible to reverse the spell. Or maybe call up another dragon. They'd fight then.'

'A sort of balance of terror, you mean?' said Vimes.

'Could be worth a try,' said Wonse earnestly. He took a few steps closer. 'Look, about your job, I know we were both a bit overwrought at the time, so of course if you want it back there'll be no prob—'

'It must have been terrible,' said Vimes. 'Imagine what must have gone through his mind. He called it up, and then found it wasn't just some sort of tool but a real thing with a mind of its own. A mind just like his, but with all the brakes off. You know, I wouldn't mind betting that at the start he really thought that what he was doing was all for the best. He must have been insane. Sooner or later, anyway.'

'Yes,' said Wonse hoarsely. 'It must have been terrible.'

'Ye gods, but I'd like to get my hands on him! All those years I've known the man, and I'd never realized . . .'

Wonse said nothing.

'Run,' said Vimes softly.

'What?'

'Run. I want to see you run.'

'I don't underst—'

'I saw someone run away, the night the dragon flamed that house. I remember thinking at the time that he moved in a funny way, sort of bounding along. And then the other day I saw you running away from the dragon. Could almost have been the same man, I thought. Skipping, almost. Like someone running to keep up. *Any of them get out, Wonse?*'

Wonse waved a hand in what he might have thought was a nonchalant way. 'That's just ridiculous, that's not proof,' he said.

'I noticed you sleep in here now,' said Vimes. 'I suppose the *king* likes to have you handy, does he?'

'You've got no proof at all,' whispered Wonse.

'Of course, I haven't. The way someone runs. The eager tone of voice. That's all. But that doesn't matter, does it? Because it wouldn't matter even if I *did* have proof,' said Vimes. 'There's no-one to take it to. And you can't give me my job back.'

'I can!' said Wonse. 'I can, and you needn't just be captain—'

'You can't give me my job back,' repeated Vimes. 'It was never yours to take away. I was never an officer of the city, or an officer of the king, or an officer of the Patrician. I was an officer of the law. It might have been corrupted and bent, but it was law, of a sort. There isn't any law now except: "you'll get burned alive if you don't watch out". Where's the place in there for me?'

Wonse darted forward and grabbed him by the arm.

'But you can help me!' he said. 'There may be a way to destroy the dragon, d'you see, or at least we can help people, channel things to mitigate the worst of it, somehow find a meeting point—'

Vimes's blow caught Wonse on the cheek and spun him around.

'The dragon's *here*,' he snapped. 'You can't channel it or persuade it or negotiate with it. There's no truce with dragons. You brought it here and we're stuck with it, you *bastard*.'

Wonse lowered his hand from the bright white mark where the punch had connected.

'What are you going to do?' he said.

Vimes didn't know. He'd thought of a dozen ways that the thing could go, but the only one that was really suitable was killing Wonse. And, face to face, he couldn't do it.

'That's the trouble with people like you,' said

Wonse, getting up. 'You're always against anything attempted for the betterment of mankind, but you never have any proper plans of your own. Guards! Guards!'

He grinned maniacally at Vimes.

'Didn't expect that, did you?' he said. 'We've still got guards here, you know. Not so many, of course. Not many people want to come in.'

There were footsteps in the passage outside and four of the palace guards padded in, swords drawn.

'I wouldn't put up a fight, if I were you,' Wonse went on. 'They're desperate and uneasy men. But very highly paid.'

Vimes said nothing. Wonse was a gloater. You always stood a chance with gloaters. The old Patrician had never been a gloater, you could say that for him. If he wanted you dead, you never even heard about it.

The thing to do with gloaters was play the game according to the rules.

'You'll never get away with it,' he said.

'You're right. You're absolutely right. But never is a long time,' said Wonse. '*None* of us get away with anything for that long.'

'You shall have some time to reflect on this,' he said and nodded to the guards. 'Throw him in the *special* dungeon. And then go about that other little task.'

'Er,' said the leader of the guards, and hesitated.

'What's the matter, man?'

'You, er, want us to attack him?' said the guard miserably. Thick though the palace guard were, they were as aware as everyone else of the conventions, and when guards are summoned to deal with one man in overheated circumstances it's not a good time for them. The bugger's bound to be heroic, he was thinking. This guard was not looking forward to a future in which he was dead.

'Of course, you idiot!'

'But, er, there's only one of him,' said the guard captain.

'And he's smilin',' said a man behind him.

'Prob'ly goin' to swing on the chandeliers any minute,' said one of his colleagues. 'And kick over the table, and that.'

'He's not even armed!' shrieked Wonse.

'Worst kind, that,' said one of the guards, with deep stoicism. 'They leap up, see, and grab one of the ornamental swords behind the shield over the fire-place.'

'Yeah,' said another, suspiciously. 'And then they chucks a chair at you.'

'There's no fireplace! There's no sword! There's only him! Now *take* him!' screamed Wonse.

A couple of guards grabbed Vimes tentatively by the shoulders.

'You're not going to do anything heroic, are you?' whispered one of them.

'Wouldn't know where to start,' he said.

'Oh. Right.'

As Vimes was hauled away he heard Wonse breaking into insane laughter. They always did, your gloaters.

But he was correct about one thing. Vimes didn't

have a plan. He hadn't thought much about what was going to happen next. He'd been a fool, he told himself, to think that you just had a confrontation and that was the end of it.

He also wondered what the other task was.

The palace guards said nothing, but stared straight ahead and marched him down, across the ruined hall, and through the wreckage of another corridor to an ominous door. They opened it, threw him in, and marched away.

And no-one, absolutely no-one, noticed the thin, leaf-like thing that floated gently down from the shadows of the roof, tumbling over and over in the air like a sycamore seed, before landing in the tangled gewgaws of the hoard.

It was a peanut shell.

It was the silence that awoke Lady Ramkin. Her bedroom looked out over the dragon pens, and she was used to sleeping to the susurration of rustling scales, the occasional roar of a dragon flaming in its sleep, and the keening of the gravid females. Absence of any sound at all was like an alarm clock.

She had cried a bit before going to sleep, but not much, because it was no use being soppy and letting the side down. She lit the lamp, pulled on her rubber boots, grabbed the stick which might be all that stood between her and theoretical loss of virtue, and hurried down through the shadowy house. As she crossed the damp lawn to the kennels she was vaguely aware that something was happening down in the city, but dismissed it as not currently worth thinking about. Dragons were more important.

She pushed open the door.

Well, they were still there. The familiar stink of swamp dragons, half pond mud and half chemical explosion, gusted out into the night.

Each dragon was balancing on its hind legs in the centre of its pen, neck arched, staring with ferocious intensity at the roof.

'Oh,' she said. 'Flying around up there again, is it? Showing off. Don't you worry about it, children. Mummy's here.'

She put the lamp on a high shelf and stamped along to Errol's pen.

'Well now, my lad,' she began, and stopped.

Errol was stretched out on his side. A thin plume of grey smoke was drifting from his mouth, and his stomach expanded and contracted like a bellows. And his skin from the neck down was an almost pure white.

'I think if I ever rewrite *Diseases* you'll get a whole chapter all to yourself,' she said quietly, and unbolted the gate of the pen. 'Let's see if that nasty temperature has gone down, shall we?'

She reached out to stroke his skin and gasped. She pulled the hand back hurriedly and watched the blisters form on her fingertips.

Errol was so cold he burned.

As she stared at him the small round marks that her warmth had melted filmed over with frozen air.

Lady Ramkin sat back on her haunches.

'Just what kind of dragon *are* you—?' she began.

There was the distant sound of a knock at the front door of the house. She hesitated for a moment, then blew out the lamp, crept heavily along the length of the kennels and pulled aside the scrap of sacking over the window.

The first light of dawn showed her the silhouette of a guardsman on her doorstep, the plumes of his helmet blowing in the breeze.

She bit her lip in panic, scuttled back to the door, fled across the lawn and dived into the house, taking the stairs three at a time.

'Stupid, stupid,' she muttered, realizing the lamp was back downstairs. But no time for that. By the time she went and got it, Vimes might have gone away.

Working by feel and memory in the gloom she found her best wig and rammed it on her head. Somewhere among the ointments and dragon remedies on her dressing table was something called, as far as she could remember, *Dew of the Night* or some such unsuitable name, a present long ago from a thoughtless nephew. She tried several bottles before she found something that, by the smell of it, was probably the one. Even to a nose which had long ago shut down most of its sensory apparatus in the face of the overpoweringness of dragons, it seemed, well, more *potent* than she remembered. But apparently men liked that kind of thing. Or so she had read. Damn nonsense, really. She twitched the top hem of her suddenly far too sensible nightshirt into a position which, she hoped, revealed without actually exposing, and hurried back down the stairs.

She stopped in front of the door, took a deep breath, twisted the handle and realized even as she pulled the door open that she should have taken the rubber boots off—

'Why, Captain,' she said winsomely, 'this *is* a *who the hell are you?*'

The head of the palace guard took several steps backwards and, because he was of peasant stock, made a few surreptitious signs to ward off evil spirits. They clearly didn't work. When he opened his eyes again the thing was still there, still bristling with rage, still reeking of something sickly and fermented, still crowned with a skewed mass of curls, still looming behind a quivering bosom that made the roof of his mouth go dry—

He'd heard about these sort of things. Harpies, they were called. What had it done with Lady Ramkin?

The sight of the rubber boots had him confused, though. Legends about harpies were short on references to rubber boots.

'Out with it, fellow,' Lady Ramkin boomed, hitching up her nightie to a more respectable neckline. 'Don't just stand there opening and shutting your mouth. What d'you want?'

'Lady Sybil Ramkin?' said the guard, not in the polite way of someone seeking mere confirmation but in the incredulous tones of someone who found it very hard to believe the answer could be 'yes'.

'Use your eyes, young man. Who d'you think I am?'

The guard pulled himself together.

'Only I've got a summons for Lady Sybil Ramkin,' he said uncertainly.

Her voice was withering. 'What do you mean, a summons?'

'To attend upon the palace, you see.'

'I can't imagine why that is necessary at this time in the morning,' she said, and made to slam the door. It wouldn't shut, though, because of the sword point jammed into it at the last moment.

'If you *don't* come,' said the guard, 'I have been ordered to take steps.'

The door shot back and her face pressed against his, almost knocking him unconscious with the scent of rotting rose petals.

'If you think you'll lay a hand on me—' she began.

The guard's glance darted sideways, just for a moment, to the dragon kennels. Sybil Ramkin's face went pale.

'You wouldn't!' she hissed.

He swallowed. Fearsome though she was, she was only human. She could only bite your head off metaphorically. There were, he told himself, far worse things than Lady Ramkin although, admittedly, they weren't three inches from his nose at this point in time.

'Take steps,' he repeated, in a croak.

She straightened up, and eyed the row of guards behind him.

'I see,' she said coldly. 'That's the way, is it? Six of you to fetch one feeble woman. Very well. You will, of course, allow me to fetch a coat. It is somewhat chilly.'

She slammed the door.

The palace guards stamped their feet in the cold and tried not to look at one another. This obviously wasn't the way you went around arresting people. They weren't *allowed* to keep you waiting on the doorstep, this wasn't the way the world was supposed to work. On the other hand, the only alternative was to go in there and drag her out, and it wasn't one anyone could summon any enthusiasm for. Besides, the guard captain wasn't sure he had enough men to drag Lady Ramkin anywhere. You'd need teams of thousands, with log rollers.

The door creaked open again, revealing only the musty darkness of the hall within.

'Right, men—' said the captain, uneasily.

Lady Ramkin appeared. He got a brief, blurred vision of her bounding through the doorway, screaming, and it might well have been the last thing he remembered if a guard hadn't had the presence of mind to trip her up as she hurtled down the steps. She plunged forward, cursing, ploughed into the overgrown lawn, hit her head on a crumbling statue of an antique Ramkin, and slid to a halt.

The double-handed broadsword she had been holding landed beside her, bolt upright, and vibrated to a standstill.

After a while one of the guards crept forward cautiously and tested the blade with his finger.

'Bloody hell,' he said, in a voice of mixed horror and respect. 'And the dragon wants to eat *her*?'

'Fits the bill,' said the captain. 'She's got to be the highest-born lady in the city. I don't know about maiden,' he added, 'and right at this minute I'm not going to speculate. Someone go and fetch a cart.'

He fingered his ear, which had been nicked by the tip of the sword. He was not, by nature, an unkind man, but at this moment he was certain that he would prefer the thickness of a dragon's hide between himself and Sybil Ramkin when she woke up.

'Weren't we supposed to kill her pet dragons, sir?' said another guard. 'I thought Mr Wonse said something about killing all the dragons.'

'That was just a threat we were supposed to make,' said the captain.

The guard's brow furrowed. 'You sure, sir? I thought—'

The captain had had enough of this. Screaming harpies and broadswords making a noise like tearing silk in the air beside him had severely ruined his capacity for seeing the other fellow's point of view.

'Oh, you *thought*, did you?' he growled. 'A thinker, are you? Do you think you'd be suitable for another posting, then? *City* guard, maybe? They're full of thinkers, they are.'

There was an uncomfortable titter from the rest of the guards.

'If you'd *thought*,' added the captain sarcastically, 'you'd have thought that the king is hardly going to want other dragons dead, is he? They're probably distant relatives or something. I mean, it wouldn't want us to go around killing its own kind, would it?'

'Well, sir, *people* do, sir,' said the guard sulkily.

'Ah, well,' said the captain. 'That's different.' He tapped the side of his helmet meaningfully. 'That's 'cos we're intelligent.'

Vimes landed in damp straw and also in pitch darkness, although after a while his eyes became accustomed to the gloom and he could make out the walls of the dungeon.

It hadn't been built for gracious living. It was basically just a space containing all the pillars and arches that supported the palace. At the far end a small grille high on the wall let in a mere suspicion of grubby, second-hand light.

There was another square hole in the floor. It was also barred. The bars were quite rusty, though. It occurred to Vimes that he could probably work them loose eventually, and then all he would have to do was slim down enough to go through a nine-inch hole.

What the dungeon did *not* contain was any rats, scorpions, cockroaches or snakes. It had *once* contained snakes, it was true, because Vimes's sandals crunched on small, long white skeletons.

He crept cautiously along one damp wall, wondering where the rhythmic scraping sound was coming from. He rounded a squat pillar, and found out.

The Patrician was shaving, squinting into a scrap of mirror propped against the pillar to catch the light. No, Vimes realized, not propped. Supported, in fact. By a rat. It was a large rat, with red eyes.

The Patrician nodded to him without apparent surprise.

'Oh,' he said. 'Vimes, isn't it? I heard you were on the way down. Jolly good. You had better tell the kitchen staff—' and here Vimes realized that the man was speaking to the rat – 'that there will be two for lunch. Would you like a beer, Vimes?'

'What?' said Vimes.

'I imagine you would. Pot luck, though, I am afraid. Skrp's people are bright enough, but they seem to have a bit of a blind spot when it comes to labels on bottles.'

Lord Vetinari patted his face with a towel and dropped it on the floor. A grey shape darted from the shadows and dragged it away down the floor grille.

Then he said, 'Very well, Skrp. You may go.' The rat twitched its whiskers at him, leaned the mirror against the wall, and trotted off.

'You're waited on by *rats*?' said Vimes.

'They help out, you know. They're not really very efficient, I'm afraid. It's their paws.'

'But, but, but,' said Vimes. 'I mean, how?'

'I suspect Skrp's people have tunnels that extend into the University,' Lord Vetinari went on. 'Although I think they were probably pretty bright to start with.'

At least Vimes understood that bit. It was well known that thaumic radiations affected animals living around the Unseen University campus, sometimes prodding them towards minute analogues of human civilization and even mutating some of them into entirely new and specialized species, such as the .303 bookworm and the wallfish. And, as the man said, rats were quite bright to start with.

'But they're helping you?' said Vimes.

'Mutual. It's mutual. Payment for services rendered, you might say,' said the Patrician, sitting down on what Vimes couldn't help noticing was a small velvet cushion. On a low shelf, so as to be handy, were a notepad and a neat row of books.

'How can you help rats, sir?' he said weakly.

'Advice. I advise them, you know.' The Patrician leaned back. 'That's the trouble with people like Wonse,' he said. 'They never know when to stop. Rats, snakes *and* scorpions. It was sheer bedlam in here when I came. The rats were getting the worst of it, too.'

And Vimes thought he was beginning to get the drift.

'You mean you sort of trained them?' he said.

'Advised. Advised. I suppose it's a knack,' said Lord Vetinari modestly.

Vimes wondered how it was done. Did the rats side with the scorpions against the snakes and then, when the snakes were beaten, invite the scorpions to a celebratory slap-up meal and eat them? Or were individual scorpions hired with large amounts of, oh, whatever it was scorpions ate, to sidle up to selected leading snakes at night and sting them?

He remembered hearing once about a man who, locked up in a cell for years, trained little birds and created a sort of freedom. And he thought of ancient sailors, shorn of the sea by old age and infirmity, who spent their days making big ships in little bottles.

Then he thought of the Patrician, robbed of his city, sitting cross-legged on the grey floor in the dim dungeon and recreating it around him, encouraging in miniature all the little rivalries, power struggles and factions. He thought of him as a sombre, brooding statue amid paving stones alive with slinking shadows and sudden, political death. It had probably been easier than ruling Ankh, which had larger vermin who didn't have to use both hands to carry a knife.

There was a clink over by the drain. Half a dozen rats appeared, dragging something wrapped in a cloth. They rathandled it past the grille and, with great effort, hauled it to the Patrician's feet. He leaned down and undid the knot.

'We seem to have cheese, chicken legs, celery, a piece of rather stale bread and a nice bottle, oh, a nice bottle apparently of Merckle and Stingbat's Very Famous Brown Sauce. *Beer*, I said, Skrp.' The leading rat twitched its nose at him. 'Sorry about this, Vimes. They can't read, you see. They don't seem to get the hang of the concept. But they're very good at listening. They bring me all the news.'

'I see you're very comfortable here,' said Vimes weakly.

'Never build a dungeon you wouldn't be happy to spend the night in yourself,' said the Patrician, laying out the food on the cloth. 'The world would be a happier place if more people remembered that.'

'We all thought you had built secret tunnels and suchlike,' said Vimes.

'Can't imagine why,' said the Patrician. 'One would have to keep on running. So inefficient. Whereas here I am at the hub of things. I hope you understand that, Vimes. Never trust any ruler who puts his faith in tunnels and bunkers and escape routes. The chances are that his heart isn't in the job.'

'Oh.'

He's in a dungeon in his own palace with a raving lunatic in charge upstairs, and a dragon burning the city, and he thinks he's got the world where he wants it. It must be something about high office. The altitude sends people mad.

'You, er, you don't mind if I have a look around, do you?' he said.

'Feel free,' said the Patrician. Vimes paced the length of the dungeon and checked the door. It was heavily barred and bolted, and the lock was massive.

Then he tapped the walls in what might possibly be hollow places. There was no doubt that it was a well-built dungeon. It was the kind of dungeon you'd feel good about having dangerous criminals put in. Of course, in those circumstances you'd prefer there to be no trapdoors, hidden tunnels or secret ways of escape.

These weren't those circumstances. It was amazing what several feet of solid stone did to your sense of perspective.

'Do guards come in here?' he demanded.

'Hardly ever,' said the Patrician, waving a chicken

leg. 'They don't bother about feeding me, you see. The idea is that one should moulder. In fact,' he said, 'up 'til recently I used to go to the door and groan a bit every now and then, just to keep them happy.'

'They're bound to come in and check, though?' said Vimes hopefully.

'Oh, I don't think we should tolerate that,' said the Patrician.

'How are you going to prevent them?'

Lord Vetinari gave him a pained look.

'My dear Vimes,' he said, 'I thought you were an observant man. Did you look at the door?'

'Of course I did,' said Vimes, and added, 'sir. It's bloody massive.'

'Perhaps you should have another look?'

Vimes gaped at him, and then stamped across the floor and glared at the door. It was one of the popular dread portal variety, all bars and bolts and iron spikes and massive hinges. No matter how long he looked at it, it didn't become any less massive. The lock was one of those dwarfish-made buggers that it'd take years to pick. All in all, if you had to have a symbol for something totally immovable, that door was your man.

The Patrician appeared alongside him in heart-stopping silence.

'You see,' he said, 'it's always the case, is it not, that should a city be overtaken by violent civil unrest the current ruler is thrown into the dungeons? To a certain type of mind that is so much more satisfying than mere execution.'

'Well, OK, but I don't see—' Vimes began.

'And you look at this door and what you see is a really strong cell door, yes?'

'Of course. You've only got to look at the bolts and—'

'You know, I'm really rather pleased,' said Lord Vetinari quietly.

Vimes stared at the door until his eyebrows ached. And then, just as random patterns in cloud suddenly, without changing in any way, become a horse's head or a sailing ship, he saw what he'd been looking at all along.

A sense of terrifying admiration overcame him.

He wondered what it was like in the Patrician's mind. All cold and shiny, he thought, all blued steel and icicles and little wheels clicking along like a huge clock. The kind of mind that would carefully consider its own downfall and turn it to advantage.

It was a perfectly normal dungeon door, but it all depended on your sense of perspective.

In this dungeon the Patrician could hold off the world.

All that was on the outside was the lock.

All the bolts and bars were on the inside.

The rank clambered awkwardly across the damp rooftops as the morning mist was boiled off by the sun. Not that there would be any clear air today – sticky swathes of smoke and stale steam wreathed the city and filled the air with the sad smell of dampened cinders.

'What is this place?' said Carrot, helping the others along a greasy walkway.

Sergeant Colon looked around at the forest of chimneys.

'We're just above Jimkin Bearhugger's whisky distillery,' he said. 'On a direct line, see, between the palace and the plaza. It's bound to fly over here.'

Nobby looked wistfully over the side of the building.

'I bin in there once,' he said. 'Checked the door one dark night and it just come open in my hand.'

'Eventually, I expect,' said Colon sourly.

'Well, I had to go in, din't I, to check there was no miscreanting going on. Amazing place in there. All pipes and stuff. And the smell!'

' "Every bottle matured for up to seven minutes",' quoted Colon. ' "Ha' a drop afore ye go", it says on the label. Damn right, too. I had a drop once, and I went all day.'

He knelt down and unwrapped the long sacking package he had been manhandling, with extreme difficulty, during the climb. This revealed a longbow of ancient design and a quiver of arrows.

He picked up the bow slowly, reverentially, and ran his pudgy fingers along it.

'You know,' he said quietly, 'I was damn good with this, when I were a lad. The captain should of let me have a go the other night.'

'You keep on telling us,' said Nobby unsympathetically.

'Well, I used to win prizes.' The sergeant unwound a new bowstring, looped it around one end of the bow, stood up, pressed down, grunted a bit . . .

'Er. Carrot?' he said, slightly out of breath.

'Yes, Sarge?'

'You any good at stringing bows?'

Carrot grasped the bow, compressed it easily, and slipped the other end of the string into place.

'That's a good start, Sarge,' said Nobby.

'Don't you be sarcastic with me, Nobby! It ain't strength, it's keenness of eye and steadiness of hand what counts. Now you pass me an arrow. Not that one!'

Nobby's fingers froze in the act of grasping a shaft.

'That's my *lucky* arrow!' spluttered Colon. 'None of you is to touch my lucky arrow!'

'Looks just like any other bloody arrow to me, Sarge,' said Nobby mildly.

'That's the one I shall use for the actual woss-name, the coup de grass,' said Colon. 'Never let me down, my lucky arrow didn't. Hit whatever I shot at. Hardly even had to aim. If that dragon's got any voonerables, that arrow'll find 'em.'

He selected an identical-looking but presumably less lucky arrow and nocked it. Then he looked around the rooftops with a speculative eye.

'Better get my hand in,' he muttered. 'Of course, once you learn you never forget, it's like riding a – riding a – riding something you never forget being able to ride.'

He pulled the bowstring back to his ear, and grunted.

'Right,' he wheezed, as his arm trembled with the tension like a branch in a gale. 'See the roof of the Assassins' Guild over there?'

They peered through the grubby air.

'Right, then,' said Colon. 'And do you see the weathervane on it? Do you see it?'

Carrot glanced at the arrowhead. It was weaving back and forth in a series of figure-eights.

'It's a long way off, Sarge,' said Nobby doubtfully.

'Never you mind me, you keep an eye on the weathervane,' groaned the sergeant.

They nodded. The weathervane was in the shape of a creeping man with a big cloak; his outstretched dagger was always turned to stab the wind. At this distance, though, it was tiny.

'*OK*,' panted Colon. 'Now, d'you see the man's eye?'

'Oh, come *on*,' said Nobby.

'Shutup, shutup, shutup!' groaned Colon. 'Do you see it, I said!'

'I think *I* can see it, Sarge,' said Carrot loyally.

'Right. Right,' said the sergeant, swaying backwards and forwards with effort. 'Right. Good lad. OK. Now keep an eye on it, right?'

He grunted, and loosed the arrow.

Several things happened so fast that they will have to be recounted in stop-motion prose. Probably the first was the bowstring slapping into the soft inner part of Colon's wrist, causing him to scream and drop the bow. This had no effect on the path of the arrow, which was already flying straight and true towards a gargoyle on the rooftop just across the road. It hit it on the ear, bounced, ricocheted off a wall six feet away, and headed back towards Colon apparently at a slightly increased speed, going past his ear with a silky humming noise.

It vanished in the direction of the city walls.

After a while Nobby coughed and gave Carrot a look of innocent enquiry.

'About how big,' he said, 'is a dragon's voonerables, roughly?'

'Oh, it can be a tiny spot,' said Carrot helpfully.

'I was sort of afraid of that,' said Nobby. He wandered to the edge of the roof, and pointed downwards. 'There's a pond just here,' he said. 'They use it for cooling water in the stills. I reckon it's pretty deep, so after the sergeant has shot at the dragon we can jump in it. What d'you say?'

'Oh, but we don't need to do that,' said Carrot. 'Because the sergeant's lucky arrow would of hit the spot and the dragon'll be dead, so we won't have anything to worry about.'

'Granted, granted,' said Nobby hurriedly, looking at Colon's scowling face. 'But just in case, you know, if by a million-to-one chance he misses – I'm not saying he will, mark you, you just have to think of all eventualities – if, by incredible bad luck, he doesn't quite manage to hit the voonerable dead on, then your dragon is going to lose his rag, right, and it's probably a good idea to not be here. It's a long shot, I know. Call me a worry-wart if you like. That's all I'm saying.'

Sergeant Colon adjusted his armour haughtily.

'When you really need them the most,' he said, 'million-to-one chances *always* crop up. Well-known fact.'

'The sergeant is right, Nobby,' said Carrot virtuously. 'You know that when there's just one chance which might just work – well, it works. Otherwise there'd be no—' he lowered his voice – 'I mean, it stands to reason, if last desperate chances didn't work, there'd be no . . . well, the gods wouldn't let it be any other way. They wouldn't.'

As one man, the three of them turned and looked through the murky air towards the hub of the Discworld, thousands of miles away. Now the air was grey with old smoke and mist shreds, but on a clear day it was possible to see Cori Celesti, home of the gods. *Site* of the home of the gods, anyway. They lived in Dunmanifestin, the stuccoed Valhalla, where the gods faced eternity with the kind of minds that were at a loss to know what to do to pass a wet afternoon. They played games with the fates of men, it was said. Exactly what game they thought they were playing at the moment was anyone's guess.

But of course there were rules. Everyone knew there were rules. They just had to hope like Hell that the gods knew the rules, too.

'It's got to work,' mumbled Colon. 'I'll be using my lucky arrow 'n all. You're right. Last hopeless chances have got to work. Nothing makes any sense otherwise. You might as well not be alive.'

Nobby looked down at the pond again. After a moment's hesitation Colon joined him. They had the speculative faces of men who had seen many things, and knew that while you could of course depend on heroes, and kings, and ultimately on gods, you could *really* depend on gravity and deep water.

'Not that we'll need it,' said Colon virtuously.

'Not with your lucky arrow,' said Nobby.

'That's right. But, just out of interest, how far down is it, d'you think?' said Colon.

'About thirty feet, I'd say. Give or take.'

'Thirty feet.' Colon nodded slowly. 'That's what I'd reckon. And it's deep, is it?'

'Very deep, I've heard.'

'I'll take your word for it. It looks pretty mucky. I'd hate to have to jump in it.'

Carrot slapped him cheerfully on the back, nearly pushing him over, and said, 'What's up, Sarge? Do you want to live for ever?'

'Dunno. Ask me again in five hundred years.'

'It's a good job we've got your lucky arrow, then!' said Carrot.

'Hmm?' said Colon, who seemed to be in a miserable daydream world of his own.

'I mean, it's a good job we've got a last desperate million-to-one chance to rely on, or we'd really be in trouble!'

'Oh, yes,' said Nobby sadly. 'Lucky old us.'

The Patrician lay back. A couple of rats dragged a cushion under his head.

'Things are rather bad outside, I gather,' he said.

'Yes,' said Vimes bitterly. 'You're right. You're the safest man in the city.'

He wedged another knife in a crack in the stones and tested his weight carefully, while Lord Vetinari looked on with interest. He'd managed to get six feet off the floor and up to a level with the grille.

Now he started to hack at the mortar around the bars.

The Patrician watched him for a while, and then took a book off the little shelf beside him. Since the rats couldn't read the library he'd been able to assemble was a little baroque, but he was not a man to ignore fresh knowledge. He found his bookmark in the pages of *Lacemaking Through the Ages*, and read a few pages.

After a while he found it necessary to brush a few crumbs of mortar off the book, and looked up.

'Are you achieving success?' he enquired politely.

Vimes gritted his teeth and hacked away. Outside the little grille was a grubby courtyard, barely lighter than the cell. There was a midden in one corner, but currently it looked very attractive. More attractive than the dungeon, at any rate. An honest midden was preferable to the way Ankh-Morpork was going these days. It was probably allegorical, or something.

He stabbed, stabbed, stabbed. The knife blade twanged and shook in his hand.

The Librarian scratched his armpits thoughtfully. He was facing problems of his own.

He had come here full of rage against book thieves and that rage still burned. But the seditious thought had occurred to him that, although crimes against books were the worst kind of crimes, revenge ought, perhaps, to be postponed.

It occurred to him that, while of course what humans chose to do to one another was all one to him, there were certain activities that should be curtailed in case the perpetrators got over-confident and started doing things like that to books, too.

The Librarian stared at his badge again, and gave it a gentle nibble in the optimistic hope that it had become edible. No doubt about it, he had a Duty to the captain.

The captain had always been kind to him. And the captain had a badge, too.

Yes.

There were times when an ape had to do what a man had to do . . .

The orangutan threw a complex salute and swung away into the darkness.

The sun rose higher, rolling through the mists and stale smoke like a lost balloon.

The rank sat in the shade of a chimney stack, waiting and killing time in their various ways. Nobby was thoughtfully probing the contents of a nostril, Carrot was writing a letter home, and Sergeant Colon was worrying.

After a while he shifted his weight uneasily and said, 'I've fought of a problem.'

'Wassat, Sarge?' said Carrot.

Sergeant Colon looked wretched. '*Weeell*, what if it's not a million-to-one chance?' he said.

Nobby stared at him.

'What d'you mean?' he said.

'Well, all *right*, last desperate million-to-one chances always work, right, no problem, but . . . well, it's pretty wossname, specific. I mean, isn't it?'

'You tell me,' said Nobby.

'What if it's just a thousand-to-one chance?' said Colon agonizedly.

'What?'

'Anyone ever heard of a thousand-to-one shot coming up?'

Carrot looked up. 'Don't be daft, Sergeant,' he said. 'No-one ever saw a thousand-to-one chance come up. The odds against it are—' his lips moved – 'millions to one.'

'Yeah. Millions,' agreed Nobby.

'So it'd only work if it's your actual million-to-one chance,' said the sergeant.

'I suppose that's right,' said Nobby.

'So 999,943-to-one, for example—' Colon began.

Carrot shook his head. 'Wouldn't have a hope. No-one ever said, "It's a 999,943-to-one chance but it might just work."'

They stared out across the city in the silence of ferocious mental calculation.

'We could have a real problem here,' said Colon eventually.

Carrot started to scribble furiously. When questioned, he explained at length about how you found the surface area of a dragon and then tried to estimate the chances of an arrow hitting any one spot.

'Aimed, mind,' said Sergeant Colon. 'I *aim*.'

Nobby coughed.

'In that case it's got to be a lot less than a million-to-one chance,' said Carrot. 'It could be a hundred-to-one. If the dragon's flying slowly and it's a big spot, it could be practically a certainty.'

Colon's lips shaped themselves around the phrase, *It's a certainty but it might just work*. He shook his head. 'Nah,' he said.

'So what we've got to do, then,' said Nobby slowly, 'is adjust the odds . . .'

Now there was a shallow hole in the mortar near the middle bar. It wasn't much, Vimes knew, but it was a start.

'You don't require assistance, by any chance?' said the Patrician.

'No.'

'As you wish.'

The mortar was half-rotted, but the bars had been driven deep into the rock. Under their crusting of rust there was still plenty of iron. It was a long job, but it was something to do and required a blessed absence of thought. They couldn't take it away from him. It was a good, clean challenge; you knew if you went on chipping away, you'd win through eventually.

It was the 'eventually' that was the problem. Eventually Great A'Tuin would reach the end of the universe. Eventually the stars would go out. Eventually Nobby might have a bath, although that would probably involve a radical rethinking of the nature of Time.

He hacked at the mortar anyway, and then stopped as something small and pale fell down outside, quite slowly.

'Peanut shell?' he said.

The Librarian's face, surrounded by the inner-tube jowls of the Librarian's head, appeared upside down in the barred opening, and gave him a grin that wasn't any less terrible for being the wrong way up.

'Oook?'

The orangutan flopped down off the wall, grabbed a couple of bars, and pulled. Muscles shunted back and forward across its barrel chest in a complex pavane of effort. The mouthful of yellow teeth gaped in silent concentration.

There were a couple of dull 'thungs' as the bars gave up and broke free. The ape flung them aside and reached into the gaping hole. Then the longest arms of the Law grabbed the astonished Vimes under his shoulders and pulled him through in one movement.

The rank surveyed their handiwork.

'Right,' said Nobby. 'Now, what are the chances of a man standing on one leg with his hat on backwards and a handkerchief in his mouth hitting a dragon's voonerables?'

'Mmph,' said Colon.

'It's pretty long odds,' said Carrot. 'I reckon the hanky is a bit over the top, though.'

Colon spat it out. 'Make up your minds,' he said. 'Me leg's going to sleep.'

Vimes picked himself up off the greasy cobbles and stared at the Librarian. He was experiencing something which had come as a shock to many people, usually in much more unpleasant circumstances such as a brawl started in the Mended Drum when the ape wanted a bit of peace and quiet to enjoy a reflective pint, which was this: the Librarian might look like a stuffed rubber sack, but what it was stuffed with was muscle.

'That was amazing,' was all he could find to say. He looked down at the twisted bars, and felt his mind darken. He grabbed the bent metal. 'You don't happen to know where Wonse is, do you?' he added.

'Eeek!' The Librarian thrust a tattered piece of parchment under his nose. 'Eeek!'

Vimes read the words.

It hathe pleased . . . whereas . . . at the stroke of noone . . . a maiden pure, yet high born . . . compact between ruler and rulèd . . .

'In my city!' he growled. 'In my bloody city!'

He grabbed the Librarian by two handfuls of chest hair and pulled him up to eye height.

'What time is it?' he shouted.

'Oook!'

A long red-haired arm unfolded itself upwards. Vimes's gaze followed the pointing finger. The sun definitely had the look of a heavenly body that was nearly at the crest of its orbit and looking forward to a long, lazy coasting towards the blankets of dusk . . .

'I'm not bloody well going to have it, understand?' Vimes shouted, shaking the ape back and forth.

'Oook,' the Librarian pointed out, patiently.

'What? Oh. Sorry.' Vimes lowered the ape, who wisely didn't make an issue of it because a man angry enough to lift 300lbs of orangutan without noticing is a man with too much on his mind.

Now he was staring around the courtyard.

'Any way out of here?' he said. 'Without climbing the walls, I mean.'

He didn't wait for an answer but loped around the walls until he reached a narrow, grubby door, and kicked it open. It hadn't been locked anyway, but he kicked it just the same. The Librarian trailed along behind, swinging on his knuckles.

The kitchen on the other side of the door was almost deserted, the staff having finally lost their nerve and decided that all prudent chefs refrained from working in an establishment where there was a mouth bigger than they were. A couple of palace guards were eating a cold lunch.

'Now,' said Vimes, as they half-rose, 'I don't want to have to—'

They didn't seem to want to listen. One of them reached for a crossbow.

'Oh, the hell with it.' Vimes grabbed a butcher's knife from a block beside him and threw it.

There is an art in throwing knives and, even then, you need the right kind of knife. Otherwise it does just what this one did, which is miss completely.

The guard with the bow leaned sideways, righted himself, and found that a purple fingernail was gently blocking the firing mechanism. He looked around. The Librarian hit him right on top of his helmet.

The other guard shrank back, waving his hands frantically.

'Nonono!' he said. 'It's a misunderstanding! What was it you said you didn't want to have to do? Nice monkey!'

'Oh, dear,' said Vimes. '*Wrong!*'

He ignored the terrified screaming and rummaged through the debris of the kitchen until he came up with a cleaver. He'd never felt really at home with swords, but a cleaver was a different matter. A cleaver had weight. It had purpose. A sword might have a certain nobility about it, unless it was the one belonging for example to Nobby, which relied on rust to hold it together, but what a cleaver had was a tremendous ability to cut things up.

He left the biology lesson – that no monkey was capable of bouncing someone up and down by their ankles – found a likely door, and hurried through it. This took him outside again, into the big cobbled area that surrounded the palace. Now he could get his bearings, now he could . . .

There was a boom in the air above him. A gale blew *downwards*, knocking him over.

The King of Ankh-Morpork, wings outspread, glided across the sky and settled for a moment on the palace gateway, talons gouging long scars in the stone as it caught its balance. The sun glittered off its arched back as it stretched its neck, roared a lazy billow of flames, and sprang into the air again.

Vimes made an animal – a mammalian animal – noise in the back of his throat, and ran out into the empty streets.

*   *   *

Silence filled the ancestral home of the Ramkins. The front door swung back and forth on its hinges, letting in the common, badly-brought up breeze which wandered through the deserted rooms, gawping and looking for dust on the top of the furniture. It wound up the stairs and banged through the door of Sybil Ramkin's bedroom, rattling the bottles on the dressing table and riffling through the pages of *Diseases of the Dragon*.

A really fast reader could have learned the symptoms of everything from Abated Heels to Zigzag Throat.

And down below, in the low, warm and foul-smelling shed that housed the swamp dragons, it seemed that Errol had got them all. Now he sat in the centre of his pen, swaying and moaning softly. White smoke rolled slowly from his ears and drifted towards the floor. From somewhere inside his swollen stomach came complex explosive hydraulic noises, as though desperate teams of gnomes were trying to drive a culvert through a cliff in a thunderstorm.

His nostrils flared, turning more or less of their own volition.

The other dragons craned over the pen walls, watching him cautiously.

There was another distant gastric roar. Errol shifted painfully.

The dragons exchanged glances. Then, one by one, they lay down carefully on the floor and put their paws over their eyes.

*   *   *

Nobby put his head on one side.

'It looks promising,' he said critically. 'We might be nearly there. I reckon the chances of a man with soot on his face, his tongue sticking out, standing on one leg and singing *The Hedgehog Song* ever hitting a dragon's voonerables would be . . . what'd you say, Carrot?'

'A million to one, I reckon,' said Carrot virtuously.

Colon glared at them.

'Listen lads,' he said, 'you're not winding me up, are you?'

Carrot looked down at the plaza below them.

'Oh, bloody hell,' he said softly.

'Wassat?' said Colon urgently, looking around.

'They're chaining a woman to a rock!'

The rank stared over the parapet. The huge and silent crowd that lined the plaza stared too, at a white figure struggling between half a dozen palace guards.

'Wonder where they got the rock from?' said Colon. 'We're on loam here, you know.'

'Fine strapping wench, whoever she is,' said Nobby approvingly, as one of the guards wheeled off bow-legged and collapsed. 'That's one lad who won't know what to do with his evenin's for a few weeks. Got a mean right knee, so she has.'

'Anyone we know?' said Colon.

Carrot squinted.

'It's Lady Ramkin!' he said, his mouth dropping open.

'Never!'

'He's right. In a nightie,' said Nobby.

'The buggers!' Colon snatched up his bow and fumbled for an arrow. 'I'll give 'em voonerables! Well-spoken lady like her, it's a disgrace!'

'Er,' said Carrot, who had glanced over his shoulder. 'Sergeant?'

'This is what it comes to!' muttered Colon. 'Decent women can't walk down the street without being eaten! Right, you bastards, you're . . . you're *geography*—'

'Sergeant!' Carrot repeated urgently.

'It's history, not geography,' said Nobby. 'That's what you're supposed to say. History. "You're history!" you say.'

'Well, whatever,' snapped Colon. 'Let's see how—'

'*Sergeant!*'

Nobby was looking behind them, too.

'Oh, shit,' he said.

'Can't miss,' muttered Colon, taking aim.

'*Sergeant!*'

'Shut up, you two, I can't concentrate when you keep shout—'

'Sergeant, *it's coming!*'

The dragon accelerated.

The drunken rooftops of Ankh-Morpork blurred as it passed over, wings sneering at the air. Its neck stretched out straight ahead, the pilot flames of its nostrils streamed behind it, the sound of its flight panned across the sky.

*   *   *

Colon's hands shook. The dragon seemed to be aiming at his throat, and it was moving too fast, far too fast . . .

'This is it!' said Carrot. He glanced towards the Hub, in case any gods had forgotten what they were there for, and added, speaking slowly and distinctly, 'It's a million-to-one-chance, but it might just work!'

'Fire the bloody thing!' screamed Nobby.

'Picking my spot, lad, picking my spot,' quavered Colon. 'Don't you worry, lads, I told you this is my lucky arrow. First-class arrow, this arrow, had it since I was a lad, you'd be amazed at the things I shot at with this, don't you worry.'

He paused, as the nightmare bore down on him on wings of terror.

'Er, Carrot?' he said meekly.

'Yes, Sarge?'

'Did your old grandad ever say what a voonerable spot *looks* like?'

And then the dragon wasn't approaching any more, it was there, passing a few feet overhead, a streaming mosaic of scales and noise, filling the entire sky.

Colon fired.

They watched the arrow rise straight and true.

Vimes half-ran, half-staggered over the damp cobbles, out of breath and out of time.

It can't be like this, he thought wildly. The hero always cuts it fine, but he always gets there just in the nick of time. Only the nick of time was probably five minutes ago.

And I'm not a hero. I'm out of condition, and I need a drink, and I get a handful of dollars a month without plumes allowance. That's not hero's pay. Heroes get kingdoms and princesses, and they take regular exercise, and when they smile the light glints off their teeth, *ting*. The bastards.

Sweat stung his eyes. The rush of adrenalin that had carried him out of the palace had spent itself, and was now exacting its inevitable toll.

He stumbled to a halt, and grabbed a wall to keep him upright while he gasped for air. And thus he saw the figures on the rooftop.

Oh, no! he thought. They're not heroes either! What do they think they're playing at?

It was a million-to-one chance. And who was to say that, somewhere in the millions of other possible universes, it might not have worked?

That was the sort of thing the gods really liked. But Chance, who sometimes can overrule even the gods, has 999,999 casting votes.

In *this* universe, for example, the arrow bounced off a scale and clattered away into oblivion.

Colon stared as the dragon's pointed tail passed overhead.

'It . . . missed . . .' he mouthed.

'But it couldn't of missed!' He stared red-eyed at the other two. 'It was a sodding last desperate million-to-one chance!'

The dragon twisted its wings, swung its huge bulk around on a pivot of air, and bore down on the roof.

Carrot grabbed Nobby around the waist and laid a hand on Colon's shoulder.

The sergeant was weeping with rage and frustration.

'Million-to-bloody-one last desperate bloody chance!'

'Sarge—'

The dragon flamed.

It was a beautifully controlled line of plasma. It went through the roof like butter.

It cut through stairways.

It crackled into ancient timbers and made them twist like paper. It sliced into pipes.

It punched through floor after floor like the fist of an angry god and, eventually, reached the big copper vat containing a thousand gallons of freshly-made mature whisky-type spirit.

It burned into that, too.

Fortunately, the chances of anyone surviving the ensuing explosion were exactly a million-to-one.

The fireball rose like a – well, a rose. A huge orange rose, streaked with yellow. It took the roof with it and wrapped it around the astonished dragon, lifting it high into the air in a boiling cloud of broken timber and bits of piping.

The crowd watched in bemusement as the super-hot blast flung it into the sky and barely noticed Vimes as he pushed his way, wheezing and crying, through the press of bodies.

He shouldered past a row of palace guards and shambled as fast as he could across the flagstones.

No-one was paying him much attention at the moment.

He stopped.

It wasn't a rock, because Ankh-Morpork was on loam. It was just some huge remnant of mortared masonry, probably thousands of years old, from somewhere in the city foundations. Ankh-Morpork was so old now that what it was built on, by and large, was Ankh-Morpork.

It had been dragged into the centre of the plaza, and Lady Sybil Ramkin had been chained to it. She appeared to be wearing a nightie and huge rubber boots. By the look of her she had been in a fight, and Vimes felt a momentary pang of sympathy for whoever else had been involved. She gave him a look of pure fury.

'You!'

'*You!*'

He waved the cleaver vaguely.

'But why you—?' he began.

'Captain Vimes,' she said sharply, 'you will oblige me by not waving that thing about and you will start putting it to its proper use!'

Vimes wasn't listening.

'Thirty dollars a month!' he muttered. 'That's what they died for! Thirty dollars! And I docked some from Nobby. I had to, didn't I? I mean, that man could make a *melon* go rusty!'

'Captain Vimes!'

He focused on the cleaver.

'Oh,' he said. 'Yes. Right!'

It was a good steel cleaver, and the chains were

elderly and rather rusty iron. He hacked away, raising sparks from the masonry.

The crowd watched in silence, but several palace guards hurried towards him.

'What the hell do you think you're doing?' said one of them, who didn't have much imagination.

'What the hell do you think *you're* doing?' Vimes growled, looking up.

They stared at him.

'What?'

Vimes took another hack at the chains. Several loops tinkled to the ground.

'Right, you've asked for—' one of the guards began. Vimes's elbow caught him under his rib cage; before he collapsed, Vimes's foot kicked savagely at the other one's kneecaps, bringing his chin down ready for another stab with the other elbow.

'Right,' said Vimes absently. He rubbed the elbow. It was sheer agony.

He moved the cleaver to his other hand and hammered at the chains again, aware at the back of his mind that more guards were hurrying up, but with that special kind of run that guards had. He knew it well. It was the run that said, there's a dozen of us, let someone else get there first. It said, he looks ready to kill, no-one's paying me to get killed, maybe if I run slowly enough he'll get away . . .

No point in spoiling a good day by catching someone.

Lady Ramkin shook herself free. A ragged cheer went up and started to grow in volume. Even in their current state of mind, the people of Ankh-Morpork always appreciated a performance.

She grabbed a handful of chain and wrapped it around one pudgy fist.

'Some of those guards don't know how to treat—' she began.

'No time, no time,' said Vimes, grabbing her arm. It was like trying to drag a mountain.

The cheering stopped, abruptly.

There was a sound behind Vimes. It was not, particularly, a loud noise. It just had a peculiarly nasty carrying quality. It was the click of four sets of talons hitting the flagstones at the same time.

Vimes looked around and up.

Soot clung to the dragon's hide. A few pieces of charred wood had lodged here and there, and were still smouldering. The magnificent bronze scales were streaked with black.

It lowered its head until Vimes was a few feet away from its eyes, and tried to focus on him.

Probably not worth running, Vimes told himself. It's not as if I've got the energy anyway.

He felt Lady Ramkin's hand engulf his.

'Jolly well done,' she said. 'It nearly worked.'

Charred and blazing wreckage rained down around the distillery. The pond was a swamp of debris, covered with a coating of ash. Out of it, dripping slime, rose Sergeant Colon.

He clawed his way to the bank and pulled himself up, like some sea-dwelling lifeform that was anxious to get the whole evolution thing over with in one go.

Nobby was already there, spread out like a frog, leaking water.

'Is that you, Nobby?' said Sergeant Colon anxiously.

'It's me, Sergeant.'

'I'm glad about that, Nobby,' said Colon fervently.

'I wish it wasn't me, Sergeant.'

Colon tipped the water out of his helmet, and then paused.

'What about young Carrot?' he said.

Nobby pushed himself up on his elbows, groggily.

'Dunno,' he said. 'One minute we were on the roof, next minute we were jumping.'

They both looked at the ashen waters of the pond.

'I suppose,' said Colon slowly, 'he can swim?'

'Dunno. He never said. Not much to swim in, up in the mountains. When you come to think about it,' said Nobby.

'But perhaps there were limpid blue pools and deep mountain streams,' said the sergeant hopefully. 'And icy tarns in hidden valleys and that. Not to mention subterranean lakes. He'd be bound to have learned. In and out of the water all day, I expect.'

They stared at the greasy grey surface.

'It was probably that Protective,' said Nobby. 'P'raps it filled with water and dragged him down.'

Colon nodded gloomily.

'I'll hold your helmet,' said Nobby, after a while.

'But I'm your superior officer!'

'Yes,' said Nobby reasonably, 'but if you get stuck down there, you're going to want your best man up here, ready to rescue you, aren't you?'

'That's . . . reasonable,' said Colon eventually. 'That's a good point.'

'Right, then.'

'Drawback is, though . . .'

'What?'

'. . . I can't swim,' Colon said.

'How did you get out of that, then?'

Colon shrugged. 'I'm a natural floater.'

Their eyes, once again, turned to the dankness of the pond. Then Colon stared at Nobby. Then Nobby, very slowly, unbuckled his helmet.

'There isn't someone still in there, is there?' said Carrot, behind them.

They looked around. He hoicked some mud out of an ear. Behind him the remains of the brewery smouldered.

'I thought I'd better nip out quickly, see what was going on,' he said brightly, pointing to a gate leading out of the yard. It was hanging by one hinge.

'Oh,' said Nobby weakly. 'Jolly good.'

'There's an alley out there,' said Carrot.

'No dragons in it, are there?' said Colon suspiciously.

'No dragons, no humans. There's no-one around,' said Carrot impatiently. He drew his sword. 'Come on!' he said.

'Where to?' said Nobby. He'd pulled a damp butt from behind his ear and was looking at it with an expression of deepest sorrow. It was obviously too far gone. He tried to light it anyway.

'We want to fight the dragon, don't we?' said Carrot.

Colon shifted uncomfortably. 'Yes, but aren't we allowed to go home for a change of clothes first?'

'And a nice warm drink?' said Nobby.

'And a meal,' said Colon. 'A nice plate of—'

'You should be ashamed of yourselves,' said Carrot. 'There's a lady in distress and a dragon to fight and all you can think of is food and drink!'

'Oh, I'm not just thinking about food and drink,' said Colon.

'We could be all that stands between the city and total destruction!'

'Yes, but—' Nobby began.

Carrot drew his sword and waved it over his head.

'Captain Vimes would have gone!' he said. 'All for one!'

He glared at them, and rushed out of the yard.

Colon gave Nobby a sheepish look.

'Young people today,' he said.

'All for one what?' said Nobby.

The sergeant sighed. 'Come on, then.'

'Oh, all right.'

They staggered out into the alley. It was empty.

'Where'd he go?' said Nobby.

Carrot stepped out of the shadows, grinning all over his face.

'Knew I could rely on you,' he said. 'Follow me!'

'Something odd about that boy,' said Colon, as

they limped after him. 'He always manages to persuade us to follow him, have you noticed?'

'All for one what?' said Nobby.

'Something about the voice, I reckon.'

'Yes, but all for one what?'

The Patrician sighed and, carefully marking his place, laid aside his book. To judge from the noise there seemed to be an awful lot of excitement going on out there. It was highly unlikely any palace guards would be around, which was just as well. The guards were highly-trained men and it would be a shame to waste them.

He would need them later on.

He padded over to the wall and pushed a small block that looked exactly like all the other small blocks. No other small block, however, would have caused a section of flagstone to grind ponderously aside.

There was a carefully chosen assortment of stuff in there – iron rations, spare clothes, several small chests of precious metals and jewels, tools. And there was a key. Never build a dungeon you couldn't get out of.

The Patrician took the key and strolled over to the door. As the wards of the lock slid back in their well-oiled grooves he wondered, again, whether he should have told Vimes about the key. But the man seemed to have got so much satisfaction out of breaking out. It would probably have been positively bad for him to have told him about the key. Anyway, it would have spoiled his view of the world. He needed Vimes and his view of the world.

Lord Vetinari swung the door open and, silently, strode out into the ruins of his palace.

They trembled as, for the second time in a couple of minutes, the city rocked.

The dragon kennels exploded. The windows blew out. The door left the wall ahead of a great billow of black smoke and sailed into the air, tumbling slowly, to plough into the rhododendrons.

Something very energetic and hot was happening in that building. More smoke poured out, thick and oily and solid. One of the walls folded in on itself, and then another one toppled sluggishly on to the lawn.

Swamp dragons shot determinedly out of the wreckage like champagne corks, wings whirring frantically.

Still the smoke unrolled. But there was something in there, some point of fierce white light that was gently rising.

It disappeared from view as it passed a stricken window, and then, with a piece of roof tile still spinning on the top of his head, Errol climbed above his own smoke and ascended into the skies of Ankh-Morpork.

The sunlight glinted off his silver scales as he hovered about a hundred feet up, turning slowly, balancing nicely on his own flame . . .

Vimes, awaiting death on the plaza, realized that his mouth was hanging open. He shut it again.

There was absolutely no sound in the city now but the noise of Errol's ascent.

They can rearrange their own plumbing, Vimes told himself bemusedly. To suit circumstances. He's made it work in reverse. But his thingys, his genes . . . surely he must have been halfway to it anyway. No wonder the little bugger has got such stubby wings. His body must have known he wasn't going to need them, except to steer.

Good grief. I'm watching the first ever dragon to flame *backwards*.

He risked a glance immediately above him. The great dragon was frozen, its enormous bloodshot eyes concentrating on the tiny creature.

With a challenging roar of flame and a pummelling of air the King of Ankh-Morpork rose, all thought of mere humans forgotten.

Vimes turned sharply to Lady Ramkin.

'How do they fight?' he said urgently. 'How do dragons fight?'

'I – that is, well, they just flap at each other and blow flame,' she said. 'Swamp dragons, that is. I mean, who's ever seen a noble dragon fight?' She patted her nightie. 'I must take some notes, I've got my memo book somewhere . . .'

'In your *nightshirt*?'

'It's amazing how ideas come to one in bed, I've always said.'

Flames roared into the space where Errol had been, but he wasn't there. The king tried to spin in mid-air. The little dragon circled in an easy series of smoke rings, weaving a cat's cradle in the sky with the huge adversary gyrating helplessly in the middle. More flames, hotter and longer, stabbed at him and missed.

The crowd watched in breathless silence.

''allo, Captain,' said an ingratiating voice.

Vimes looked down. A small and stagnant pond disguised as Nobby grinned sheepishly up at him.

'I thought you were dead!' he said.

'We're not,' said Nobby.

'Oh. Good.' There didn't seem much else to say. 'What do you reckon on the fight, then?'

Vimes looked back up. Smoke trails spiralled across the city.

'I'm afraid it's not going to work,' said Lady Ramkin. 'Oh. Hallo, Nobby.'

'Afternoon, ma'am,' said Nobby, touching what he thought was his forelock.

'What d'you mean, it's not going to work?' said Vimes. 'Look at him go! It hasn't hit him yet!'

'Yes, but his flame has touched it several times. It doesn't seem to have any effect. It's not hot enough, I think. Oh, he's dodging well. But he's got to be lucky every time. *It* has only got to be lucky once.'

The meaning of this sank in.

'You mean,' said Vimes, 'all this is just – just *show*? He's just doing it to *impress*?'

'S'not his fault,' said Colon, materializing behind them. 'It's like dogs innit? Doesn't really dawn on the poor little bugger that he's up against a big one. He's just ready for a scrap.'

Both dragons appeared to realize that the fight was the well-known Klatchian standoff. With another smoke ring and a billow of white flame they parted and retreated a few hundred yards.

The king hovered, flapping its wings quickly.

Height. That was the thing. When dragon fought dragon, height was always the thing . . .

Errol balanced on his flame. He seemed to be thinking.

Then he nonchalantly kicked his back legs out as though hovering on your own stomach gases was something dragons had mastered over millions of years, somersaulted, and fled. For a moment he was visible as a silver streak, and then he was out over the city walls and gone.

A groan followed him. It came from ten thousand throats.

Vimes threw up his hands.

'Don't you worry, guv,' said Nobby quickly. 'He's – he's probably gone to, to have a drink. Or something. Maybe it's the end of round one. Or something.'

'I mean, he ate our kettle and everything,' said Colon uncertainly. 'He wouldn't just run away after eating a kettle. Stands to reason. Anyone who could eat a kettle wouldn't run away from *anything*.'

'And my armour polish,' said Carrot. 'It was nearly a whole dollar for the tin.'

'There you are then,' said Colon. 'It's like I said.'

'Look,' said Vimes, as patiently as he could manage. 'He's a nice dragon, I liked him as much as you, a very nice little chap, but he's just done the sensible thing, for gods' sake, he's not going to get burned to bits just to save us. Life just doesn't work like that. You might as well face it.'

Overhead the great dragon strutted through the air and flamed a nearby tower. It had won.

'I've never seen that before,' said Lady Ramkin. 'Dragons normally fight to the death.'

'At last they've bred one who's sensible,' said Vimes morosely. 'Let's be honest: the chances of a dragon the size of Errol beating something that big are a million-to-one.'

There was one of those silences you get after one clear bright note has been struck and the world pauses.

The rank looked at one another.

'Million-to-one?' asked Carrot nonchalantly.

'Definitely,' said Vimes. 'Million-to-one.'

The rank looked at one another again.

'Million-to-one,' said Colon.

'Million-to-one,' agreed Nobby.

'That's right,' said Carrot. 'Million-to-one.'

There was another high-toned silence. The members of the rank were wondering who was going to be the first to say *it*.

Sergeant Colon took a deep breath.

'But it might just work,' he said.

'What are you talking about?' snapped Vimes. 'There's no—'

Nobby nudged him urgently in the ribs and pointed out across the plains.

There *was* a column of black smoke out there. Vimes squinted. Running ahead of the smoke, speeding over the cabbage fields and closing fast, was a silvery bullet.

The great dragon had seen it too. It flamed defiance and climbed for extra height, mashing the air with its enormous wings.

Now Errol's flame was visible, so hot as to be almost blue. The landscape rolled away underneath him at an impossible speed, and he was accelerating.

Ahead of him the king extended its claws. It was almost grinning.

Errol's going to hit it, Vimes thought. Gods help us all, it'll be a fireball.

Something odd was happening out in the fields. A little way behind Errol the ground appeared to be ploughing itself up, throwing cabbage stalks into the air. A hedgerow erupted in a shower of sawdust . . .

Errol passed silently over the city walls, nose up, wings folded down to tiny flaps, his body honed to a mere cone with a flame at one end. His opponent blew out a tongue of fire; Vimes watched Errol, with a barely noticeable flip of a wing stub, roll easily out of its path. And then he was gone, speeding out towards the sea in the same eerie silence.

'He miss—' Nobby began.

The air ruptured. An endless thunderclap of noise dragged across the city, smashing tiles, toppling chimneys. In mid-air, the king was picked up, flattened out and spun like a top in the sonic wash. Vimes, his hands over his own ears, saw the creature flame desperately as it turned and became the centre of a spiral of crazy fire.

Magic crackled along its wings. It screamed like a distressed foghorn. Then, shaking its head dazedly, it began to glide in a wide circle.

Vimes groaned. It had survived something that tore masonry apart. What did you have to *do* to beat it? You can't fight it, he thought. You can't burn it, you can't smash it. There's nothing you can do to it.

The dragon landed. It wasn't a perfect landing. A perfect landing wouldn't have demolished a row of cottages. It was slow, and it seemed to go on for a long time and rip up a considerable stretch of city.

Wings flapping aimlessly, neck waving and spraying random flame, it ploughed on through a debris of beams and thatch. Several fires started up along the trail of destruction.

Finally it came to rest at the end of the furrow, almost invisible under a heap of former architecture.

The silence that it left was broken only by the shouts of someone trying to organize yet another bucket chain from the river to douse the fires.

Then people started to move.

From the air Ankh-Morpork must have looked like a disturbed anthill, with streams of dark figures flowing towards the wreck of the dragon.

Most of them had some kind of weapon.

Many of them had spears.

Some of them had swords.

All of them had one aim in mind.

'You know what?' said Vimes aloud. 'This is going to be the world's first democratically killed dragon. One man, one stab.'

'Then you've got to stop them. You can't let them kill it!' said Lady Ramkin.

Vimes blinked at her.

'Pardon?' he said.

'It's wounded!'

'Lady, that was the intention, wasn't it? Anyway, it's only stunned,' said Vimes.

'I mean you can't let them kill it like *this*,' said Lady Ramkin insistently. 'Poor thing!'

'What do you want to do, then?' demanded Vimes, his temper unravelling. 'Give it a strengthening dose of tar oil and a nice comfy basket in front of the stove?'

'It's butchery!'

'Suits me fine!'

'But it's a dragon! It's just doing what a dragon does! It never would have come here if people had left it alone!'

Vimes thought: it was about to eat her, and she can still think like this. He hesitated. Perhaps that *did* give you the right to an opinion . . .

Sergeant Colon sidled up as they glared, white-faced, at one another, and hopped desperately from one squelching foot to the other.

'You better come at once, Captain,' he said. 'It's going to be bloody murder!'

Vimes waved a hand at him. 'As far as I'm concerned,' he mumbled, avoiding Sybil Ramkin's glare, 'it's got it coming to it.'

'It's not that,' said Colon. 'It's Carrot. He's arrested the dragon.'

Vimes paused.

'What do you mean, *arrested*?' he said. 'You don't mean what I think you mean, do you?'

'Could be, sir,' said Colon uncertainly. 'Could be. He was up on the rubble like a shot, sir, grabbed it by a wing and said "You're *nicked*, chummy", sir. Couldn't believe it, sir. Sir, the thing is . . .'

'Well?'

The sergeant hopped from one foot to the other. 'You know you said prisoners weren't to be molested, sir . . .'

It was quite a large and heavy roof timber and it scythed quite slowly through the air, but when it hit people they rolled backwards and stayed hit.

'Now *look*,' said Carrot, hauling it in and pushing back his helmet, 'I don't want to have to tell anyone again, right?'

Vimes shouldered his way through the dense crowd, staring at the bulky figure atop the mound of rubble and dragon. Carrot turned slowly, the roof beam held like a staff. His gaze was like a lighthouse beam. Where it fell, the crowd lowered their weapons and looked merely sullen and uncomfortable.

'I must warn you,' Carrot went on, 'that interfering with an officer in the execution of his duty is a serious offence. And I shall come down like a ton of bricks on the very next person who throws a stone.'

A stone bounced off the back of his helmet. There was a barrage of jeers.

'Let us at it!'

'That's right!'

'We don't want guards ordering us about!'

'Quis custodiet custard?'

'Yeah? Right!'

Vimes pulled the sergeant towards him. 'Go

and organize some rope. Lots of rope. As thick as possible. I suppose we can – oh, tie its wings together, maybe, and bind up its mouth so it can't flame.'

Colon peered at him.

'Are you serious, sir? We're really going to *arrest* it?'

'Do it!'

It's *been* arrested, he thought, as he pushed his way forward. Personally I would have preferred it to drop in the sea, but it's been arrested and now we've got to deal with it or let it go free.

He felt his own feelings about the bloody thing evaporate in the face of the mob. What could you do with it? Give it a fair trial, he thought, and then execute it. Not kill it. That's what heroes do out in the wilderness. You can't think like that in cities. Or rather, you *can*, but if you're going to then you might as well burn the whole place down right now and start again. You ought to do it . . . well, by the book.

That's it. We tried everything else. Now we might as well try and do it by the book.

Anyway, he added mentally, that's a city guard up there. We've got to stick together. Nobody else will have anything to do with us.

A burly figure in front of him drew back an arm with a half-brick in it.

'Throw that brick and you're a dead man,' said Vimes, and then ducked and pushed his way through the press of people while the would-be thrower looked around in amazement.

Carrot half-raised his club in a threatening gesture as Vimes climbed up the rubble pile.

'Oh, hallo, Captain Vimes,' he said, lowering it, 'I have to report I have arrested this—'

'Yes, I can see,' said Vimes. 'Did you have any suggestions about what we do next?'

'Oh, yes, sir. I have to read it its rights, sir,' said Carrot.

'I mean apart from that.'

'Not really, sir.'

Vimes looked at those parts of the dragon still visible under the rubble. How *could* you kill one of these? You'd have to spend a day at it.

A lump of rock ricocheted off his breastplate.

'Who did that?'

The voice lashed out like a whip.

The crowd went quiet.

Sybil Ramkin scrambled up on the wreckage, eyes afire, and glared furiously at the mob.

'I said,' she said, 'who did that? If the person who did it does not own up I shall be *extremely* angry! Shame on you all!'

She had their full attention. Several people holding stones and things let them drop quietly to the ground.

The breeze flapped the remnants of her nightshirt as her Ladyship took up a new haranguing position.

'Here is the *gallant* Captain Vimes—'

'Oh gods,' said Vimes in a small voice, and pulled his helmet down over his eyes.

'—and his *dauntless* men, who have taken the *trouble* to come here today, to save your—'

Vimes gripped Carrot's arm and manoeuvred him down the far side of the heap.

'You all right, Captain?' said the lance-constable. 'You've gone all red.'

'Don't *you* start,' snapped Vimes. 'It's bad enough getting all those leers from Nobby and the sergeant.'

To his astonishment Carrot patted him companionably on the shoulder.

'I know how it is,' he said sympathetically. 'I had this girl back home, her name was Minty, and her father—'

'Look, for the last time, there is absolutely *nothing* between—' Vimes began.

There was a rattle beside them. A small avalanche of plaster and thatch rolled down. The rubble heaved, and opened one eye. One big black pupil floating in a bloodshot glow tried to focus on them.

'We must be mad,' said Vimes.

'Oh, no, sir,' said Carrot. 'There's plenty of precedents. In 1135 a hen was arrested for crowing on Soul Cake Thursday. And during the regime of Psychoneurotic Lord Snapcase a colony of bats was executed for persistent curfew violations. That was in 1401. August, I think. Great days for the law, they were,' said Carrot dreamily. 'In 1321, you know, a small cloud was prosecuted for covering the sun during the climax of Frenzied Earl Hargath's investiture ceremony.'

'I hope Colon gets a move on with—' Vimes stopped. He had to know. '*How?*' he said. 'What can you do to a cloud?'

'The Earl sentenced it to be stoned to death,' said Carrot. 'Apparently thirty-one people were killed.' He pulled out his notebook and glared at the dragon.

'Can it hear us, do you think?' he said.

'I suppose so.'

'Well, then.' Carrot cleared his throat and turned back to the stunned reptile. 'It is my duty to warn you that you are to be reported for consideration of prosecution on some or all of the following counts, to whit: One (One) i, that on or about 18th Grune last, in a place known as Sweetheart Lane, the Shades, you did unlawfully vent flame in a manner likely to cause grievous bodily harm, in contravention of Clause Seven of the Industrial Processes Act, 1508; AND THAT, One (One) ii, that on or about 18th Grune last, in a place known as Sweetheart Lane, the Shades, you caused or did cause to cause the death of six persons unknown—'

Vimes wondered how long the rubble would hold the creature down. Several weeks would be necessary, if the length of the charge sheet was anything to go by.

The crowd went silent. Even Sybil Ramkin was standing in astonishment.

'What's the matter?' said Vimes to the upturned faces. 'Haven't you ever seen a dragon being arrested before?'

'—Sixteen (Three) ii, on the night of 24th Grune last, you did flame or cause to flame those premises known as the Old Watch House, Ankh-Morpork, valued at two hundred dollars; AND THAT, Sixteen

(Three) iii, on the night of 24th Grune last, upon being apprehended by an officer of the Watch in the execution of his duty—'

'I think we should hurry up,' whispered Vimes. 'It's getting rather restive. Is all this necessary?'

'Well, I believe one can summarize,' said Carrot. 'In exceptional circumstances, according to Bregg's Rules for—'

'It may come as a surprise, but these *are* exceptional circumstances, Carrot,' said Vimes. 'And they're going to be really *astonishingly* exceptional if Colon doesn't hurry up with that rope.'

More rubble moved as the dragon strained to get up. There was a thump as a heavy beam was shouldered aside. The crowd began to run for it.

It was at this point that Errol came back over the rooftops in a series of minor explosions, leaving a trail of smoke rings. Dipping low, he buzzed the crowd and sent the front rank stumbling backwards.

He was also wailing like a foghorn.

Vimes grabbed Carrot and stumbled down the heap as the king started to scrabble desperately to get free.

'He's come back for the kill!' he shouted. 'It probably took him all this time just to slow down!'

Now Errol was hovering over the fallen dragon, and hooting shrilly enough to bust bottles.

The great dragon stuck its head up in a cascade of plaster dust. It opened its mouth but, instead of the lance of white fire that Vimes tensed himself to expect, it merely made a noise like a kitten.

Admittedly a kitten shouting into a tin bath at the bottom of a cave, but still a kitten.

Broken spars fell aside when the huge creature got unsteadily to its feet. The great wings opened, showering the surrounding streets with dust and bits of thatch. Some of it clanged off the helmet of Sergeant Colon, hurrying back with what looked like a small washing line coiled over his arm.

'You're letting it get up!' Vimes shouted, pushing the sergeant to safety. 'You're not supposed to let it get up, Errol! Don't let it get up!'

Lady Ramkin frowned. 'That's not right,' she said. 'They never usually fight like that. The winner usually kills the loser.'

'Right on!' shouted Nobby.

'And then half the time he explodes with the excitement in any case.'

'Look, it's *me*!' Vimes yelled, as Errol hovered unconcernedly over the scene. 'I bought you the fluffy ball! The one with the bell in it! You can't do this to us!'

'No, wait a minute,' said Lady Ramkin, laying a hand on his arm. 'I'm not sure we haven't got hold of the wrong end of the stick here—'

The great dragon leapt into the air and brought its wings down with a *whump* that flattened a few more buildings. The huge head swung around, the bleary eyes caught sight of Vimes.

There seemed to be some thought going on inside them.

Errol arced across the sky and hovered protectively in front of the captain, facing the thing down. For a moment it looked as though he might be turned into a small flying charcoal biscuit, and then the dragon lowered its gaze in a slightly embarrassed way and started to rise.

It climbed in a wide spiral, gathering speed as it did so. Errol went with it, orbiting the huge body like a tug around a liner.

'It's – it's as though he's *fussing* over it,' said Vimes.

'Add up the bastard!' shouted Nobby enthusiastically.

'Total, Nobby,' said Colon. 'You mean "total".'

Vimes felt Lady Ramkin's gaze on the back of his neck. He looked at her expression.

Realization dawned. 'Oh,' he said.

Lady Ramkin nodded.

'Really?' said Vimes.

'Yes,' she said. 'I really ought to have thought of it before. It was such a hot flame, of course. And they're always so much more territorial than the males.'

'Why don't you fight the bastard!' shouted Nobby, at the dwindling dragons.

'Bitch, Nobby,' said Vimes quietly. 'Not bastard. Bitch.'

'Why don't you fi – what?'

'It's a member of the female gender,' explained Lady Ramkin.

'What?'

'We meant that if you tried your favourite kick, Nobby, it wouldn't work,' said Vimes.

'It's a *girl*,' translated Lady Ramkin.

'But it's sodding *enormous*!' said Nobby.

Vimes coughed urgently. Nobby's rodent eyes slid sideways to Sybil Ramkin, who blushed like a sunset.

'A fine figure of a dragon, I mean,' he said quickly.

'Er. Wide, egg-bearing hips,' said Sergeant Colon anxiously.

'Statueskew,' Nobby added fervently.

'Shut up,' said Vimes. He brushed the dust off the remains of his uniform, adjusted the hang of his breastplate, and set his helmet on squarely. He patted it firmly. This wasn't where it ended, he knew that. This was where it all got started.

'You men come with me. Come on, hurry! While everyone's still watching them,' he added.

'But what about the king?' said Carrot. 'Or queen? Or whatever it is now?'

Vimes stared at the rapidly shrinking shapes. 'I really don't know,' he said. 'That's up to Errol, I suppose. We've got other things to do.'

Colon saluted, still fighting for breath. 'Where we going, sir?' he managed.

'To the palace. Any of you still got a sword?'

'You can use mine, Captain,' said Carrot. He handed it over.

'Right,' said Vimes quietly. He glared at them. 'Let's go.'

The rank trailed behind Vimes through the stricken streets.

He started to walk faster. The rank started to trot to keep up.

Vimes began to trot to keep ahead.

The rank broke into a canter.

Then, as if on an unspoken word of command, they broke into a run. Then into a gallop.

People scurried away as they rattled past. Carrot's enormous sandals hammered on the cobbles. Sparks flew up from the scads of Nobby's boots. Colon ran quietly for such a fat man, as fat men often do, face locked in a scowl of concentration.

They pounded along the Street of Cunning Artificers, turned into Hogsback Alley, emerged into the Street of Small Gods and thundered towards the palace. Vimes kept barely in the lead, mind currently empty of everything except the need to run and run.

At least, nearly everything. But his head buzzed and resonated manically with those of all city guards everywhere, all the pavement-pounding meatheads in the multiverse who had ever, just occasionally, tried to do what was Right.

Far ahead of them a handful of palace guards drew their swords, took a second look, thought better of it, darted back inside the wall and started to close the gates. They clanged together as Vimes arrived.

He hesitated, panting for breath, and looked at the massive things. The ones that the dragon had burned had been replaced by gates even more forbidding. From behind them came the sound of bolts sliding back.

This was no time for half measures. He was a captain, godsdammit. An officer. Things like this didn't present a problem for an officer. Officers had

393

a tried and tested way of solving problems like this. It was called a sergeant.

'Sergeant Colon!' he snapped, his mind still buzzing with universal policemanhood, 'shoot the lock off!'

The sergeant hesitated. 'What, sir? With a bow and arrow, sir?'

'I mean—' Vimes hesitated. 'I mean, open these gates!'

'Sir!' Colon saluted. He glared at the gates for a moment. 'Right!' he barked. 'Lance-constable Carrot, one stepa forwarda, *take*! Lance-constable Carrot, inna youra owna timer! Open these gatesa!'

'Yes, sir!'

Carrot stepped forward, saluted, folded an enormous hand into a fist and rapped gently on the woodwork.

'Open up,' he said, 'in the name of the Law!'

There was some whispering on the other side of the gates, and eventually a small hatch halfway up the door slid open a fraction and a voice said, 'Why?'

'Because if you don't it will be Impeding an Officer of the Watch in the Execution of his Duty, which is punishable by a fine of not less than thirty dollars, one month's imprisonment, or being remanded in custody for social enquiry reports and half an hour with a red-hot poker,' said Carrot.

There was some more muffled whispering, the sound of bolts being drawn, and then the gates opened about halfway.

There was no-one visible on the other side.

Vimes put a finger to his lips. He motioned

Carrot towards one gate and dragged Nobby and Colon to the other.

'Push,' he whispered. They pushed, hard. There was a sudden eruption of pained cursing from behind the woodwork.

'Run!' shouted Colon.

'No!' shouted Vimes. He walked around the gate. Four semi-crushed palace guards glowered at him.

'No,' he said. 'No more running. I want these men arrested.'

'You wouldn't dare,' said one of the men. Vimes peered at him.

'Clarence, isn't it?' he said. 'With a C. Well, Clarence with a C, watch my lips. Either you can be charged with Aiding and Abetting or—' he leaned closer, and glanced meaningfully at Carrot – 'with an axe.'

'Swivel on that one, doggybag!' added Nobby, jumping from one foot to the other in vicious excitement.

Clarence's little piggy eyes glared at the looming bulk that was Carrot, and then at Vimes's face. There was absolutely no mercy there. He appeared to reach a reluctant decision.

'Jolly good,' said Vimes. 'Lock them in the gatehouse, Sergeant.'

Colon drew his bow and squared his shoulders. 'You heard the Man,' he rasped. 'One false move and you're . . . you're—' He took a desperate stab at it – 'you're Home Economics!'

'Yeah! Slam 'em up in the banger!' shouted

Nobby. If worms could turn, Nobby was revolving at generating speeds. 'Doucheballs!' he sneered, at their retreating backs.

'Aiding and Abetting what, Captain?' said Carrot, as the weaponless guards trooped away. 'You have to aid and abet something.'

'I think in this case it will just be generalized abetting,' said Vimes. 'Persistent and reckless abetment.'

'Yeah,' said Nobby. 'Can't stand abettors. Slime-breaths!'

Colon handed Captain Vimes the guardhouse key. 'It's not very secure in there, Captain,' he said. 'They'll be able to break out eventually.'

'I hope so,' said Vimes, 'because the very first drain we come to, you're going to drop the key down it. Everyone here? Right. Follow me.'

Lupine Wonse scurried along the ruined corridors of the palace, *The Summoning of Dragons* under one arm, the glittering royal sword grasped uncertainly in one hand.

He halted, panting, in a doorway.

Not a lot of his mind was currently in a state sane enough to have proper thoughts, but the small part that was still in business kept insisting that it couldn't have seen what it had seen or heard what it had heard.

Someone was following him.

And he'd seen Vetinari walking through the palace. He *knew* the man was securely put away. The lock was completely unpickable. He remembered the Patrician being absolutely insistent that it be an unpickable lock when it was installed.

There was movement in the shadows at the end of the passage. Wonse gibbered a bit, fumbled with the doorhandle beside him, darted in, slammed the door and leaned against it, fighting for breath.

He opened his eyes.

He was in the old private audience room. The Patrician was sitting in his old seat, one leg crossed on the other, watching him with mild interest.

'Ah, Wonse,' he said.

Wonse jumped, scrabbled at the doorhandle, leapt into the corridor and ran for it until he reached the main staircase, rising now through the ruins of the central palace like a forlorn corkscrew. Stairs – height – high ground – defence. He ran up them three at a time.

All he needed was a few minutes of peace. *Then* he'd show them.

The upper floors were more full of shadows. What they were short on was structural strength. Pillars and walls had been torn out by the dragon as it built its cave. Rooms gaped pathetically on the edge of the abyss. Dangling shreds of wall-hanging and carpet flapped in the wind from the smashed windows. The floor sprang and wobbled like a trampoline as Wonse scurried across it. He struggled to the nearest door.

'That was commendably fast,' said the Patrician.

Wonse slammed the door in his face and ran, squeaking, down a corridor.

Sanity took a brief hold. He paused by a statue.

There was no sound, no hurrying footsteps, no whirr of hidden doors. He gave the statue a suspicious look and prodded it with the sword.

When it failed to move he opened the nearest door and slammed it behind him, found a chair and wedged it under the handle. This was one of the upper state rooms, bare now of most of its furnishings, and lacking its fourth wall. Where it should have been was just the gulf of the cavern.

The Patrician stepped out of the shadows.

'Now you have got it out of your system—' he said.

Wonse spun around, sword raised.

'You don't really exist,' he said. 'You're a – a ghost, or something.'

'I believe this is not the case,' said the Patrician.

'You can't stop me! I've got some magic stuff left, I've got the book!' Wonse took a brown leather bag out of his pocket. 'I'll bring back another one! You'll see!'

'I urge you not to,' said Lord Vetinari mildly.

'Oh, you think you're so clever, so in-control, so *swave*, just because I've got a sword and you haven't! Well, I've got more than that, I'll have you know,' said Wonse triumphantly. 'Yes! I've got the palace guards on my side! They follow me, not you! No-one likes you, you know. No-one *ever* liked you.'

He swung the sword so that its needle point was a foot from the Patrician's thin chest.

'So it's back to the cells for you,' he said. 'And this time I'll make *sure* you stay there. Guards! Guards!'

There was a clatter of running feet outside. The door rattled, the chair shook. There was a moment's silence, and then door and chair erupted in splinters.

'Take him away!' screamed Wonse. 'Fetch more scorpions! Put him in . . . *you're not the*—'

'Put the sword down,' said Vimes, while behind him Carrot picked bits of door out of his fist.

'Yeah,' said Nobby, peering around the captain. 'Up against the wall and spread 'em, motherbreath!'

'Eh? What's he supposed to spread?' whispered Sergeant Colon anxiously.

Nobby shrugged. 'Dunno,' he said. 'Everything, I reckon. Safest way.'

Wonse stared at the rank in disbelief.

'Ah, Vimes,' said the Patrician. 'You will—'

'Shut up,' said Vimes calmly. 'Lance-constable Carrot?'

'Sir!'

'Read the prisoner his rights.'

'Yes, sir.' Carrot produced his notebook, licked his thumb, flicked through the pages.

'Lupine Wonse,' he said, 'AKA Lupin Squiggle Sec'y pp—'

'Wha?' said Wonse.

'—currently domiciled in the domicile known as The Palace, Ankh-Morpork, it is my duty to inform you that you have been arrested and will be charged with—' Carrot gave Vimes an agonized look – 'a number of offences of murder by means of a blunt instrument, to whit, a dragon, and many further offences of generalized abetting, to be more specifically ascertained later. You have the right to remain silent. You have the right not to be summarily thrown into a piranha tank. You have the right to trial by ordeal. You have the—'

'This is madness,' said the Patrician calmly.

'I thought I told you to shut up!' snapped Vimes, spinning around and shaking a finger under the Patrician's nose.

'Tell me, Sarge,' whispered Nobby, 'do you think we're going to *like* it in the scorpion pit?'

'—say anything, er, but anything you do say will be written down, er, here, in my notebook, and, er, may be used in evidence—'

Carrot's voice trailed into silence.

'Well, if this pantomime gives you any pleasure, Vimes,' said the Patrician eventually, 'take him down to the cells. I'll deal with him in the morning.'

Wonse made no signal. There was no scream or cry. He just rushed at the Patrician, sword raised.

Options flickered across Vimes's mind. In the lead came the suggestion that standing back would be a good plan, let Wonse do it, disarm him afterwards, let the city clean itself up. Yes. A good plan.

And it was therefore a total mystery to him why he chose to dart forward, bringing Carrot's sword up in a half-baked attempt at blocking the stroke . . .

Perhaps it was something to do with doing it by the book.

There was a clang. Not a particularly loud one. He felt something bright and silver whirr past his ear and strike the wall.

Wonse's mouth fell open. He dropped the

remnant of his sword and backed away, clutching *The Summoning*.

'You'll be sorry,' he hissed. 'You'll all be *very sorry*!'

He started to mumble under his breath.

Vimes felt himself trembling. He was pretty certain he knew what had zinged past his head, and the mere thought was making his hands sweat. He'd come to the palace ready to kill and there'd been this *minute,* just this *minute,* when for once the world had seemed to be operating properly and he was in charge of it and now, now all he wanted was a drink. And a nice week's sleep.

'Oh, give *up*!' he said. 'Are you going to come quietly?'

The mumbling went on. The air began to feel hot and dry.

Vimes shrugged. 'That's it, then,' he said, and turned away. 'Throw the book at him, Carrot.'

'Right, sir.'

Vimes remembered too late.

Dwarfs have trouble with metaphors.

They also have a very good aim.

The Laws and Ordinances of Ankh and Morpork caught the secretary on the forehead. He blinked, staggered, and stepped backwards.

It was the longest step he ever took. For one thing, it lasted the rest of his life.

After several seconds they heard him hit, five storeys below.

After several more seconds their faces appeared over the edge of the ravaged floor.

'What a way to go,' said Sergeant Colon.

'That's a fact,' said Nobby, reaching up to his ear for a dog-end.

'Killed by a wossname. A metaphor.'

'Dunno,' said Nobby. 'Looks like the ground to me. Got a light, Sarge?'

'That was right, wasn't it, sir?' said Carrot anxiously. 'You said to—'

'Yes, yes,' said Vimes. 'Don't worry.' He reached down with a shaking hand, picked up the bag Wonse had been holding, and tipped out a pile of stones. Every one had a hole in it. Why? he thought.

A metallic noise behind him made him look around. The Patrician was holding the remains of the royal sword. As the captain watched, the man wrenched the other half of the sword out of the far wall. It was a clean break.

'Captain Vimes,' he said.

'Sir?'

'That sword, if you please?'

Vimes handed it over. He couldn't, right now, think of anything else to do. He was probably due for a scorpion pit of his very own as it was.

Lord Vetinari examined the rusty blade carefully.

'How long have you had this, Captain?' he said mildly.

'Isn't mine, sir. Belongs to Lance-constable Carrot, sir.'

'Lance—?'

'Me, sir, your graciousness,' said Carrot, saluting.

'Ah.'

The Patrician turned the blade over and over

slowly, staring at it as if fascinated. Vimes felt the air thicken, as though history was clustering around this point, but for the life of him he couldn't think why. This was one of those points where the Trousers of Time bifurcated themselves, and if you weren't careful you'd go down the wrong leg—

Wonse arose in a world of shades, icy confusion pouring into his mind. But all he could think of at the moment was the tall cowled figure standing over him.

'I thought you were all dead,' he mumbled. It was strangely quiet and the colours around him seemed washed-out, muted. Something was very wrong. 'Is that you, Brother Doorkeeper?' he ventured.

The figure reached out.

METAPHORICALLY, it said.

—and the Patrician handed the sword to Carrot.

'Very well done, young man,' he said. 'Captain Vimes, I suggest you give your men the rest of the day off.'

'Thank you, sir,' said Vimes. 'OK, lads. You heard his lordship.'

'But not you, Captain. We must have a little talk.'

'Yes, sir?' said Vimes innocently.

The rank scurried out, giving Vimes sympathetic and sorrowful glances.

The Patrician walked to the edge of the floor and looked down.

'Poor Wonse,' he said.

'Yes, sir.' Vimes stared at the wall.

'I would have preferred him alive, you know.'

'Sir?'

'Misguided, yes, but a useful man. His head could have been of further use to me.'

'Yes, sir.'

'The rest, of course, we could have thrown away.'

'Yes, sir.'

'That was a joke, Vimes.'

'Yes, sir.'

'The chap never grasped the idea of secret passages, mind you.'

'No, sir.'

'That young fellow. Carrot, you called him?'

'Yes, sir.'

'Keen fellow. Likes it in the Watch?'

'Yes, sir. Right at home, sir.'

'You saved my life.'

'Sir?'

'Come with me.'

He stalked away through the ruined palace, Vimes trailing behind, until he reached the Oblong Office. It was quite tidy. It had escaped most of the devastation with nothing more than a layer of dust. The Patrician sat down, and suddenly it was as if he'd never left. Vimes wondered if he ever had.

He picked up a sheaf of papers and brushed the plaster off them.

'Sad,' he said. 'Lupine was such a tidy-minded man.'

'Yes, sir.'

The Patrician steepled his hands and looked at Vimes over the top of them.

'Let me give you some advice, Captain,' he said.

'Yes, sir?'

'It may help you make some sense of the world.'

'Sir.'

'I believe you find life such a problem because you think there are the good people and the bad people,' said the man. 'You're wrong, of course. There are, always and only, the bad people, *but some of them are on opposite sides.*'

He waved his thin hand towards the city and walked over to the window.

'A great rolling sea of evil,' he said, almost proprietorially. 'Shallower in some places, of course, but deeper, oh, so much *deeper* in others. But people like you put together little rafts of rules and vaguely good intentions and say, this is the opposite, this will triumph in the end. Amazing!' He slapped Vimes good-naturedly on the back.

'Down there,' he said, 'are people who will follow any dragon, worship any god, ignore any iniquity. All out of a kind of humdrum, everyday badness. Not the really high, creative loathesomeness of the great sinners, but a sort of mass-produced darkness of the soul. Sin, you might say, without a trace of originality. They accept evil not because they say *yes*, but because they don't say *no*. I'm sorry if this offends you,' he added, patting the captain's shoulder, 'but you fellows really need us.'

'Yes, sir?' said Vimes quietly.

'Oh, yes. We're the only ones who know how to make things work. You see, the only thing the good people are good at is overthrowing the bad people.

And you're *good* at that, I'll grant you. But the trouble is that it's the *only* thing you're good at. One day it's the ringing of the bells and the casting down of the evil tyrant, and the next it's everyone sitting around complaining that ever since the tyrant was overthrown no-one's been taking out the trash. Because the bad people know how to *plan*. It's part of the specification, you might say. Every evil tyrant has a plan to rule the world. The good people don't seem to have the knack.'

'Maybe. But you're wrong about the rest!' said Vimes. 'It's just because people are afraid, and alone—' He paused. It sounded pretty hollow, even to him.

He shrugged. 'They're just people,' he said. 'They're just doing what people do. Sir.'

Lord Vetinari gave him a friendly smile.

'Of course, of course,' he said. 'You have to believe that, I appreciate. Otherwise you'd go quite mad. Otherwise you'd think you're standing on a feather-thin bridge over the vaults of Hell. Otherwise existence would be a dark agony and the only hope would be that there is no life after death. I quite understand.' He looked at his desk, and sighed. 'And now,' he said, 'there is such a lot to do. I'm afraid poor Wonse was a good servant but an inefficient master. So you may go. Have a good night's sleep. Oh, and do bring your men in tomorrow. The city must show its gratitude.'

'It must *what*?' said Vimes.

The Patrician looked at a scroll. Already his voice was back to the distant tones of one who organizes and plans and controls.

'Its gratitude,' he said. 'After every triumphant victory there must be heroes. It is essential. Then everyone will know that everything has been done properly.'

He glanced at Vimes over the top of the scroll.

'It's all part of the natural order of things,' he said.

After a while he made a few pencil annotations to the paper in front of him and looked up.

'I said,' he said, 'that you may go.'

Vimes paused at the door.

'Do you believe all that, sir?' he said. 'About the endless evil and the sheer blackness?'

'Indeed, indeed,' said the Patrician, turning over the page. 'It is the only logical conclusion.'

'But you get out of bed every morning, sir?'

'Hmm? Yes? What is your point?'

'I'd just like to know *why*, sir.'

'Oh, do go away, Vimes. There's a good fellow.'

In the dark and draughty cave hacked from the heart of the palace the Librarian knuckled across the floor. He clambered over the remains of the sad hoard and looked down at the splayed body of Wonse.

Then he reached down, very gently, and prised *The Summoning of Dragons* from the stiffening fingers. He blew the dust off it. He brushed it tenderly, as if it was a frightened child.

He turned to climb down the heap, and stopped. He bent down again, and carefully pulled another book from among the glittering rubble. It wasn't one of his, except in the wide sense that all books came under his domain. He turned a few pages carefully.

'Keep it,' said Vimes behind him. 'Take it away. Put it somewhere.'

The orangutan nodded at the captain, and rattled down the heap. He tapped Vimes gently on the kneecap, opened *The Summoning of Dragons*, leafed through its ravaged pages until he found the one he'd been looking for, and silently passed the book up.

Vimes squinted at the crabbed writing.

Yet draggons are notte liken unicornes, I willen. They dwellyth in some Realm definèd bye thee Fancie of the Wille and, thus, it myte bee thate whomsover calleth upon them, and giveth them theyre patheway unto thys worlde, calleth theyre Owne dragon of the Mind.

Yette, I trow, the Pure in Harte maye stille call a Draggon of Power as a Forse for Goode in thee worlde, and this ane nighte the Grate Worke will commense. All hathe been prepared. I hath laboured most mytily to be a Worthie Vessle ...

A realm of fancy, Vimes thought. That's where they went, then. Into our imaginations. And when we call them back we shape them, like squeezing dough into pastry shapes. Only you don't get gingerbread men, you get what you are. Your own darkness, given shape ...

Vimes read it through again, and then looked at the following pages.

There weren't many. The rest of the book was a charred mass.

Vimes handed it back to the ape.

'What kind of a man was de Malachite?' he said.

The Librarian gave this the consideration due from someone who knew the *Dictionary of City Biography* by heart. Then he shrugged.

'Particularly holy?' said Vimes.

The ape shook his head.

'Well, noticeably evil, then?'

The ape shrugged, and shook his head again.

'If I were you,' said Vimes, 'I'd put that book somewhere very safe. And the book of the Law with it. They're too bloody dangerous.'

'Oook.'

Vimes stretched. 'And now,' he said, 'let's go and have a drink.'

'Oook.'

'But just a small one.'

'Oook.'

'And you're paying.'

'Eeek.'

Vimes stopped and stared down at the big, mild face.

'Tell me,' he said. 'I've always wanted to know . . . is it *better*, being an ape?'

The Librarian thought about it. 'Oook,' he said.

'Oh. Really?' said Vimes.

It was next day. The room was wall-to-wall with civic dignitaries. The Patrician sat on his severe chair, surrounded by the Council. Everyone present was wearing the shiny waxen grins of those bent on good works.

Lady Sybil Ramkin sat off to one side, wearing a few acres of black velvet. The Ramkin family jewels glittered on her fingers, neck and in the black curls of today's wig. The total effect was striking, like a globe of the heavens.

Vimes marched the rank to the centre of the hall and stamped to a halt with his helmet under his arm, as per regulations. He'd been amazed to see that even Nobby had made an effort – the suspicion of shiny metal could be seen here and there on his breastplate. And Colon was wearing an expression of almost constipated importance. Carrot's armour gleamed.

Colon ripped off a textbook salute for the first time in his life.

'All present and correct, sah!' he barked.

'Very good, Sergeant,' said Vimes coldly. He turned to the Patrician and raised an eyebrow politely.

Lord Vetinari gave a little wave of his hand.

'Stand easy, or whatever it is you chaps do,' he said. 'I'm sure we needn't wait on ceremony here. What do you say, Captain?'

'Just as you like, sir,' said Vimes.

'Now, men,' said the Patrician, leaning forward, 'we have heard some remarkable accounts of your magnificent efforts in defence of the city . . .'

Vimes let his mind wander as the golden platitudes floated past. For a while he derived a certain amount of amusement from watching the faces of the Council. A whole sequence of expressions drifted across them as the Patrician spoke. It was, of course, vitally important that there be a ceremony like this. Then the whole thing could be neat and *settled*. And forgotten. Just another chapter in the long and exciting history of eckcetra, eckcetra. Ankh-Morpork was good at starting new chapters.

His trawling gaze fell on Lady Ramkin. She winked. Vimes's eyes swivelled front again, his expression suddenly as wooden as a plank.

'. . . token of our gratitude,' the Patrician finished, sitting back.

Vimes realized that everyone was looking at him.

'Pardon?' he said.

'I *said*, we have been trying to think of some suitable recompense, Captain Vimes. Various public-spirited citizens—' the Patrician's eyes took in the Council and Lady Ramkin – 'and, of course, myself, feel that an appropriate reward is due.'

Vimes still looked blank.

'Reward?' he said.

'It *is* customary for such heroic endeavour,' said the Patrician, a little testily.

Vimes faced forward again. 'Really haven't thought about it, sir,' he said. 'Can't speak for the men, of course.'

There was an awkward pause. Out of the corner of his eye Vimes was aware of Nobby nudging the sergeant in the ribs. Eventually Colon stumbled forward and ripped off another salute. 'Permission to speak, sir,' he muttered.

The Patrician nodded graciously.

The sergeant coughed. He removed his helmet and pulled out a scrap of paper.

'Er,' he said. 'The thing is, saving your honour's presence, we think, you know, what with saving the city and everything, or sort of, or, what I mean is . . . we just had a go, you see, man on the spot and that sort of thing . . . the thing is, we reckon we're entitled. If you catch my drift.'

The assembled company nodded. This was exactly how it should be.

'Do go on,' said the Patrician.

'So we, like, put our heads together,' said the sergeant. 'A bit of a cheek, I know . . .'

'Please carry *on*, Sergeant,' said the Patrician. 'You needn't keep stopping. We are well aware of the *magnitude* of the matter.'

'Right, sir. Well, sir. First, it's the wages.'

'The wages?' said Lord Vetinari. He stared at Vimes, who stared at nothing.

The sergeant raised his head. His expression was the determined expression of a man who is going to see it through.

'Yes, sir,' he said. 'Thirty dollars a month. It's not right. We think—' he licked his lips and glanced behind him at the other two, who were making vague encouraging motions – 'we think a basic rate of, er, thirty-five dollars? A month?' He stared at the Patrician's stony expression. 'With increments as per rank? We thought five dollars.'

He licked his lips again, unnerved by the Patrician's expression. 'We won't go below four,' he said. 'And that's flat. Sorry, your Highness, but there it is.'

The Patrician glanced again at Vimes's impassive face, then looked back at the rank.

'That's *it*?' he said.

Nobby whispered in Colon's ear and then darted back. The sweating sergeant gripped his helmet as though it was the only real thing in the world.

'There was another thing, your reverence,' he said.

'Ah.' The Patrician smiled knowingly.

'There's the kettle. It wasn't much good anyway, and then Errol et it. It was nearly two dollars.' He swallowed. 'We could do with a new kettle, if it's all the same, your lordship.'

The Patrician leaned forward, gripping the arms of his chair.

'I want to be clear about this,' he said coldly. 'Are we to believe that you are asking for a petty wage increase and a domestic utensil?'

Carrot whispered in Colon's other ear.

Colon turned two bulging, watery-rimmed eyes to the dignitaries. The rim of his helmet was passing through his fingers like a millwheel.

'Well,' he began, 'sometimes, we thought, you know, when we has our dinner break, or when it's quiet, like, at the end of a watch as it may be, and we want to relax a bit, you know, wind down . . .' His voice trailed away.

'Yes?'

Colon took a deep breath.

'I suppose a dartboard would be out of the question—?'

The thunderous silence that followed was broken by an erratic snorting.

Vimes's helmet dropped out of his shaking

hand. His breastplate wobbled as the suppressed laughter of the years burst out in great uncontrollable eruptions. He turned his face to the row of councillors and laughed and laughed until the tears came.

Laughed at the way they got up, all confusion and outraged dignity.

Laughed at the Patrician's carefully immobile expression.

Laughed for the world and the saving of souls.

Laughed and laughed, and laughed until the tears came.

Nobby craned up to reach Colon's ear.

'I *told* you,' he hissed. 'I *said* they'd never wear it. I *knew* a dartboard'd be pushing our luck. You've upset 'em all now.'

Dear Mother and Father [wrote Carrot] You will never guess, I have been in the Watch only a few weeks and, already I am to be a full Constable. Captain Vimes said, the Patrician himself said I was to be One, and that also he hoped I should have a long and successful career in the Watch as well and, he would follow it with special interest. Also my wages are to go up by ten dollars and we had a special bonus of twenty dollars that Captain Vimes paid out of his own pocket, Sgt Colon said. Please find money enclosed. I am keeping a little bit by though because I went to see Reet and Mrs Palm said all the girls had been following my career with Great Interest as well and I am to come to dinner on my night off. Sgt Colon has been telling me about how to start courting, which is very interesting and not at all complicated it appears. I arrested a dragon but it got away. I hope Mr Varneshi is well.

I am as happy as anyone can be in the whole world.

Your son, Carrot.

Vimes knocked on the door.

An effort had been made to spruce up the Ramkin mansion, he noticed. The encroaching shrubbery had been pitilessly hacked back. An elderly workman atop a ladder was nailing the stucco back on the walls while another, with a spade, was rather arbitrarily defining the line where the lawn ended and the old flower beds had begun.

Vimes stuck his helmet under his arm, smoothed back his hair, and knocked. He'd considered asking Sergeant Colon to accompany him, but had brushed the idea aside quickly. He couldn't have tolerated the sniggering. Anyway, what was there to be afraid of? He'd stared into the jaws of death three times; four, if you included telling Lord Vetinari to shut up.

To his amazement the door was eventually opened by a butler so elderly that he might have been resurrected by the knocking.

'Yerss?' he said.

'Captain Vimes, City Watch,' said Vimes.

The man looked him up and down.

'Oh, yes,' he said. 'Her ladyship did say. I believe her ladyship is with her dragons,' he said. 'If you like to wait in 'ere, I will—'

'I know the way,' said Vimes, and set off around the overgrown path.

The kennels were a ruin. An assortment of battered wooden boxes were lying around under an oilcloth awning. From their depths a few sad swamp dragons whiffled a greeting at him.

A couple of women were moving purposefully among the boxes. Ladies, rather. They were far too untidy to be mere women. No ordinary women would have dreamed of looking so scruffy; you needed the complete self-confidence that comes with knowing who your great-great-great-great-grandfather was before you could wear clothes like that. But they were, Vimes noticed, incredibly good clothes, or had been once; clothes bought by one's parents, but so expensive and of such good quality that they never wore out and were handed down, like old china and silverware and gout.

Dragon breeders, he thought. You can tell. There's something about them. It's the way they wear their silk scarves, old tweed coats and granddad's riding boots. And the smell, of course.

A small wiry woman with a face like old saddle leather caught sight of him.

'Ah,' she said, 'you'll be the gallant captain.' She tucked an errant strand of white hair back under a headscarf and extended a veiny brown hand. 'Brenda Rodley. That's Rosie Devant-Molei. She runs the Sunshine Sanctuary, you know.' The other woman, who had the build of someone who could pick up carthorses in one hand and shoe them with the other, gave him a friendly grin.

'Samuel Vimes,' said Vimes weakly.

'My father was a Sam,' said Brenda vaguely. 'You can always trust a Sam, he said.' She shooed a dragon back into its box. 'We're just helping Sybil. Old friends, you know. The collection's all to blazes, of course. They're all over the city, the little devils. I dare say they'll come back when they're hungry, though. What a bloodline, eh?'

'I'm sorry?'

'Sybil reckons he was a sport, but I say we should be able to breed back into the line in three or four generations. I'm famed for my stud, you know,' she said. 'That'd be something, though. A whole new type of dragon.'

Vimes thought of supersonic contrails crisscrossing the sky.

'Er,' he said. 'Yes.'

'Well, we must get on.'

'Er, isn't Lady Ramkin around?' said Vimes. 'I got this message that it was essential, she said, for me to come here.'

'She's indoors somewhere,' said Miss Rodley. 'Said she had something important to see to. Oh, do be careful with that one, Rose, you silly gel!'

'More important than *dragons*?' said Vimes.

'Yes. Can't think what's come over her.' Brenda Rodley fished in the pocket of an oversized waistcoat. 'Nice to have met you, Captain. Always good to meet new members of the Fancy. Do drop in any time you're passing, I'd be only too happy to show you around.' She extracted a grubby card and pressed it into his hand. 'Must be off now, we've heard that some of them are trying to build nests on the University tower. Can't have that. Must get 'em down before it gets dark.'

Vimes squinted at the card as the women crunched off down the drive, carrying nets and ropes.

It said: *Brenda, Lady Rodley. The Dower House, Quirm Castle, Quirm.* What it meant, he realized, was that striding away down the path like an animated rummage stall was the dowager Duchess of Quirm, who owned more country than you could see from a very high mountain on a very clear day. Nobby would not have approved. There seemed to be a special kind of poverty that only the very, very rich could possibly afford . . .

That was how you got to be a power in the land, he thought. You never cared a toss about whatever anyone else thought and you were never, ever, uncertain about anything.

He padded back to the house. A door was open. It led into a large but dark and musty hall. Up in the gloom the heads of dead animals haunted the walls. The Ramkins seemed to have endangered more species than an ice age.

Vimes wandered aimlessly through another mahogany archway.

It was a dining room, containing the kind of table where the people at the other end are in a different time zone. One end had been colonized by silver candlesticks.

It was laid for two. A battery of cutlery flanked each plate. Antique wineglasses sparkled in the candlelight.

A terrible premonition took hold of Vimes at the same moment as a gust of *Captivation*, the most expensive perfume available anywhere in Ankh-Morpork, blew past him.

'Ah, Captain. So nice of you to come.'

Vimes turned around slowly, without his feet appearing to move.

Lady Ramkin stood there, magnificently.

Vimes was vaguely aware of a brilliant blue dress that sparkled in the candlelight, a mass of hair the colour of chestnuts, a slightly anxious face that suggested that a whole battalion of skilled painters and decorators had only just dismantled their scaffolding and gone home, and a faint creaking that said underneath it all mere corsetry was being subjected to the kind of tensions more usually found in the heart of large stars.

'I, er,' he said. 'If you, er. If you'd said, er. I'd, er. Dress more suitable, er. Extremely, er. Very. Er.'

She bore down upon him like a glittering siege engine.

In a sort of dream he allowed himself to be ushered to a seat. He must have eaten, because servants appeared out of nowhere with things stuffed with other things, and came back later and took the plates away. The butler reanimated occasionally to fill glass after glass with strange wines. The heat from the candles was enough to cook by. And all the time Lady Ramkin talked in a bright and brittle way – about the size of the house, the responsibilities of a huge estate, the feeling that it was time to take One's Position in Society More Seriously, while the setting sun filled the room with red and Vimes's head began to spin.

Society, he managed to think, didn't know what was going to hit it. Dragons weren't mentioned once, although after a while something under the table put its head on Vimes's knee and dribbled.

Vimes found it impossible to contribute to the conversation. He felt outflanked, beleaguered. He made one sally, hoping maybe to reach high ground from which to flee into exile.

'Where do you think they've gone?' he said.

'Where what?' said Lady Ramkin, temporarily halted.

'The dragons. You know. Errol and his wi – female.'

'Oh, somewhere isolated and rocky, I should imagine,' said Lady Ramkin. 'Favourite country for dragons.'

'But it – *she's* a magical animal,' said Vimes. 'What'll happen when the magic goes away?'

Lady Ramkin gave him a shy smile.

'Most people seem to manage,' she said.

She reached across the table and touched his hand.

'Your men think you need looking after,' she said meekly.

'Oh. Do they?' said Vimes.

'Sergeant Colon said he thought we'd get along like a *maison en Flambé*.'

'Oh. Did he?'

'And he said something else,' she said. 'What was it, now? Oh, yes: "It's a million-to-one chance",' said

Lady Ramkin, 'I think he said, "but it might just work".'

She smiled at him.

And then it arose and struck Vimes that, in her own special category, she was quite beautiful; this was the category of all the women, in his entire life, who had ever thought he was worth smiling at. She couldn't do worse, but then, he couldn't do better. So maybe it balanced out. She wasn't getting any younger but then, who was? And she had style and money and common-sense and self-assurance and all the things that he didn't, and she had opened her heart, and if you let her she could engulf you; the woman was a city.

And eventually, under siege, you did what Ankh-Morpork had always done – unbar the gates, let the conquerors in, and make them your own.

How did you start? She seemed to be expecting something.

He shrugged, and picked up his wineglass and sought for a phrase. One crept into his wildly resonating mind.

'Here's looking at you, kid,' he said.

The gongs of various midnights banged out the old day.

(. . . and further towards the Hub, where the Ramtop Mountains joined the forbidding spires of the central massif, where strange hairy creatures roamed the eternal snows, where blizzards howled around the freezing peaks, the lights of a lone lamasery shone out over the high valleys. In the courtyard a couple of yellow-robed monks stacked the last case of small green bottles on to a sleigh, ready for the first leg of the incredibly difficult journey down to the distant plains. The box was labelled, in careful brush-strokes, 'Mstr. C.M.O.T. Dibbler, Ankh-Morpork'.

'You know, Lobsang,' said one of them, 'one cannot help wondering what it is he does with this stuff.')

Corporal Nobbs and Sergeant Colon lounged in the shadows near the Mended Drum, but straightened up as Carrot came out bearing a tray. Detritus the troll stepped aside respectfully.

'Here we are, lads,' said Carrot. 'Three pints. On the house.'

'Bloody hell, I never thought you'd do it,' said Colon, grasping a handle. 'What did you say to him?'

'I just explained how it was the duty of all good citizens to help the guard at all times,' said Carrot innocently, 'and I thanked him for his co-operation.'

'Yeah, and the rest,' said Nobby.

'No, that was all I said.'

'Then you must have a really convincing tone of voice.'

'Ah. Well, make the most of it, lads, while it lasts,' said Colon.

They drank thoughtfully. It was a moment of supreme peace, a few minutes snatched from the realities of real life. It was a brief bite of stolen fruit and enjoyed as such. No-one in the whole city seemed to be fighting or stabbing or making affray and, just for now, it was possible to believe that this wonderful state of affairs might continue.

And even if it didn't, then there were memories to get them through. Of running, and people getting out of the way. Of the looks on the faces of the horrible palace guard. Of, when all the thieves and heroes and gods had failed, of *being there*. Of nearly doing things nearly right.

Nobby shoved the pot on a convenient window sill, stamped some life back into his feet and blew on his fingers. A brief fumble in the dark recesses of his ear produced a fragment of cigarette.

'What a time, eh?' said Colon contentedly, as the flare of a match illuminated the three of them.

The others nodded. Yesterday seemed like a lifetime ago, even now. But you could never forget something like that, no matter who else did, no matter what happened from now on.

'If I never see any bloody king it'll be too soon,' said Nobby.

'I don't reckon he was the right king, anyway,' said Carrot. 'Talking of kings: anyone want a crisp?'

'There's no right kings,' said Colon, but without much rancour. Ten dollars a month was going to make a big difference. Mrs Colon was acting very differently towards a man bringing home another ten dollars a month. Her notes on the kitchen table were a lot more friendly.

'No, but I mean, there's nothing special about having an ancient sword,' said Carrot. 'Or a birthmark. I mean, look at me. I've got a birthmark on my arm.'

'My brother's got one, too,' said Colon. 'Shaped like a boat.'

'Mine's more like a crown thing,' said Carrot.

'Oho, that makes you a king, then,' grinned Nobby. 'Stands to reason.'

'I don't see why. My brother's not an admiral,' said Colon reasonably.

'And I've got this sword,' said Carrot.

He drew it. Colon took it from his hand, and turned it over and over in the light from the flare over the Drum's door. The blade was dull and short, and notched like a saw. It was well-made and there might have been an inscription on it once, but it had long ago been worn into indecipherability by sheer use.

'It's a nice sword,' he said thoughtfully. 'Well-balanced.'

'But not one for a king,' said Carrot. 'Kings' swords are big and shiny and magical and have jewels on and when you hold them up they catch the light, *ting*.'

'*Ting*,' said Colon. 'Yes. I suppose they have to, really.'

'I'm just saying you can't go round giving people thrones just because of stuff like that,' said Carrot. 'That's what Captain Vimes said.'

'Nice job, mind,' said Nobby. 'Good hours, kinging.'

'Hmm?' Colon had momentarily been lost in a little world of speculation. Real kings had shiny swords, obviously. Except, except, except maybe your *real* king of, like, days of yore, he would have a sword that didn't sparkle one bit but was bloody efficient at cutting things. Just a thought.

'I say kinging's a good job,' Nobby repeated. 'Short hours.'

'Yeah. Yeah. But not long days,' said Colon. He gave Carrot a thoughtful look.

'Ah. There's that, of course.'

'Anyway, my father says being king's too much like hard work,' said Carrot. 'All the surveying and assaying and everything.' He drained his pint. 'It's not the kind of thing for the likes of us. Us—' he looked proudly – 'guards. You all right, Sergeant?'

'Hmm? What? Oh. Yes.' Colon shrugged. What about it, anyway? Maybe things turned out for the best. He finished the beer. 'Best be off,' he said. 'What time was it?'

'About twelve o'clock,' said Carrot.

'Anything else?'

Carrot gave it some thought. 'And all's well?' he said.

'Right. Just testing.'

'You know,' said Nobby, 'the way *you* say it, lad, you could almost believe it was true.'

Let the eye of attention pull back . . .

This is the Disc, world and mirror of worlds, borne through space on the back of four giant elephants who stand on the back of Great A'Tuin the Sky Turtle. Around the Rim of this world the ocean pours off endlessly into the night. At its Hub rises the ten-mile spike of the Cori Celesti, on whose glittering summit the gods play games with the fates of men . . .

. . . if you know what the rules are, and who are the players.

On the far edge of the Disc the sun was rising. The light of the morning began to flow across the patchwork of seas and continents, but it did so slowly, because light is tardy and slightly heavy in the presence of a magical field.

On the dark crescent, where the old light of sunset had barely drained from the deepest valleys, two specks, one big, one small, flew out of the shadow, skimmed low across the swells of the Rim ocean, and struck out determinedly over the totally unfathomable, star-dotted depths of space.

Perhaps the magic would last. Perhaps it wouldn't. But then, what does?

THE END

THE COLOUR OF MAGIC
Terry Pratchett

'One of the best and funniest
English authors alive'
Independent

*Twoflower was a tourist, the first ever seen on the
discworld. Tourist, Rincewind decided, meant idiot.*

SOMEWHERE on the frontier between thought and
reality exists the Discworld, a parallel time and place
which might sound and smell very much like our
own, but which looks completely different. It plays by
different rules. Certainly it refuses to succumb to the
quaint notion that universes are ruled by pure logic and
the harmony of numbers.

But just because the Disc is different doesn't mean
that some things don't stay the same. Its very existence
is about to be threatened by a strange new blight: the
arrival of the first tourist, upon whose survival rests the
peace and prosperity of the land. But if the person
charged with maintaining that survival in the face of
robbers, mercenaries and, well, Death, is a spectacularly
inept wizard, a little logic might turn out to be a very
good idea...

'Like Jonathan Swift, Pratchett uses his other
world to hold up a distorting mirror to our own,
and like Swift he is a satirist of enormous
talent...incredibly funny... compulsively readable'
The Times

'Pratchett is a comic genius'
Daily Express

0 385 608640

THE LIGHT FANTASTIC
Terry Pratchett

'A true original among contemporary writers'
The Times

'What shall we do?' said Twoflower.
'Panic?' said Rincewind hopefully. He always held that
panic was the best means of survival.

WHEN THE very fabric of time and space are about to be put through the wringer – in this instance by the imminent arrival of a very large and determinedly oncoming meteorite – circumstances require a very particular type of hero. Sadly what the situation does not need is a singularly inept wizard, still recovering from the trauma of falling off the edge of the world. Equally it does not need one well-meaning tourist and his luggage which has a mind of its own. Which is a shame because that's all there is…

'He is a satirist of enormous talent… Incredibly funny, compulsively readable'
The Times

'He would be amusing in any form and his spectacular inventiveness makes the Discworld series one of the perennial joys of modern fiction'
Daily Mail

'Pure fantastic delight'
Time Out

0 552 15259 5

EQUAL RITES
Terry Pratchett

'Persistently amusing, good-hearted and shrewd'
Sunday Times

They say that a little knowledge is a dangerous thing, but it is not one half so bad as a lot of ignorance.

THERE ARE some situations where the correct response is to display the sort of ignorance which happily and wilfully flies in the face of the facts. In this case, the birth of a baby girl, born a wizard – by mistake. Everybody knows that there's no such thing as a female wizard. But now it's gone and happened, there's nothing much anyone can do about it. Let the battle of the sexes begin...

'Pratchett keeps getting better and better...It's hard to think of any humorist writing in Britain today who can match him'
Time Out

'If you are unfamiliar with Pratchett's unique blend of philosophical badinage, you are on the threshold of a mind-expanding opportunity'
Financial Times

0 552 15260 9

TERRY PRATCHETT'S FAMOUS DISCWORLD® SERIES NOW AVAILABLE ON TAPE AND CD!

Twenty-nine titles in the now legendary Discworld® series
are available in Corgi audio.

'Pure fantastic delight'
Time Out

All tapes are abridged on two tapes lasting approximately three hours.

All CDs are abridged on 3 or 4 CDs lasting approximately three hours.

0552 14017 1	THE COLOUR OF MAGIC	£9.99 incl VAT
0552 15222 6	THE COLOUR OF MAGIC CD	£14.99 incl VAT
0552 14018 X	THE LIGHT FANTASTIC	£9.99 incl VAT
0552 15223 4	THE LIGHT FANTASTIC CD	£14.99 incl VAT
0552 14016 3	EQUAL RITES	£9.99 incl VAT
0552 15224 2	EQUAL RITES CD	£14.99 incl VAT
0552 14015 5	MORT	£9.99 incl VAT
0552 15225 0	MORT CD	£14.99 incl VAT
0552 14011 2	SOURCERY	£9.99 incl VAT
0552 15226 9	SOURCERY CD	£14.99 incl VAT
0552 14014 7	WYRD SISTERS	£9.99 incl VAT
0552 15227 7	WYRD SISTERS CD	£14.99 incl VAT
0552 14013 9	PYRAMIDS	£9.99 incl VAT
0552 15298 6	PYRAMIDS CD	£14.99 incl VAT
0552 14012 0	GUARDS! GUARDS!	£9.99 incl VAT
0552 15299 4	GUARDS! GUARDS! CD	£14.99 incl VAT
0552 14572 6	ERIC	£9.99 incl VAT
0552 14010 4	MOVING PICTURES	£9.99 incl VAT
0552 15300 1	MOVING PICTURES CD	£14.99 incl VAT
0552 14009 0	REAPER MAN	£9.99 incl VAT
0552 15301 X	REAPER MAN CD	£14.99 incl VAT
0552 14415 0	WITCHES ABROAD	£9.99 incl VAT
0552 15302 8	WITCHES ABROAD CD	£14.99 incl VAT
0552 14416 9	SMALL GODS	£9.99 incl VAT
0552 15303 6	SMALL GODS CD	£14.99 incl VAT
0552 14417 7	LORDS AND LADIES	£9.99 incl VAT
0552 14423 1	MEN AT ARMS	£9.99 incl VAT
0552 14424 X	SOUL MUSIC	£9.99 incl VAT
0552 14425 8	INTERESTING TIMES	£9.99 incl VAT
0552 14426 6	MASKERADE	£9.99 incl VAT
0552 14573 4	FEET OF CLAY	£9.99 incl VAT
0552 14574 2	HOGFATHER	£9.99 incl VAT
0552 14684 6	JINGO	£9.99 incl VAT
0552 14650 1	THE LAST CONTINENT	£9.99 incl VAT
0552 14653 6	CARPE JUGULUM	£9.99 incl VAT
0552 14720 6	THE FIFTH ELEPHANT	£9.99 incl VAT
0552 14793 1	THE TRUTH	£9.99 incl VAT
0552 60188 3	THIEF OF TIME	£9.99 incl VAT
0552 14898 9	NIGHT WATCH	£9.99 incl VAT
0552 15074 6	NIGHT WATCH CD	£14.99 incl VAT
0552 15161 0	MONSTROUS REGIMENT	£9.99 incl VAT
0552 14940 3	MONSTROUS REGIMENT CD	£14.99 incl VAT
0552 14942 X	GOING POSTAL	£9.99 incl VAT
0552 14228 5	GOING POSTAL CD	£14.99 incl VAT

All Transworld titles are available by post from:
Bookpost, P.O. Box 29, Douglas, Isle of Man IM99 1BQ.

Credit cards accepted.

Please telephone +44(0)1624 836000, fax +44(0)1624 837033,
Internet http://www.bookpost.co.uk or e-mail: bookshop@enterprise.net for details.

Free postage and packing in the UK.

Overseas customers allow £2 per book (paperbacks) and £3 per book (hardbacks).

A LIST OF OTHER TERRY PRATCHETT TITLES
AVAILABLE FROM CORGI BOOKS

The prices shown below were correct at the time of going to press. However,
Transworld Publishers reserve the right to show new retail prices on covers which
may differ from those previously advertised in the text or elsewhere.

All Transworld titles are available by post from:
Bookpost, P.O. Box 29, Douglas, Isle of Man IM99 1BQ.

Credit cards accepted.
Please telephone +44(0)1624 836000, fax +44(0)1624837033,
Internet http://www.bookpost.co.uk or e-mail: bookshop@enterprise.net for details.

Free postage and packing in the UK.
Overseas customers allow £2 per book (paperbacks) and £3 per book (hardbacks).